Coleman Northwest
Regional Library

# The Secret Life of Winnie Cox

D1284897

*Also By:*

Of Marriageable Age
The Small Fortune of Dorothea Q

# The Secret Life
## of *Winnie Cox*

SHARON MAAS

**bookouture**

Published by Bookouture

An imprint of StoryFire Ltd.
23 Sussex Road, Ickenham, UB10 8PN
United Kingdom
www.bookouture.com

Copyright © Sharon Maas 2015

Sharon Maas has asserted her right to be identified
as the author of this work.
All rights reserved. No part of this publication may be
reproduced, stored in any retrieval system, or transmitted,
in any form or by any means, electronic, mechanical,
photocopying, recording or otherwise, without the
prior written permission of the publishers.

ISBN: 978-1-910751-51-0

This book is a work of fiction. Names, characters,
businesses, organizations, places and events other than
those clearly in the public domain, are either the product
of the author's imagination or are used fictitiously. Any
resemblance to actual persons, living or dead, events or
locales is entirely coincidental.

*For Aliya*

# Chapter One

## 1910 – British Guiana

A telegram! There it sat, in its innocence and its power, staring at us in silence from a silver platter on the hall sideboard. Waiting. Unsuspecting, we had gambolled in from tennis, sweaty and exhausted, chattering and laughing as young girls do; Yoyo was fourteen and I sixteen, as blithe and blind as our age and our daydreams. And then we saw it, and an axe of reality fell through our little carefree world, cutting off our prattle mid-sentence; and we remembered: Mama. My heart lurched and slid to the soles of my feet; the tennis racket slipped from my hand. Yoyo gasped and her hand flew to her mouth. Such is the power of an unopened telegram.

It paralyzed us. We simply stared. It stared back, daring us to rip it open and read – which of course we couldn't. My first panicked thought – once I could think again – was, *Mama's ship has sunk.* The second was, *or has been captured by pirates.* One heard such dreadful stories about the Atlantic crossing. One sang hymns *For Those in Peril on the Sea.* One prayed and hoped and yet still imagined the worst at the sight of that little grey envelope:

THE HON ARCHIBALD COX
PLANTATION PROMISED LAND
BERBICE COUNTY
BRITISH GUIANA

Papa was out in the cane-fields and wouldn't be home for another two hours at least. Once we had recovered our minds and our speech we ran to Miss Wright, our governess: we begged her to let us ride out to Papa, to deliver it ourselves, but she was adamant.

'You know the rules, girls! Either we'll send it with one of the yard-boys, or we'll wait till your father returns.'

We did know the rules: the fields were forbidden territory for us girls. We pleaded; we reasoned: 'But surely Papa would want to know at once, and have us all together, for support?' But no, Miss Wright was adamant. Yoyo and I looked at each other; she raised her eyebrows and I nodded. There was no question: we couldn't send it with a yard-boy. We sighed and surrendered to Miss Wright's decision. We would wait. I knew this of Yoyo and she knew it of me. That's how close we were in those days: we read each other's minds.

We had to be there when Papa opened the envelope. We need-ed to read his face as he read it – distorted with pain, or smiling in relief. And so, pacing the gallery and glancing out the windows every few seconds, or running downstairs to the drive and out to the gate, we waited and watched for Papa's return; we listened for his horse's hooves, the creak of the gate when the guard-boy opened it, the barking of the watchdogs.

As luck would have it, Papa was late that day and the six o'clock bee had already started its punctual screech before we finally heard the longed-for hooves on the driveway. Yoyo and I flew down the front stairs. Papa, unsuspecting, flung himself off his horse and handed over the reins to the waiting groom, only to find himself beleaguered by two desperate daughters leaping at him, grabbing his hands and dragging him up the stairs, crying into his ears in a jumbled chorus.

'Papa, Papa, Papa! There's a telegram, Papa, from England! Quick, hurry! We've been waiting ever so long!'

Thankfully, Papa picked up on our urgency and hurried over to the sideboard where the little grey envelope still sat waiting on its platter. His eyes widened. He turned pale, just as we had. Yet still he would not be hurried. He picked up the silver platter, placed it on the side-table next to the Berbice chair. He removed his pith helmet and handed it and his whip to the hovering house-boy. He sat himself down in the chair and held out his legs for the boy to remove his boots. He slipped his feet into the waiting slippers. He removed a big handkerchief from the pocket of his breeches and wiped his face free of sweat and dust. He drank the entire contents of the water-glass held out to him by the boy, not without first taking the time to squeeze a sliver of lime into it. And only then did he pick up the telegram. By this time I had almost wet myself with desperation. It might be indecorous to mention this, but it's true.

We watched his face, hardly daring to breathe. I'm sure my heart must have slowed to a stop as I waited for him to slit open the envelope, remove the slip of paper within, unfold it, and read. As he read, Papa's moustache turned upwards at the ends with the curl of his smile.    'Everything's fine, girls!' he said as he passed it to us to read: RUTH AND KATHLEEN ARRIVED SOUTH-AMPTON STOP LETTER CONCERNING HEIR ON WAY GOOD NEWS STOP PERCY.

We breathed again.

❅ ❅ ❅

'I wonder what Uncle Percy means about an heir,' Yoyo mused later, as she climbed under the mosquito net to join me in the big bed we shared. I held the sheet back for her and covered her as she lay down.

'What does it matter?' I replied. 'Mama's safe, and that's the important thing. And Kathleen.'

Kathleen, our eldest sister, was the ostensible excuse for Mama's voyage to England. Hungry for the London season and, hopeful of finding a suitable husband, Kathleen had begged to go too. Mama was to be her chaperone. But we all knew that Mama's illness was the real reason for the journey.

But Yoyo frowned. 'It must mean something!' Yoyo's mind, even then, was sharp and critical, less trusting than mine. Though we were close we were so very different. Yoyo – the childhood pet name that had stuck, short for Johanna, pronounced the German way, Mama's way – was the one more likely to rebel, to protest, to challenge and break the rules. I was the gentle, compliant one, all of which makes my story all the more improbable. My story should have been Yoyo's. The story of my transformation from a girl into a woman.

But on that day, I felt safe and comforted, as safe and comforted as a girl can feel when her mother is so very far away. It was the calm before the storm. Our very last days in the artificial paradise of Promised Land.

✳ ✳ ✳

**Two Months later**


I was in the middle of my afternoon violin practice – Elgar's *Salut D'Amour* – when Yoyo burst in, a vision to behold. Her clothes were disarrayed. Her blouse that hung out from the waistband of her riding culottes was not only limp from the heat and sweat of her body but strangely mud-splattered, and her face was spotted with brown, and tear-smudged. She was wearing her riding boots – strictly forbidden indoors. Her cheeks were ruddy with some violent emotion and her eyes wide, and wild, and red. Her hair was dishevelled, falling free from its molly, and her voice was shrill with dismay.

'Winnie! You've got to come with me! Now!'

'Yoyo! What on earth … Why …'

'I'll explain. Just come. I need you to come. Please, Winnie. *Please*!' She took the violin from my hands, peeled my fingers from the bow, and laid both on the table. I moved to put them away properly, but she would not let me.

'Yoyo, really ...' Miss Wright, sitting at the piano, interjected. Yoyo ignored her.

'Come *on*!' She pulled at my arm. 'Khan's saddling Tosca for you.'

'We're riding? I need to change!'

'Yes, but hurry! *Hurry*!'

I hurried – up to my room and then back down the stairs to the bottom house where I sat and pulled on my riding boots. That done, Yoyo grabbed my hand and pulled me to my feet. Infected by her urgency, I dashed across the sandy forecourt behind her to the stables, where Khan had already saddled a second pony for me. Yoyo's own pony, Pascale, was as splattered with mud, or worse, as she was. His flanks still heaved from what had obviously been a punishing ride back from ... somewhere. Khan handed us our helmets. We put them on; Yoyo mounted.

Both of us rode astride; we had given up our side-saddles a year ago and rejoiced in the freedom of riding like men. Papa had of course protested, saying it was most unladylike. But who cared about being ladylike out here on the plantation? We were Sugar Princesses in a magical realm, a sunlit, wind-blown bubble of sweetness: sugar was our livelihood, sugar determined the seasons, sugar was our world. When your father is a Sugar King you grow up basking in such sweetness and light you think it will last forever. You grow up never knowing how fragile that bubble is, and that one day, it must burst.

I was about to swing myself up into the saddle when the ringing of a bicycle bell caused Tosca to leap away. I stumbled behind her, hanging on to the reins, and looked around.

A darkie was sailing up the drive on a bicycle. Not one of *our* darkies; I'd never seen this young man before. He approached with carefree abandon, his bicycle swinging down the drive in wide curves; as he drew nearer he flung one arm into the air in greeting. Yoyo, already mounted, and I, still on foot, watched in mute surprise as he rode right up to us, swung his leg over the cycle's saddle and dismounted. His clothes were clean but worn: long khaki trousers, a short-sleeved khaki shirt and a peaked khaki cap: almost a uniform, a little too large for his lanky frame, a little too short for his height, for the trousers stopped well above the scuffed brown shoes. He wore no socks.

He carried a canvas bag slung around his shoulder, and into that bag he pushed a hand as he greeted us with an affable 'Good afternoon, Miss!' – and looking up at us, grinned, first at Yoyo, and then at me. He looked me straight in the eye, which I found strange; darkies always looked down when they addressed us. Yet his gaze was not impertinent; there was no disrespect in it, but also no deference. Instead, a playful innocence, coupled with such self-possession as I had never before seen in a darkie: frank, unfettered by convention. His eyes, I noticed, were almost black, deepset and wide apart in a smooth-skinned face of burnt bronze. His voice, when he spoke, was deeper than one would assume for his apparent youth; a rich voice, with a pleasant Creole lilt.

'You mus' be Miss Cox? A letter for ...' he removed a small white envelope, and read the name on it, 'The Honourable Archibald Cox.'

Did I detect a mocking note as he spoke the words *the honourable*? I must have been wrong, for his face showed nothing but innocent candour.

'Yes, that's our father,' Yoyo replied, although he had addressed me; but I had lost my tongue. 'There's a letter-box at the gate – didn't you see it?'

The young man scribbled in the air. 'Registered delivery, Miss! Somebody gotta sign.'

I stepped forward to sign, Tosca's reins slung over my arm, but Yoyo spoke out. 'No, we've no time, Winnie' She looked down at him, twirled Pascal around to show her impatience. 'Take the letter to the door; give it to the housekeeper. She'll sign.'

I finally found my voice.

'Where's Mr Perkins?' I asked. Our letters were usually delivered by genial old Mr Perkins who lived above the Post Office in the village.

'He retired, Miss,' said the youth. 'I'm the new postman, temporarily at least. I …'

'We have to go,' said Yoyo, interrupting impatiently. He nodded, touched his cap – I noticed he had not removed it – smiled again, placed his cycle on its stand, and walked towards the main entrance to the house.

'No!' called Yoyo, 'The *back* door: you have to walk around the house, to the kitchen!'

'Ah! Righty-ho, Miss!' He grinned, again – looking at me, not at Yoyo – and then marched off to the back of the house. He turned around one more time, grinned again, touched his cap, and disappeared behind the building.

'Winnie! Come *on*!' Still whirling on Pascal, Yoyo was red-faced with displeasure.

'No,' I said simply. 'I'm not going anywhere until you tell me what's wrong? Where are we going?'

Yoyo had a tendency to overdramatize events; she also possessed the skill of infecting others with her zeal before they were aware of what they were doing. For all I knew she had trodden on a beetle and wanted me to save its life. Not that I didn't think a beetle's life worth saving. I just needed to know.

'It's Nanny! She's *dying*!' It was a cry that would rend the heart of a statue. Her voice broke. 'I was out riding on the back dam … I met Gopal … he told me.'

'Oh!' was all I said, and swung myself into the saddle without a further word. Yoyo had already spurred Pascale and leapt away, towards the gate. I cantered off after her, down the driveway and out the gate onto the gravel road outside. This road ran east-west, parallel to the coast, but soon met a junction, a wider road that

ran south towards the back dam and north towards the senior
staff compound, the Promised Land village, and the East Coast.
Yoyo turned north and spurred her pony into a gallop. I followed
suit. The road cut through the cane fields, the growing canes now
at half height were almost six feet tall. They acted as a funnel for
the strong Atlantic breeze, which whipped the wide legs of my
culottes high up around my thighs. Ahead of me, Yoyo lashed
Pascale with her crop, urging him on. The gap between us widened.

Where on earth were we going? I had no idea where Nanny
lived, and as far as I knew, neither did Yoyo. But perhaps she
did? Gopal must have told her where to find her. In the village
perhaps, as we were headed in that direction.

Nanny had left us years before, dismissed by Papa and replaced
by Miss Wright. We were too old for a nanny, Papa had said, and
Nanny was too old to work. Yoyo, the youngest of us all and the
closest to Nanny, had thrown a tantrum, but Papa was adamant:
Nanny must go. Nanny had gone and we'd never seen her again.
More concerned with trying to win back Mama's love and attention than by Nanny's dismissal, I had forgotten her. Yoyo hadn't.
I had always been aware of the little notes she sent Nanny via her
grandson, Gopal, our gardener. Nanny never replied, as far as I
knew; but then, Nanny couldn't read or write. I assumed someone had read the notes out to her. I hadn't taken much interest. I
hadn't even thought of Nanny again before today.

The village was just over two miles away, but we weren't anywhere near the first house before Yoyo slowed to a trot and then to
a walk. She seemed to be looking for something in the cane field,
and before long found it: an opening, barely visible between the
man-high canes, and an overgrown stone bridge over the trench
that ran beside the road.

She turned to me. 'This must be it,' she said. She walked Pascale over the bridge into the opening, which was, in fact, a well-

hidden path; so well hidden that I had never noticed it before. We often rode to the village, where we would buy a packet of boiled sweets from Chan's grocery, or crispy *mittai* from Singh's bakery, or a variety of other treats. The village belonged to the plantation, and served the people who worked there. We knew the villagers and they knew us, and would smile and salute us, the men removing their hats if they wore them, and the women curtsying as we rode past, and we would smile, wave, and greet them, sometimes by name, in return.

Some instinct told me that this path was taboo, hidden as it was between two cane fields and made of earth, not of gravel or sand, and I hesitated. Narrow and crude, it was no path for a sugar princess to venture down. It felt alien, wrong; I had an intimation of venturing into forbidden territory, a vague sense of peril. But Yoyo had no such scruples. Without a word she led the way. She turned in the saddle, and gestured to me to come. I followed.

It was the beginning of the rainy season and it had rained on and off all day: a burst of rain lasting for five or ten or twenty minutes, followed by sunshine in a brilliant blue sky and fluffy white clouds drifting by until the next cloud came with a new downpour. As a result the earth on this path had turned to mud. Yoyo slowed to a walk and our ponies' hooves squelched as they moved. Now and then we came across a puddle that filled the entire path, and still in single file, we waded through it. I called out:

'Are you *sure* this is the right way, Yoyo?'

She half turned in the saddle. 'Yes. Gopal told me. Just follow.'

So I followed and mud from the hooves splattered up onto my culottes – now decorously around my legs again – and fronds of green from the cane on either side reached over and stroked my bare arms as the path grew narrower, and my heart beat faster for I did not like this place at all.

After twenty minutes of this my nostrils became aware of a pungent smell, a smell that grew into a stench as we continued.

'Yoyo ... I think ...'

'Be *quiet!*' she commanded, and I left the sentence unfinished. On a normal ride, even if we were far apart, she would be chattering away gaily of this and that and I would be smiling and nodding. Now, I understood her silence; I knew well that death made people silent. I had learned that from Mama, after Edward John's death. Dear little Edward John, our baby brother, his life snapped shut before it had even begun.

❄ ❄ ❄

Yoyo's attachment to Nanny began long before Edward John's death. For years before that sad day, Mama had been drifting away from us, losing herself in a melancholy none of us could pierce. Yoyo, too young to cope with the gradual withdrawal of motherly affection, turned with full force to Nanny, who responded in kind. Nanny took Mama's place in Yoyo's heart; quite literally a *Mutterersatz*, as Mama would say in her own tongue.

We did not know the source of Mama's sorrow; we suspected a part of it was mere homesickness, yearning for Austria, her homeland – but so extreme? It was puzzling. We only knew that she buried that sadness in the keys of her piano, and for years the Plantation Promised Land reverberated with Beethoven, Brahms, and Bach, incongruous on the hot flat plains of the Courantyne Coast.

Edward John's death – finally broke her. Little Edward John, the only son and long-awaited heir – dead in his cot, a week after his birth – just when it seemed that Mama was returning to life, and rediscovering lost joy. His death almost took Mama with him. Her body recovered; her soul never.

And if Nanny was now dying – well, no wonder Yoyo was too distraught to speak. I understood it. But right now, disquiet was slowly seeping through me, and the silence made me shiver in spite of the heat of the afternoon, and it had nothing to do with death.

The silence, and the stench. The stench grew worse and I pulled out a handkerchief and held it against my nose and was just about to call out to Yoyo to insist that we return home as I could not breathe, when the first glimpse of a rooftop rose above the green of the waving cane. Two seconds later we were there, and at last she drew to a halt. I walked Tosca up to stand beside her and we both stared in silence.

'We have to go in there,' Yoyo said at last, and we looked at each other and I nodded. 'Nanny's in there. But ...'

She looked at me in anguish. She did not need to complete her sentence. I nodded again, understanding, and searching for words. I knew where we were. I knew we couldn't go any further. This was finally, that *other* world. Up to now we had only played on its outskirts, pretending we knew it, but this was the real thing. These were the *logies*.

You couldn't live on a plantation, in a plantation owner's household, without occasionally hearing that word and grasping, however vaguely, that the *logies* were the homes of the coolies. The words would be dropped casually into conversation when Papa had visitors, maybe one of the managers, or a planter from one of the neighbouring estates, Dieu Merci or Roosendaal or Nieuw Haarlem, and they would discus in grim tones the Labourer Problem. Somewhere at the back of my mind I had picked up the knowledge that the coolies lived in *logies*, but I had had no idea where these *logies* were or what they looked like. Why, I hardly took note of the coolies themselves.

The coolies were a part of the landscape. They belonged, quite simply, to the backdrop of life in this grand Kingdom of Sugar. Riding out along the back dam, or even from our bedroom windows, we saw them: half-naked men, their skin dark brown and shiny with sweat, their muscles rippling as they hacked at the cane with their cutlasses or bound the cane into bundles and carried those bundles to the canals and loaded the punts. Coolie women, fully clothed, up to their waists in water, pulled the loaded punts along the canals. Coolies were everywhere, so ubiquitous one never even noticed them, and with the wisdom of hindsight I'm ashamed to make these confessions. Why, I even thought it romantic: coolies at work in the fields, coolies in the trenches. An essential part of the scenery we loved so much, to be taken for granted.

'Let's go back,' I said eventually.

'We can't,' Yoyo replied. 'I have to see Nanny. She's *dying*, don't you understand? I have to see her; I have to go in there. We have to go.'

She was crying openly by now. Yoyo never cried. She had not cried when Mama boarded the ship that would take her away. She had not cried when Edward John died. She had last cried, as far as I remembered, when her beloved dog Frisky died, three years ago. I on the other hand, wore my heart on my sleeve, and cried easily. I cried at a litter of new-born kittens, at music too beautiful to bear, at exquisite poetry, at sad endings of novels. Yoyo never read novels; she considered love-stories soppy and sentimental, a waste of time. She wore a sheath of hard-edged cynicism to protect her from the world, whereas I – I was raw and exposed, my soul laid bare to the elements. But now it was Yoyo who cried, not me.

'Yoyo …'

She looked at me, and fire burned in her eyes. 'Nanny lives in there, Winnie. Somewhere. I have to see her before she dies. I have to say goodbye. I …' Her face crumpled. She rubbed her eyes with her knuckles. I realised, in many ways, she was still a child. I realised, too, how important it was that she should see Nanny again. I realised I would have to take her in. In there. Into this … this horror before us.

It was a city set in mud. The houses, if you could call them that, were ramshackle windowless shacks that seemed held together with nothing more than luck. They were made of no recognizable building materials, though here and there a wooden plank was to be seen, or a broken sheet of corrugated iron for a roof. Mostly they were made of coconut palms and rice sacks, pieces of tarpaulin or canvas, crumbling mud bricks: bits and pieces haphazardly fitted together to do no more than provide a rudimentary protection from sun and rain. Two raggedy lines of such shacks stretched away before our eyes along a narrow lane of oozing black slush, and several more such lines lay to our left and right. On either side of the lane ran two ditches, overflowing with some kind of sickening black ooze. Over the entire area hung that abominable stench that had assaulted my nostrils some time back and had now grown so strong as to be unbearable. I still held a handkerchief to my nose; the sight had distracted from the stench for a while, but now I realised just how ghastly it was, a melange of offal and excretion and rotting flesh and various other unidentifiable but equally nauseating odours.

And the flies. Oh, the flies, swarms of them nestled on the ground. Flies, whirring around the eyes of small children and the sores on dogs' backs. Perhaps they gorged on stench.

It was, quite simply, horrendous. To think of Nanny, our beloved Nanny, living within this abomination – it was unbearable. Did Papa know she lived here? Had he sent her away, knowing she would move here? Had he knowingly thrown her into a pigsty?

By this time word had spread and people, that is, small children, young women with babies and toddlers, old women, and old men, for every able-bodied coolie was working in the canes, had emerged from the nearest shacks and come forward and now stood watching us. Silently. Just stood there, waiting for us to do something. Dogs, too, had gathered, and stood there barking, warning us to keep away, but coming no closer, no doubt wary of our horses and their hooves. The overseers rode horses. Overseers and their horses were dangerous beasts.

Beside me, Yoyo seemed to wake up. She straightened her back, signalled to one of the women nearest us, and called.

'Come!'

Come the woman did, but reluctantly, taking time to move away from the little crowd outside her hut and looking around as if to see it was really she who had been addressed. She arrived at our side and Yoyo said, looking down at her, 'We're looking for – for …'

She looked at me, seeking an answer. She could hardly ask for Nanny, but she had never called her anything else. Luckily, I knew Nanny's name

'Yashoda,' I said to the woman. 'We're looking for Yashoda. Gopal's grandmother.'

'Gopal?' she repeated, looking up and shaking her head, 'plenty people name Gopal. Plenty people name Yashoda.'

She wore a faded, tattered strip of cloth as a sari. Her thinning hair, grey and shiny with coconut oil, was pulled back behind her neck. It would be gathered into a long plait down her spine in the style of the coolie women.

'Gopal …Gopal the gardener. At Mr Cox's house, our house. The gardener! His grandmother is Yashoda.'

I had the feeling the woman knew exactly which Gopal I wanted, and which Yashoda. That she was being deliberately ignorant. To spite us. Because we were who we were. Yoyo must have come to the same conclusion, because she said now, sharply, and more in keeping with her natural character:

'You *know* which Gopal! His grandmother is Yashoda and she's dying. Take us to her!' There was a cutting edge of impatience in Yoyo's voice. It made me nervous.

'Please!' I added, but already the wrongness of our demand had become clear to me. I reached over and touched Yoyo's elbow.

'Yoyo, come, let's go. This isn't right,' I pleaded. She simply nudged me away, not looking away from the woman on the ground, who seemed more hostile than ever. She looked around at the other *logie* dwellers, looked down, and clenched the ragged skirt of her sari. Finally she raised one skinny arm and gestured vaguely into the settlement.

'Over there,' she said. 'But Gopal in't there now. He workin.'

'It's Yashoda we want to see,' said Yoyo. 'Nanny. It's her we want to visit. Show us the way.'

'Please,' I added again.

What choice did the poor woman have? She hesitated again, then shrugged and walked away with a 'follow me' gesture, into the central lane between the rows of huts, and Yoyo urged Pascale on. Off they walked.

I followed, urging Tosca on, into the mud. Mud, that sucked at our horses' hooves and splattered up as we walked by; past those abominable hovels. At several huts, old women and young children came out to stare, and mangy dogs came out to bark, though keeping well away. Swarms of flies rose up at our passing in a restless buzzing cloud, parting to let us through

Horrified thoughts raced through my mind as we passed by. This could not be happening on our property, under our very noses! And if it was, then Papa must be informed. He could not possibly know! Papa was a gentleman, a decent, caring man. A Christian. He would not allow such loathsomeness to blight our Promised Land. Papa must be brought here, to see for himself; he would be as horrified as we were, and put an end to it. I was eager, almost, to see more, to make a full report, and my initial impulse to whisk Yoyo away turned to gratitude that she had found this place. I needed to know everything, to suppress my own revulsion in the interest of helping these people. I needed to observe it all so as to describe it in detail to Papa.

The people, for instance. The coolies who emerged from their shacks to stare silently as we passed by, showed none of the deferential nodding of heads and curtseying we were used to when riding through the village; there were none of the polite calls of 'Good-day Miss!' and the obsequious smiles of the villagers. The eyes that looked down the moment I sought them – to smile, to greet, to show my solidarity – were neither obsequious nor shy.

With a start I realized: these people were hostile. And hostility was a thing I had never in all my life encountered. We moved deeper into the – well, what shall I call it – village? Community? No. Slum was more like it; a rural slum plonked bang in the middle of Paradise. And as we progressed, turning right into another identical lane and left again into an even narrower, but similarly stinking, alleyway, the more my worry increased: how could Papa *not* know about this? And if he knew, then why … I could think no further.

Looking behind me, I saw that we were being followed by a rag-tag group of old women and young children. The lanes grew ever narrower and muddier the hovels more rudimentary, the glares more hostile. Presently I became aware of a moaning, keening sound, more animal than human. It grew louder as we progressed. Finally, we approached a group of women standing in the lane at the entrance to one of the shacks. The noise came from them; they were swaying and bowing and beating their breasts, clinging to each other, bawling and moaning and howling a most pitiful lament whose meaning was obvious. They wore worn saris that had once been white, and their hair was undone and hanging loose over their shoulders, instead of being plaited neatly down their backs. We needed no explanation. We were too late: Nanny had passed away.

'NO!' cried Yoyo and swung her leg over Pascale's back. Oblivious to the mud she plunged forward and right through the group to the opening that stood in as a door. A short, steep flight of dilapidated steps rose up to the door – for the *logies* were built, like all British Guiana houses, on stilts, albeit short stilts – and there she stopped. A stony-faced woman emerged from the hut's interior, and arms crossed before her chest, blocked Yoyo's entrance. Yoyo, weeping, tried to push past; the woman would not let her. The mourners abruptly stopped their moaning, and stared. Yoyo tried again to climb the stairs but the woman held out a hand and pushed her back. She stumbled and almost fell, righted herself, swung around and glared at the women and children gathered around, both mourners and the spectators who had followed us here.

'Go away! Stop *staring*!' She made a shooing gesture, and when no one stepped away, looked past them to me.

'Winnie, say something! Talk to her, please! I *need* to go in there! I need to see Nanny! Even if she's dead I need to see her!'

She was crying again by now, weeping with an anguish that shook her from head to foot. She buried her face in her hands and collapsed in a desolate heap on the mud at the bottom of the steps. Only then did the mourners back away a little, as if in deference to genuine grief. At the same time, the spectators drew nearer, the better to take in the unfolding drama. I dismounted, and took up Pascale's reins – which Yoyo in her haste had simply dropped – and gestured to an older boy to come nearer. I handed him the reins of both ponies and gestured again for him to wait there; though I need not have, for where else would he have gone? I stepped up to the hut. The gathering of mourners parted to let me through. I bent down, clasped Yoyo under her arms, and raised her up. Up she came, limp and sobbing, and clung to me. I patted her on the back and looked pleadingly at the woman in the doorway, presumably Nanny's daughter or daughter-in-law or granddaughter or niece.

'Please,' I said, 'please let us in. We both loved Nanny – Yashoda. We came to say goodbye.'

'Yashoda dead,' said the woman unnecessarily.

'I know,' I said. 'That's why we came. Is her body in there? Can you let us see her? Please?'

The emaciated being scrutinised me as if to divine my secret wicked thoughts. Perhaps she found nothing threatening, for eventually she shrugged and gestured to our feet, first mine then Yoyo's. I understood at once, and bent down to remove my muddy boots. This much I knew about coolies: they remove their shoes, if they had any at all, before entering a home. I whispered to Yoyo to follow suit – for she stood there numb and speechless – and she too bent over to remove her riding boots. We placed our footwear outside the hut. The woman stepped aside to allow us to pass by. We climbed the steps and bending low, entered. There was no door, of course, only a doorway, a dark hole and a rice-sack curtain tied to one side.

Inside it was dark for there were no windows. Dark, small, and crowded. We were the only standing occupants; everyone else – all old women, their hair loose and hanging over their shoulders – were sitting on the floor filling every last space, and at their centre was a stretched- out figure lying on the ground. A tiny lamp burned at the figure's head, and in its glow I made out Nanny's cold, pale features.

There is something so final, so chilling about death. There were Nanny's familiar features, older now, but the same, yet devoid of that vital element that separates the animate from the inanimate. She could have been carved in stone. They had tied a cloth around her jaw, knotted on the crown of her head, presumably to keep it closed. It was just a body. Nothing was in it. Nanny was truly gone. Absent. This cold thing had nothing to do with her.

I sank to my knees, head bowed; so did Yoyo. It was an involuntary gesture, as if Death itself had pointed to the floor and silently commanded such deference. Outside, the moaning and keening began anew, and now the women sitting cross-legged around the body began to moan and keen and lament as well. 'Eeeeeeiiiiiiiiiiih!' they cried and 'Ooooooooooowwwww!' they howled.

Yoyo and I, kneeling near the entrance, sank back to sit on the floor like the women. It was of wooden planks, widely gapped; black, yet, as far as I could tell, clean. My eyes, finally accustomed to the half-light, scanned the rest of the room, beyond and above the heads of the mourners. The family's meagre possessions were stacked neatly on rudimentary boxes acting as shelves against the walls. Above our heads, a few dented pots and tins (I recognised the empty *Cow & Gate* powdered milk tins that we threw out regularly) hung on pieces of twine from the ceiling; to collect rainwater, it seemed, from, no doubt, the leaking roof.

The room itself was smaller than Mama's dressing room. Now, with the two of us, the five or six women sitting on the floor, as well as Nanny's body, it was full. A sling made from an old piece of sari-cloth hung from a board in the ceiling; it seemed to contain a lump of something, but now the woman – Nanny's daughter, or daughter-in-law, or granddaughter – removed the lump and it turned out to be a baby. It started to cry, a thin high wail. She placed it to her breast, pulled away the rags of her sari, and it fell silent.

We sat there for some time. It was impossible to measure the passing minutes. An incredible sadness descended on me: grief for Nanny; that she should have lived out her last days in such a dreadful place; despair at the conditions in which the coolies lived; helplessness; anger; disgust. *Weltschmerz,* Mama would have called this collective gloom. Mama was an expert at the various nuances of misery. I wallowed in this darkness for a while, cocooned by the clamour of moans and wails, and when I could stand it no longer, I squeezed Yoyo's hand and we rose somewhat shakily to our feet and made silent signs of gratitude and leave-taking to Nanny's daughter, or daughter-in-law, or granddaughter; we left the hut, put on our boots, reclaimed our ponies, mounted them, and returned the way we had come. The boy who had held the ponies led the way.

Down those stinking, muddy lanes lined with their ramshackle hovels not even fit for pigs. All the coolies came out to watch us leave. They stood before their miserable dwellings in silence, and stared at us as our horses clip-clopped past them, their hooves making sickly sucking sounds in the sludge. Sullen, empty eyes followed us. Not even the children – the littlest ones pressed against their mother's skirts as if shrinking from us – uttered a word. Not a baby cried. Dogs barked and snarled, but at a cringing distance from the hooves. Yoyo rode with her head held high, her eyes dry now, but her cheeks more tear-smudged than ever. I looked down.

At last we left the *logies* and were once again on the path that led through the cane fields. I would have loved to race home, but the condition of the path made this impossible; we rode single file, Yoyo leading the way. In silence. I could not stand the silence. There was so much to say, and too much to bear. The enormity of what we had seen weighed so heavily upon me I thought I would break under it, but Yoyo stayed stubbornly mute and I – well, words failed me.

I found my voice when we reached the stables and dismounted and handed our ponies over to the groom. I looked around me.

'Compared to our coolies,' I said to Yoyo, gesturing all around to indicate the neat, clean stables with the cobbled yard and wooden loose boxes made of best timber, painted white, 'our ponies live in palaces.'

❊ ❊ ❊

## Mama's Diary: Salzburg, 1889

*Liebes Tagebuch,*

*I cannot contain it! I am simply bursting with it all but I have to tell someone or else I will explode! Oh, I will! How I wish I had a friend, a sister of my heart! Since I do not, dear diary, YOU must be that friend. I am in Love!*

*It is madness. No other word can describe it. But it is not a bad thing for I am mad with love! Oh, yes I am! Don't look at me like that, dear diary – shaking your sensible head! Because I am sure you are sensible! Yes, I can almost see you and you are frowning and saying things like 'silly girl!' and 'get down from your cloud'! But I won't because I like it up here on my cloud and love is just the most wonderful, magnificent thing that has ever happened to me in all my seventeen years! Yes! Go ahead and disapprove, deny, deride!*

*I'll tell you about it – I know you are curious. You know that Father was invited to Vienna to stay with the Bonhoffers – Dr Bonhoffer being Father's old friend from University. They have a daughter, Liese, who is around my age so I was invited as well. And so we all went to Vienna for a fortnight. I love Vienna! I love it more than ever now, for that is where I met HIM!*

*We went to the Kaiser's ball. Well, it so happened that Dr Bonhoffer has a good friend named Dr von Brandt who also went to the ball. And this Dr von Brandt had a young friend staying with him; that is, the young friend is the son of an English friend – someone he had met in Cambridge many years ago – Cambridge, you know, is an important University town in England. That is, he met the father of this young man, not the young man himself. Oh, it all sounds so complicated but it isn't!*

*His name is Archibald Cox – The Honourable! Archibald Cox! (The son, I mean – the father wasn't there.) Archie, for short.*

*And he is the handsomest, most charming, most delightful young man in the entire world! Are all Englishmen this handsome, this charming? No. He is special, unique. Mine! And we danced – oh how we danced! He whirled and twirled me around beneath the chandeliers and the orchestra played the Blue Danube and I will never ever dance with another to that music, for it is ours alone – we have claimed it! And as we swirled I laughed, and so did he – and his arms were strong and his eyes were blue and if there is a heaven on earth, this is it. I am still dancing in my heart, dear Diary. I will always dance in my heart. I want to keep this memory alive forever, and this is why I have written you this letter. So that I will never ever forget.*

*The best thing is that Dr von Brandt has invited us all to dinner tomorrow evening – the Bonhoffers, and us! I will see my Archibald again. Oh, I cannot wait!*

*(By the way, I wore a beautiful green satin dress, cut wide along the shoulders, with puffed sleeves – and I will keep this dress forever!)*

*(Oh and I should mention, though I don't want to make a fuss about this but afterwards Dr Bonhoffer told me that Archie is the son of an Earl. Imagine that!)*

# Chapter Two

After Edward John's death, and Mama's final and complete with-drawal. I mourned our mother as if she too had died. I mourned her with a dry-eyed silence that gradually grew into a tendency to introspection and a yearning for – well, I can certainly define it with long impressive words but finally I can only call it Love. Love with a capital L. Mama left a space, a vacuum, that had to be filled.

As for Kathleen, at nineteen and the eldest, she was cut from a different fabric. Yoyo and I loved British Guiana, Berbice County, the Courantyne Coast, Promised Land; this was our home. For Kathleen, as for Papa, England was Home. Born in Norfolk, Kathleen laid much value on being the granddaughter of an Earl, and aspired to heights Yoyo and I were oblivious of and indiffer-ent to. And so it was Kathleen who was sent to England when she reached marriageable age. It was Kathleen who won Mama for herself when she sailed across the ocean, bound for that mag-nificent Norfolk manor which Yoyo and I knew only from the painting in the library. Mama went as chaperone; but I suspect that Mama needed her more than she needed Mama; that ac-companying Kathleen across the ocean was simply the excuse that Papa, in his solicitude, needed to get Mama back to Europe. First to England, to deliver Kathleen to the Cox family, then on to her people in Austria, to Vienna, and to that famous doctor who had agreed to cure her. Dr Freud was his name. Freud, meaning *joy* in German. He would return the joy to Mama's heart. That is what Papa told us; what we hoped.

The day we saw them off on the Georgetown wharf was the day my heart shattered into a million shards, a mirror crashed against stone. How could Mama leave us behind? She had not been a mother to us for many years now, but at least she had been *physically* with us. At least she had filled the house with her music, reminding us of her presence. At least we could see her face, pinched and drawn and soulless though it was. At least she was *there*. How could she leave us? I did not understand it. Kathleen could surely have found another escort – another English woman returning Home, maybe. I burned with jealousy: why should Kathleen have Mama all to herself, when I was the one who needed her the most! And this Dr Joy – well, hopefully he would cure her and she would return. Soon. But there had been little talk of Mama's return. None, to be quite honest. Whenever I asked, Papa would hem and haw and mumble something about these things taking time. I might be an adult before I saw her again! And then the dreaded day arrived.

How could I ever forget that day? The whole family at the Georgetown dock, Papa to the fore, pushing a way through the crowd like a coolie forging his way through a dense cane field. The rest of us came single file behind him. Three porters behind us carried the luggage on their heads and under their arms. At the gangplank, Papa brandishing the tickets, spoke to a liveried official of some sort, and then turned to wave us all to gather round. The man nodded and signalled for us to pass, and across the gangplank we walked, single file again, Papa leading.

I was already sick to my stomach. I would have preferred to say my goodbyes elsewhere. At the Park Hotel, or better yet, back home at Promised Land. Why postpone the agony? But then we were there, in the first class cabin Mama would share with Kathleen. Kathleen, bright-eyed and eager, chattering away, her head full of hairstyles and hats, Mama, silent and stricken. Papa, stern and watchful. Yoyo, dry-eyed and tight-lipped and pale, clasping my hand tightly, and I hers. My own eyes stinging with unshed tears.

And then Mama seemed to wake up out of a trance. She rushed forward and swept me into the first embrace she had given me in years, and as she held me she shuddered and whispered the words into my ears: *Ich wollte es nicht, mein Schatz; ich wollte es nicht!* I didn't want it, my treasure, I didn't want it!

I clung to her but then she let me go and hugged Yoyo, and then I grabbed her again, howling now, but Papa clutched my arms and pulled me away. And there was Mama, miraculously crying, calling my name and reaching out for me, and I knew she loved me still; but it was all too late.

'Don't go, Mama, don't go!' I wailed, and I reached for her even as Papa pushed me out of the cabin and into the corridor, and then he shut the cabin door and dragged me away, Yoyo following, and took us home. At some point, through my devastation, I realized Mama had not taken leave of Papa, nor he of her.

That was how I lost Mama a second time. Home, Promised Land, had been empty for me ever since. A home without a heart.

❋ ❋ ❋

Promised Land plantation had been in our family's possession for many generations, and passed down from father to son, had been competently managed by a series of English and Scottish men engaged for the task. Papa, being the Earl's third son and therefore with no prospects of his own in England, came here as a young man, temporarily leaving behind his wife and baby daughter. Mama and two-year-old Kathleen followed once Papa had established himself as one of the legendary Sugar Kings who ruled the colony. He built a palace worthy of his status. It was constructed of sturdy greenheart wood in the Dutch Colonial style, typical of the land. Sparkling white in the sunlight, with filigree fretwork and the lattices that provided its ventilation and curlicues on the jutting Demerara windows, it resembled a fairytale castle made of lace. This was our home.

Yoyo and I were born into this palace of wood. We loved every nook and cranny of it. We loved the staircases and the tower, the breeze-filled verandas, the rafters for little girls to swing on, the balustrades for little girls to balance on. Most of all we loved the garden: the orchard that brought forth fruit of every imaginable variety, every month a different and more delicious kind; the mango tree with its low-slung branches inviting us to climb. Birdsong and flowers framed our little perfect kingdom: the call of the kiskadee; the wing-whirr of the hummingbird; the huge bunches of purple, pink and vermillion blooms hanging low from the towering bougainvillaea that climbed our porticos and porches, not to mention the hibiscus, and frangipani, and oleander, and the rose-fragrance that wafted through it all, carried on the wings of a cool sea-breeze.

We grew up indifferent to the apples and pears and grapes Mama described to us in the early years of her motherhood, trying to entice us, to lure us, into her own European world. We cared not for rhododendrons and tulips and edelweiss, golden autumn and budding May. We did not yearn for snow and mountains, as she did. We had the vast sky with its puffy clouds, the ocean and the breeze-brushed emerald cane. Yoyo and I ran free and laughing through our paradise. We turned from little girls into adolescents, barefoot princesses only vaguely aware that one day we must grow up to marry one of our kind. But where was the guidance towards that blessed state? Who would teach us about Love?

For many years, Mama had been a withdrawn, silent being whose only lifeline had been her music, but after Edward John's death, she was in utter despair. Papa, of course, busy as he was with estate business, had no time to offer us more than affectionate pats on the head and expensive gifts from Georgetown. Yoyo found comfort in Nanny's arms. Kathleen yearned for London. Behind the laughter, the fun and freedom of estate life, unseen by all, I nurtured a great big hole in my heart where Mama had once dwelled.

* * *

We arrived home in time to change for dinner. Yoyo and I shared a large upstairs bedroom; though there were rooms to spare in the house, we preferred to be together, sleeping in the same wide bed under the ghostly white tent of the mosquito net where we could talk into the night until our eyelids grew heavy and our breath long. We changed in silence, each occupied with her own thoughts. I found myself praying – not to God, but to Mama. *Hold her tongue!* I begged her. *Don't let her lash out at him!*

My fear was that Yoyo would create a scene, blaming Papa for Nanny's appalling last years; that the two of them would have one of their ghastly shouting matches. But I need not have worried: Papa pre-empted any drama on Yoyo's part by presenting a little furore of his own, one that momentarily banished all our own concerns and cancelled the planned confrontation. He strode into the dining room that evening chortling with mirth.

It was always possible to divine Papa's mood by the shape of his moustache. Long, blonde, and copious, it literally drooped, dull and unkempt, and turned down at either end, when his mood was low – all too often in these days. On his good days it stretched out long with the upward curve of his lips, neat and almost boyish in the way it curled up at the ends, constantly stroked into shape by preening fingers. This was such a day. Papa's pale blue eyes sparkled as he took his place at the head of the table. He had, of course, changed from his khaki work clothes into evening wear, long black trousers, a white long-sleeved shirt and a tie; as always, he looked as crisply neat as a perfectly peeled egg.

He guffawed a hearty greeting to each of us in turn. We both looked up, at each other and at him; such good cheer was rare, for times were tough on the plantation. He beamed back at us: a handsome man, in his mid-forties, his sun-bronzed skin leathered from the outdoor life, his features sharp, his chin firm and square, his blonde hair trim. Settling into his seat with great ceremony, he adjusted his cutlery carefully before reaching into the top button of his white evening shirt, removed an envelope, and waved it at us – the same envelope that had been delivered by registered mail that very afternoon by the cocky dark youth on a bicycle.

'Girls!' he said, as he removed the letter it held, 'I have some excellent news! Excellent. This here is a letter from your Uncle Percival. Let me read it to you.' He flapped open the letter, perched his spectacles on his nose and, holding the letter on high, read it out:

'"Dear Archie, I hope – etc etc etc – Please forgive the months of silence; you will be wondering by now if I ever even received your last. I did, but truth be told I was reluctant to write earlier, since my initial endeavours regarding the mission you requested of me proved fruitless.

Initially, certain of an eager response, I waved the splendid prospect of inheriting a sugar plantation in British Guiana before all the eligible young men in our extended family, but to no avail. To my everlasting astonishment, there were no offers of acceptance. I am afraid the great British Pioneer Spirit seems to be all but absent in the younger generation, for all the young men so approached, refused. They are reluctant, it seems, to abandon their familiar life in England for, as they are prone to call it, 'the backwaters of the New World' – demonstrating, if you ask me, a decided lack of the very pluck and fortitude that has been the backbone of the British Empire, and has placed the Great in Great Britain. Our forefathers must be turning in their graves! No – our young men would not be tempted. I am afraid the pleasures of Ascot, the Hunting Season, the comforts of their paternal country manors, and, last but not least, a new flock of fresh-faced young debutantes waltzing their way into the London scene each year have proved enough to outweigh the temptation of becoming one's own man on foreign shores. Alas! Manhood is at a premium in these leisurely days – a spineless generation. For us who fought in the Boer War these modern chaps certainly seem a spoiled, foppish lot. That's what happens when boys are reared in pampered comfort – life is too easy. But don't let me get into that – you know my feelings.

"Be that as it may, I now have great pleasure in reporting an unmitigated success. The young man in question is my wife's nephew – no relation to the Cox's, which is actually a <u>positive</u> detail; one does hear that marriage between cousins occasionally has troubling ramifications for the health of the offspring. But that is by-the-by. His name is Clarence Smedley – the youngest son of Lord Smedley. A fine chap, if I may say so – now approaching his 30th birthday. Lord Smedley is eager to see him settled, and as far away as possible. Do not let this last alarm you. It is true that he has got himself into a spot of bother of late – nothing too serious; a bit of bad luck at the races, and I believe there was some scandal with a young woman of ill-repute – but boys will be boys, as you yourself know, and it is nothing that the responsibilities of learning the ropes of plantation business will not cure. It will make a man of him, if you ask me, and I am sure those are exactly Lord Smedley's thoughts and intentions.

"I am aware of your worries regarding the fortunes of the plantation and I am delighted to inform you that Clarence will be endowed with his portion of his inheritance upon his arrival in BG. This will enable you to build the sugar-processing factory that will, I presume, reverse your fortunes, and chase away the bloodthirsty Booker vultures. So, good news for all concerned, and several birds killed with one stone – an heir for Promised Land, money for the proposed factory, a second chance and a manly future for young Clarence, a pre-emptive move to prevent that Booker beast from destroying everything we have built over the generations, and last but not least, God willing, a husband for one of your daughters, and a father for your grandsons!

"Young Smedley will be ready to sail the moment we receive confirmation from you that you approve of this plan. If at all possible, send a telegram – a simple 'yes' or 'no' will be quite sufficient, but I am already assuming the 'yes' and I know that the Smedleys are similarly positively inclined. Indeed, this seems like the answer to all your prayers.

"Ethel" – no, I'll skip that. Let me see – there's something about your mother – ah, here it is: "Ruth and Kathleen have not yet arrived at the time of writing. Their ship is due next week and I shall be there to meet them at Southampton. I'll send you a telegram when they do arrive. We greatly look forward to the pleasure of their company, and I can tell you in confidence that we have lined up several immensely eligible young men to whom we will introduce Kathleen at the earliest opportunity. We'll have her walking up the aisle in no time, and I shall be delighted to act *in loco parentis* and take her on my arm. Once Kathleen has settled in we shall send Ruth on to Salzburg, as you requested. We shall find a suitable companion for her. You need not worry about a thing.

I am etc etc etc."

'Well, girls, what do you say to that? Magnificent news, eh? Eh?'

When we made no response, he continued: 'I know you girls will be particularly interested in the hints of marriage; at your age, your thoughts will be drifting more and more towards your futures and I have to admit, I myself was rather worried; most of the eligible young men in the colony are unfortunately Booker men. We don't want that, do we? Well, I suppose you girls wouldn't know the ramifications of that, and I'm afraid I've broken a few of my own rules today, by inadvertently bringing business matters to the dining table – but it's practically impossible to extract one's own personal prospects from plantation matters; it's imperative to keep Promised Land out of the claws of Bookers and I want you both to be very aware of that when the time comes. Your mother – this should have been her job ...'

He paused here and a shadow momentarily wiped the smile from his face, as if the thought of Mama had erased the pleasure the letter had brought. The ghost of Mama swirled over our heads. Mama, gone forever from us. I was sure of that. Unless this Dr Joy healed her. But even if he did, my great fear was that she would never return. That Europe would claim her and never let her go again.

Papa dismissed whatever distressing thoughts had fleetingly distracted him, and, as we still did not speak – not even Yoyo, who usually added her comments at every turn of a conversation – he continued, somewhat absentmindedly, as if speaking to himself.

'Yes, yes. Keep that in mind, and you might as well write it behind your ears right now: no Booker husbands for you! Fortunately, there are no leering young bachelors from Glasgow and Dieu Merci. No immediate danger.'

Glasgow, to the east, and Dieu Merci, to the west, were our neighbouring plantations. Papa was correct in that business affairs were kept strictly from our ears, but we would have had to have been living under a bush not to have known that the great behemoth Booker Brothers was taking over the colony's smaller, privately owned plantations one by one.

Papa's nemesis, the Booker clan. The gargantuan Liverpool company, Booker Brothers, was a malignant beast crawling up and down British Guiana's coastline devouring all the smaller, floundering estates. One by one, the privately owned plantations fell into the jaws of Bookers. There remained only Promised Land, belonging to us, and Albion, belonging to the Campbells, further west, towards New Amsterdam on the Berbice River, *not* in the claws of Bookers. It was no secret that Promised Land was next on the agenda; that offers had been made, and rejected.

Booker Brothers practically owned the colony. Sugar, shops and shipping were now all in the Booker domain. People joked that BG – as we all fondly referred to British Guiana – actually stood for Booker Guiana.

It did not help that we lacked our own processing factory – that we had to pay ever more exorbitant fees to use the Booker factory at Dieu Merci. At grinding season we could hear it chugging away day and night, a great growling monster at the edge of our world as if eager to devour us all. We needed a factory of our own. But all this was vague knowledge, picked up here and there by accident, mostly through chit-chat with the darkies – according to Papa's firm belief that business must be kept away from Home and Women.

A moment's silence followed. Yoyo and I exchanged looks; and then I spoke.

'Does this mean, Papa,' I said, 'that you expect one of us to marry Clarence Smedley?'

'That is the intended outcome, indeed,' said Papa. 'What I mean is this: I would like you – you especially, Winnie, as the elder – to cultivate an attitude of *positive inclination* towards him, as he certainly will towards you. Human nature will do the rest. It always does.'

'But, Papa – what about *love*?'

'Love – ha! That is exactly what I mean by human nature doing the rest. I know that you in particular have developed a certain sentimentality in this regard, Winnie, and I blame it on the novels of that Miss Austen you so relish. But that is just a fantasy. In fact, what we call love is better built on practicalities than on flighty emotions. Take it from me: the violins in the sky soon outplay themselves when faced with harsh reality. I know whereof I speak.'

Indeed, he did. We knew the story. Papa met the pretty, young, gay Ruth Birnbaum when hardly out of his teens, in Vienna. He was on the Grand Tour of Europe customary for young people of the English aristocracy. She was enjoying the opera season with her Austrian family. They were introduced by a mutual family friend, and it was mutual love at first sight. Archie held her in her arms, and as they waltzed to the Blue Danube at a Viennese ball, they vowed never to part.

Mama was from a cultured, wealthy, but not aristocratic family. Both sets of parents objected to the match; Papa's, because she wasn't English, had no title, and worse yet, was Jewish; and Mama's because marriage would mean her leaving Austria for England, which was simply too far away, and worse yet, because he was a *goy*. They never dreamed that in fact, she would end up in South America, almost at the end of the world. It would have been inconceivable. But Papa and Mama were young and in love: they knew better. They eloped, and the deed was done. Eventually, both families forgave them, especially after Kathleen's birth. Mama converted to Christianity; but then the Earl banished Papa to the New World, to take over the floundering fortunes of Promised Land. As a younger brother with few prospects in England it was, in fact, a sensible decision and got him and his foreign wife conveniently out of the way.

It wasn't banishment to them; it was an exciting new adventure, and they believed their love would conquer all. So the story went – romantic and sentimental and heroic – causing me to dream of a similar True Love waiting for me in the wings of time.

But the romance ended with Mama's arrival in British Guiana. She had never been happy here. She had come for love, stuck it out for love: a devoted wife and mother who masked her nostalgia for her homeland, her *Heimat* Austria, with the role of busy housewife, and tried to introduce her daughters – with little success as far as Yoyo and Kathleen were concerned – to a culture as far removed from the raw splendour of the Courantyne cane fields as the moon was from the earth. For we were British Guianese, born and bred.

But Mama was like a tender garden flower transplanted to the wilderness; she could not flourish in the torrid heat of British Guiana, in the isolation of Plantation Promised Land. Papa tried his best, by giving her the best, biggest, coolest room in the house, the Seaview Room on the second story, whose man-high windows stayed open all day to catch the cool Atlantic breezes and whose private shaded balcony kept the sun from pouring through those windows. This was Mama's personal realm; here she kept her memories and dreams: the trunk with Edward John's baby clothes, the desk where she wrote her letters home, her bookshelves filled with books in the German language, the oil painting on one of the walls – a wedding-present – of the snow-capped mountains surrounding Salzburg. There were other pictures of the Alps placed at strategic points all over the house; as if Mama needed these reminders of her true home wherever her eyes rested. And now she was gone. She had chosen those snow-capped mountains, and left us behind. *She had no choice,* I kept reminding myself. *She had to go. She is ill. Dr Joy will cure her.*

'What I want for each of you,' my solicitous father continued now, 'is a sensible marriage with a wealthy young man who can offer you a continuation of the security and comfort you have found in Promised Land. There are a few such young men in the colony, and when the time comes I shall certainly ensure that you are introduced to them – I'm thinking of you, now, Yoyo, assuming that Winnie and young Clarence are mutually compatible.'

Father guffawed. 'We can only hope and pray,' he added, 'that Clarence does not fall for one of the delightful Booker damsels!'

Booker Brothers sat like a huge spider on the perimeters of Promised Land, waiting to pounce. We two girls, of course, were prime victims as prospective brides, for then the takeover would be assured. For Clarence, as heir, to fall for and marry a Booker girl – well, it would be the death knell for our little kingdom.

'But, Papa …' Yoyo's face was as red as a tomato. I was anxious, fearing she might say something inappropriate. I was sure she was thinking exactly as I was – that life would never be the same again, after what we had seen today. That Promised Land was anything *but* what its name implied. That the whole concept of its existence was based on error, and that this error must be put right before we could even *think* of importing eligible young men of fortune. This was *my* worry, and we needed to tread carefully when we discussed it with Papa. I didn't want Yoyo plunging in with premature accusations; she could get emotional when she caught the bit between her teeth. But Yoyo had other concerns.

'Papa, is he qualified? What does he know about the sugar business? He sounds a bit of a dandy to me. Is he capable of running the business, making it profitable?'

'Now don't you worry your pretty little head, Yoyo! You are far too young to be concerned with marriage and future plans for the plantation. Enjoy what is left of your youth; for it will be over all too soon. Now, if you will excuse me – Miss Wright, do you have a moment? Will you join me in the library?'

The meal was over. Yoyo and I had eaten little, but Papa had not noticed, just as he had not noticed the subtle change in our demeanour. We ourselves – and at that stage I could speak confidently for Yoyo, for we were still of one mind – were hanging in vague uncharted territory as far as Papa was concerned, unsure of who he really was and how to respond to him. Up to now, he had been our hero, our Sir Galahad who could do no wrong. The knowledge we had gained this day had tarnished that once-shining armour. But then again, we could not be *certain*. I wanted so very much to *believe* in Papa: that he was as good and honourable as we had always thought. That the wrongdoing occurred on a level below his authority, and that he remained blissfully unaware of it. I hoped and prayed that it was so: that he lived in ignorance of the horror taking place on his own property, under his very nose. It could not be his fault. No, it couldn't! Papa was a *good* man. Hadn't he always supported Mama in all her little 'causes'?

Mama in her own pensive way had imbibed us with the concept of *Doing Good to Others Less Well Off.* One of the highlights of the Christmas season was always Boxing Day, when each of the house servants was given a hamper filled with special things to eat, and the half-day off to spend with their families – on a rotating schedule, of course, so that there was always a skeleton staff of darkies to look after us. And sweets were distributed to the children of the coolie workers. How we enjoyed those days of largesse! Yes, we were good people, Christian and kind. Including Papa.

We may only have been young girls, but Papa was fond of us and it was certainly within the realm of possibility that he would hear our pleas on behalf of the coolies. He was a good-hearted man, and what we had witnessed that afternoon was completely contrary to the courteous and civil manner with which he treated our house servants. Didn't they all live in their own pretty little cottages at the back of the compound, behind the orchard and the vegetable patch, the wood as sparkling white as our own house, and, though small, perfectly clean? Weren't we brought up to be polite to our servants under all circumstances? Hadn't we been allowed, when we were very young, to play with the darkie children who lived in the servants' quarters? Hadn't Iris, Mildred's granddaughter close to me in age, been almost my best friend, in spite of being a darkie?

I had been so fond of Iris; she had taken on the role of big sister to me, a role which Kathleen had failed to fulfil. Then, when she was twelve, Iris was brought into the house to work as a maid, our own personal maid, at which time our friendship had been deemed inappropriate by Papa. And then, a year ago, Iris had disappeared, without a goodbye. When I asked Mildred, she only shook her head; as I persisted, she only said, 'Iris belly swell'. She refused to say another word. I remembered Iris now with a pang of guilt. Perhaps I should have continued our friendship in spite of Papa's command; sought out Iris, found her, persisted. Life was so hard; how could one ever know what was right or wrong?

※ ※ ※

It was our habit to withdraw to the gallery after dinner; sometimes Papa and Miss Wright joined us and, in the past, so had Mama, and sometimes even Mrs Norton, our English housekeeper. Tonight, though, Yoyo and I were alone, and I was glad of it. We took our places in the wicker chairs next to the gallery's glass-topped table. Nora brought out our evening drinks, our Twilight Twizzles – fruit punch made from whatever was in season; now it was passion-fruit – and placed them on the table.

Evening was upon us. The *crapauds* were out in full force down below, croaking their good-night serenades, while the buzz of night beetles lent a shrill, constant accompaniment to their tuneless song – a twilight chorus of a thousand invisible singers. Far away to the north, the sky was still streaked with gold though the sun had sunk beneath the Atlantic. I slapped a mosquito on my arm. We were both silent; the night noises grew louder. In the distance, a baby cried in the overseers compound. A dog barked, and set off a torrent of barking as one dog after the other joined in. In the village, towards the coast, a donkey brayed, the sound carried clearly on the Atlantic breeze that played with my hair and now and then puffed out my blouse. The breeze was cool but never cold, not even in the fully-fledged rainy season; and yet I shivered.

I needed to talk. So much had happened today – first the *logies*, then this letter from England, and yet something else, something big, some unidentified *thing* looming in the recesses of my memory, so vague and yet on the other hand huge, like a mountain towering in the background of a landscape. What was it? I could not for the life of me identify the third momentous event of that day. I only sensed it.

Night had completely fallen. The steady flame of a kerosene lamp cast an orange glow on Yoyo. She sat next to me as still as a statue, eyes closed. I realised what her unusual silence meant: she was grieving for Nanny. In the half-light I saw that her cheeks were wet.

I turned to her: 'Yo …'

In that moment she turned to me. 'Winnie …'

We smiled in unison, understanding. We had this day been tried to the limits of our endurance; we had reached that place where our basic unity could have broken apart. Our differences could have wrapped themselves around each one of us and pulled us into separate shapes which no longer fit comfortably – pieces of a jigsaw incorrectly placed instead of slotting into a unified whole. Without saying a single word, we each of us reached and grasped the other's hand.

We sat in silence as night wrapped closer around us and folded us into its chant. Eventually, a background rhythm gently merged into the soprano cricket chorus; a pounding bass, rising and falling with the wafting of the wind; it drifted in from over the savannah, night's irregular heartbeat. A distant throbbing: tum-tum, tum-tum, tum-tum, alternating with a rapid tum-tum-tum-tum, sometimes silent, then picking up again, a steady yet arrhythmic pulse, sometimes rolling like thunder, sometimes staccato; a deep tuneless voice that seemed to hold in its thrall the entire savannah – the land and the cane, the sky and the ocean, the very moon and the stars and the wind, and us two listeners, and who knows how many more. We often heard the drums at night, but usually later, after midnight, and further away, from Dieu Merci, our neighbour to the west.

'Gracious! The drums sound so close tonight!' said Yoyo.

'Yes,' said I. 'I say … could it be coming from the village?'

'Yes, I think so … Oh! Maybe it's a wake! A wake for Nanny!'

'Yes,' I said. 'That must be it. A wake. For Nanny.'

'I wish we could be there. It just seems so unfair.'

'Yoyo: we wouldn't be welcome. Didn't you see those *faces*?'

❀ ❀ ❀

## Mama's Diary: Salzburg, 1889

*Liebes Tagebuch,*

*I am back from that dinner I told you about and it fulfilled every one of my expectations. Archibald Cox sat opposite me at the table – a long table with a white cloth and sparkling silver – and as servants floated in and out serving food and everyone else was chattering away about who knows what, Archie – as he asked me to call him – and I just kept gazing at each other, and each time our eyes met my heart went pitter-patter, pitter-patter, and I could hardly breathe, and I just wanted to smile, smile, smile! My cheeks are sore from all that smiling! Sometimes people spoke to me, trying to engage me in conversation. I was placed next to Liese Bohoffer and she had a thousand things to say, but I can't remember a thing she told me. I must have appeared so very rude, but frankly, I don't care! Thank goodness Liese was sitting next to Dr von Brandt's son, and I think it was deliberate; I think there is some matchmaking going on there, and so she was distracted for much of the time, leaving Archie and me to have our secret conversation across the table.*

*After dinner, the men repaired to the study for whatever men do when they are among themselves and we women repaired to the sitting room. But I managed to escape. I am so wicked! I went in search of him and he in search of me and we met in the hallway and he whisked me through a door and we were alone at last, in the Morning Room!*

*He did not waste time. He drew me into his arms the moment we were alone and kissed me, and I will never forget that kiss just as I will never forget a word he spoke – few were the words, but every one was pertinent. His German is not very good, and neither is my English, but he knew the right words and said it in both languages. 'I love you,' He said. 'Ich liebe Dich.' He loved me from the first moment he saw me, he said in stumbling German. Just as I loved him! It was real and strong and everlasting. 'We must marry!' he said. 'As soon as possible!'*

*And that was when the first drop of bitter vermouth entered my heart. It must have shown on my face for he then asked, 'What's the matter, my darling Ruth?'*

*I did not have the words to tell him. My English is faltering and weak – how I wish I had paid more attention to my governess! But I much preferred French and now I must pay the price for my inattention. So I just told him the essentials.*

*'I am Jewish!' I said. I'm not sure if he understands the implications. He seemed not to care, for he only kissed me again. And that kiss swept away my own fears, my own concerns … what a magical moment!*

*There was a desk in the corner of the room, with a writing pad and a pen on it. We exchanged addresses, for he is to leave for England in a day or two. At the thought of not seeing him again the second drop of vermouth entered my heart. 'We must write!' he said, and I nodded, but deep inside my heart was crumbling. How could I not see him again! How could I not marry him!*

# Chapter Three

We went to bed, calmed and somehow recovered. There could be no thought of sleep, and so, lying side by side in bed, we finally spoke of the matter of the *logies*. Something within me wished I had never seen what I had seen, that Yoyo had never stumbled upon that horror, had never drawn me into its implications, had never forced me to follow her down that stinking alley, had never pulled me into Nanny's dreadful hovel. It was an abomination, unlike anything I'd ever known outside of a novel.

I am not made of the stuff of heroes. I am drawn to things of beauty: flowers and art and music. But if one thing was clear now it was this: *we had to do something.* It's one thing to live in a happy world of sweet song and dance, blithely oblivious of any nasty shadow that the world might be casting on others; quite another to know the ugly truth and turn away. We had to do something. But what? And how? What could we do, young as we were? The only way was through Papa, and there our differences came to light.

Yoyo believed in confrontation. She thought we should hold Papa responsible for the eyesore on his own property, demand an explanation, and jointly discuss with him the ways and means of its removal.

I disagreed. 'We must give Papa the benefit of the doubt!' I told her firmly, speaking with all the authority granted by my seniority. Yoyo well knew how her impulsive, unconsidered responses to life's little hurdles sometimes caught her up in unfortunate nets of discord; it was always I who freed her. Calmness trumps agitation any day. And so now she listened as I explained how I thought we should approach this problem.

'Papa is not responsible for the living conditions of the coolies,' I told her confidently. 'You can't expect him to push his nose into every little detail of plantation management! He has supervisors for these things. There's Mr McInnes. Now, there's a nasty piece of work! I can quite imagine him being perfectly indifferent to the well-being of our coolies.'

Mr McInnes was the estate manager, Papa's second-in-command. A hard, mean, cruel man. I could easily see him as responsible for this atrocity, and hiding it from Papa.

'And what about the head foreman? What's his name now?'

'Mr Howarth …' said Yoyo. It seemed to be the beginning of a sentence, but before she could continue I did.

'Papa is the plantation *owner*, at the head of the whole operation. He doesn't concern himself with the little day-to-day practical details of how it's run, or how the workers live. Other men do that, and report to him. That's why it's up to us to tell him what we have discovered. I am sure he'll be just as shocked as we are.'

'I suppose you're right.' I felt rather than saw Yoyo nodding in agreement, and breathed out in relief. My worst nightmare was that she would burst into unwarranted accusations that would anger him, put his back up, and force him into a position of resistance which he could hardly retreat from without losing face. Yoyo and Papa were so alike in that way. Once hardened into a particular standpoint they would defend it simply for the sake of defence, even if it was obvious to others they were wrong. I was fortunate to have caught Yoyo before she had fixed her opinion regarding our manner of approach.

That decided, we moved onto more pleasant ruminations. We thought of what we would do once Papa was made aware of the deplorable living conditions of our coolies, and the changes that would subsequently be made. Our vision was of a field on the back dam, donated by us for the creation of a coolie village, where each family would have a pretty little white cottage, not unlike the staff housing in our own compound. Little wooden cottages on stilts, with marigolds and hibiscus in the front gardens and small plots for provisions at the back. Coolies loved to grow vegetables. They loved gardening. They loved cows.

'We could erect a cowshed for them,' Yoyo said, and I thrilled at the thought.

'And give them cows,' I said. 'And then we'll buy milk from them. It will give them a new source of income!'

'Chickens!' cried Yoyo.

'Eggs!' said I.

The house servants kept a chicken run in their own compound at the back fence, and when we were small we had enjoyed running up there every day to collect fresh eggs for the family breakfast. We had loved feeding the hens, and of course the little chicks were adorable.

'A school!'

'A surgery! With its own doctor!'

'Nurses and midwives!'

On we dreamt, creating the most perfect community of coolies BG had ever known. Plantation Promised Land would be a lamp of goodwill and charity in the entire colony, a living example to other plantations. This would be the crowning glory of our benevolence, for it meant transforming a little hell into a little heaven. The coolie village we planned would be a place where all our labourers would live lives very much like our own, only on a smaller scale; if we were the Sugar Kings then they were our subjects, and it was our responsibility to ensure their contentment and gratitude. I remembered with a shudder the hostile eyes that had stared at us as we walked through the logies, that sank rather than meet our own eyes. The sullen faces, the silent covert watching. In our dreams and plans those eyes would be friendly and grateful, those faces smiling; voices would call to us in good cheer as we passed, hands would wave, flowers would be pressed into our hands, strewn at our feet. It was all settled. Those atrocious *logies* would be razed to the ground, and every last splinter of them burnt. We would all watch, and cheer. Yoyo and I would be saviours, heroes. Our coolies would adore us.

'And then,' said Yoyo, with a giggle, 'Then I'll marry Clarence Smedley!'

'You! No you won't! Bags I Clarence! Because I'm the elder!'

'Oh, but I'll flirt with him and steal him from you! Mark my words!'

'Don't you dare!'

Yoyo giggled. 'I bet he's got a paunch! Like Mr Watkins – he's old too – thirty!'

'No – he'll be wearing a pince-nez. "My dear Miss Cox," he'll say to me, "would you do me the honour of accepting my wrinkled hand in marriage?"'

'No, he'll say it to me. "Oh, Mr Smedley," I'll say, "indeed I will; but I do wonder about a certain lady of ill-repute; I trust you did not bring her in your trunk?"'

We both spluttered with laughter; it was our only means, right now, of dealing with the further menace of Clarence Smedley.

We hugged and kissed, and settled for the night.

'Good night, Yoyo.'

'Good night, Winnie.'

✳ ✳ ✳

Papa always rose at dawn and never joined us for breakfast; he took his lunch in the senior staff compound along with all the managers, and so we would not see him all day. On this occasion, it was completely to our advantage. It would give us time to carefully plan our benevolent assault during the evening meal: the words we would use, who would speak when, and so on. Papa loved us; he would listen.

We rose to the gleeful chirping of a kiskadee on the mango tree outside, and the morning sun slanting in through the slats of the Demerara windows of the corner room we shared. To the front, on the north side, the sash window stood open and a cool morning breeze swept in and out; away in the distance the Atlantic glimmered grey and silver.

Some people might call the view from our window monotonous. This was the season of growing cane. Already, some of the canes were over six feet high and at full maturity could grow to up to twelve, towering high above you if you walked the roads between the fields. From up here, as far as the eye could see, was a vast, flat sea of vivid green – a shining emerald expanse stretching out to the east, west and south horizons. Stroked by the strong breeze wafting in from the Atlantic, it rippled and swayed as if brushed by an invisible hand. The northern view was different, for that horizon was indeed of the ocean, a glittering silver stripe in the distance.

The vista was not entirely unbroken; the red roofs of the European quarters were still visible above the cane, but still, the greenness seemed as solid as if painted on to the earth. And above the green, the blue of the sky. Oh, the vastness of the Courantyne sky! Perhaps it was the flatness of the cane fields that made that sky so big – an endless sapphire blue as deep as it was wide, sometimes empty of clouds, sometimes dotted with balls of white fluff that fled across it as if chased by wind-dragons. Sometimes cumulous clouds gathered on the horizon and crept forward to cover the sky; sometimes those clouds grew dark and heavy and seemed so low you could touch them, and then they would break: and the rainy season is a chapter in itself.

There are only two seasons in BG: the rainy and the dry. But on a plantation there are many more. Plantation seasons are dictated by the rhythm of sugar, and we knew each season by the sights, sounds and smells of the sugar cycle, field by field. Full growth, when all would be green as the cane stretched up to its full height. The burning of the trash, when the field would be set alight and the green would be consumed by flames and all around us the ocean would be of fire and smoke and the air smelled of scalded, syrupy, smoky cane-juice, almost intoxicating in its pungency. Then the harvest: swarms of half-naked coolies wielding cutlasses, shouting and swearing as they slashed their way through the fields, felling those giant scorched denuded canes. The loading of the punts; the cane-cutters, their bodies, now smudged black with soot, ash and cane-juice, bent low with the weight of the bundles on their backs. The loaded punts, pulled along the canals by mules, several of them chained together, on the way to the factory. Grinding season, when the factory over at Dieu Merci would groan and chug day and night like a monster waiting in the wings to devour us all. The harvested fields ugly as hell must be, disfigured by endless miles of hacked off stumps black from the burning. Then the flood-fallowing, when the young green shoots, the *ratoons*, would grow out from fields now glistening with water, and the coolie women bent low in the water as they weeded; or else, every few years, the planting of new canes.

It was magnificent. It was breathtaking. It was romantic. It was my life, my world. It was all I knew; sugar was in my blood. I had never questioned it. Until now.

❁ ❁ ❁

Yoyo and I floated down to breakfast smiling, almost singing. Miss Wright was already at the table, and noticed at once our spirited mood.

'You girls look very gay today,' she said, smiling herself. We were both most fond of Miss Wright; we regarded her as a member of the family, rather than an employee.

'Yes!' said Yoyo, eyes gleaming. 'We've got big future plans. Haven't we, Winnie?'

We looked at each other in secret complicity and laughed in unison.

'Well, they must be grand plans indeed! Do let me into the secret!'

'We will, and very soon!' I said.

Mildred appeared behind me and poured my coffee. I added sugar – brown crumbling Demerara sugar, from our very own cane – and milk. The milk was made from powder: Cow & Gate. Soon, I thought, we would have our own fresh milk; Promised Land would earn its name, not just for us, the planter family, but for our coolies too. They would live as well as did our darkies.

I wondered fleetingly about the two varieties of humans who lived on our land and worked under our jurisdiction: the darkies in the house and garden compound, and the coolies in the cane-fields. What were they doing here? How did they get here? I knew that coolies came originally from India and darkies originally from Africa; I knew that both Africa and India were part of the great British Empire, that Empire upon which the sun never set, of which father was so proud. There was a globe in our schoolroom, and we could both easily find Africa and India on it; the colonies, including British Guiana, were all pink. But how far was BG from Africa, and even more so, from India! BG, a little pink splodge perched precariously on the north-eastern shoulder of South America, conspicuous amid the expanse of dark green that formed the rest of the continent. India, on the other side of the globe! I would have to ask Miss Wright.

Mildred's ebony hand shook as she poured Yoyo's coffee and it spilled all over the table.

'Wah! Ah too sarry, Missy Winnie!' She tried to mop it up with her apron. The coffee ran across the polished surface of the dining table and dripped over the edge – I pushed away my chair and stood up.

'Nora!' cried Mildred to the kitchen girl. 'Fetch a cloth! Quick time! An' a mop!'

Nora ran in from the kitchen with mop and cloth; she and Mildred soaked up the coffee, Mildred apologising all the while: 'Sarry, Missy, sarry, ah too sarry'.

'It's all right, Mildred,' I said soothingly. 'I didn't get any on my clothes and look, it's all gone.'

Indeed, it had. Mildred and Nora bustled out to the kitchen and Mildred bustled in again with a platter loaded with warm bakes, puffed and golden and smelling delicious. But even before she reached the table something happened – I don't know what – and the platter tumbled to the ground and the bakes bounced away across the polished floor.

Mildred spluttered further apologies and Nora, alerted by the noise, rushed back out and both scrambled around picking up bakes and replacing them on the platter; bakes, which of course, could no longer be eaten.

'We gon' make more, Missy, Cooky gon' make more quick time!' promised Mildred.

Miss Wright was frowning. 'You're very clumsy today, Mildred!' she said.

'Yes, Miss, ah sarry, a too sarry – is jus' – is dem coolie-man outside de gate, ah frighten bad!'

'What coolies? What are you frightened of?'

'Dem coolie-man, Miss. Outside de gate. You 'en see dem yet? Massa done gone out to dem, tryin' to calm dem down.'

Miss Wright half rose from her chair, dropping her table napkin on the table. Yoyo and I stared at each other. Mildred seemed pleased to have an excuse to distract us from the spilled bakes, and continued in great excitement.

'Outside de gate! Missy! If yuh go to de window yuh gon' see! A tousan' a dem, shoutin' an' screamin' an' wavin' cutlass an' t'ing!'

We all three ran to the north window of the dining room. It was wide open, but due to the curved shape of the driveway we could not see through to the gate. We could hear, though, the commotion coming from beyond the curve. The three of us ran up the stairs and into Father's bedroom, which had the best north view over the treetops towards the ocean. And there we saw everything.

The double wrought-iron gates to our compound were closed. Before it, on the inside, stood Papa, along with several of the male darkies, our yard boys. On the outside, stood a swarm of coolies. Hundreds of them. A seething mass of half-naked brown flesh, arms waving, gesticulating. Even from here, we could see some of the foremost faces behind the gate, faces distorted by anger; mouths open, shouting; we could hear the shouts, feel the rage. Some of those waving arms ended in waving sticks, slashing the air.

Miss Wright gasped. 'Oh my good Lord!' she cried. 'It's a riot!'

My heart lurched and I too cried out! 'Papa!'

Yoyo simply turned and ran, leaping down the stairs. I swung around and ran behind her. Miss Wright came last.

❋ ❋ ❋

Papa didn't see us coming. His back was turned to us: he wore his work clothes now, khaki short trousers, khaki short-sleeved shirt, khaki knee socks, white pith helmet. He stood arms akimbo at the gate, gazing outward, unaware of our approach. Not until we were right beside him, to his right and left at the gate, did he notice our presence and even then it was only to swing around and shout at us to 'Go away!'

We did not go away. Yoyo shouted back: 'Papa, Papa, tell us, what are they doing here? What's going on? Why are they all so angry?'

The rage engulfed us like a tidal wave swept in by the ocean: a terrible roaring beast that would have dashed us to pieces were it not for the protection of the gate; and even that protection seemed fragile, for brown hands grasped the iron staves and curlicues, rattling, pushing, pulling. On the other side, brown men screaming: words I could not decipher for the rage that filled them, for the hatred that hurled them. Some of the hands reached through the staves and snatched at air, fingers grasping; one touched a curl of mine and I stepped back as if slapped.

Papa was shouting back but most of his words were drowned in the tumult; but then he leaned towards me, grasped my arm and screamed into my ear.

'Winnie, I command you to take Yoyo back to the house! This is *nothing* for you girls!'

I tried to obey; I rushed over to Yoyo and grabbed her hand but by this time she was pulling at his arm and shouting at Papa, and she shook me off as she would a fly. I grabbed her by the waist, and pulled, and this time she came away. Papa turned back to the mob and cried some indecipherable words: as ineffectual as shouting at a hurricane to calm it. By this time some of the hands reaching through the gates held sticks in them, bludgeons that swiped randomly and dangerously close to Papa, who took a step back. Behind the gate, brown men were climbing on the shoulders of other brown men; now the rampaging beast was two tiered, battering the gate, attempting to climb it.

On our side, the darkies did nothing, said nothing, only watched, knowing themselves safe behind the gate: they might be outnumbered, but the raging mob was caged. Most of the darkies were armed with wooden staves or cutlasses; they stood there almost smiling, as if enjoying the show. Now, though, some of them leapt forward and battered at the coolies attempting to breach the gate, pushing at them with the staves so that they fell backwards, or hammering at the hands on the gate's upper bars.

Behind the gate, the uproar's discord was settling into a steady rhythm, and at last formed words. A drum-beat, threatening and dark, pulsating with fury: *No More Massa. No More Massa. No More Massa.*

So this was it – the rumoured protest movement, *Massa Day Done.* Try as he would to keep it from our ears, Papa, the Master, could not keep us entirely in the dark. We both knew that the coolie labourers were agitating to be rid of us. But never had that agitation reached our gates. How could the Master's day be done? We *were* Sugar! If we were gone – then what?

Yoyo and I stood watching, hand in hand, paralyzed with fear. At least I was; perhaps Yoyo's temporary paralysis was bewilderment rather than fear. Miss Wright had run with us to the gate, but stayed at a safe distance when we rushed up to Papa. Now, she stepped up behind us and placed a hand on each of our shoulders, drawing us back even more.

'Come, girls,' she said soothingly. 'Let's go back inside.'

We both wriggled free, and turned to face her.

'What's going on, Miss Wright? Why are they so angry?' I cried out, and Yoyo too looked up at Miss Wright, her eyes pleading for an explanation.

'Come inside with me and I'll try to tell you,' said Miss Wright firmly, and with that assurance we at last turned our backs on Papa. Back at the house we raced up the two flights of stairs to Papa's room, to the only window in the house that offered an unobstructed view of the gate. We found all the house servants, every one of them, even the cook and kitchen maids, clustered round that window, and Mrs Norton, who should have known better, in their midst. Mrs Norton was a ghost-like creature who managed the household of countless servants with invisible efficiency. She was an Englishwoman, married to one of the overseers, and slept in the senior staff compound; apparently she had two children of her own, older than us; but we had never seen them, and she never spoke of them. Everything about Mrs Norton was businesslike and scrupulous. For Mrs Norton to be mixed up in the general excitement, to even show interest, was totally out of character and indicated something serious was at play.

Miss Wright assumed responsibility and chased them all away, except Mrs Norton, and we three took their places. In silent shock we stared at the mayhem below: now the coolies were all scrambling against the gate trying to climb over, and the darkies were beating them back. Father had given up his shouting; he paced up and down the driveway, stopping every now and then to watch. The noise of it all! The chant of the coolies, the shouts of the darkies, the whacking of the staves against metal and flesh.

'Tell us!' begged Yoyo at last, and Miss Wright drew a deep breath before speaking the words that would strip us of our innocence.

'There's been trouble for some time,' she said. 'The coolies have been restless, agitating against your father. It's happening in all the plantations up and down the coast. All the planters have to deal with it, not just us. Anger erupting in waves: threats and violence. Many of the planters have had to deal with revolts such as this one.'

'But – but why?' I asked, still safely cushioned in my little bubble.

'Well – they want better working conditions,' Miss Wright explained. 'They believe they work too hard for too little pay. And then of course their living conditions are said to be distressing to them …'

Yoyo and I glanced at each other, before turning back to Miss Wright. Yoyo spoke next:

'But why doesn't Papa simply raise their pay and let them work less and – and …'

'And improve their living conditions?' I completed her sentence.

Miss Wright sighed, and pressed our hands. 'Girls, you are both too young to understand. A plantation is a *business*, you see. A business has to make a profit, otherwise it falls apart, and the business owner is a failure. To make a profit the income has to exceed the expenditures. It's quite simple arithmetic. Therefore, expenditures must be kept to a minimum. To – to make changes in the allocation of expenses, such as raising pay and spending more money *generally* on the running of the plantation means less profit. Less profit means more likelihood of failure. Failure would mean – why, for you girls it would mean your father would be compelled to sell the plantation and return in disgrace to England. You don't want that now, do you? You're so happy here.'

'You mean it's all about – about *money?* Our coolies? The way they work, the way they live?'

'Well, basically, yes, actually. You could say it's all about money.'

And so it was Miss Wright who, with that single word, money, pierced the bubble of my childhood innocence, burst apart my little world of sunshine and rainbows.

Miss Wright looked embarrassed. She was a tall, slim woman, with smooth brown hair knotted into a soft round molly in the nape of her neck; not too old, but not young either, perhaps 30, a spinster who had come to us eight years ago. Papa had employed her primarily for Kathleen's sake. Previously, all three of us had attended school in the senior staff compound with all the other staff children: offspring of the managers and overseers and other British plantation employees. Yoyo and I had enjoyed it, for besides learning it meant making friends, after-school visits, and the like. There was a playground in the compound, a tennis court and a swimming pond; fun and games are better with many than with two.

But as Kathleen grew older, the more she objected. She thought some of the children were common; their language was vulgar, their accents – most of them were the children of Scottish farmers – unintelligible. They were beneath us in status. Father gave in and got her a governess, and to make the expenditure worth its while he took Yoyo and me out of school as well, so that we could benefit from private tuition. Miss Wright, found by our relatives in England and imported by Papa, was perfect. She taught us English, Arithmetic, History, Geography, French, and German, as well as Music and Art. Yoyo had expressed an interest in Science, but Papa had rejected it, reasoning that girls had the wrong brains for Science, as indeed for any mathematics beyond basic sums. And Mama had insisted on a governess who could teach German; I needed formal lessons in her native language, and Kathleen and Yoyo should learn the basics, even if reluctantly.

As a result of Miss Wright's employment, our contact with the compound children weakened; we saw less of them and more of each other. For me, only Emily remained: Emily Stewart was a red-haired, outspoken Scottish girl just a month younger than me; but Emily and her mother now lived in New Amsterdam during term time, so that Emily could attend secondary school. And so we had drifted apart. We now saw each other only in the holidays and on occasional Saturday visits to New Amsterdam, when Papa would visit his own friends and drop Yoyo and me off at Emily's. Mama would stay at home during those Saturday excursions, but Miss Wright would come with us and enjoy a day out without us. We often wondered where she went, but didn't dare to ask. Yoyo and I suspected she had a gentleman friend.

'I bet she kisses him,' Yoyo whispered, giggling, to me one night, but I couldn't imagine Miss Wright kissing anybody. Her amiability was of the cool, distant sort. We liked her; we did not love her. We showed her respect, not deference, and certainly not love. She taught us facts; she did not teach us principles. Certainly, though, on that morning she gave our illusions the stab of death. Money!

Money was a dirty word in the Cox family. For us girls it hardly existed. We had no need to think of it. We hardly ever touched it. We had our weekly pocket money, with which we'd cycle down to the village and buy sweets, and that was the extent of our dealings with it. We dropped the change into our piggy banks, and forgot it. We certainly never spoke of it. Sometimes the word 'wealth' was mentioned, but more in a philosophical context. Wealth did not mean money; it meant status and importance. We knew we were wealthy, but we knew it in an abstract sense. All it meant was that this was our plantation and here we ruled supreme; that the servants were in our employ, our subjects, and had to do as we said; but that too was abstract because we took it all for granted; it was simply the reality we had always known. It was because it was; because there was nothing else beyond that reality. We had known no alternative. And it was this way in the plantations up and down the coast from the Berbice River to the Courantyne, and I assume along the Demerara coast and the Essequibo coast, as well: each planter a king in his own realm.

'They want more money,' Miss Wright said simply. 'Money for food, for clothes and medicine. They want new houses.'

'And Papa won't give it to them?'

'I just explained to you why not.'

'But ...' to me it sounded most un-Christian. Weren't we supposed to give to the poor? How could Papa –

Miss Wright looked stricken, as if this revelation of the basic truth of our existence was far beyond the call of duty, as if every word must be wrenched from her.

'Winnie, look! The overseers!'

I turned back to the window. Three men were approaching, on horseback, galloping up the sand road behind the throng of coolies.

'It's Mr Grant!' cried Yoyo. 'And Mr Stewart!'

'Mr McInnes, too,' I added.

The men on horseback had reached the coolies, and that's when the real horror began. Out of nowhere, a pistol appeared in Mr McInnes' hand, and was pointed at the sky. Three shots rang out. The horses pulled up rearing and snorting and whips cracked and flew and snapped. Coolies screamed; the chanting stopped and they turned to face the overseers, suddenly silenced.

We could not see from that distance what exactly was going on but it seemed that Mr McInnes was speaking to one of the coolies. And then the crowd parted and Mr McInnes rode through it, accompanied by a coolie. They reached the gate, and Papa. Another conversation. And then the smaller, side gate opened to let that one coolie in. He was a young man, half-naked like most of them; even from this distance his upper body glistened in the early morning sunlight. It seemed he and Papa were going to have a civil discussion. The pounding of my heart slowed down; peril had been averted; Papa had saved the day.

But then, all of a sudden, the horror began again. Papa seemed to give Mr McInnes some kind of a sign and a whip passed between the gate-bars and two of the guards grabbed the young coolie and turned him around, struggling and fighting, and Papa whipped him. Whipped him like an animal, hurling the whip against the bare back again and again and again. Even from our upstairs window we could see red streaks appear on the young man's back. He squirmed and writhed but the guards held him fast so that he could not escape.

'No! No! Stop it! Stop it!' Yoyo and I screamed, watching helplessly from above, but our words were useless and the beating went on. My own voice was frantic, desperate. I was blubbering like a baby by now, hammering the window-sill with impotent fists. Yoyo screamed, in fury: 'Stop it! Stop it! No!' and she leaned forward as if she would propel herself through the window and fly through the air to stop the madness. But the beating went on, interminably.

Miss Wright seemed to wake out of a trance. 'Come, girls, come away; this is nothing for you.'

'No, no, I have to see!' cried Yoyo, and I did too. We struggled physically as Miss Wright tried to pull us away, and finally she capitulated and let us watch; I suppose she did not want to miss the show herself.

Papa was using was one of the whips the overseers carried with them when they went out to the fields; I always thought they were pretty things, with their long snaking thongs. This one cracked and snapped in the air and lashed at the writhing brown body that thrashed and struggled but could not escape.

Then the man lay on the ground and Papa kicked him. Kicked him again and again and he tried to curl into a ball but Papa continued to kick and kick and kick until he lay still. And then the gate opened again and the man was thrown out, into the crowd.

I broke down in tears. I let Miss Wright drag me away to my room, and then I collapsed in a heap on my bed in sobbing, spluttering anguish. I may have passed out, for I have no recollection of what happened next; except that, sometime later, we all three sat in the schoolroom while Nora served us the breakfast we had missed. We were all much subdued; but for me it was more serious. Something had shifted within me: a stone curtain of naiveté had rolled away; a veil of sentimentality had lifted. I had collapsed on the bed as a little girl, and stood up a woman.

None of us ate much, and none of us spoke. Yoyo nibbled at a bake in sullen silence; Miss Wright looked more embarrassed than ever, and I – I was in a state of suspended shock, whose only outlet were the tears that continued to leak from behind my eyes no matter how much I forced them back. Miss Wright gave me her handkerchief and I snorted into it and dabbed my eyes but doing so brought out yet more tears.

Nora carried away the remnants of breakfast and we settled in for morning lessons.

'Girls, now let's put that unpleasant business behind us and get down to work,' said Miss Wright briskly, but unconvincingly, plonking a pile of textbooks down onto her desk. The words 'unpleasant business' made me howl out in outrage and evoked a new burst of tears. Yoyo, not understanding the epic shift of mood that I had undergone, looked at me with contempt.

'Oh, don't be such a snivelling baby! I *told* you he knew all about it! I told you Papa was …'

'Girls! Stop arguing this minute!' Miss Wright tried to put authority into her voice but I knew, I could tell, that she was just as distressed as we were. 'And please control yourselves. Your father must *not* know that you saw – what you saw. Do you understand!'

I looked at her through my tears and indeed, I understood. I understood more than she thought I did. Her distress had nothing to do with what we'd seen. *She had known.* What we had seen was no surprise to her, but it had been her duty to keep us away from it, and she had failed, and now she feared Papa's reaction to that failure.

'You don't care, do you?' The words slipped out; the outrage erupting like a burst ulcer. 'You don't care about those poor coolies … you don't! You only care about your own hide – that Papa will be angry at you for allowing us to watch!'

'I bet she enjoyed it!' cried Yoyo. 'Like Papa did! Papa enjoyed it! Did you see, Winnie? He liked it! And you did too!' Jabbing her finger at Miss Wright's face, Yoyo's eyes were hard and cold with fury.

'I saw!' I agreed. 'I hate Papa! I hate him! And I hate you too!'

This to Miss Wright. Poor Miss Wright. She was not responsible for what had happened but now she bore the brunt of our wrath, a lightning rod in the teacup storm of adolescent rage. But what else could we do? We could hardly go down and rebuke the overseers, or our darkies who had watched, or Papa who had wielded that awful whip.

Miss Wright held up both hands as if to push away the wave of fury unleashed on her, and said, quite calmly,

'Girls, don't be silly. You saw what the coolies were doing. What do you think would have happened if they had not been beaten back? What if they had breached the gate and come to the house? Do you know what would have happened to us? I can't believe you're taking their side against ours! It was *clearly* self-defence. Clearly. They had to be taught a lesson, and that's what your father did. Teach them a lesson. A lesson they will never forget.'

'But …'

'Do you know what would have happened if the coolies had breached the gate? Can you even imagine? Why, we would all have been dead! Or even worse – we women violated! By a horde of savages! What can you be thinking to defend them! How could they possibly have been stopped, if not by force? Now stop being silly and let's get back to our lessons.'

And then, as suddenly as it had started, we were spent. Emptied, limp, like balloons that have lost their air. The morning was half over. Miss Wright began her lessons: Arithmetic, and then French, and then History. Listless, distracted, we complied. But then, in the middle of History – which had always bored me, but today more so than ever – I snapped back into form. I slammed shut my book.

'I don't care!' I cried. 'I don't care about these English and Scottish kings and queens, Henry the Fourth and William the Eighth or whatever! I can't remember their dates and I don't *care*!

What has this got to do with *me*, with *us*? Why can't you teach us *proper* history? Something *real*, something *relevant*? What are we doing here, for instance, we planters? If Papa is English why is he here in South America and not in England? Why did he get to own a plantation and plant sugar and get rich and have all these coolies and darkies working for him and what gave him the right to make them work for him, and make them live like pigs, and whip them? I don't understand. I just don't. Tell me. Tell us! You're our teacher, so teach us, for goodness' sake!'

Miss Wright and Yoyo both stared at me. Miss Wright's jaw dropped open. Yoyo smiled, and found her voice.

'She's right! I want to know as well!'

Miss Wright could only stutter. 'Girls, I – the curriculum! I don't think – I don't know ...'

'If you don't know we'll have to find out ourselves, won't we, Winnie?'

I nodded. 'Yes. Let's go to Papa's library and look for books.'

'Girls! Please!'

But this time we would not be silenced. We were already on our feet and clattering down the stairs to the large dark study at the back of the house where Papa had his desk, where he did his private business and kept his books. We were not allowed in here unless summoned in by Papa. Papa had told us there was nothing that would interest girls in here. And indeed, it was dark and gloomy and smelled of stale tobacco and floor polish and dried men's sweat and old rum. This was where Papa entertained his friends, the other plantation owners and senior managers from up and down the Courantyne Coast. Sometimes, even men from Georgetown; they came with their whole families, and while the wives and the children enjoyed the peculiar delights of a Courantyne sojourn, the husbands retreated to Papa's musty cave with their cigars and their rum and talked about who knows what.

One entire wall of the library was a fitted bookcase; the books were all behind glass doors, to keep the insects and the dust out. Yoyo and I stormed the bookshelves, breached the glass walls, grabbed the books, and blew away the dust that had somehow crept in through the cracks. Some of them, when we held them in our hands, almost fell apart for they had been attacked by termites, which had eaten tunnels into the pages. They smelt old, and musty like history itself. We searched their titles and tables of contents. We carted the most promising books to the table in the centre of the room where Papa and his cronies would sit with their drinks and talk away the night. We scoured those books for Truth, impatiently scanning the pages for mention of BG. We didn't find it.

Finally, though, we found a volume entitled History of the British Empire. Yoyo and I bent over it together, leafing through the pages to find some reference to our own country. Most of it was devoted to the continents of Africa and Asia. There were whole sections, several chapters long, on Canada and Australia. The West Indies were allocated a single chapter. In that chapter, three paragraphs were devoted to British Guiana.

'Here it is!' I cried. 'I'll read it aloud.'

And that I did. We learnt that the country had belonged to the Dutch and the French before the British; but we had known that anyway. That's why some of the places had names like Stabroek and New Amsterdam, Mon Repos and Dieu Merci. We learned that the Dutch had built the sea defences and prepared the coastline for agriculture with their expertise in land drainage, canals and *kokers*; that they had built the Demerara seawall. But we had already known that too; it's one of those facts you pick up in the course of BG childhood. We learned that the British came and changed the name of the capital, Stabroek, to Georgetown. That made sense, but didn't impress us much.

Cotton, we learnt, was the first crop, but was driven to failure by the more successful cotton industry in the southern states of North America. We learned that sugar was the next successful industry. We learned that labourers from Africa were brought in to work the fields. We learned that 'after Emancipation', first Chinese and then Portuguese labourers replaced the Africans. We learned that subsequently, labour was recruited in India; that East Indians came in their hundred-thousands as indentured servants, to replace the slaves … *slaves*. The word leapt out at us.

'Miss Wright,' I said, looking up at her with great solemnity. 'Did the Cox family own *slaves*?'

And from the annals of my memory the Troublemaker re-emerged. How could I have forgotten that terrible night, the Night of the Troublemaker!

❊ ❊ ❊

### Mama's Diary: Salzburg, 1890

*Liebes Tagebuch*

*I have not written to you for many months because when I write at all, it is to him! So please forgive my neglect of you. I will keep his letters forever – they are so funny, in his broken German! Yes, he studied my language but never perfected it so it is quite amusing to see how he stumbles over the language. I admit it must be difficult for him. I write back in German, for his comprehension is superb – he has a dictionary! I told him to write me in English and I will use a dictionary too, but he insists on his broken German – how droll! How charming!*

*He has repeated his proposal of marriage. He repeats it every time. I have not said yes even though I scream it in my heart. I have tried to explain to him the difficulties involved but he does not understand. Father will never allow me to marry a goy. Though we are not practising Jews, and Father is indeed quite liberal, I do know that that is written in stone. Oh, how I wish Mother were still alive! I'm sure I could have confided in her, and she would have persuaded him. Mother was a great believer in Love. But I am all Father has left now, and he is so protective of me! Now that my brothers have all moved out and married he is focused on me entirely – I am his family. He wants to see me well settled – I believe there is a friend of Rudolf's they are all hoping to see me engaged to. Never!*

*My heart is heavy, dear diary. Sometimes I feel I am under water, unable to breathe. Unable to reach the freedom of fresh air where I will be in his arms, his lover, his wife. It has to be! But how! I have told him a thousand times but he won't believe me. We will find a way, he keeps saying. Love will find a way. Love will conquer. I would love to believe it but I can't.*

*Father suspects nothing. I always manage to get my hands on the post first, and fish out his letters. If they knew they would put a stop to it. But I won't let them! No! I must sustain this love as long as I can! Sometimes I dare to believe him: Love will find a way!*

# Chapter Four

I don't remember the name of the Troublemaker; just that he made Trouble, and most rudely, at the dinner table. Our parents had given one of those elaborate dinner parties that Promised Land, back then, had been famous for. I hadn't been listening to the adult conversation; I was only about eleven at the time and Mama's darkness had not yet descended. On the contrary: she was in the prime of her womanhood, beautiful, spirited, charitable and gentle, the perfect hostess. Papa was proud of her; we girls adored her. She was one of those people who, without ever trying, somehow became the centre of attention; she had a natural charm. She spoke quietly, yet with vigour, for what she had to say was never frivolous but always heartfelt.

All I remember of that particular conversation is that the word 'slavery' featured prominently in it. The Troublemaker was not a planter; I vaguely remember him as being a Bookers man, possibly involved in shipping. Other Bookers men and their wives sat at the table – the sugar planters' aristocracy. As dinner progressed, the conversation became more and more heated, and ever more divided: it was the planters united against him, this Troublemaker. Eventually, Yoyo and I listened in, but as we were but children we did not understand, and only one sentence, spoken slowly and with great force and dignity by the Troublemaker, remains clear in my memory:

*'Indenture is slavery in all but name; nothing has changed.'*

I had no idea what indenture was; I had never heard the word before. But I could tell it was important. The table fell silent. Everyone seemed to hold their breath, Yoyo and I included. And then Mama, like all the other women silent until now, spoke up. Her voice was calm, but firm, and she spoke only two words, 'I agree.'

And then the table exploded. All the men began speaking at once, shouting, in fact, at the Troublemaker, who shouted back.

Mama remained silent for a few minutes. Then she turned to me and said, 'Winnie, take your sister upstairs.' Too scared to protest, we fled. Mildred brought up our puddings, and much confused, we ate them at the schoolroom table.

We could hear the shouting well into the night. At breakfast – for of course everyone stayed the night – there was nothing but silence. The Troublemaker had apparently left at dawn. The other guests left after breakfast. The following day was spent in silence. And that night, Mama and Papa had their big quarrel. They tried to keep it from our ears, but BG houses are built to circulate the air, they are full of louvres and vents that carry sound as well as they do breezes. Though we could not follow the substance of the argument, its heat and passion were palpable. I was terrified; so was Yoyo. I assume Kathleen was too; but she was older and living on different principles from us, as became clear in the following days when Mama and Papa made up and things returned to normal.

For of course, we wanted to know. What was *slavery*? we asked, tentatively. What was indenture? Instead of an explanation, Mama handed us a little book – apparently the Troublemaker had given it to her, secretly, before leaving – and told us to read it, secretly, and give it back when we had finished. The name of the book, I have forgotten; it was a first-hand account of a North American slave, and told us all we wanted to know. We were horrified.

When the three of us had read the book, Mama said simply, 'That was going on here in BG as well. Do you understand?' Yoyo and I nodded; Kathleen shrugged.

Then Mama told us that slavery had been abolished, and thank goodness; but the shortage of labour had forced the planters to bring in labourers from other parts of the world than Africa: Portuguese and Chinese and, most successfully, Indians. The

Indians, Mama explained, came on a five-year contract known as indenture; but, in practice, it was just the same as slavery. As she spoke those words, tears gathered in her eyes; but she wiped them away and said, fiercely, as if to herself, and in German: '*and that is what I have to live with*'.

Of the three of us, only I understood the words, but I did not understand their deeper meaning. A few months later, Edward John was born, dead. Mama fell into her darkness. The quarrel faded into non-existence in the shadow of that tragedy; we had lost not only our potentially much-loved little brother, also our very real and very loving Mama. That was our tragedy. What did we care about slavery, indenture, and quarrels that Mama and Papa may have had on the subject? The Troublemaker, the quarrel, the book: they disappeared, forgotten. Until now.

Now, I realized, that little book might still be in Mama's room, somewhere; possibly hidden away, as she had kept its existence a secret from Papa. I reminded Yoyo of the quarrel; her memory of it was much vaguer than mine, but she remembered the book and together we searched Mama's room. In the end, it wasn't hidden away at all: it was right there on the shelf with all her German books, next to a copy of Rilke poems. The title of it was: *A Narrative of the Adventures and Escape of Moses Roper, from American Slavery*; and it was written by Moses Roper himself.

We read that book, and now, with our greater maturity and understanding, the horror of it rose like bile in our throats, for we now understood Mama's revulsion: slavery might have been abolished, but the fortunes of the Cox family, our wealth, our status, our very lives, was built upon an atrocity! And furthermore, what we had seen over the last few days made clear to us that the Troublemaker and Mama were right; indenture was slavery in all but name, and indenture was alive and well and flourishing under our very noses.

❋ ❋ ❋

Papa hardly ever came home for lunch, but today he did, and he did so with a slamming of doors and a stomping of boots on wooden floors and a roar that we heard right up in the schoolroom.

'Winnie! Yoyo! Come down here right this *minute*!'

There was no disobeying that voice; but we did not hurry. The 'this minute' part of the command was certainly thwarted, for it was the only rebellion we could reasonably afford. We closed our books and walked down stairs to the front hall, knocked on the library door where Papa waited, and arrived not *right this minute* but the next. We stood before him, hands behind out backs like good little girls. My heart hammered within my breast. But I held my head up high.

'Yes Papa?'

'Is it true,' he said, and his voice was slow and rather low, the anger behind it constrained. 'Is it true that you two girls went out to the *logies* yesterday?'

'Yes Papa.'

'You walked through the *logie* compound and you went to one of the homes?'

'Yes Papa.'

'You *entered* Yashoda's *logie*?'

'Yes Papa.'

Papa by now was marching up and down. He still held his riding whip in his right hand, and both his hands were behind his back, as were ours; and as he marched the riding whip twitched as if eager to fulfil his purpose.

I stole a look at Yoyo in alarm. Could it be that Papa might actually whip *us*? If he could whip the coolies why not us?

It was a thought that would never have occurred to me before that morning. Papa was Papa: a kind, dear man who loved us with a boundless affection; who had tried to compensate us for Mama's withdrawal with extra portions of kindness and paternal consideration. I had no idea how other fathers treated their daughters, but certainly we had no complaints. He never forgot our weekly pocket money with which we could spoil ourselves with sweets from the village shop; he praised us when Miss Wright reported on our diligence and intelligence; he patted my head when I played a violin tune for him, and Yoyo's when she finished the Times crossword puzzle, and Kathleen's when she showed off a new silk gown. Yes, he had a temper, and when we did wrong he let us know in no uncertain terms, but his anger was short-lived and his punishments were fair. Sometimes, he and Yoyo had heated arguments, but they blew over quickly. He had never spoken an unkind word to any of us. We adored him.

I glanced at Yoyo out of the corner of my eye, and my left hand reached out, behind my back, fumbling at her skirt until her right hand closed around it. Our fingers intertwined, and our two hands clasped, palm against palm.

I squeezed her hand. *Don't,* I was trying to say, *just don't. Don't attack him, don't argue with him, don't let your outrage erupt.* My brave, headstrong sister! How often she plunged into conflict carried only by the passion of the moment, speaking or acting before thinking; and how often that impulse only served to complicate the conflict. How often it was left to me to speak the calming words that would quiet the waves. How many storms, fanned by her own unrestrained temper, we had thus ridden out together! She had no fear of Papa; she would clash with him without a further thought, as always in the past; but this was not the time. This was different. A different Papa; a Papa we did not know. A stranger.

'Could you,' he said now, his voice still calm and collected but with an undercurrent of wrath, 'could you please explain to me what in the good name of all Christian folk you were doing there?

What devil whispered into your ear told you to set foot in that – that …' he searched for a word, and found it: 'that *nigger yard?*'

I started as if truly whipped. I had never heard the word before, but from the way he spat the word, the way his eyes glared cold and hard, the way his lips curled and his face darkened, I sensed a slagheap of ugliness, a mire of utter abhorrence. My soul cringed; my body wanted to curl into a ball to protect itself from such speech. That Papa, always so particular about our language, always correcting us should we fall into the vernacular used by the servants, should let slip such an expletive in our presence was beyond comprehension.

Yoyo must have felt the same, for her fingernails dug into the palm of my hand. We stood before Papa in shocked silence, neither of us daring to speak.

'I'm waiting,' he said. He now stood before us, legs apart; he held the whip in his right hand and absent-mindedly tapped his open left palm with it. We remained silent.

'Give me an answer!' he shouted. 'You, Winnie!'

He aimed the whip at me, pointing me out like a convicted criminal.

'Papa, I – I don't know. We were just …'

'It was my fault, Papa!' Yoyo had finally found her voice. 'Please don't be angry with Winnie! It was all my fault. I took her there. She didn't even want to go. I'm to blame. I wanted to see Nanny. Nanny was dying. Nanny *died,* Papa!'

'Aha,' said Papa. 'So now we're slowly approaching the truth. Can you now tell me what induced you to take your sister, and yourself, into places that don't concern you? That are not your *damned* business?'

Another expletive! A word Papa had never, ever used in our presence. A profanity, a sacrilege, a bolt of lightning. Our clasped hands squeezed tighter than ever.

'Papa, I'm very sorry. I …' Yoyo stopped, took a deep breath, and repeated, 'I'm very sorry, Papa. I won't go there again.'

'I should think not!' Papa bellowed; but Yoyo's contriteness worked its magic. To my relief, he placed the whip on the table, folded his arms on his chest, and said, in a much milder tone of voice, 'remember, from now on the *logies* are out of bounds for you girls. Absolutely and completely out of bounds. You are never, ever to set foot in that place again. Do you understand?'

'Yes, Papa,' we said in chorus. Papa now seemed completely pacified. His voice gradually turned into the old familiar Papa-voice, the voice he used to explain the world to us growing girls. Paternalistic, authoritative, but concerned and kind. It was the Papa we knew; but the words he spoke were foreign, and as he came to the end of his speech, we recognized them as lies.

'There are certain matters which do not concern you whatsoever. In particular, the running of this plantation. That has nothing to do with you. Keep out of it. It's not your business. Do you know what trouble you set into motion? A riot! The situation is volatile as it is, but two rich white girls walking through the nigger yard …' that word again! I inwardly cringed 'to gloat at the conditions of the coolies is the last thing we need on this plantation. Do you know what could have happened? Do you know the fuse you lit? Thank goodness I was able to talk the coolies into submission! They are a very emotional people, you know; sometimes they do erupt and one needs to take them in hand though firmly. They are like children, like you, Yoyo. A stern word or two, and they are back in their place. Sometimes, even, a good flogging does the trick.'

I heard Yoyo's sharp intake of breath and I pressed her hand as hard as I could: *say nothing! Be quiet! Don't contradict him!* Glancing at her again, I saw the tight clench of her jaw, the pulsing vein in her neck. She was about to burst. Extremely anxious, I squeezed her fingers again in warning. *Don't. Keep it down.*

As if completely exhausted, Papa flung himself into the high-backed leather armchair which had been among the furniture shipped from England, and was his favourite. He smiled at us. I could not look at him, nor meet his gaze. I kept my eyes lowered. I saw only his heavy boots – astonishingly, he had kept them on! – and khaki socks, and the hairy bare knees above them.

'Come,' he said in a different voice, and he gestured to us both to approach, then held open his arms. In the old days, that is, just a day earlier, we would both have rushed into those waiting arms, laughing with affection; we would have hugged him and sat on his knobbly knees, left and right, and known all was right again with our world. We would have forgiven him the scolding at once; our hearts would have lifted to hear the familiar fatherly cadence of his speech as he explained himself. We would have *believed.*

'It's not easy being a planter in British Guiana,' he said in a tone of deep confidentiality. 'It's tough work; it toughens you. Thickens your skin. Emotionally tough, emotionally draining, even for a man. There are hard decisions to be made; decisions no woman could make, or ever understand. Business decisions. Now, I want you girls to trust me, to know that everything I do, each decision I make, each step I take, it is all for *you,* for your comfort and well-being. That is all I care about. This is our home; I must protect it the way I think best. An Englishman's home is his castle, but I share it with you and *you* come first. It is a place of peace and well-being, a refuge. I do not want the travails and the hardships of business to ever enter these walls. They must be kept out. That is why I have this rule: plantation business stays outside every room except my study. That is why we never discuss plantation business at the table. That is why I want you girls to keep your pretty little heads pretty. There are words I never want you to speak within these walls. There are some aspects of this business I never want you to think about. I want you to be happy and carefree, and up to now you have been – is that not true?'

Papa seemed not to have noticed that this time, we had not come to him. We were not perched on his knees, drinking in his words and nodding at their wisdom. We still stood, facing him, stiff and speechless, our hands still joined. All of this a clear signal to him, had he been observant enough to notice, that we were united against this new entity, this stranger who had, I now realized, always lurked in the shadows of Papa's geniality. The stranger had always been there, but hidden from our eyes, kept away from our awareness. A cold shudder passed through my body, which might have given me away, but Papa did not notice.

He sighed. 'I know you girls miss your mother. She has not been a mother at all these last few years. Misfortune has changed her almost beyond recognition; at this time in your lives she should be with you, guiding you, advising you, helping you to take your first steps into the world of adults, which in the case of a female means ushering you into the social world where you will eventually find your husbands. It's not easy in British Guiana, which is why we decided to send Kathleen back to England – it was anyway, her wish. The social world among the planters is a rather isolated business here, especially on the Courantyne Coast. There are no young people of your own age and standing on Plantation Glasgow or Dieu Merci and we can hardly expect you to mix with overseer's children or even senior management ... not at this stage in your lives. Much less find your husbands there.'

He paused, and scratched his chin. Yoyo and I looked at each other; I raised my eyebrows, she mouthed words I could not decipher. Papa continued.

'It's difficult, being a father of girls. Especially so for a planter. Now, if you had been boys it would have been different; I would have introduced you into plantation affairs long ago so that one day you could take over from me. But now your education is drawing to a close – Miss Wright has done an excellent job and I expect you both to pass your School Certificates; but what then? Miss Wright has intimated that you are both capable of attending Bishops' High School in Georgetown to get your Higher Certificate, but I do believe that education is wasted on a woman – what will you do with a Higher Certificate as the wife of a planter? One hears such atrocious stories of these suffragettes in England – all due to too much education. No. I can't send you to Bishops. Were we in England you would long have been part of the London scene, even if you had not officially come out. But here – I can hardly send you to your uncle, as I have done Kathleen – you are both far too rough around the edges. You're such wild things. I dare say you would not be happy in London. Yes, Mr Smedley will be coming soon, but you are still too young to marry.' He paused. Yoyo and I looked at each other, wondering what was coming next.

'Don't mind me, girls. I'm just thinking aloud. These are worrying times in many ways. But remember your interests are my first concern and I will find a solution before long. Now do come here and kiss your Papa goodnight. I do love you so much, you know. Don't worry your little heads about anything you may have seen – remember that this is your home, and my whole life is dedicated to your comfort and well-being. Trust me. Now run along both of you.'

❋ ❋ ❋

That night I could not sleep; there was just too much to digest. The events of the last two days tumbled over and over again in lurid pictures; my thoughts were not in words but in bold images of brown bodies scrambling against a gate, horses plunging, whips cracking, men shouting and screaming; and then the *logies*, silent and grim and lined with coolies whose hostile gazes burned my flesh. And coolies with cutlasses sweating in the cane fields. Coolie women up to their waists in water, pushing the punts along the canals. Coolie men carrying loads of cane. The story of Moses Roper.

And there was yet another thing I couldn't put my finger on, that large looming Something that refused to show itself.

Hour after hour I tossed and turned. But as the night grew deep and old, the violent knots within my mind began to unravel and their noise became less thunderous. The night chorus of beetles settled into a steady silver buzz. A darker sound punctuated the night, a deep rhythmic pulse so natural it was like the earth's heartbeat. The drums. I listened to the drums for a while, and my breathing calmed and the next thing I knew it was morning.

❃ ❃ ❃

## Mama's Diary: Salzburg, 1890

*Liebes Tagebuch,*

*Archie loves the idea of an elopement! He has already started planning – we must lose no time, he says. Almost a year has passed since we met, and he can wait no longer. He is supposed to be going to Paris next month to visit an aunt. He will pretend to go, but instead, make his way to Salzburg. I am to write back to him and suggest a good place to meet, and a date and a time. We will then make our way to London, posing as a married couple.*

*I am so thrilled I can hardly sleep, but at the same time a little bit scared. This is such a preposterous thing to do! Father will be devastated, and so worried – but when he knows I am alive and well he will be so relieved he will finally bless the union and we can be married properly. I will write to him as soon as we are at some distance from Salzburg, and let him know I am safe with Archie. No – I will leave a note. It is the only way. I will write to Archie tonight with my instructions – and a date! Oh, how I hope nothing goes wrong!*

# Chapter Five

Sometime in the early dawn I woke up with the words poring through my mind: German words, addressed to Mama. German was our secret language; our special bond, for my sisters had refused to speak it, and eventually forgot whatever they had learned. Not me; I loved German, for it connected me with her. So Mama had ensured that I not only speak but also read and write German; she shared her precious books with me, and taught me the words to Schubert's songs, to Bach's cantatas and to Rilke's poems. When I was ten, she arranged for me to correspond with the daughter of the woman who had been her best friend back in Austria, and even now, Miriam Gottlieb and I exchanged at least three letters a year.

Mama grew up in Salzburg, in an upper class Jewish family. She grew up in a world of music, ballet, theatre and opera, and everyone told me that I had inherited my quiet nature, reserved disposition and love of artistic beauty from her. She was a gifted violinist, and had it not been for her prolonged mourning the two of us would surely have enjoyed many hours of exquisite music-playing – duets, and with Miss Wright's arrival – trios, for like Mama, Miss Wright was an excellent pianist, and she also played the flute.

The upright piano in Mama's morning room now stood mostly closed and silent. Her Stradivarius – given to her as a wedding present by her devastated but forgiving family – had returned to Europe with her; Mama had often hinted that the tropical climate would destroy it; perhaps it could now be rescued from that ruin.

How different from the old days! In the old days, before Edward John's death, on some special evenings, we would push the drawing-room furniture against the walls, roll back the carpets, and

Mama and Papa would dance. Oh, how they would dance! There was no music, no one to play the piano for them, much less an orchestra, but we would all sing the music, and sometimes I would play my violin: Da-da-da-da-da, da-da, da-da! Da-da-da-da-da, da-da, da-da! Laughing, they'd waltz to the Blue Danube, Papa's long legs in his evening suit striding out as he swirled her around the room, Mama bent back over his arm, her head thrown back, her skirt swishing around her legs, her dark hair swinging, and always laughing. They would glide through the room as if on air, laughing, singing, and we children would clap and laugh too, and sometimes we'd join in and dance with them, spinning barefoot around the polished drawing room floor. Sometimes Mama would twirl herself free of Papa's arms and dance alone, arms swinging, eyes closed, and we'd know she was back in Salzburg under the chandeliers in an exquisite, sparkling gown, dancing to a full orchestra. Papa would watch with eyes glowing in admiration. Then he'd step up to her with open arms and she'd sail back to him and they'd dance the last coda together, ending it all with a flourish, she with a dainty curtsy, he with a deep bow, removing an imaginary hat; and we girls would clap excitedly and cry for an encore.

'*Wunderbar*! Ach, how I wish you girls could hear the orchestra!' she would cry, and sigh in frustration, for this she could not offer us; there was no orchestra in the whole of BG. But we could hear the music by the way she danced, by the light in her eyes, by her radiant beauty, by her cries of '*Wunderbar*!'

And then the singing stopped, and the dancing, and the cries of *Wunderbar*! I missed those evenings so much, the gaiety and the joy of seeing Mama and Papa, such a beautiful couple, happy and dancing together, palpably in love; but when I tried to speak of them to Yoyo, she would only sneer.

'*Schmalz*!' said Yoyo of my nostalgia. 'Pure *Schmalz*.'

If Papa missed those dance evenings he never spoke of it to us; Kathleen had moved on to a better, more exciting life; and so it was left to me alone to yearn and pine for better days, and for Mama.

Mama and I, I always believed, shared a special link in spite of her sorrow. Of her three daughters, Kathleen and Yoyo were fair, like Papa, whereas I was dark-haired, like her. There was the music we both loved, the violin lessons she had given me from the time I was a small child; Kathleen and Yoyo were bored by music. Then there was language. Mama had spoken to us all in German when we were little. It was our first language, literally our mother tongue, but after a while, my sisters refused to speak it, and Papa forgot the few words he had learned as a youth, forcing her to switch to English. So German became our own private language. Mama clung stubbornly to her little German gems of comfort, such as pronouncing Yoyo's full name, Johanna, the German way – *Yohanna* – and sprinkling her speech with *ja's* and *nein's* and calling us girls *Liebes* or *Schatz*, and Papa, *Liebling*.

In the old days, the good days, that language was our link. Even through Mama's silences, and the sadness that clung to her like a miasma, I felt it. I was the one who could best reach her. I shared her beloved books; I understood her melancholy; I knew her depths. When Mama sat at the piano and sang those wistful Schubert *Lieder,* I tuned in to the wellspring of yearning at the core of her being. When she spoke longingly of the Austrian seasons, I could empathize.

'*Schnee*!' Mama would sigh, and in her clipped Austrian accent, add, 'Snow! There is nothing in the world so beautiful!' conjuring up a vision of a thick white silent blanket that covered the world in cold pristine beauty. Mama's *Heimat:* her home. Not mine. I never longed for that *Heimat;* I was happy right here, in my own. Mama lived in a world that was purely emotional, consisting of nostalgia and homesickness and grief and memories of friends and family and places she would most likely never see again. Young girls never think much about their own mothers'

cares and sorrows, and it was only much later that I pieced together Mama's story and understood how unhappy she must have
been in BG.

❄ ❄ ❄

Now, lying in bed, I longed for her so much that tears pricked my
eyes. I wanted to deposit the entire burden of this dramatic day in
her lap. Have her guide me through the storm, tell me what to say
to Papa, how to manage a situation that was far too complicated
for a girl of sixteen. Even in her withdrawn, sorrowful state, she
was still Mama, and I could draw strength from her. Mama – the
real, original Mama, not the ghost of her we had known these last
few years – would do something about those *logies*. I was sure of it.

The *logies*! Oh, those *logies*! And *Nanny*! Living out her life in
the midst of such foulness! The memory of Nanny burst into my
consciousness with the immediacy of a bomb blast, casting out
all worry of Mama; grief overcame me for the first time, the grief
that had been displaced by the general shock of what we had seen.
Her face, gleaming brown with coconut oil, loomed before me:
the kind eyes wrinkled around the edges, the thin greying hair
tied back in a plait down the back of her neck, her softness when
she gathered us into her arms, Yoyo and me. The Hindi words we
had learnt from her; her voice, always warm, always calm: 'don'
worry, *beti*, everyt'ing gn' be all right.' But everything wasn't all
right for her. She never *said* … she never spoke. She never told us
of her real home in the *logies*.

And then Papa. His fury. The whipping of the coolie. It was
just too much.

I needed to talk to Mama. I needed to talk to her desperately.
And since I couldn't I had to write. In the half-light, I slipped
from the double bed I shared with Yoyo, taking care not to wake
her as I ducked beneath the mosquito net and tiptoed barefoot
across the floorboards to the door. Across the hall to the school-

room, avoiding the board that creaked, into the schoolroom, and straight to the desk. I removed a pad of paper from the top drawer, found my pen, and dipped it into the bottle of Quink. I did not have to think; it was as if it were already written and all I did was to take dictation.

*Liebe Mama,* I wrote, and continued, in German:

*It has only been a few months since you left us and already it seems like a lifetime since we waved goodbye on the Georgetown wharf. How I miss you! I have so much to tell you and I wish so much you were here! …*

It was an outpouring; words erupted from me such as I would never have been able to say to her face. It was the longest letter I had written in my life. I told her everything. I told her of my loneliness and isolation; I told her of the *logies* and the whipping and Miss Wright. I told her I remembered the Troublemaker, the book about slavery. I did not stop writing once. I did not read it over to correct spelling or other mistakes, as Miss Wright would have insisted. It was not a well-written letter. But it came from my heart and it said all the things I wanted Mama to know; so before I could have doubts and second thoughts I folded it, pushed it into an envelope, sealed it with red sealant, and stamped it with the Promised Land stamp. There. It was done. I slipped it into the neck of my nightgown and returned to bed, at peace. The next thing I knew it was morning.

❊ ❊ ❊

After breakfast, I told Yoyo what I had done – that I had written to Mama and wanted to go to the post office to post it.

'You wrote to Mama? Why, you should have told me – I would have added a few words and then she would have heard from both of us. Really, Winnie, you can be so selfish at times. Wait a few minutes and I'll add a letter of my own. Or have you already sealed the envelope?'

For a moment, I held my breath: would she insist on opening it? Read the letter? It was so private, so intimate! Then I remembered it was in German; she could not read German. I nodded.

'Bother!' said Yoyo, and, 'really, you should have told me. We could have written together. I do hope you told her what is going on here! Did you? Good. Well, then that's done and I won't bother to write this time – I do hate writing letters. Especially since I'm sure she won't write back – but she does need to know the situation here. I hope you told her in no uncertain terms what we think of Papa! Really, I'm quite furious and I don't know if I can ever forgive him. Very well, then, let's go down to the village.'

So we collected our bicycles and rode down to the village. Usually Harry our house-boy did this, but it was Saturday, so there were no lessons, and we had our weekly pocket money to spend. Papa had left for Georgetown before dawn, so we did not see him before we left, and I was glad of it; the more time passed between the incidents of the last few days the less inclined I was to meet Papa face to face. The inevitable confrontation was postponed, and I was glad of it. I now realised how carefully we had to tread. Papa had become a stranger.

It was good to escape the house, which more and more was beginning to feel less like a home and more like a prison – a place that kept us away from a world briskly striding forward. I had never thought about this before – that out there, across the river that separated us from the more progressive county of Demerara and across the ocean that lapped almost to our doorstep, events took place – that the dramas I read about in my beloved novels had their counterparts in real life. And that, but for the accident of our birth and the isolation of our geography, we too would have been a part of that bustling world, knowing things, seeing things we could only dream of, and living lives worthy of being written about in novels.

As we rode along the sandy path towards the village, I noticed for the very first time the coolies working in the cane fields that lined the road. I mean, really *noticed* them, which is different from merely *seeing*. I had never really seen them before as *people*; they were simply an integral part of the landscape; their dark shiny bodies glistening in the sunshine were as familiar to me as the emerald green cane or the cobalt blue of the sky. I even had thought it beautiful – part of the Courantyne charm. I had taken them for granted.

But wait – no. A young child takes nothing for granted. I *had* noticed them, when I was very young. I had asked questions. *Who are those brown people?* I had once asked Mama. *Why are they not wearing clothes? Why are they cutting cane? Why are they in the water? Why are they so unfriendly, not greeting us?*

'They are the Poor Unfortunate,' Mama had replied. 'We must pray for them.' And she had. Every evening when Mama led our prayers at our bedside she had added, after we had prayed for all our family members, 'and bless the Poor Unfortunate'. After Edward John's death Mama had no longer led the prayers, and we had forgotten the Poor Unfortunate, and that is when they became part of the landscape. Only bodies. A part of the background of my existence: not really people, with homes, families, children, cares, sorrows, and the propensity to be happy and love and plan and care about their own lives.

Guilt struck me as a bolt from heaven. How could I have been so blind, so wrapped in my own world? How could it be? It was like emerging from a thick black fog; like sight returning to the blind. A great sense of helplessness and despair descended on me. I was a prisoner of history, of my ancestry. It held me captive within thick walls that I, alone or even with Yoyo, could not break down. What would we do? What *could* we do, two young girls dependent on the very keeper of that fortress for their own survival?

The village started with a few straggling cottages. A darkie woman in her front garden waved and smiled as we rode past, and a man carrying a bulging bag across his shoulder removed his

cap; we were well known. The post office was on this main road.
We dismounted, placed our cycles on their stands, and entered.

It was no more than a single room on ground level, divided by
a waist-high counter, the larger portion of the room being behind
the counter. The walls of the behind-counter area were lined with
shelves and cupboards; there were drawers and cubbyholes and a
rather large desk with a chair; and at the desk someone sat with his
back to us. Strange clicking noises seemed to be coming from the
desk. The front door was wide open, and we made no sound as we
crossed the threshold, and so this someone did not hear our entry,
and jumped when Yoyo called out, 'good morning'. He sprang to
his feet, almost toppling his chair, and turned towards us.

My heart stumbled unaccountably as I recognised him. It was
the lad who had delivered Uncle Percy's letter. Of course it was!
Hadn't he said that he was replacing Mr Perkins? The various
dramas that had followed in the wake of our first encounter had
wiped his memory entirely from my mind, and only now I remembered – what? Nothing, really; nothing real. Simply an acute
sense of his presence, and bemusement at his entire demeanour,
and an odd sensation I could not identify for I had never known
it before; not ever, not with anyone, and certainly not with a
darkie. The nearest I can come to describing it is this: it was an
overwhelming sense of *recognition*. As though I already knew
him, even though I didn't. As if we had already met, even though
we hadn't. As if we were already friends, even though we weren't.
All of those feelings, combined and vague, and distinctly foreign:
it was the other Big Thing of the last few days. And that Big Thing
was back. My breath stopped as he leaped across the room to join
us at the counter.

'Good mornin', ladies, Miss Cox, mornin'; what can I do for
you?' he said, and looked from me to Yoyo and back, smiling
that very same smile as before, a grin that Papa would certainly
have described as 'too familiar for a darkie', and yet it wasn't:

it contained nothing but simple friendliness. A heart-warming smile that made you want to smile back, so I did, and, I'm afraid to say, I blushed; at least, my cheeks grew hot so I knew that they were red. Ashamed of that blush, I lowered my eyes from his; I was strangely sure my eyes gave me away, that he could read me like a book.

When I looked up again I found he was engaged with Yoyo, who, unlike me, seemed perfectly composed; she had, apparently, looked beyond him to the desk at which he had been sitting.

'What's that thing?' she asked, pointing.

'What? Oh, that. I'll show you.'

He bounded over to the desk and back and placed the object in front of us. It was a strange, rather crude contraption: a small wooden board, on top of which a wooden lever was balanced on a metal hinge; it had a knob on one end, and on the other a metal spike on the lever, which touched a small metal plate on the board. Underneath it was a spring. As he showed it to us he grasped the knob end and tapped a few times; the noise that we had heard emerged, an arrhythmic staccato sound.

'It's a Morse machine – a Morse key,' he said. 'I made it myself! I'm practicing the Morse code. Look, see, you tap this li'l thing here, and normally, it would have wires attached to it that you send out long and short pulses down the wire, codes for letters, words. And someone on the other end of the wire, even far away, gets the message and writes it down. Hey presto: a telegraph! You have to learn the combinations of dots and dashes – really. They're called dits and dahs, but we like to call them 'dots' and 'dashes' anyway. Look how it works:'

He tapped several times on the machine again, and then looked up with an expression of pure delight. 'See? You know what that was?'

I watched him as he spoke, taking in his features; they pleased me. Today he was without his khaki postman's cap; his hair was cropped short, in the darkie style. His hairline started far back on a shiny high forehead – a stark black curving line that swept in and out along the natural contours of his forehead, the hair springy like black moss against the smooth dark brown of his skin. His eyes were large, set wide apart beneath finely drawn brows. A generous smile revealed pearly white teeth set in a strong jaw with a dimple in the middle. On the counter, long-fingered hands moved in time to his speech to demonstrate his words, tapping at the machine.

'No,' said Yoyo. 'What was it?'

'Everybody knows that! SOS! Dot-dot-dot, dash-dash-dash, dot-dot-dot: 'S-O-S'. Save our souls – the emergency call!'

'Oh, well, our souls don't need saving.'

She nudged me then, and I woke up. All this time, while he had been speaking, he had looked from one of us to the other: mostly to Yoyo, as she had posed the questions and he was, of-ficially, answering her; and yet he kept glancing at me as if to include me in the conversation, or as if to – oh, I don't know. It was more than that. It was as if there were two conversations go-ing on, one on the surface, a spoken one, with Yoyo, and another beneath the surface, a silent one, with me; and only he and I knew the silent one. But then again maybe it was all my own rabid imagination, this thing about a silent conversation, and I was just being silly and over-sensitive and taking my 'inner feel-ings too seriously', which is what Yoyo would say.

The nudge she gave me was as good as an accusation. 'Oh!' I said, as I jumped to attention. 'I have a letter!' And pulled it out of my purse.

The young man looked even more delighted. 'A letter!' he said, and, looking at the address, 'to Norfolk, England. That will be twopence.' He pronounced Norfolk phonetically, Nor-folk, which I found endearing.

But Yoyo laughed. 'It's pronounced Nor-*fuck*,' she said.

I gasped in shock, my ears burning. I'm sure I turned beetroot red. How could she say that word! In a *man's* presence! A word we'd heard whispered about, giggled about, with the other youths from the senior staff compound, the dirtiest word of all! Yoyo only giggled, enjoying her moment. I met his eyes; his lingered in mine, and I saw embarrassment there. I turned away, fumbled in my purse, and handed him the money. I watched as he tore a stamp from a large sheet, brushed it with glue, and stuck it on the envelope.

I was scrambling for something distracting to say, for Yoyo's last word still hung in the air. I reached for the Morse key, and tapped a few times on it. Each time, it clicked.

'So every letter is made up of dots and dashes?' I asked.

'Yes,' he said, relief in his voice. 'I taught myself. It's easy – after a while you know the whole alphabet just as dots and dashes, so you could theoretically write a whole letter an' sen' it by telegraph. This letter, for example. You could write it in Morse and the recipient would get it mebbe even the same day. Think of it! Normally it would take weeks to get to Norf ... to England, right? But the same day!'

'But I thought telegrams were always short?' That was me again; I had finally found a way out of my debilitating embarrassment, for I was genuinely curious. What if I could write to Mama and have my letters delivered the same day! What a miracle! How wonderful! But how could I write to her in telegraph form? Telegrams, after all, leave out all the superfluous words, and thus all the essential emotion.

'That's why I said *theoretically*,' he replied. 'Telegraph can't replace letter-writing; it is a short-cut, like an instant message, with only the really important words. In a letter, you get to say everything with all the words you want; you put all your soul into the envelope. I like delivering a letter into somebody's hand, 'stead of into a letter-box. It makes people smile – mostly, people are happy when they get a letter. It's true, sometimes it's bad news – but still!

'A telegram is different. It's only for urgent news, the essentials. Let's say a boy wants to tell his sweetheart how much he loves her. He can't do that in a telegram. It wouldn't work. He would have to write a letter. Say he wants to propose marriage. He would just say, 'marry me'. And that's the best way to get a marriage refusal – it sounds rude. So, letters are better for *feelings*. Telegrams are better for *information* – urgent information, news. Telegrams are just for important things, and you say it in a few words. I think if you were to get a telegram you would be frightened – because – is it bad news?'

He now spoke in a curious melange of simplistic Creole, multisyllabic vocabulary, bad grammar and educated content, all spoken in a rich, melodic voice that was somehow fascinating and – to me at least – hypnotic.

He tapped again into the machine.

'What was that?' asked Yoyo. Her eyes, too, sparkled; she seemed every bit as fascinated by the young man's story as I was.

'*Yes,*' he replied. 'dash-dot-dash-dash-dot-dot-dot-dot.'

'What's *no*?'

He tapped it out quickly, speaking as he tapped: 'dash-dot-dash-dash-dash.'

'So you know the whole Morse alphabet?' Yoyo asked. 'By heart?

'Yes,' he said. 'I taught myself. All I got to do now is practise, practise, practise so I can do it quick on the machine. As quick as handwriting. Quicker. I tryin' to increase my speed. See, this machine isn't connected to a cable so I can use it to practise. When it's connected it sends electrical currents through the cable, and the person on the other end gets the signal and interprets it and writes it down in words and sends it to the recipient in a telegram. Easy!'

'What about telephone?' Yoyo asked. 'Have you seen one? I heard some people are getting them in Georgetown. Surely that's even better than telegraph? I mean to actually *speak* to people over a distance – that's even more miraculous, isn't it?'

But he shook his head in dismissal. 'The problem with telephone,' he said, 'is that you got to set up a cable between the people who want to communicate. Plenty people got it in Georgetown, is true, and they even got lines all up the coast to the Berbice River. They ain't yet manage to get it to New Amsterdam. And to cross the sea – country to country? No. I can't imagine that happening. Maybe, a long time from now – who knows? No – telegraph is the thing. And one of these days I goin' to be a telegraph operator. I goin' to work for the West India and Panama Telegraph Company, Limited. And one of these days, I want to be the one runnin' de whole telegraph company.'

Such pride in those words, such ambition!

'Really!' said Yoyo. 'Can you – I mean – usually – I mean to run an office …'

She stopped, plainly embarrassed, but I knew what she meant and so too did the young man, for he scratched his head in obvious discomfort and rushed to explain.

'I know is maybe too high-up for a coloured but I got a good education an' if I can get some experience an' learnin' I can do it.'

'What education do you have?' I asked

'Queen's College!' he said, and his grin spread wider than ever; Queen's College, as everyone knew, was the most prestigious boy's secondary school in the colony, and few darkies attended it.

'I won a scholarship and I was able to attend till I got my School Certificate. An' then I had to leave an' the only job I could get was postman. But don't matter – I like it. I was postman in Georgetown for a year, deliverin' letters in North Cummingsburg. An' then this job in Berbice came up an' nobody wanted to take it, because it's so far away, not even for six weeks till they find someone permanent from up here and train him in Georgetown, an' I took it because I reasoned, if I do it, when the time come, an' I want to work in the telegraph office, they gon' remember me.'

'So you don't like it here?' I asked. 'I dare say it must be a bit lonely for you.'

'Oh, I *love* it here!' said the young man. 'Nice and quiet an' it gives me time to study, an' the people are nice and friendly, not so rough like in Georgetown. Already I got a hundred friends in the village.'

I could easily believe that. He seemed to me the kind of person who drew others to him like a magnet, who might light up a room the moment he walked in. Like Mama. Like Mama used to be, that is. Yoyo was one of those people as well. There were such people, and there were shrinking violets, like myself, those who went unnoticed, a plain little weed.

There were only two differences to that situation on this occasion. He was the only *darkie* sunflower I had ever met. And he had *definitely* noticed me.

As he spoke his eyes drifted back to mine again and again, and I felt, I knew, that it cost him an effort to turn back to Yoyo, that he did so only for the sake of politeness; that he would rather look at me, even in silence; that he did not find me stupid and awkward and nondescript. He told me so with deep dark eyes more eloquent than a thousand words; eyes I could read as I read a book for they spoke a plain language uncomplicated by subterfuge; nothing hidden, nothing masked. All else, speech, language, words, were as a fog drifting above that essential clarity. I knew, without being told, that what I felt, this connection so intimate it was beyond speech, beyond all common methods of communication, was shared by him. He knew. I knew. It was something secret, powerful, and completely and utterly preposterous.

So preposterous it had to be all my imagination. I was making it up. It was only my starved romantic longings running wild. I was just a foolish little girl. Yes, that was it. Foolish, silly me.

'What's your name?' I heard Yoyo ask the question through the fog, and I was glad of it, for in this new country of secret power and shattering doubt I was a stranger, and speechless.

'George Theodore Quint,' he replied, glancing from her to me. From the first I loved that name. It had something noble and strong and independent about it. Something different; something unique.

'How old are you?'

'Nineteen, Miss. Twenty next month.'

'And already running the Post Office?'

He chuckled. 'Young, yeah; but you know how it is in BG. Nobody don' wan' to go into the country. Nobody wanted to work in de Courantyne, not even for two-three months. I volunteered to come because it gon' help me later on, when I look to become a telegrapher. An' another thing – I got *lines*.'

He leaned forward and almost whispered the last word, hinting at some mysterious process by which influential people of anonymous identity had placed him into high position. This was the way many promotions worked in BG, though in this particular case it seemed less of a promotion than banishment to an unpopular post that nobody else wanted.

I would have loved to hear more about his *lines*, more about him, but Yoyo was growing restless, and bored, adjusting her clothing and tapping her fingers on the countertop. She looked at me and arched her eyebrows, asking if we should go. I nodded; not that I really wanted to go, but a nervous Yoyo was not good company.

'Well, George, it was lovely speaking to you,' She said now, and held out her hand for him to shake. He took it.

'You are Miss …?'

'Miss Johanna,' she said firmly. 'And my sister is Miss Winnie.'

It was my turn. I hesitated before I took that outstretched hand. His long fingers curled around mine and it was as if a current ran between us, passing from one to the other as if for those few moments we were joined, one entity, and my eyes met his again and I knew that he knew. Those eyes of his! They drew me in, and told me things that words could never tell. His hand lingered around mine, and I did not pull away. For those few moments we stood in silence, linked by our clasped hands, those locked eyes, and I sensed a parting of the ways, as if a river coursing down a mountainside suddenly discovered a new path, a hidden one between the rocks and off its well-worn course. As if our joined hands and locked eyes sealed some momentous pact with history.

An outsider, looking on, might see this: the Honourable Archibald Cox's oldest daughter lowering herself to shake hands with the postman, a common darkie: a travesty. I knew only that there was no higher or lower. No white lady and darkie postman. There was only this: one soul. Unity. I had read of love at first sight, and doubted its reality. Surely it was mere imagination? Surely love came slowly, after long acquaintance, long conversation. Yet here it was, instant, and real.

'Come on, Winnie; let's go.' Yoyo was already at the door. How could I pull my eyes away? His were hypnotic; they held me bound. We stood still for several seconds, joined by our gaze, our smiles. Then I took a deep breath, summoned all my strength, pulled away both my gaze and my hand. I smiled with secret knowledge, and turned to leave.

I was so much in a daze as I left the Post Office that I didn't look where I was going and ran straight into a giant of a Someone as I turned to retrieve my bicycle. The next thing I knew, two giant paws were gripping my arms and I was looking up at the bluest eyes and the bushiest beard I ever did see. The eyes were set in a leathery face as brown as a light-skinned darkie, but the wild hair that surrounded it was brown, not black; and anyway the eyes' brilliant blueness gave him away as European. And the beard! It was at least a foot long, all crinkles and frizz, darker than the hair on his head but still dark brown rather than black, fanning out from his chin in a glorious semi-circle of bush.

I cried out in shock: shock, first at the collision itself, then at the sight, then at the realization of who this was; who it could only be: Mad Jim.

I had seen Mad Jim before, several years previously; Papa had pointed him out one Sunday as we drove in our coach over to Sunday lunch at Glasgow. He – Mad Jim – had been walking along the road towards us, leading a donkey. On the donkey was perched a darkie woman. She had looked up at us as we passed; one glimpse of those striking dark eyes, and then she was gone; they were both gone. I looked backwards once we had passed, but Papa called me to attention.

'Mad Jim,' he said. 'That's what becomes of a man who abandons his own people. Pah!' He spat over the edge of the coach. 'Mad as a hatter.'

But I had heard of Mad Jim, and even if Papa wouldn't tell us more, the rumours in the English compound told me enough. He was, indeed, mad; a white man who had lived in the fearsome bush, the jungle backlands, for several years with a darkie woman, and produced a horde of children from her – a pack of wild animals, they said. Then for some reason, he had moved to the outskirts of Promised Land village and mixed only with darkies and coolies; which, it seemed, was the chief symptom of his madness.

Now, as I looked into those sparkling bluer-than-blue eyes, I saw no madness but only keen interest; and the moustache that concealed his lips curved upwards in what could only have been a smile.

He pushed me gently away, still holding my arms in a firm, yet gentle grip. He seemed to search my face as if looking for some secret characteristic; and then he let go, touched his head as if to remove a hat, and said only, in a voice that was deep and gruff and tinted with a Creole melody, 'Watch where you goin', Miss Cox!'

I mumbled a quick apology and a good-day, grabbed my bicycle, and wheeled it to the road where Yoyo stood waiting. I looked back at Mad Jim; he was still looking at me and grinning. Then he touched his hat again, made a slight bow, turned and continued on his way. Yoyo and I rode off.

Only when we arrived back home did we realize: we had forgotten to buy our sweets.

❄ ❄ ❄

### Mama's Diary: Salzburg, 1890

*Liebes Tagebuch,*

*Tonight is the night! I am so excited! Tonight, the first Tuesday of the month. Papa will be away from home till midnight, for it's the night his favourite chamber music quartet plays. He is always there, winter and summer alike; we will have an early dinner, as always, and then off he will go to the Mozart Hall, and I will be alone at last. My bag is already packed – I have hidden it away so that Else, the maid, will suspect nothing. I have also already told Else that I have a headache and I might sleep in late tomorrow morning. That way my absence won't be discovered till late tomorrow. I have written a note to Father, which I will hide in my bed, under the covers, for Else to find. Hopefully by the time he reads it I will be halfway across Germany!*

*Just as Archie, right this minute, is halfway across Germany, on his way to pick me up! He is taking various trains from Paris – but tonight, once he has picked me up, we shall be boarding the Orient Express, back to Paris! How romantic that sounds! I can hardly believe it – Archie and I, on the Orient Express, to Paris! He will come to my house at nine; the coach will wait for him around the corner, and he shall come on foot, and I shall escape and meet him on the street.*

*I am beside myself with trepidation. Will all go according to plan? Yes! It must! I will be his tonight! (Though we will wait till Paris for The Main Event – I'm not quite sure what that means, but it's what Archie said.) We will exchange our marriage vows in Paris – he says we should do it in Notre Dame Cathedral. He seems to have forgotten that I am Jewish. I will have to remind him. And I thought Notre Dame is Catholic, and he isn't? But it is his God, and he will know what to do. I will have to let him know, though. Perhaps we can find a rabbi in Paris.*

*After that we move on to Calais, cross the English Channel, and on to Norfolk, his home.*

*He says his parents will be shocked but will get over it once it is all a* fait accompli, *and once they see how pretty and charming I am. I certainly hope so! And so, Liebes Tagebuch, I say goodbye to you for now. I don't suppose I will have time to visit you in the next few days – the next time, it will all be over, and I shall be in Norfolk!*

*Poor Father. He will be frantic. But he will read the note and know that I have not been kidnapped by bandits, or anything like that. Though no doubt it will appear that way to him.*

*I am simply bursting with excitement!!!*

# Chapter Six

This much I know: it is not easy for a Sugar Princess to find a husband. She knows, more by instinct than by explicit instruction, that she may only love a man she is allowed to marry. And she may only marry a man of equal standing, that is to say, a Sugar Prince. Those are the unspoken rules.

At the time I met George Theodore Quint I was well aware of the paucity of suitable Sugar Princes: most of the plantations along the Courantyne Coast were by now, owned by the Booker Brothers and Company. Booker Brothers ate businesses for breakfast.

Promised Land *must* escape the Booker beast. However much we girls were shielded from the realities of the sugar business – that much we knew. That much Papa made sure we knew. Marry we must, but it had to be to a man who could ensure the survival of our family legacy – the plantation, founded by pioneers, that had brought wealth and well-being to the family back home.

A son – Edward John – would have been raised as the one who would continue this epic fight for independence. A daughter's duty was to fling the bonds of marriage around a suitable groom: a planter's son, or, second best, a high-ranking manager from a plantation in similar circumstances, one owned by an absentee landlord. There were now in total only three such plantations: Houston on the East Bank of Demerara, Windsor Castle on the West Coast of Demerara, and Albion further down the Courantyne Coast, belonging to the Campbells, who also owned Ogle Estate on the East Coast Demerara. Unfortunately, the Campbells were absentees. Houston belonged to a Portuguese family, and Papa let us know in no uncertain terms that the Portuguese were beyond the pale. That left only Windsor Castle: owned by a solidly functioning family whose several sons were regularly married off to brides imported from the Motherland.

I remembered all of this that evening as Yoyo and I sat in the evening air on the veranda. The certainty that had for a few fleeting moments overcome me in the Post Office had faltered, then flown, and as I sat hugging my twilight twizzle I realized with growing alarm that I had lit a fuse that afternoon; that my only option was to stamp on it until it was well and truly dead. Me, marry a darkie Postman! The idea was so ludicrous I had to ask myself if I had gone momentarily mad.

But no! The cry came from deep inside; it had been no madness, but the very opposite: an insight of such dazzling clarity it seemed that those few minutes in the Post Office were sanity and that my entire state of being before *that* was the madness.

And yet: George was so far beneath me socially he could just as well not have been a man, but an animal. Papa may not have ever said so in so many words, but my upbringing to this point had taught me that, and I knew it without telling. Realization descended on me in a curtain of gloom. I could not speak; I did not trust my voice. Silence was my only strength.

Yoyo broke the silence. 'Papa must never find out about George, you know!'

I started – however did Yoyo know? Had it been that obvious? Was Yoyo that observant?

'What do you mean?' I asked tentatively.

'Well, you know. For us to hob-nob with a darkie, even if George does seem rather well educated, it's not quite the done thing, is it? I did like him, though; he's quite unusual – different, somehow, and I even wondered if he was presumptuous, or simply naïve. To talk to us like that, almost as equals! It was quite an adventure, wasn't it! If Papa saw us he'd explode! To think that we have a darkie friend! Especially after all that has happened in the last few days – all this bother with the coolies! It's quite clear that Papa has no intention of improving their living conditions and perhaps the only way we can fight back is like this – defying him in our own way. That's why he must never know.'

I nodded in the darkness – my secret was safe; she had no idea. I smiled to myself. If even hob-nobbing with a darkie was so very scandalous, what would actually *marrying* one be!

❈ ❈ ❈

The following day was Sunday. As usual, we attended Church in the senior staff compound.　Usually after Church one of the managers would invite us all back for lunch, or we would invite a manager and his family back to our home. Yoyo and I would spend the rest of the day with the young people of the compound; it was our day of rest, leisure and pleasure. There was a tennis court in the officer's compound, and a swimming pool; the latter was cleared of men for two hours each Sunday afternoon so that the ladies could bathe. We all welcomed stripping off our heavy gowns – our lady's maids, of course, would be there to help with the fastenings, the corsets, and petticoats – and donning our bathing costumes for an hour or two in the deliciously cool water.

Today was no different, except that Papa was absent; Yoyo and I had Sunday lunch with the Marshalls. Mrs Marshall was the kindest of ladies and envisioned herself as some kind of substitute mother, though Yoyo conjectured that behind it all was the wish to see her son – now quite old, in his early twenties and still unmarried, and studying Law in England – engaged to one of us. After lunch, we young people all sat on their veranda playing Chinese Chequers with their two girls, both slightly younger than ourselves, and went for our afternoon bathe.

During the August holidays, Ladies' Bathing Time was a jolly occasion. All the teenage boys were back from their schools in Georgetown or England; and their one ambition was to witness the ladies bathing. They would climb onto the roof of the Clubhouse or scramble on each other's shoulders behind the hibiscus hedge in order to peek at us in our bathing costumes. We would all squeal and scream and hide our half-naked bodies by jumping into the pool where we would all squeal and scream some more and hug each other in mock fear. Everyone would have the appropriate hysterics and the boys would giggle and fall over themselves and the darkie guards would chase them away and the mothers would waggle their fingers and a good time would be had by all. But this was off-season; all the boys were absent, as well as most of the girls our age. There was no squealing or screaming; no hysterics, just a quiet leisurely bathe. I floated on my back, gazing up into the vast Courantyne sky.

Something had happened. Something so big, so fundamental that I seemed lost and wandering in an alien world; as if the identity I had worn up to that day had been stripped from me, a mere hull discarded as a lizard discards its skin, leaving me exposed and raw, for no new identity had yet grown to replace the one that was lost. The Sugar Princess was no more; I knew not what to say; I could not play my part. I spent that Sunday in a daze. Conversation at lunchtime had seemed vacuous and thin. My attention wandered as I played board games and I lost them all. And now I could only float and gaze up at the endless sky and dream. And I saw there a swarthy face and a loving smile and deep dark eyes like pools into which I longed to fling myself and drown.

❊ ❊ ❊

Late Monday morning, Marigold, one of the housemaids, knocked on the schoolroom door and entered when Miss Wright bid her in.

'Excuse me, Miss,' she stammered. 'But Police at de door.'

'Police? What do you mean? Who for?'

'Dey sayin' dey want to speak to de Master, Miss. When I say Master gone Georgetown, dey askin' fuh you.'

'For me? Dear, dear. There must be some mistake. But I'd better go down. Girls, stay here and finish off that chapter. I'll be back as soon as I've dealt with this.'

She bustled off, closing the door behind her. Yoyo opened it, and listened; we heard voices at the bottom of the stairs, but could not decipher the words. A few minutes later, Marigold was back. She looked from one of us to the other, eyes wide with fear.

'Miss Johanna, Miss Winifred – police want talk to you too.'

Yoyo and I went downstairs. In the main hallway stood the two policemen; one of them needed no introduction as the more important one, for he was big and ruddy and seemed about to burst out of his dark blue uniform, and fixed us with steely grey eyes. The other, a thin darkie, cringed in the background. Miss Wright stood to one side wringing her hands and staring at us intensely, shaking her head and mouthing words we could not understand.

'I am Chief Inspector Armstrong,' said the very important one. 'I am sorry to interrupt your morning but I have a few questions I need to ask you girls.'

Miss Wright took a step forward. 'I'm very sorry but the girls are minors. They may not give statements to the police in the absence of their father.'

'I'm not looking for an official statement,' said the chief inspector. 'Just a little conversation – girls, there has been a ...' he cleared his throat, 'a complaint. Some of your coolies have reported a flogging that took place last Friday. We are here to investigate; we need witnesses to the alleged flogging.'

'The girls may not say a word!' cried Miss Wright. 'Girls, do not say a word! There was nothing. You saw nothing. Chief Inspector, this is most irregular. I must ask you to return when Mr Cox is present. I must ask you to leave. How dare you discuss this in full view of the servants!'

For indeed, the door to the kitchen was open and Mildred, Nora and Shirley stood in the doorway gaping. Marigold, a duster in her hand, looked down from the top staircase landing, and through the open door to Papa's library, Mrs Norton could be seen hovering near the desk.

Miss Wright had assumed the position of acting head of house, and filled that role admirably. She and the chief inspector stared each other down. Finally, the chief inspector nodded, acknowledging defeat.

'Very well. I will return in a few days' time. In the meanwhile, though, I shall be interviewing your servants and other employees ...'

But Miss Wright stood her ground; I have to say she managed to adopt an attitude that held a very fine balance between authority, deference, resolve and appeasement.

'I'm sorry, Chief Inspector, I cannot permit this. I must ask you to leave, and to return for your interviews when the plantation owner has returned from his business in Georgetown. I'm quite sure there is some – misunderstanding. I'm quite sure he will be able to clear things up when he returns – if you know what I mean.'

Watching them both, it was quite clear to me that Miss Wright knew exactly what she meant, and so did the chief inspector, for immediately his attitude changed; now he was the one seeking appeasement and reconciliation. The last remnants of belligerence melted away under Miss Wright's stern gaze; his own eyes dropped, he smiled, and said, 'I understand, Miss Wright. I apologize for my former discourtesy, and you're perfectly right; it is indeed better to discuss the incident when the master of the house is here. I'll take my leave now, and return at a more convenient time. Please extend my apologies to Mr Cox – I'm sure there's some reasonable explanation for – for – never mind.'

He looked around him as he spoke those words and for perhaps the first time became aware of the several pairs of listening ears. Miss Wright took care of that with one unambiguous sweeping gesture of her hand; at once all the doors slammed shut. Marigold disappeared into the kitchen, and Yoyo and I fled up the stairs and huddled together on the upstairs landing, listening.

The Chief Inspector's boots stamped across the hall; the front door opened and slammed shut and he was gone, and Miss Wright was coming up the stairs. Yoyo and I stood up to meet her. Guilt was written all over Yoyo's face, and I can only conjecture the same of my own, for guilt was what I felt: for myself and Miss Wright and most of all, for Papa. Miss Wright ushered us both back into the schoolroom with a no-nonsense, 'come girls, we need to talk' manner, though she did not speak a word. Once there, we sat at our desks and she stood before us and explained the situation.

'Girls, this is more serious than we first thought,' she began. 'And I need you to promise me sincerely once more: your father must never know that I allowed you to watch from the bedroom window. *He must never know,* do you understand? That's the three of us cleared; you two are, anyway, too young to be called to the witness stand without your father's permission but I am not and since I have already told him a white lie – that I was with you in the schoolroom – I must now maintain that lie or else – or else there will be trouble. There is already trouble. Your father has been accused of flogging. Flogging is against the law. That is the simple situation. The coolies have reported the incident to the police. The overseers deny flogging. It's the coolies' word against ours. True, there is the question of wounds – welts on the backs of one of the coolies. Medical examinations and such and such. This could mean trouble for your father. I don't know what will happen but your father is a clever and rich man and I have no doubt that he will be able to deflect the charge. But there must be no witnesses from this house. The darkies can be relied on not to say a word. I am sure of that. But you girls – you must promise me. You must promise me. Your father does not know that you saw, and he must never know. Otherwise … otherwise …'

'You'll be in trouble,' finished Yoyo, speaking the words I was already thinking.

'Yes,' said Miss Wright. She was humble now, and pleading, knowing that her future was in our hands. 'You see – your father wants to keep the more unpleasant aspects of the plantation away from you. He means well; he does it out of love. He has told me this quite unequivocally, and on that one day I failed you. I can't imagine what came over me. I should never have let you go down to the gate; and once we were sent away I should never have taken you to the window. I confess – it was my own curiosity that made me do so. Curiosity that swept away every last vestige of responsibility for you. Now you have seen, and I don't know what to do. He must never know. Can you promise me this one thing?'

Yoyo and I looked at each other, nodded in unison, and gave our promise.

❊ ❊ ❊

**Mama's Diary: Norfolk, 1890**

*Liebes Tagebuch,*

*Here I am, in Norfolk, England! It all went according to plan, right up to the moment that Archie brought me to his home. What a grand home it is too! I still feel quite overwhelmed. What a to-do our arrival caused. His parents were torn between being furious with him, and their need to be polite to me – they are so well-mannered, as I assume all English people are, that they could not in any way rebuke me. And so I was escorted to a ladies' drawing room where I was forced to make polite conversation with his mother, his two sisters, his grandmother, and a maiden aunt! Now THAT was a conversation to behold, considering my knowledge of English is that of a two-year-old child, and theirs of German non-existent! We spent the whole time nodding and smiling and drinking constant cups of tea, poured by a maid in a blue uniform and white frilly apron! I felt as if I were in one of those old English novels.*

*In the meantime my poor Archie was marched off to some other
meeting among the men: his father, elder brother, an uncle or two.
Two other brothers arrived in the course of the afternoon. I can
hardly tell them apart at this point in time, but I expect I shall
soon learn.*

*'Don't worry,' dear Archie told me on the way here, 'There is noth-
ing they can do to tear us apart. It is too late.' For of course, the
Main Event has taken place in Paris, as he promised, and no,
dear Tagebuch, I shan't give you any details on that as you should
know there is such a thing as privacy! Suffice it to say that now,
more than ever, I am his.*

*Now two days have passed by and things have calmed down con-
siderably. They are all still worried about the scandal, and about
my Jewishness. But Lord Cox – for that is Archie's father's title,
goodness me! – has sent a telegram to Father informing him of the
situation, and we will all await his instructions. They have put
me up in a lovely room in the guest wing, and though Archie and
I are separate at night we do spend many hours together during
the day and I could not be more content. I am learning more
English day by day. I have also decided to become a Christian.
Father won't like it but I understand that I must adapt to the
English ways.*

*For me anyway, it is all one God – what does it matter in which
way we worship, or what label we place on him? Surely it's the
heart that counts, and God can see into that, and know whether
there is love there or not? Yes, I will become Christian. It is decided. That will make them love me more.*

# Chapter Seven

I spent the next two days in a state of complete and utter turmoil. One emotion after the other chased through my mind: hope, courage, elation would swing me up to the heights of euphoria; the meeting with George had opened some hidden spring within my soul out of which gushed the most delightful of waters, all rushing at top speed into the gap left by Mama's departure. And no sooner would I find myself swinging among the stars, than a net of black despair at the hopelessness of it all would fling itself around me, holding me captive, dragging me down to earth where I would wallow in a swamp of doubt and despair.

I could not love this man! But I did! Oh, I did!

I reasoned with myself, sternly. After all, I had only met him once – no, twice, counting the first encounter on his bicycle – and Love cannot grow from such casual acquaintance! *Oh, but I can! I can!* Love cried within me. *I am here, see! How can you deny me!*

*No!* I called back. *I cannot permit you! You have no reason, no foundation! Get away from me! Go back whence you came!* And I would push Love back into the cave of my heart, to wait for a more suitable recipient, a more appropriate prospect. But Love would only bounce back into my being, fresher and more spirited than ever before, lifting me into previously unknown heights. *Here I am!* It would call, kindly mocking, smiling, forcing me to smile.

Until now I had known love only second-hand, vicariously through the characters in the books I devoured. I had understood it in theory, and longed for the direct experience. This had to be it, surely! But no. It could not be! Not from so fleeting an acquaintance, and for such a forbidden subject! And so, when despair washed through me as it did time and time again, it was total: total blackness, total hopelessness, leaving me an abject puddle on the ground.

I hid this all from Yoyo. Never could I share this with her. I was able, through superb acting, to continue as ever before, playing the character of myself while under the surface this inner battle raged. Only at night when I could not sleep, and she lay lost to the world beside me, I let myself go, pressing my face into my pillow while the tears soaked into the softness. *Oh, help me, help me!* The cry came from the bottom of my soul as I tossed and turned in my bed, and I bit into the fabric of my pillow so that no sound would escape me. Who was I crying to? Mama? God? It did not matter. The silent cry rose up into nothingness, and there came no reply, and no help.

Sometimes I left my bed and paced the floor, walking to the window and gazing out into the moonlit sky, to the north, towards the ocean and the village and him. When would I see him again? If ever? I dared not go to the village, the Post Office – what would I do, what would I say! I could not bear it!

Ironically it was Yoyo who took the next step in this most impossible of romances. On Monday morning, before we went down to breakfast, she said to me,

'Let's go and visit George again, this afternoon!'

'George?'

'Yes – don't you remember? That friendly darkie in the post office. The one with the Morse machine. He's so interesting, and I'm so bored!'

'Oh! But … why? I mean, what purpose do we have? What shall we tell him?'

'Nothing! We'll just visit, and ask to see that Morse machine again, and play with it. Do you have anything better to do? A book to read, perhaps? Violin practice?'

Her last words were mocking; Yoyo thought books and music a complete waste of time, possibly because when I indulged it left her with nothing to do and nobody to do it with. Yoyo disliked being on her own. She liked to talk, and needed someone to talk *to,* constantly, and that was, more often than not, me. Mostly, when left alone she would go out riding and talk to Tosca.

'All right,' I said now. 'Let's go.' And as I said it my heart turned somersaults because I could not wait to see his face again, and I would have hugged Yoyo and squeezed the life out of her in gratitude, if only she knew.

❈ ❈ ❈

We parked our bicycles and climbed the steps to the post office, and entered through the open door. As before, George sat with his back to us, bent over his Morse key. We could hear it clicking away in rapid staccato.

'Good afternoon, Mr Quint!' called Yoyo. Startled, he leapt to his feet and his chair fell backwards. While bending to pick it up he turned and looked up and, seeing us, stumbled and dropped it again. We approached the counter, he righted himself and the chair, and came up to us.

'Do call me George!' He said. 'Good afternoon, Miss Winnie and Miss Johanna! You are back already! You have more letters to post?'

'No,' said Yoyo. 'We just thought we'd come. We wanted to see that Morse machine again. Didn't we, Winnie?'

She looked at me for confirmation, and I gave it with a vigorous nod of my head. Just like the last time, my tongue seemed stuck to the bottom of my mouth, and I knew I was blushing. He looked straight at me, into my eyes, and held my gaze for just a second. And then he smiled, turned and fetched the machine, and was about to bring it to us when he stopped, and pointed to a table pushed against the back of our half of the room. It was a wooden table with a single chair pushed up against it, its surface scuffed, scratched, and ink-stained, and on it lay a fountain pen on a chain next to a round jar containing ink, as well as a smaller jar containing glue with a brush sticking out of it, and a wad of blotting paper.

'Let's sit over there,' said George, placing the machine on the table. 'I'll bring more chairs.'

He returned for his own chair and walked around the counter towards the table. He set the chair down, pulled out the one already there, and gestured for us to take a seat.

'I'll just go and get another chair, from the back office!' he said, and dashed off while we sat down on either side of the table. In an instant he was back, bearing a stool, which he placed before the third side of the table, facing the wall, between the two of us.

He had brought something else: a folded piece of paper, which he now unfolded and laid on the table next to the machine.

'The Morse code!' he said, and a moment later he had launched into his lesson. He was a good teacher. He passed the machine from one to the other of us, letting us tap in the dashes and dots for each letter, letting us create words, of three letters, then four letters, then, even little sentences. It was fascinating; the most interesting thing I had done in weeks. We were so totally absorbed in our tapping that we did not notice when a customer entered the post office; but George did, and jumped to his feet to serve the customer. I looked up; it was Mr Persaud, the greengrocer, buying stamps. He was staring at us in curiosity, no doubt wondering what we were doing there, but I did not care.

Having served Mr Persaud, our teacher returned to us and continued his lesson. Another customer entered, and this time I heard him for he came in with a loud, 'Hello, hello, hello, Georgie boy!' I looked up, as I was facing the door. It was Mad Jim, who stopped just inside the building, placed his hands on his hips, and guffawed.

'Well, well, well, Georgie! Lady visitors! Don't let me interrupt!'

George seemed embarrassed; he jumped up from his stool and opened his mouth to speak, but Mad Jim had turned and walked out again. George sat down, his demeanour flustered. I remembered seeing Mad Jim here the last time I came, which was only three days ago. He must write a lot of letters, I thought.

George quickly regained his composure. 'You know what?' he said, 'You take this paper with you and practice at home. Next time you come you might be fluent!'

He folded the paper and handed it to me; it seemed the lesson was over. It was strange; being here with him this time was completely different from the last time, and not what I had expected. Gone were the eddies of emotion that had plagued me these last few days. Today, once I had stopped blushing and my heart stopped pounding, I had settled into a state of complete – what can I call it other than *normality*? I felt calm this time, relaxed, at home in George's presence. And though I felt a quickening whenever his eyes caught mine – as they did, frequently – or his hand touched mine – seemingly by accident – that too seemed not something extraordinary but simply *right*. Perfect. As if I were, somehow, at *home* within myself. Grounded. And even my disabling shyness had flown, and I found my tongue, now, at last.

'Thank you!' I said. 'That was so interesting! It must feel like a miracle to send a real telegram – I mean, one with the wires attached – and to know someone in a far off country will receive it!'

'One day, I gon' be doing that!' said George, laughing. 'If all goes well. When I return to Georgetown.'

'You're going back to Georgetown?'

'One day, Miss. When they find someone permanent for here. And then I gon' to try and get a job in the telegraph office, sending messages around the world. And receiving them.'

My heart dipped a little when he mentioned leaving – *but what about* me! – it cried. And I looked at him with a question in my eyes: *do you?* And clearly, so clearly, I saw the reply in his own eyes: *Yes, oh yes!* I saw it as clearly as if he had spoken the words. Yes. There was something there between us, something so fine and yet so strong there was no need of words, of verbal confirmation. I relaxed once more.

Morse: in itself it seemed a code for what we had between us. A metaphor for the secret messages we sent each other, reading each other's eyes, and, I was sure, even each other's mind. The covert joining of hearts by wires so thin they had to be felt rather than seen. A connection in which words and touch were nothing more than decoration, so solid the innate knowledge of its presence. I smiled, and he smiled back, and in that moment Yoyo, who had been tapping away at the machine, looked up and spoke, destroying the moment of intimacy.

'How does it work?' she asked. 'How do the messages get delivered? I mean, how do they get from place to place? It does seem extraordinary!'

'Through cables,' he answered. 'Cables linked between overhead posts, or buried underground, even on the ocean bed!'

'On the ocean bed!' I was astonished.

'Yes! At the bottom of the ocean!'

'How?' Yoyo asked.

It was the cue he was waiting for.

'Oh, Miss! That is one of the greatest achievements of the last century! The laying of the transatlantic cable! The linking of the continents!'

And he was off. Off on the story of the almost insurmountable difficulty of laying the cable, the failed attempts. Two ships, one from the continent of North America and one from Ireland, setting sail to meet in mid-ocean, each one laying cable. The cables had then to be spliced, he said, linking the continents beneath the sea. But one attempt after the other failed; the ships had to return to shore.

'The problem,' he said, 'was weight. See – the copper cables that transmit the signals had to be protected so they're enclosed in a kind of rubber: *gutta percha* from Malaya. There was many types of cable dependin' on water depth; the shore ends were real heavy – sixteen tons per mile!'

The cable was so heavy, he said, that it kept breaking; it had to be paid out slowly, over a wheel above the propeller at the stern of the ship. And then, on August 5th 1858, the miracle: the cable was complete! The continent of Europe was connected to North America! It reduced the communication time between the continents from the ten days it took to deliver a message by ship to a matter of minutes. Congratulatory messages passed between Queen Victoria to the American President James Buchanan, and the world would never be the same again.

George's excitement was palpable; his eyes glistened as he spoke, and his voice filled with a fervour that lent a thrill to every word he spoke.

'And then,' he continued, 'they laid the cables joining islands of the Caribbean. Just imagine! Imagine all those islands connected to each other and to the mainland by submarine cable: from Cuba to Jamaica to Panama and all over. Jamaica had two lines going off from Kingston: to Puerto Rico and Antigua; Guadeloupe, Dominica, Martinique, St. Lucia, St. Vincent, Barbados. And then St. Vincent, Grenada, Trinidad, and from Trinidad across the mouth of the Orinoco to British Guiana. The line passes from Georgetown all the way down the coast, through New Amsterdam to Dutch and French Guiana, and then by more land lines down Brazil to Rio de Janeiro and Monte Video in Argentina!'

By this time he could hardly contain his excitement.

'Imagine it! BG is the entrance for the entire East Coast of South America. That cable to Jamaica connects us to North America and from there to Europe and India and the whole world! Think of it! Think of someone in Rio sending a message to India or China in the blink of an eye! And it passes right under our noses, up the coast to Georgetown. Think of all those messages flying around the world! Think how small the world has become! Messages going here and there and everywhere! Anywhere you want to send a message to, it can get to the recipient in minutes, instead of days and weeks and months! The world is growing smaller – the continents closer!'

His eyes glowed with ardour. The words poured out of him; I could hardly follow, for he used words I had never heard before. He spoke of *electromagnetic pulses*, and *magnetic permeability* and *ferromagnetic material,* and I heard the words without knowing their meaning. He wove images with words, metaphors to describe the disappearance of distances in the giant world – he said it was a spider-web, a wide-flung network linking countries and continents, a crocheted doily, threads criss-crossing and linking and messages shooting back and forth along them. He told us of the flood of information moving across the globe with the speed of light. He used his hands to demonstrate, fingers zipping back and forth. He formed his hands into a wide ball, fingertips touching, to show the cable lines that bound the globe, and then slipped them into each other to show the closing of the network. It was beyond belief; not even the horseless carriage, he said, could match the importance of the telegraph. News could pass from one country to the next in the wink of an eye. What a difference this would make for commerce! For the stock market! For international politics! For personal relationships! If someone in Russia died who had a relative in Chile, that relative could find out in a day instead of a month!

'And all because of this little machine!' And he held up his crude little home-made Morse machine with the pride of someone who had walked on the moon.

Yoyo and I left soon after. I let her walk out first, just so that I could linger a little longer with George, share a little moment alone with him. And so I was the only one of us who heard his last words, spoken quietly when Yoyo was already out of the door, his eyes fixed on mine:

'Come again – I'll give you another lesson if you like!'

Were those words meant for me alone? Oh, how I wished they were! I clung to him with my eyes alone. We just stood there, both of us, smiling, our gaze locked. His eyes were like deep dark pools, soft as water, luring me to fall into them, let myself go. Lose myself. Is that what love is? Letting go of self, to melt into the Beloved?

Yoyo called, and I pulled myself away, reluctantly. Some enormous thing had shifted within myself, and somehow I had to find my way forward.

❊ ❊ ❊

## Mama's Diary: Norfolk, 1890

*Liebes Tagebuch,*

*It's been a long time, hasn't it? More than two months, and now I have so much to tell you! First of all, we are married! Yes, officially (the Notre Dame wedding wasn't enough for them, unfortunately.) Father came for the wedding! And though he pretended to be angry, he wasn't half as furious as I had thought – in fact, he told me I should have confided in him! And I would not have had to run away after all! And then he told me a big secret – Mother was a gentile! He met her in Berlin and fell in love and she converted to Judaism in order to satisfy his parents' conditions for their marriage. Her German parents, however, disowned her, and that's why I don't know my maternal grandparents – they are not dead, as I was led to believe.*

*It was a very quiet ceremony with a Justice of the Peace. Of course, every girl, Jewish or not, longs for a beautiful big wedding but I have long accepted that it was not to be, and so Archie and I are now officially man and wife, and share a bedroom.*

*More exciting news: it seems – but I dare not say it out loud for fear I will somehow jinx it – that we are to be parents! But I will say no more on that.*

*Archie however seems to have a bit of a problem, but he won't tell me what it is. He is always arguing with his father, but out of reach of my ears. It is some secret they share. I am sure I shall find out in due time.*

*Father brought me a wonderful new violin as my wedding present – a Stradivarius! – and I spend many hours playing. There is a beautiful grand piano in the lounge here, and everyone is very impressed with my musical skills. They have all warmed towards me considerably. My English has improved by leaps and bounds, and I am now officially a Christian – yes! I am a convert!*

# Chapter Eight

Sometimes, Lady Fate plays her cards exactly right. That next day, Papa came home at lunchtime; he had news for us.

'Yoyo,' he said, 'I believe you are friends with Margaret Mc-Innes? The daughter of my estate manager? She is your age.'

'Yes,' said Yoyo. 'Maggie and I are great friends; she's a very jolly girl. But she goes to school in New Amsterdam, so I hardly ever see her during term time.'

'Well, my dear, that is going to change. Mrs McInnes is expecting another child, and will close down her New Amsterdam house and move back to her husband in the Senior Staff quarters. And Maggie will join you for lessons with Miss Wright. It's all been decided. I hope you're pleased!'

'Pleased! Oh Papa, I'm *delighted*! Hurrah! She and I shall have such fun together!'

And with that, George, the transatlantic cable, the Morse Code, vanished from Yoyo's mind. That very afternoon she ran off to visit Maggie at the senior staff quarters, and I was left alone.

As soon as I could, I picked up my bicycle and almost flew the distance to the post office. As usual, he was sitting at his desk but turned around the moment I walked in as if he were waiting for my footstep. He scraped back his chair, and almost bounded across the room to meet me. His smile seemed to light up everything within me; my whole soul smiled back. I rushed to the counter and we faced each other in silence, joined by this one marvellous smile; words were superfluous.

'Your sister did not come today?' he said at last.

'No,' I replied. 'She's gone to visit a friend. But I'd like another lesson in Morse, so I came alone.'

He hesitated just a second too long, and in that second I realised why – was it within the rules of propriety, for me to be alone with him? Yet even to think there might be anything improper in our association was ludicrous. Only we knew what was between us. It might be unusual for a darkie to teach a Sugar Princess, but for anyone to suspect more – well that would be so ridiculous, it was shocking; not on my behalf or George's but on the person who harboured such a suspicion. George might be a man, but he was a darkie, practically a servant.

'It's all right,' I said. 'Come on over – bring the machine!'

What a delightful time we spent! George gave me the Morse booklet and a pencil and paper and while he tapped out words I meticulously translated them and wrote them down. Then the other way around: I would look up the code for certain words and tap them into the key. And so we conversed, exchanging simple pleasantries by way of code; and all in complete silence. Soon it began to feel natural to converse in this way, as if I were having a normal conversation with a friend, an equal. The inequalities of our birth simply melted away. The awkwardness I felt at being alone with a man, a man who made me feel like a bud opening in the sunlight, gave way to a sense of rightness and complete calm. He was a teacher, I was his pupil, and perhaps that relationship was the great equalizer, for him as well as for me, for he too appeared more relaxed, more at ease with me, laughing and joking as we conversed in code.

My name. Then his name.

'Faster!' said George, and I'd tap again.

'Faster yet!' and I'd try again, a second speedier.

'You're really good!' Admiration was in his voice, and it propelled me to try faster and faster yet. The dots and the dashes in all their combinations began to feel natural, as natural as the letters of the alphabet. I tapped out an entire sentence.

'*Do you have brothers and sisters?*'

He took the machine from me.

'*I have two sisters,*' he tapped.

I took back the machine.

'*So do I,*' I tapped. I became audacious. Cheeky, even.

'*Love,*' I tapped. Over and over again, until I knew it by heart. '*Marriage,*' That really was mischievous. I looked up as I tapped it, and to my consternation he seemed uncomfortable; his smile had left him and beads of sweat dotted his forehead.

He took the machine, and hesitated a moment. Then he tapped, slowly, a longer sentence. I wrote down the dots and dashes, deciphered them, and smiled.

'*She has such pretty eyes.*'

I blushed, and looked up, meeting his gaze. His eyes were large, dark, luminous – the black forest creeks in the interior, as clear as mirrors; and indeed, I felt myself mirrored in them, as if I could see myself in that gaze, as if that gaze probed deep into my heart, penetrated every little nook and cranny of my soul, saw all there was to see, absorbed my last little secret; and it was good. I could not pull away from that gaze – but he did, with a quick shake of his head as if flinging away the magic, breaking the spell.

*I am happy I met you,* he tapped into his machine, which seemed an anti-climax after the intensity of that gaze, but I understood – we had to return to the real and mundane world, and that, for the moment, was this – the tapping out of words on a primitive Morse key. A code, a common link in our so disparate lives.

And then everything changed. George took the key from me and began tapping, quickly, much too quickly for me to note the dots and dashes and write them down, much less to interpret them. On and on he spoke in the language of Morse, a whole paragraph, a speech. What was he saying?

'George, stop! Stop! I can't follow! Do it slowly so I can write it down!'

He stopped his tapping and his shoulders slumped. His face was serious, and somehow sad, when he spoke: 'Miss Winnie, I don't *want* you to understand.'

There it was again, that obnoxious 'Miss Winnie'. 'Don't call me that!' I said. 'Call me Winnie. Please do!'

He shook his head, and his eyes glistened, perhaps with tears. A sadness had descended upon him and I was at a loss at how to shake it off. The message he had sent me vanished into space, never to be retrieved. What had he said? Was it something he'd never dare to tell me to my face?

At that moment someone entered the Post Office. There had been one or two interruptions today, and George had left the table to serve his customers, then returned immediately. But this person entered in such a whirlwind of hostility that I looked up. It was a young Indian man, and he bristled with rage. He did not look at me, but stepped in front of the table, arms akimbo.

'You lost your senses, George? What you doin' with this white girl, the boss' daughter? You mad or what?'

George, so happy and confident just a few minutes ago – before his Morse speech, that is – crumbled. 'Bhim, I – I ...' he began, but the man broke in.

'Get rid of her. Now! I need to talk to you.'

'Win – Miss Winnie, I think you'd better leave ...' George began, but I was already on my feet and on my way to the door, my cheeks burning. I felt as if I had been whipped. I cycled home, in tears. Who was that man, and why was he so rude? And why had George not defended me? Wasn't it *his* post office? What had he done wrong?

I had to find out. I would return the next day, for certain.

\* \* \*

I could not sleep at all that night, and was silent for most of the evening. I listened to Yoyo as she chattered about the wonderful time she had spent with Maggie, and what they had planned for the morrow. My own plans for the morrow were clear. I had to speak to George. He had to answer my questions.

All night I tossed and turned, going over in my mind the events of the afternoon.

As always, when my thoughts needed calming, I began to talk internally to Mama, and at once the words began to pour out, tumbling over each other in my need for expression. And so I decided to give them that expression, to write her another letter. How much could I tell her? This time, the answer came clear and strong: *Everything!* Mama would understand.

And so I sat myself down at my desk, dipped my pen into the bottle of Quink, and let the words pour out on to the page. Afterwards, I felt lighter, relieved of a burden. Indeed, writing to Mama had helped. And I would have to post it, I realized; tomorrow. I would see George, and ask him face- to-face what had happened. Why he had been so rude to me! I deserved an answer, an explanation. Why had he let this Bhim control him? Why? Why?

❉ ❉ ❉

I was practically quivering with anticipation as I walked up the steps to the post office and through the door. George was standing at the counter today, attending to a customer; he looked up as I entered and some strange emotion flitted across his features.

'One minute, please, Miss Winnie!' he said, and turned back to his customer. I waited at the back of the room. My moment would come. I would not confront him, not accuse him, I had decided. I would tell him of my feelings. There was far too much secrecy between us, too much left unspoken. Then he would tell me of his feelings for me that I was certain he harboured. I had seen it in his eyes, felt it at the touch of his hand. I knew. We would declare our love for each other. It had to be out in the open, no matter what would come of it. And once it was out in the open I would question him about the disastrous end to yester-day's session. Yes, that was the way to do it.At last, the customer left, and I approached the counter, smiling. But George did not smile back. His eyes met mine, but the warmth and acknowledg-ment I had seen there on Monday, and on Friday, failed to shine within them. Instead, all that met me was a blank gaze.

'How can I help you, Miss Winnie,' he said. It wasn't even a question; it was a statement, as if he did not *care* about helping me. I was completely thrown. And he had called me Miss Win-nie. Again.

'I-I have a letter to p-post,' I said. I couldn't control the stutter, or the shyness coursing through me. Thank goodness I *did* have a letter. Unthinkable the embarrassment had I turned up without a valid excuse!

The tension between us was excruciating. Debilitating. My knees turned weak, as if they would give way and I would faint, but I held myself together as George dealt with my letter. I had imagined he would have made a joke, about my sending a second letter so quickly on the heels of the first, to the very same recipi-ent, but he made no comment; he simply cut away the required stamp and pasted it on to the envelope without a word, without a glance at me. It was almost rude, considering the intimacy we had shared just two days previously. What on earth was going on? I died several deaths before, at last, he was finished and I could flee. Flee the building and flee him. Oh, the humiliation! The devastation! I grabbed my bicycle and tore home, tears stinging my eyes and my soul ripping to pieces in the wind.

❀ ❀ ❀

### Mama's Diary: Norfolk, 1890

*Liebes Tagebuch*

*Again, many moons have passed and my suspicions are more than confirmed – our first child is to be born in three months' time! As you can imagine, I am thrilled beyond measure – we are to be parents!*

*I now also know what Archie's dire secret is. I really don't know why he is making such a fuss. It seems that the family owns a sugar plantation in Africa or somewhere like that – I can't remember the exact name of the country – and Archie is to be sent there to manage it, as it is losing money. Archie says the real reason is to get rid of him, to punish him for marrying me (I didn't know this at first but it seems they had planned a different bride for him, and that alliance would have enriched the family no end, and they are still peeved about that.)*

*'They are banishing us!' Archie says. But frankly, I don't care. Wherever he goes, I shall go too. Isn't that what my namesake Ruth of the Old Testament says? The circumstances may have been different but the essence of what she says remains. He is my husband, my beloved, and I will follow him to the ends of the earth. I am happy to go wherever he goes. I will give my life to him, love him with all my heart and soul. He is truly the best husband on the world. Not only handsome and charming, but so kind and loving. He adores me. I am his Princess, his Queen! We will go to Africa, then, and reign there! I have told him I am happy to go – as long as we have each other, what does it matter what soil is under our feet!*

*And besides, it sounds like a jolly adventure! I love that English word, jolly, and I use it all the time, now. It's my favourite word! Yes, a jolly adventure I shall have, in Africa, on a sugar plantation! It will surely be all sweetness and light – what else could it be, surrounded by sugar! I shall eat pudding and cake all day and grow fat on sweetness! The plantation is called Promised Land! If that is not a harbinger for wonderful things to come, then what is!*

# Chapter Nine

Early the following morning, long before dawn, a cannon's boom jolted me out of sleep. I shot up in bed, deafened and dazed. A crack of light, another bang, and I knew: thunder, lightning. The next instant the sky opened and an ocean poured down on to the roof and the whole world roared. The rainy season had arrived. It would mean being confined to the house for weeks on end while the water rose around us, rose and sank as the drainage channels carried it away again, rose and sank, rose and sank. It meant rain. Rain, rain and more rain. Rivers of rain pouring from the sky. How very fitting, I thought. Nature giving expression to my soul.

British Guiana is a country whose coastal lands lie six feet beneath sea level. Were it not for the Dutch, the strip of coast lapped by the Atlantic would actually be submerged; but the Dutch, who had colonized the country before the British, had converted these Netherlands into arable, liveable, agricultural terrain by a complicated system of canals and *kokers, kokers* being the sluices that regulated the water in the canals. For the rest, the Courantyne coast was protected from the sea by an inviolable dyke running all the way from the Berbice River to the Courantyne. Westwards from us, down in Demerara, they had the famous seawall, a solid brick wall wide enough to walk upon, running the entire length of the coast between the Demerara and the Berbice. The management of water was what the Dutch did well, and it was only thanks to that nation of dam-and-canal builders that plantations such as Promised Land could exist at all. At high tide in the rainy season, the water rose, converting the area into a lake. At low tide the *kokers* were opened, the water released, and the water drained off. This was the reason why our houses, all the houses, were raised on stilts.

As a child I had loved the rainy season; what child would not! We three girls would run out into the rain and scream and spin with joy; when the house became an island trapped in a lake of knee-high water, and the rain let up for an hour or two, we would build rafts and play at pirates; barefoot, bare-legged, our dresses soaked from hem to neckline, we cavorted like three foals let loose in a green pasture; Mama, laughing herself, would watch us sitting on the front stairs, knowing it was useless to bind us.

Now, I slipped from my bed and repaired to the veranda to watch the water fall from the dry safety of the house: and a waterfall it truly was, cascading all around, enclosing the house in a dry safe bubble.

I huddled in one of the rattan chairs and wrapped a thin cotton shawl around me; the air was cool and close and very damp. The rain fell in huge flat sheets, like water sloshed from a bucket. No spaces between the drops. Surrounded by a globe of solid water, I let the roar of the downpour drown out every feeling, every thought. Eventually it drew me into itself; I became a part of that roaring, rushing flood, without thought and yet so vibrantly present and alive as never before.

My skin turned to gooseflesh, like the skin of a plucked chicken; cool on the outside, I nevertheless felt a sweet, melting warmth that came from within, simply by watching the rain. It was as if the noise and the wetness washed through me, draining away the gloom and despair that had filled me the previous evening, and transforming it into a shivery elation, a peculiar sense of gladness. George's coldness of yesterday faded into the background, inconsequential.

I sat there for an age, watching, listening, huddled under my shawl, free of all thought, merged in the downpour. It was bliss. Then I jumped, for someone had touched my shoulder. I looked around and it was Yoyo.

'Winnie!' she cried. 'What on earth are you doing here? We've been looking for you everywhere! It's time for breakfast!'

Her words jolted me back to reality. I sprang to my feet, gathered up my shawl and turned to follow her into the house. Just as I passed the threshold I turned around to look once again into the rain. And that's the moment when reality truly jolted me awake. One thought:

*What can it be like in the logies?*

I stopped dead in my tracks at the thought. A vision of horror encompassed me. Those muddy tracks between the houses: now open sewers. Those makeshift roofs: as protective as treetops. The wood for their stoves: sodden through. How would they cook? Where would they sleep? What would they use as toilets when all around them, there was only water? Would the plantation management be there for them?

This much I knew about our coolies: they were our responsibility. The plantation hired them, housed them, paid their wages, looked after their welfare such as it was. They came from India at our bidding, because we needed them. We provided for them for the duration of their contract. Outside of us, they had nothing.

This much I knew now about plantation management: it didn't give a fig. And Papa was at the top. Papa *was* plantation management. I grabbed Yoyo's arm, pulled her to me, and pointed into the deluge.

'The *logies!*' I said. It was enough; she grasped my dismay immediately.

Her eyes widened. We stared at each other, united again in the awareness that the world did not begin and end at the little doorstep called *me*; that what little aches and pains we felt were pinpricks against the gut-wrenching misery that lay beyond our bubble of paradise; that the gilded privilege we took for granted was agonizingly paid for by others. Her eyes mirrored the *Weltschmerz* that now submerged me, sweeping away every last vestige of yesterday's heartbreak, every last memory of George. How trivial my own cares and problems in the light of that misery!

'What can we do?' I whispered. 'I feel so helpless!'

She nodded. That was the worst of it; the knowledge that there was not one thing she or I could do. But I had to do something; if only to assuage the appalling sense of guilt.

'We *must* do something!' I said. 'I know we can't change things – but there must be *something* we can do to help? To show, at least, that we care?'

'I know.'

We stood there, hands clasped, staring at each other. Beyond the veranda's balustrade the rain continued to sluice down. Dry and safe, we were; but all I wanted, right now, was to run through the rain screaming every last breath from my lungs. I hated my bubble. Hated my privilege. Hated my very skin. My perfect bubble of paradise – well, it was pierced, and could never again be whole.

❊ ❊ ❊

We breakfasted in glum silence. Lessons that morning passed by as in a dream; if Yoyo was anything like me then she too was listening far more to the thunder of the rain on the rooftop than to the drone of Miss Wright's voice. I racked my brain for that one little gesture of guilt-assuaging solidarity that would, perhaps patch one of the holes in my once-perfect world.

Then I had an idea, and after class I shared it with Yoyo. 'Their clothes must get soaking wet,' I reasoned. 'Wouldn't it be helpful if at least they had some dry clothes to change into? Why don't we give them our old dresses from the charity box? At least the women would be helped that way.'

'But they don't wear dresses,' Yoyo answered. 'They wear saris!'

'Surely if you're soaking wet you'll wear anything you can get your hands on! I think we should just do it. Or do you have a better idea?'

She didn't. By lunchtime the rains had ceased for a while, and so, after lunch, the two of us found the key to the downstairs store-room, stole into it, and opened the charity box. It had been started by Mama to collect our cast-off clothes to send to the Anglican vicar in New Amsterdam to distribute to the poor. Mama hadn't attended to the box for several years now, but Mrs Norton had continued the tradition; our maids would pass our outgrown dresses, skirts and blouses on to her, laundered and neatly folded, and they would end up in this trunk.

'How many shall we take?' Yoyo asked as I lifted the top layer. A whiff of moth-balls rose up from the trunk, so astringent I coughed. 'Phew!' She added. 'These stink!'

'As many as we can carry,' I replied. 'There are a lot of women down there. Let's take the whole trunk!' I lifted one of the leather straps. 'Oh! I said. 'It's so heavy! We should take little bundles one by one.'

Yoyo tried one of the straps and realized I was right.

'If we're going to take it all,' she said, 'let's give away Mama's things as well.'

I had opened the trunk lid again; I dropped it and it slammed shut. I glared at Yoyo.

'Give away Mama's things! You mean her dresses? Her clothes?'

Yoyo smiled, and it seemed to me there was something like triumph in that smile.

'Well, she won't be needing them anymore, will she? Or do you think she'll send for them? After all, she's not coming back.'

'Yoyo, how could you even say such a thing! Of *course* she's coming back!'

Yoyo shrugged, as if to say, if that's what you believe, then go ahead. 'At the very least, we could give them Edward John's clothes. *He* won't be needing them. And they had a baby – remember?'

I did remember; the little bundle hanging in a sling from the roof in Nanny's hut. And I remembered Edward John's clothes, stored in the window-seat in Mama's bay window. Most of those garments had been individually sewn by Mama's private seamstress, and embroidered by Mama herself; tiny suits, cotton jackets. No dresses; they had hoped desperately for a boy and to prepare girls' clothes would no doubt have shown lack of faith in Mama's prayers. They were beautiful garments; some of them quite exquisite. We girls had often wondered if Mama would pass them on to us when we had sons of our own. I thought she would. Yoyo thought she wouldn't. Mama was too attached to them; they anchored her in her grief. Whenever her sorrow reached a low ebb she would open the lid on Edward John's clothes, lift the garments, raise them to her cheek, stroke them, and sigh. Grief would come rolling back with all its power, and Mama would be soothed again, for Mama was only soothed while wallowing in grief.

'Yes,' I said now, firmly. 'Edward John's clothes must go. But not Mama's. Mama will return. We can't give away her things.'

So up we traipsed to the Seaview Room and down again with as many of Edward John's clothes as we could carry, and prepared to pack our bundles of goodwill.

It felt good to be doing this! Good and kind and compassionate – Christian. I wished I could see the beaming faces of the coolie women when they unpacked the sacks. Surely they would gasp in joy at our English-cut skirts, dresses and blouses, our petticoats and bodices! Everything was still in best condition, almost new: cotton skirts for every-day and tailored blouses to go with them, fancier dresses for special occasions. Of the latter there were few, for the dinners and garden parties and balls for which Promised Land had once been famed had come to an abrupt halt with Edward John's death; still, we were occasionally invited out and had to dress appropriately.

Now, the lovely silk and satin dresses, specially sewn from us by Millicent, a darkie seamstress from New Amsterdam who came to measure and fit us and recreate the fashions we pointed out in the magazines sent to us from London, brought *oohs* and *aahs* and 'do-you-remembers' to our lips. Not that either of us was as fashion-conscious as Kathleen; but what young lady does not like to see herself in a glimmering evening dress, if only on occasion? We were growing girls, though, and hardly had we worn one dress once than it no longer fitted. Our social life was simply too limited. And the baby clothes were exquisite. The coolie mother of that baby would be delighted. She'd hold them up and admire the embroidery and stroke the beautiful fabric in wonderment, and smile up at us in gratitude.

Except that we would not be there to see that smile: neither of us dared to return to the *logies*. No: we had to find Gopal. Now that the rain had ceased he would be at work, somewhere in the acre of garden that surrounded the house; while it rained he, along with the other gardeners and yard-boys, would have taken shelter in the roundhouse or one of the pavilions or garden sheds scattered amid the bougainvillea and honeysuckle bushes.

In a corner of the storeroom was a neat pile of gunnysacks, once used for rice. Had I been more astute I would have remembered that many of the *logies* were patched together with gunnysacks, and that they were probably of more use than the clothes. But I wasn't thinking. We each grabbed a sack and filled it with as many clothes as it would be practical to carry; and off we walked into the drizzle, each with a sack over her shoulder.

We found him in the rose garden, restoring the bushes that had been battered by the morning's downpour, and clearing up the petals that littered the beds. Yoyo called out to him; we hoisted our skirts (for the path was wet and there were many puddles) and ran over to him, and when we had reached him we held out our sacks, beaming with pride.

'This is for you!' said Yoyo.

'For your wife!' I corrected. 'And the other ladies. We hope you like them!'

Gopal looked mystified. He stuck the secateurs he was holding into the waistband of his trousers and took both of the sacks; holding them both, he opened one and peered into its depths.

'Our dresses!' said Yoyo, flushed with excitement. 'And skirts and blouses – all really good quality; some of them we haven't worn much at all! And I know we are only girls but your women are quite thin, aren't they, and small – much thinner and smaller than we are – so they should fit nicely. Some of the dresses are real silk!' She paused, waiting for Gopal's response, and when none came, repeated: 'We do hope you like them! And there's more where those came from – much more!'

'And baby clothes!' I added. 'We saw you have a baby – a young baby. There are lots of baby clothes in there, as well!'

Gopal closed the sack and looked into the other one, as if to ascertain that its contents were similar. He looked at us, from one to the other, still not speaking. We looked back, waiting for his thank you. It did not come. The smiles faded from our lips; we looked at each other, and then at him. Finally he spoke.

'Miss Winnie, Miss Johanna,' he said, speaking to the air between us, 'is very kind of you-all to give we these things. But I can't take it. We don't want you old clothes.'

'But,' said Yoyo, 'They're not really *old*! They've only been worn once, most of them! The poor women in New Amsterdam adore them! They are so grateful! Mildred told us! Nothing's wrong with them, nothing at all! And the baby clothes: they are quite new, never worn and perfectly exquisite! Why, you couldn't even buy baby clothes as good as those, not even in London! They are hand-embroidered, by Mama! And …'

Yoyo, oblivious to the sensitivity of the moment, not noticing the hardness in Gopal's face, prattled on. I pinched her then, and she stopped. Gopal had placed the clothes he had removed back in the sack. He closed the sack with determined finality.

'See,' he said, 'we don't like charity, we Indians. We don't like it at all.'

Shock and shame rushed through me in a red-hot tide; I was melting from the top down. I looked at Yoyo; she was red as a tomato, as I most likely was myself.

Yoyo spoke again, but now it was just a stutter. 'I-I … we … d-didn't think … I-I

m-mean …'

But Gopal had started to speak again, and with such confidence as I had never heard in a coolie.

'I sorry if I is rude, Miss. I don' want to be rude – or ungrateful. I know you does mean well. I know you is good girls. But – we don't want no charity.'

'We only wanted to help – a little,' I heard myself say. 'We were so sorry – about what happened – we wanted to help. We thought you'd be so wet – in the rain – we wanted you to have some dry clothes – I know it's just a drop in the ocean but we wanted to show …'

'We don't need your help,' said Gopal. He stood tall and straight before us. He pointed to the rejected gifts. 'And this don't help at all. A li'l cloth is not what gon' help we.'

'We meant well,' I managed to say. Now it was Yoyo who, for once, seemed tongue-tied. Gopal softened his stance. His voice, when he spoke again, was gentler.

'See,' he explained, 'we Indians been here ten, twenty, thirty years in BG. Them that din' die in de boats, that din' die on the field, that din' die from exhaustion and disease, survived to this day, and we gon' survive longer. Before us, the slaves. We learn to deal wit' the heat an' the rain and the punishment. We don't need charity. We is strong.'

'But …'

'We need more than charity,' said Gopal. 'We need change, but change in't gon' come from you white people. Change got to come from we, weself. We gon' change we own situation. You is good girls, both a you. You got good hearts. But is not enough. Change gon' come, but not from you. It happenin' already. You stay out of it. Take care. Don't worry 'bout we.'

I had no words; I could only stare at him. Tears pricked my eyes: tears at the knowledge of what he and his people endured, tears too of shame: that it was my people who put them through this hell. Tears of helplessness. As for Yoyo, she was still red, bowed, and speechless.

I reached out, took the sacks, handed one of the sacks to her, and said, 'I'm sorry, Gopal, if we insulted you. Come, Yoyo, let's go.'

❄ ❄ ❄

It rained solidly for the next few days, making it impossible to leave the house. On the third day, above the rattle of rain on the roof, we heard a strange honking from the yard; Yoyo and I ran to the gallery window and looked out. There, standing in the forecourt, half hidden by the veil of water falling from above, was a black motor car. Emerging from the front seat was a tall, thin figure in black; another figure in black ran around from the other side of the car and held an open umbrella over the first.

'Papa!' shrieked Yoyo. 'He's got a *motor car*! At last!'

She ran to the front door, down the stairs and into the rain to greet him. I was more circumspect; once upon a time I too would have flung myself into Papa's arms when he returned from a trip to Georgetown, especially so with a motor car. Those days belonged in the past. I was an older, wiser being now; a woman who knew that even a beloved father can have a dark side, a side kept hidden like an ugly beast caged in a dungeon. I had seen the beast; I could not return to the carefree days of naive girlhood. Yoyo now, she was different; she could continue in her role as Papa's favourite; it may have been an act, or maybe it wasn't. Maybe she still loved him just the same as before; maybe her love was unspoiled by any wrong he could do. And maybe, even, hers was the higher form of love, unconditional. Who was I to judge?

I watched from the dry refuge of the gallery as Yoyo, ignoring the rain – as she always did; she loved getting soaked through – danced around the car, darted in and out of its doors, hugged Papa who stood watching under the umbrella, danced around the vehicle again, and finally, took Papa's hand and led him inside. I waited in the house for them both to come in. Still holding the umbrella, papa entered and closed it immediately. Yoyo laughing and chattering, hung on to his arm. Water collected around them in puddles on the floorboards. He removed his raincoat, handed it to Mrs Norton who had glided up out of nowhere, and reached out for me, talking all the time.

'I bought it in Georgetown,' he was saying; 'It really wouldn't do for me to be the last of the planters with a horseless carriage! How do you like it, from what you can see? I shall take you both for a drive the moment the rain lets up. Now we'll be able to dash into New Amsterdam and back in the space of a morning! And we can drive to Georgetown, too, now and then, instead of taking the train. Girls, this is a new era!'

'Oh Papa! It's heavenly! What fun we shall have! Can you drive it yourself? Did you learn to drive already? Is it hard to drive? Can I learn to drive?'

Yoyo, jumped up and down in excitement, with the water still dripping from her hair and clothes. Mrs Norton rushed up with a cloth to mop the floor. Papa, this stranger, stuck the wet umbrella in the stand next to the front door, and approached me with arms spread wide.

'Winnie, my dear!' he said as he enfolded me in his embrace. 'You haven't said a word about the car. You do like it, I hope?'

'Yes, Papa,' I replied dutifully. 'It looks lovely.'

I let him embrace me; he did not notice my lack of response.

Over his shoulder I saw Miss Wright descend the stairs, her face grim. Papa heard her footsteps and turned around.

'Miss Wright!' he began and stepped towards her with out-stretched hand. Really, Papa was behaving as if he'd been gone a year instead of just five days. Miss Wright, instead of shaking his hand, gestured with her chin in the direction of Papa's study. He let his hand drop, turned from her, and opened the door to let her in. He entered himself, and the study door closed on them. Yoyo and I exchanged a look and a shrug and went upstairs to continue our game of cards.

Half an hour later the car door slammed, easy to hear because now the rain was little more than a trickle and the windows were open. Yoyo rushed to the window.

'Oh, Winnie, look!' she called. 'Papa's going for a drive! I'm going to go with him!'

She dashed to the door and a moment later her feet clattered on the stairs. I stayed behind and watched. The chauffeur – I could see him clearly now the rain had let up – a tall thin darkie, wearing the dark blue Promised Land uniform, was cranking at a handle at the front of the car; Papa was already inside it. A few moments later Yoyo, skirt raised the better to run and hair dishevelled, flew down the front stairs and up to the car window. There she stood, obviously arguing with Papa, and obviously being refused, for she turned away, stamped her foot and stood watching in the drizzle as the car puffed and shuddered, and the chauffeur climbed in, and drove off down the drive.

❊ ❊ ❊

At dinner it was raining heavily again and Papa's mood was sombre. He hardly spoke; he answered Yoyo's questions regarding the car and the journey and Georgetown in a series of monosyllables. Mildred cleared the dishes of the main course, served the pudding, and retreated into the kitchen. Papa looked from Miss Wright to Yoyo, and to me and finally spoke.

'I heard the police have been here,' he said. 'And I'm happy to hear that you can support me in my insistence that the cause of the mischief lies entirely in the hands of the coolies. You didn't see what happened! It was an attack! A riot! They tried to storm the gate, intent on violence. This is our home, our castle; we defended it admirably and no harm was done. I have been to the estate manager's quarters and had a word or two with Mr McInnes. We are all in agreement: all that we did was defend our property, as is our right. Defend our lives: the coolies were, after all, armed. Heaven knows what would have happened if the gate had been open, if they had gained entrance! Everything was quite above board. It seems they were impertinent enough to report a whipping. I ask you. A whipping! It never happened. Mr Stewart and Mr McInnes both agree, there was no such thing as a whipping. I can't believe that Mr Armstrong tried to involve you girls in this preposterous affair, asking you for statements. Why, you could have been hurt! Young girls! You saw them: they were armed!

'Anyway, enough is enough. Tomorrow I'm going to drive down to New Amsterdam to speak to Mr. Armstrong. I have no doubt that the misunderstanding can be cleared up, and then we'll hear not a further word on the matter. And I want you girls to put it all out of your heads and simply enjoy your lives. Oh! I almost forgot to give you your presents! You shall have them after dinner.'

Indeed, after dinner we all retired to the drawing room. The chauffeur – whose name, we now learned, was Poole – brought several large packages wrapped in brown paper into the room and carefully deposited them on the carpet. Papa instructed us to open them. That we did, with the usual *oohs* and *aahs* of gratitude; but mine, at least, were artificial. I was playing the game, for Papa's benefit.

Yards of silk and satin spilled on to the carpet: yellow and blue and pink, bolts of it, enough for several ballroom dresses. We opened hat-boxes, shoe-boxes, producing delicate bonnets and silken shoes, all in the latest fashions. More *aahs* and *oohs* and thank yous emerged from our lips. We tried on bonnets and shoes while Papa looked on in satisfaction – and held up yards of silk against our skirts. Yoyo was beside herself with glee, but I – I was pretending. Any other day, any day in the past, I would have been truly delighted. Not today. As for Yoyo – she was young, so young. She lived in the moment, and this moment was one of rare glamour and genuine delight. How could it not be, among such gorgeous gifts?

Papa smirked and clapped. Miss Wright fingered the silk and declared it Best Quality. 'Really, Mr Fogarty is outdoing himself!' she added. Papa complained that the ladies in Georgetown were wearing their skirts so short their ankles showed and declared that we wouldn't have any such lasciviousness on Promised Land. I was too upset to care. Yes, I loved fashion and new clothes and radiant silk and bonnets like any young girl anywhere in the world, and any other day in the past I would have been squealing in genuine pleasure. But now, distress outweighed pleasure.

When it was all over Papa slapped his forehead. 'I almost forgot to tell you!' he cried. 'The biggest news of all! You haven't forgotten Mr Smedley, I hope?' He winked, and with a jolt I remembered – our would-be suitor, chosen by Uncle Percy! Papa looked from one to the other of us to make sure we understood, and when we nodded, he pulled a piece of paper from his pocket. A telegram! He waved it at us, and continued.

'Mr Smedley is sailing for BG this summer – he shall be arriving in September!'

The words hardly sank in. I was staring at the telegram itself. When had it arrived? Had George come to deliver it without my ever noticing? Had I missed him? When? My heart thumping wildly, I dared put the question: 'When did the telegram come, Papa?'

'Oh, it didn't come *here*. I sent my 'Yes' telegram from Georgetown and that's where Archie sent his reply – care of the Georgetown Club.'

✵ ✵ ✵

**Mama's Diary: Norfolk, 1890**

*Liebes Tagebuch,*

*And now our darling daughter is with us – her name is Kathleen! Our joy would be complete, were it not for the fact that Archie is to leave in a month's time for this sugar plantation I told you about. I made a mistake – it's not in Africa at all, but in South America. My geography is terrible! He showed me where it is on the globe and I am no longer as sanguine about it as I was. It is across the ocean, in the New World! I am terrified about the Atlantic Crossing. One hears such things. Sometimes in church – for I am now a regular church-goer! – we sing this hymn:*

Oh hear us when we cry to Thee

For those in peril on the sea!

*And indeed there is great peril – not only pirates, but storms, hurricanes, great waves that will toss the ship around as if it were but a leaf. He will go first on his own and once he is settled there he will send for me, and then it is my turn, our turn, mine and Kathleen's! I am terrified!*

*Sometimes at night I cry and he takes me in his arms and comforts me, and reminds me that most ships do cross safely; that worrying will not change one little thing. We must have faith, he says. Faith will make us strong. What a gentle, caring, kind husband I have! He adores me. And he is such a good father to our little Kathleen!*

*Father came to visit, and he too is delighted with his granddaughter. He is not delighted by the news that we are to be sent away; in fact, he was quite angry with my father-in-law but nothing can be done about it now. All the arrangements have been made.*

*Archie says it's because he's the younger son. The plantation is not as profitable as it could be and it needs a family member to run it, and that lot falls to him. There is a smaller plantation owned by the family, and this is in Barbados. Archie's youngest brother Donald is to be sent there. So it is not Archie alone who is being banished.*

*The family, in the meantime, have accepted me completely. They love me, and I love them. It's a good thing, for otherwise I could not bear to be left behind. It will break my heart to part with Archie but there is nothing to be done, except pray for his safe passage. And that I will do.*

# Chapter Ten

It rained all night. I fell asleep to the rattle on the roof and woke up to the very same rattle. A deep melancholy descended into my being and took root. Everything seemed so hopeless, so unfinished, so impossible. Everything in my life fed into the misery that engulfed me. The coolies, the discovery of Papa's secret cruelty, Mama's absence – and then, yes, George.

The moment of Truth that had overcome me in the Post Office – that exquisite moment when I had *known* to the depths of my being that I loved George Theodore Quint. That I would love him forever. That sense of communion that had lent me wings, had vanished completely. It all now seemed only like the hysterical imagination of a silly, overwrought girl. It had only been an illusion. That last meeting with him had told me all I wanted to know. The black despair that had crept over my spirit intermittently in my days of trust and hope and confidence had finally seeped through my being and taken possession of it. It was as if the sheer joy of love had gouged a hole into my soul, which was now filled with a dark, heavy sludge from which I could not escape.

The darkness gnawed at me from the inside; I stood at my window and gazed out northwards, at the huge sheets of water gushing from above as if from an inexhaustible source. I had managed to push him from my mind for a short while, but now it was back, the longing, the yearning. Oh, for just a glimpse of that lost joy!

My yearning was that of the watchman waiting for dawn, my emptiness that of the landlocked seaman far from the ocean. I visualised eyes that melted deep into my own; I heard a rich deep voice that spoke of conductor-wires but resonated with – but no.

There was a word I dared not say even to myself. A thing that forced its way up through smothering layers of dark, like a rose-bud covered in earth and bearing upwards to the light, its petals pushing outwards as they unfold. Something tight and closed within my soul swelling with an indomitable force. I would not, could not name it again. Love was an illusion, a delusion, a figment of an overwrought imagination. Pure emotion, unstable, as a house built on sand, transient, and ultimately false. I had fallen into a trap that day in the post office. Imagined things that did not exist. In me surged an ocean of unreleased tears. George was no more. I must banish him from my mind, banish all hope and allow darkness to settle in my mind.

Somewhere out there was a village and a post office and a young man whose eyes spoke louder than words. It was that silent voice I yearned to hear, not the roar of rain; I yearned to feel again what I had once felt, but the moment had come and gone and it would never return. It had been a dream. Unreal. Lost forever.

※ ※ ※

Papa drove off into the rain soon after breakfast. He returned just before lunch, his humour entirely restored.

'Everything's fine,' he announced. 'I've taken care of it. I spoke to Chief Inspector Armstrong and he agrees that the whole matter has been atrociously exaggerated – a man has a right to defend himself, his castle and his family. All charges have been dropped. No need to worry.'

Mildred placed a bowl of steaming hot potatoes on the table and Papa slid several on to his plate, cut them open and drowned them in gravy.

'Nevertheless,' he continued, 'I want you girls to be careful. The coolies are getting restless – not just here, but up and down the Courantyne, and in Demerara. Ours wasn't the only plantation where they rioted that day – imagine! Dieu Merci and

Glasgow had troubles too, and even as far up as Skeldon, but not as serious as ours. It was almost as if there was some sort of conspiracy – but hardly possible, considering the distances involved. And in Demerara there have been strikes. These coolies will never understand. If we were to give in to their ridiculous demands …' He stopped mid-sentence.

'Then what, Papa?'

'Then the entire sugar industry would break down. The plantations would fold. It would be over. BG would collapse. But – that's not for you girls to worry about. We planters are taking care of it. They don't call us sugar kings for nothing. Government supports us. Great Britain supports us. That's all you need to know. But – that's enough. Remember the rule – no business at the table. So what have you girls been up to while I was away?'

'Papa, what are their demands?' I had not forgotten the *logies*. Why was everyone telling us not to worry, not get involved? Not only Papa, but Gopal too, who just like Papa had told us – warned us – not to worry. Both sides were telling us to keep away; it was beginning to bother me that there was a huge *situation* brewing away right on our doorstep and we weren't allowed to think about it. Thinking about it was what I needed to do.

'Winnie, I said, *don't worry about it.* It doesn't concern you. You don't need to know these things. It's a complicated situation and nothing for young women to worry about. There's all that beautiful silk I brought for you. That will give you enough to think about – a perfect occupation for a rainy day. Think about what dresses you'll have made. Now we have the car I can have Miss Whatever's-her-name brought up from New Amsterdam and back in a morning. I want to see you looking beautiful – there'll be a big party at the Georgetown Club once the rains are over, and I want you two to be the most beautiful girls there. It's a good thing women are still women here in BG – none of this suffragette nonsense. A plague of harridans is the last thing we need.'

Yoyo and I let him talk on for the rest of the meal. Eventually, he and Miss Wright entered into some conversation about the situation in Europe – it seemed there was trouble brewing there too, and Papa had brought back a stack of newspapers from Georgetown. Miss Wright was eager for his opinion, which he gave as pompously as ever. I felt as if I had awakened from a dream; that my kind, sweet, perfect dream Papa had turned into this stranger whose every word made me want to curl up in embarrassment or anguish or even revulsion. In that dream I had been blind to the faults of my beloved father; faults that in any other person would have been as glaring as if they had been wearing horns and carrying a pitchfork.

Could I still love Papa, with all these faults? After all, he was still my father. And he loved me; there was no doubt about that. Papa was a family man; we were everything to him, and he let us know it without reservation. How could I detest someone who loved me? Was it possible to love the person, but detest their personality? How did that work? Did George have faults I would detest, if only I were not too blind to see them? Did Mama love Papa in spite of his faults? Had she seen them as clearly as I now did? Was it those faults that drove her away, rather than the reasons Yoyo and I had surmised?

So many questions. So few answers. And so much rain.

❊ ❊ ❊

The rain came down and the floods came up. The *kokers* opened and closed. The water on the land rose and fell. The ditches and canals overflowed. The roads were awash with water, emerging from the floods only when the *kokers* opened. From the sky, water poured down. It plunged and plummeted, sometimes in a perpendicular rush like a one-drop waterfall, sometimes, when the winds were high and fierce, slanted and biting, a vicious horde of silver mosquitoes. It seemed there would be no end to it; that there was an inexhaustible ocean in the sky filling all of the universe; that heaven's sluice-gates had opened and all there would be was water till the end of our days. That the ocean up there was trying to drown the earth, and here were we in this mansion, trapped in a dry bubble while around us the ocean on earth filled up. But then the *kokers* opened and the water sank but more water came from above. Water, water, water.

Papa went off to work each day in his car – how he loved that car! – but I had no idea what work could be done in a solid downpour that never let up for more than a few minutes at a time.

❊ ❊ ❊

Rain. Days of it. A solid week of rain. I watched it, listened to it, smelt it, and breathed it. Even our dry spaces were damp, the air moist and warm, sticky with vapour; but sometimes cool, so that I drew my shawl around my shoulders and pulled it close and shivered. My hair and my clothes hung limp as I paced the floor, wandered up and down stairs, stood at windows staring out into the rain, curled up in armchairs with books whose pages were soft and tired, soaked with humidity. I tried playing the violin, but the roar from outside drowned out the sound and I gave up.

Was it my imagination; that this was the heaviest rain we had had in my memory? Or did it only appear that way because of my longing to escape it? Because it so mirrored my soul, the melancholy that flooded me.

And in my misery a crack appeared and I remembered the *logies,* and I knew that for all my gloom and all my misery, here in my white wooden mansion, I was still high and dry and privileged beyond measure. Guilt flooded through me, soul-destroying guilt, and I wept. I wept for those out there in the rain and the mud, for the weightlessness of my own complaints, for my helplessness in the face of true suffering. I wept for my doomed love; how trivial it seemed in the light of that comparison! And I walked out into the rain and stood there weeping, allowing it to soak me down to the skin in a feeble, foolish and pathetic attempt at solidarity.

\* \* \*

As for Yoyo: every morning Papa sent the motor car to the senior staff quarters to fetch Maggie McInnes, and Maggie would spend the rest of the day with us, learning with us in the mornings and playing with Yoyo in the afternoons, retuning home only in the evening. She and Yoyo found enough to occupy themselves through all the rain. They played games: Chinese Checkers, and Ludo, and huddled together giggling and chatting, unconcerned with the weather.

As a distraction, I had only my books. But I soon finished all the books. I had a pile to be returned to the library and exchanged for new ones, and I would have to wait for a long enough pause in the rain to venture out. It did not take longer than twenty minutes to walk from the gate, north up the road, and through the senior staff compound to the library. I had already made my way through most of the novels there, for it was a small library; however, it was constantly replenished by books donated by staff members. I had not been back for several weeks, and I hoped to find a few that would lure me into faraway worlds, allowing me to escape, if only for a few hours a day, the melancholic vacuum of my real life.

Finally, one morning, during the lessons, the rain gradually diminished to a light shower, then to a sprinkling, and then, after lunch, it stopped completely and the layer of clouds covering the sky thinned out to a glowing white veil bearing the promise of sunshine – a thing we had not seen now for almost two weeks.

I quickly changed into an outdoor skirt and blouse, and put the five or six books to be returned into a cotton bag. I went out the back door, through the kitchen porch, stopping only to pull on a pair of wellington boots, for the road, though drained, was wet and full of puddles. Breathing in the sweet damp air, I set off buoyed by a sense of freedom, freedom from the cloying tedium of the house.

But hardly five minutes past the gate my footsteps faltered and my heart gave a deep lurch and my breath stood still. I had rounded the corner and turned north and I saw him immediately – cycling towards me – sailing nearer by the second. I stopped altogether. My feet refused to walk. I could not breathe. My heart hammered and my thoughts stopped.

I could only watch in stillness as he drew nearer. His gaze, fixed on me, was a magnetic thread that pulled him closer, closer, closer until he was right there in front of me. His leg swung over the bicycle saddle and he sprang to the ground before me. There he stood, and our eyes locked. I held my breath and swallowed the lump in my throat. I wanted to say something, anything, a greeting, his name. Nothing came. He too was silent. And yet we spoke; oh, how we spoke! I could read his eyes like a book. They had been so cold and blank that last day in the post office, yet now they spilled over with feeling, saturated with that *thing* I could not name; they melted me with their eloquence. The lump rose in my throat again and I swallowed. I tried to speak but only a croak emerged.

The sky darkened and growled. We both looked upwards. Shadowy clouds had gathered and now huddled into an angry dark shroud thick with rain. A deafening crack like a whiplash rent the air, and thunder grumbled. The softness in George's eyes turned to concern, and finally the spell broke and he spoke.

'Rain gon' fall in a minute,' he said. 'You have a raincoat?'

I shook my head.

'You better go back home,' he said. 'You gon' get soaked.'

I shook my head again. The thought of returning to the house to be cooped up again for however many weeks it would rain when it started again was unbearable. Now I was out I would continue to the library. I would get wet. So what!

'I'm going to the library!' I said, and my voice was a croak. 'In the senior staff quarters – it won't take long. I've got some books …' I patted the bag hanging over my shoulder.

'Then take my raincoat. I don' wear it anyway. I don' mind getting' wet. You can't let the books get wet!'

Still speaking he opened one of his saddlebags and removed a roll of material; it turned out to be a big midnight-blue mackintosh. He placed his bicycle on its stand, shook the mac open, and stepped towards me with it, holding it up by the shoulders. Truly, I hadn't thought about the books; and they indeed *would* get wet if I continued through the rain; and so I allowed him to dress me in his mackintosh. He held it up as I pushed one arm then the other into the sleeves; then he buttoned it up the front, and raised the hood so my head was covered. He never once touched my body while doing all this; but all the while his eyes clung to mine and mine to his. Neither of us spoke as he dressed me.

Lightning flashed. The heavens broke and a waterfall gushed over us. We stood still, barely a foot apart. Not moving, not speaking, not reacting to the rain. He was soaked through within a moment; he seemed not to care. He only gazed at me through the rain.

And then he spoke, at last, and said the word.

'Miss Winnie – oh. I love you so much. I just love you so much. I can't stop thinking of you. I just love you so much …'

And then his hands were on my cheeks, cupping my face, and he was leaning forward, tilting my head up by the chin, drawing my face closer, kissing me, kissing my forehead and my cheeks, my nose, my chin, my closed eyelids, and at last, my lips. The slanting rain beating my cheek from the north was hard and cold and harsh, but his lips were soft and warm and sweet. Then he drew away and looked at me through the rain. His face was blurred and wet and I knew not if it was from rain or tears, because his face was a crumpled mask of abject misery.

'I just love you so much! I'm sorry!'

He turned away then, away from me, and wheeled his bicycle off its stand and jumped on to it and rode away from me through the rain. I stood watching him ride away, into the water. He never looked back. And then I turned and continued on my way to the library.

※ ※ ※

I no longer walked. I ran, I danced. I twirled and skipped through the rain. I laughed, I sang, I yelled, I flung out my arms to the rain and the sky and the sodden earth; I grew wings; I flew, I sailed, I whirled and waltzed all the way to the senior staff compound. A puzzled guard opened the gate and I danced past him in a twirling, prancing, laughing, waving, rain-sodden gambol, a foal let out to play. He must have thought me mad; and mad I was. Mad with an ecstasy too huge to hold; mad with a sweet euphoria bubbling up through my being, a rush of golden splendour. The guard shook his head and smiled to himself as if to say, *these white people!*

On I spun, dancing through the compound. The rain still fell in a steady cascade, lighter now after the first rush yet still enough to keep people indoors, and so I arrived at the library out of breath, grinning from ear to ear, without any further human encounters, and only one animal: Rummy, the librarian's dog who usually waited patiently on the bottom step, ran out from beneath the house and greeted me with her usual overflowing joy. Elation exuding from every pore of my body, I stooped down and patted her soggy fur. It wasn't enough. I flung my arms around her, cuddled her and laughed with her and she, enjoying such unabashed ardour, whined and wagged her tail and licked the rain from my face. I hugged her one last time, laughed goodbye, and ran up the stairs to the library.

The library wasn't really a full-time library. It was a private venture of Miss Hull, one of the European primary school teachers, whose passion was literature. It had started with her extensive private collection, which she lent out to the book-starved members of the senior staff compound. The demand was so heavy that this casual lending needed to be administered; that is, book borrowers needed to be monitored, and the lent books tracked. The books were duly indexed, classified, and given a room of their own in Miss Hull's home; borrowers had to become library members, and were allowed access three days a week for two hours. In these two hours Miss Hull acted as honorary librarian. Books reached her from many sources; they were donated to her by senior staff members, and sometimes there were library book exchanges between other plantations. We would never run out of new books.

Still grinning from ear to ear, I opened the front door and burst into Miss Hull's gallery – her door was never locked – and water sloughed off of me onto her polished floor.

'Oops!' I cried, and exited again. On the sheltered porch I removed George's mackintosh, laid it across the railing, took off the wellingtons, and re-entered the house. Miss Hull, drawn by the opening and closing of doors and my cry, now entered the gallery herself. Seeing me, she rushed up.

'My dear Winnie! What on earth! Why, you're soaking wet!'

I had not noticed; how could I have, in the oblivion of ecstasy? In my reckless cavorting the hood from the mackintosh had fallen from my head and my hair was wet, and so was the hem of my skirt, all the way up to my knees, for I had skipped and danced through puddles without thought or care. Water had trickled past the mackintosh's collar as well, down my neck and wetting my blouse thoroughly. It had even eased in through the tops of my wellingtons; my stockings were soaked. What did I care!

But Miss Hull cared. She bustled away and returned with a towel and went about briskly rubbing down my hair while muttering comforting things like *tut-tut* and *silly girl* and *come, dear!* The towel was not enough. She ushered me into her own bedroom and made me change into clothes of her own: a skirt that was far too wide and long, which she rolled at the waist so that I would not tread on the hem, and a blouse that was far too loose at the front, Miss Hull being rather big-bosomed. She dried my feet and eased them into thick, hand-knitted woolly socks, the kind no one ever wore in BG.

That done, she took a second look at my face. She frowned, and her lips puckered. 'Whatever were you thinking, my dear, to come here through the downpour? And why on earth are you smirking like a Cheshire cat?'

'Oh, Miss Hull, I'm just so happy!' I replied, and added, 'I *love* the rain, don't you?'

And then I hugged her.

Unaccustomed to being hugged by her ex-pupils, and nonplussed by my out-of-character exuberance, she could only purse her lips some more, mutter a few more *silly girls* and pull away. She picked up my wet clothes from the floor and laid them over a clothes horse; and then she picked up the bag that had been slung over my shoulder.

'Oh! Oh look!' she cried. 'These books are *wet!* They're *quite* sodden! Oh, Winnie, *really!* You *might* take better care of our precious books! Oh, how careless of you! Oh, what a shame! They're ruined!'

I took them from her hands. 'No,' I said. 'See? Only the top one got wet, and it's only a few drops. It's just a bit moist, that's all; it will dry. Just lay it in the sun for a while. It's only water, not tar or anything.'

'What sun? I haven't seen the sun for weeks. Oh Winnie, this is just so *tiring* of you. Whatever were you *thinking*?'

'I wasn't,' I admitted. 'I'm so sorry, Miss Hull. Truly I am. I'm afraid I got carried away a little.'

'By the rain? I never knew the rain could have such an effect on you. Are you *sure* that's the reason?' She peered into my face as if looking for some hidden source of foolishness. My cheeks turned hot.

'You're blushing, my dear; I think there's more to this than meets the eye. However, I won't pry. What you young people get up to in your spare time is your own business and that of your parents, not mine. It's such a pity about that book, however. Mr Dickens would be horrified at the way you treat his precious words. Haven't I always taught you all to treat books with very special care? Oh dear, oh dear. And even of it dries out, it will be warped.'

'I'm sorry,' I repeated, truly sorry now. 'If it does end up warped, Papa will replace it.'

'That's the trouble with you planter children,' said Miss Hull in her sternest teacher voice. 'Spoilt silly. "Papa will replace it", indeed. That's exactly the reason you take no care in the first place. If you had to pay for damaged goods with your own hard-earned money you would think twice before cavorting through the rain with my library books! Now, I suppose you want to borrow some more, so run along and choose a few, and please take better care next time! No running around in the rain with them! And in fact I'm not going to send you home until this weather lets up. If it doesn't let up I'll order a coach. Now run along, chop-chop.'

Half an hour later I had chosen my books and the rain had diminished to a light drizzle. Miss Hull packed my damp clothes into a dry bag, wrapped up the books carefully and placed them in another, waterproof bag, and placed an umbrella in my hand as I left the house.

'You can return it next time you come – I've got another one,' she said as I pulled on my wellingtons. 'Now take care, my dear!'

I said goodbye and left the house. Over the porch railing lay George's mackintosh. I picked it up and lay it lovingly over my left arm. I raised the umbrella over my head and walked down the stairs. Rummy jumped up at me, wetting my skirt with her paws, but I had no hands free to return her greeting so I only smiled at her and said 'good girl'.

Actually, I was thinking of the mackintosh. One fine day I would return it to George. I could hardly wait.

❋ ❋ ❋

### Mama's Diary: Norfolk, 1890

*Liebes Tagebuch,*

*I keep resolving to write to you more often but everything gets in the way and holds me back. Kathleen grows bigger by the day, and fills me with delight – if not for her I would surely be pining away, I miss Archie so much. I have an excellent nursemaid for her, who loves her almost as much as I do – well, that is an exaggeration, but she is such a devoted nurse and I am grateful for her loving care. She is almost a friend. But I can't let the family know. I am sometimes shocked and appalled by the way the servants are treated in this household. It is as if they are mere chattels. It is so un-Christian! It seems to me that I, though born Jewish, have a far more Christian heart than my in-laws. For instance, one of the maids, a slight, fearful girl younger even than I am, tripped on the carpet and fell, and in falling she dropped the vase of flowers she was carrying and it broke, and water splashed all over the floor, wetting the carpet. Her head hit the corner of a table and she had a cut on her forehead. We were all there as witnesses. But instead of showing concern for her injury, Lady Cox shouted at her for her clumsiness, and informed her that the price of the broken vase will be taken off her wages! And the servants earn so little to begin with! I could not bear it – I was so embarrassed, mortified by her arrogance and cruelty. The poor little maid.*

*I managed to slip away once the maid had cleaned up and I went in search of her. I found her and ensured she was well looked after, and spoke a few words of sympathy. She was crying, and I longed to take her in my arms, but that of course would not do.*

*I did take her hand and squeeze it, to let her know that I at least cared. She is human, just as we are, and it is not her fault she is born into lowly circumstances, just as it is not our accomplishment that caused us to be born into more advantageous conditions. As a new Christian I have taken the teachings of Our Lord to heart and does He not say we should treat each other with love and kindness? I just do not understand it. If this is the English upper class – well, I do not want to be a part of it.*

*I almost forgot to mention that Archie has arrived safely in the colony of British Guiana – for at last I have memorized the name of my new home! – and seems to have settled in nicely. I cannot wait to join him, but we must wait till Kathleen is a little bit bigger and stronger. Thank goodness, my nursemaid – Elsa is her name – will be travelling with us.*

*I look forward to it, and am no longer frightened by the Atlantic Crossing. I have found faith, as Archie instructed me, and now look forward to joining him at our new home across the seas. What an adventure it will be!*

*I do feel homesick sometimes. I miss the mountains, the snow in winter, the cobbled streets of Salzburg; the music, the concerts, the opera, the balls. Occasionally, we do go to stay in the town house in London but it just isn't the same. Most of all, I miss my language. Though I am now fluent – but very far from perfect! – in English, I miss conversing in German. How glad I am to be able to write to you,* Liebes Tagebuch. *I would surely forget my own language otherwise.*

# Chapter Eleven

The soaking was too much for me. The next day I woke up with a bad cold and a fever that kept me bedridden for over a week. I didn't care; I relished it even, and understood. The fever seemed more a thing of the soul than of the body; or rather, it seemed to me that the fever of the body was a reflection of the fever of my soul, burning away at everything in me that was impure, heavy and dark, everything that was not of that great shining central essence of me, Love. It was a fever that sapped my heart of everything that might distort or cloud that essence; everything that was dross, or shallow, or of the self.

And even as I tossed and turned in the single bed they moved me to, in the single room across the way from my old room, at the back of the house, so as not to infect or disturb Yoyo, even in the heat of my physical fever, I rejoiced and understood the great thing that had happened. And even as the doctor from the senior staff compound read the thermometer that refused to go down and shook it and frowned and *tut-tutted* and whispered to Miss Wright in a corner of the room, even as the nurse they hired from New Amsterdam wiped my body with cool flannels and changed my wet nightgowns and helped me to the potty and back, even then I smiled to myself, and knew; and when they left me to myself I hugged myself and basked in the deliciously sweet memories of that day on the way to the library. The kiss. I played it over and over and over again in my mind. I saw his face, bent low to mine, dark and wet with rain and maybe tears, his eyes, limpid with love. I felt his fingers on my chin, gently tilting my face up to his, the warm, soft touch of his lips on my cheeks, my eyelids, my mouth. And each time I replayed that scene visually, I once more went through that metamorphosis: the spectacular opening of a closed bud into the sunshine. Darkness became light. Sadness became joy. I felt, I knew, it would last forever, if only I could remember that scene and keep it present within me. It was real, it was present, it was the truth of my whole being.

❊ ❊ ❊

Sometimes, often, in fact, Yoyo came to visit, and of course wanted to talk. As the week wore on, the fever subsided, but the cold persisted and the doctor said I should keep to my bed. Yoyo, sometimes with Maggie in her wake, brought board and card games to entertain me; she offered to teach me chess, and even, if I were too weak to hold a book, to read to me – a great concession from Yoyo, who considered the reading of fiction a waste of time. But I did not want to be entertained, and I feigned weariness just to make her go away. Papa came too, of course, his brow at the beginning furrowed with worry. As the week wore on and I began to recover, his face took on its usual weather-beaten crispness. Papa's presence was even more unwanted than Yoyo's, and even more, I feigned weariness and heavy-eyed sleep, so that he would not stay long.

The only company I wanted was the rain, and it did not disappoint. Day after day it poured down, a constant hammering on the roof. We were now in the fourth week of almost interminable rain. With it came a delicious sweetness, for it reminded me of *him,* and that precious stolen moment. I closed my eyes, curled up in a ball beneath the sheet, hugged my legs tightly, and smiled to myself, basking in the glow of my secret.

I was not a secret-keeper. Papa would say fondly that I wore my heart on my sleeve and it was true: I had always, before the dramas of this season, blurted out all I felt and thought. But never had I felt anything of this magnitude, of this substance, and of this consequence. This new heart of mine I would not wear on my sleeve. *This* secret was precious, a treasure that was mine alone, all the more priceless because nobody else could even begin to understand. On the contrary: they would revile and rebuke me for it. Even Yoyo, I feared. And so I pushed away the thought of others and kept my heart as tightly locked as a vault.

They say distance makes the heart grow fonder, and I now understood why. The distance between us, both in time and space, could only be breached by reaching out from within – my soul stretching out across the abyss to meet his. I did not need to see him, to talk to him, for love to grow. It grew as a plant grows, in silence; and the fact that it was forbidden was only nourishment, for love pushed against resistance and grew muscles. It would prevail!

❈ ❈ ❈

But after a while, I began to yearn for someone to confide in. I longed to share my secret, tell of my joy; doing so would surely double the delight. If only I had a friend, a girl my age, a sister of my heart! Yoyo could not fill that role. She with her mocking judgments and proclamations of *Schmaltz*. And besides, Yoyo now had Maggie, and preoccupied with her new friendship, she had turned away from me. There was only Mama, and she was far away.

Nevertheless, I wrote to her. One early morning, I slipped down once again to the study and Papa's desk. Once more, I poured out my heart to her. I did not edit or understate my rapture; she must know it just as it was, raw and abundant in its flowering. She might never read these words; still she must know. Mama was an invisible god who must know each tiny movement of my soul; I told her all. What I did not tell her were the details of George's person. I merely said: '*He is of a social standing Papa will deem beneath me: but, Mama, Love shall conquer all. This much I know.*'

I folded the pages and put them in an envelope, sealed and addressed it, and hid it in my desk till the time should come to post it. The very word 'post', if only in thought, caused my heart to leap.

As my illness subsided so did the rain, and by the time I was back on my feet it had diminished to only a light drizzle. I returned to the classroom and to the daily life of the household, physically weakened and much thinner; and also, a changed person.

❊ ❊ ❊

I was almost fully recovered when the note arrived, the call to action. Nora passed it to me one evening as I left the dining room. She placed a finger on her lips and slipped it into my hand, a piece of paper folded many times so that it was a small square hardly bigger than a thumbnail.

I hid it in my bodice and unfolded it later, when attending to nature's needs. Just a few scribbled words: 'Please come to the post office as soon as possible.' And George's initials. I could hardly contain my cry of joy; instead, I closed my eyes tight and clasped the paper to my breast; then I folded it as tightly as before, slipped it back into my bodice, and went to bed. Tomorrow, it must be.

I have often noticed that, once a decision is made in thought, outer events fall into place even without further planning; it is as if the individual, in forming that resolve, has simply fallen into line with a greater plan and must wait only for it to unfold. So it was on the following day.

Unusually, Papa joined us for breakfast. 'Girls,' he said before long, 'I promised to take you for a drive in the motor car – do you remember?'

Yoyo beamed. 'Yes, Papa! Of course!' Her eyes shone with expectation.

'Well, today is as good a day as any – the sun's out for the first time. I'm driving down to Albion Estate to speak to Mr Bee – plantation business. How would you like to come along for the drive? The last few weeks have been so dreary – I'm sure you'll enjoy it. I'll be gone all day – I'll free you from lessons, and we'll have lunch at Albion. Miss Wright, you're welcome to come along as well. Maggie, of course, is also welcome. What do you say?'

He looked from one of us to the other. Yoyo leapt from her seat, rushed over to his chair at the head of the table, and hugged him from behind. It was as if all memory of the *logies* and Nanny and the whipping had fled from her mind; as if she had forgiven him everything. Miss Wright flashed Papa a huge smile before frowning and looking at me.

'I'm not sure,' she said, 'Winnie has fallen behind in her studies …'

'Oh, fiddlesticks!' cried Yoyo. 'She'll catch up in time; she can't miss this. Can you, Winnie?'

Papa looked concerned. 'I hadn't thought of that. Miss Wright, do you think …' Then his face cleared. 'Yoyo is right. Fiddlesticks! You're girls – what's a few missed lessons?'

But I would not let this opportunity pass. I spoke up, firm and clear, the mature, responsible daughter.

'No, Papa, Miss Wright is right. I really need to catch up. There's some reading I need to do, and some French conjugations to learn; I'm happy to stay and study on my own. I'm sure there'll be lots of chances to drive in the motor car in future. The four of you – just go. I'm happy to stay at home alone.'

'Oh, *Winnie*! No! Don't be a spoilsport! What a bore!'

I smiled at Yoyo. 'I'm still a bit shaky on my feet, Yoyo; I think it's a bit early for an excursion. Don't worry about me. You know I'm just a boring old fogey who likes to be buried in books.' After more discussion – needless in my eyes for I was quite determined – my decision was accepted. With many kisses and exclamations of regret and apology, Yoyo and Miss Wright, in a flurry of goodbyes and hugs and kisses and a splattering of gravel under wheels, drove off in Papa's car, and the house was empty of all but the servants and me. I couldn't have asked for a better outcome if I had deliberated for weeks.

They left. I stood watching till the vehicle was out the gate, and then sprang into action: up the stairs, back into the house, up to my room, a quick change into outdoor clothes and shoes. I grabbed Mama's letter from my desk, then went down again and on to my bicycle. Only once did I indulge in a sense of guilt – where had the innocent, guileless *me* gone? Never in my life had I had need for subterfuge, secrecy, and lies, and now I was up to my neck in all three. Does love change a person that much, for the worse? But no, I argued with myself. It was not love that had changed me; it was the knowledge that this perfect love of mine would be seen as less than perfect by those who would never understand. Subterfuge, secrecy and lies were necessary to protect that which was pure and good and grand. One day, they would all understand.

I reached the village, and the post office, and placed my bicycle on its stand. Then I took a deep breath, reached into the pocket of my skirt to remove the letter and the postage money. I stepped into the open doorway already smiling – and came to a full stop.

My Beloved was not there, sitting at the desk, with his back to me. I saw instead grey grizzled hair, and recognized the familiar hunch of an ageing back. I knew that figure.

'Mr Perkins?' My voice faltered as I spoke, as if I doubted the evidence of my eyes.

He turned around, and, seeing me, stood up with some difficulty and, taking up a stick that leant against the desk, hobbled over to the counter. He smiled broadly as he came. 'Ah, Miss Cox!' he said. 'You see! Can't keep an old dog down! Here I am again!'

'Mr Perkins …' confusion made me stutter. 'It …it's good to see you back but-but … I thought …'

Mr Perkins had taken the letter from my hand, peered at the address, and bent down to remove the cardboard box containing stamps from under the counter. He opened the box, tore several stamps from a sheet, and proceeded to prepare the envelope for dispatch.

'Sitting around all day …not for me. I insisted. And me wife complaining – she tired of me moping around. And we need the money too. Nobody can't live from twopenny pension. So, I said, I goin' back to work! I goin' to deliver letters till I fall down dead! Brought me grandson to help me – I deliver in the village, he can deliver to the estate on he bike.'

He stamped the letter firmly with the date, hobbled back across the room and tossed it into a wire basket.

'That's nice, that's good, but …' But George had summoned me! Where was George?

'I missed it you know! Missed it somethin' terrible. I suppose one day I'll have to retire but till then …oh, by the way, seein' you reminds me …'

He raised the flap on the counter and moved out into the customer's space. Gesturing to me to follow, he shambled across to the open door. Once there, he placed his fingers to his lips and emitted a piercing whistle, once, twice, three times. He stood watching the house across the road for a while. A woman appeared at a window. He waved, she waved back, and a few seconds later a small darkie boy, no older than six or seven, emerged from the house and ran over the street to join us.

'Hello, Freddie-boy!' said Mr Perkins, and gestured to me. 'Here's the lady. Off you go, Miss Cox! I've been left instructions for you – you're to follow this little boy. There's somebody waitin' to see you.'

It seemed as if I'd been holding my breath all this long time, for I gave a sigh so deep it must have been audible to Mr Perkins. All right, so the old postmaster was back at work but that didn't mean that George himself was gone. He was waiting for me, somewhere; he had sent for me. This little boy ...

'Let's go,' I said to Freddie, and descended the steps to the street. Freddie, who, it seemed, could not speak, gestured to me to follow and off we went on foot. Freddie himself was barefoot, and wore nothing but a ragged pair of short trousers and a torn singlet. His limbs emerged from those rags like twigs covered in a layer of shiny brown skin. His shoulder-blades were sharp, his neck piteously thin. In spite of these signs of undernourishment he showed no lack of energy, sprinting forward down the village street. I ran behind him in shoes that seemed far too heavy for the task.

'Wait, wait,' I called. 'Not so fast!'

The boy slowed down without a word and I caught up with him. We walked down the village street. A few heads turned as we passed, and people smiled; though of course I did not know the villagers by name – except for the shop-owners – they certainly knew me, and greeted me with their usual deference, though obviously surprised to see me on foot. Whenever we came, Yoyo and I, it was on bicycle or horseback. I smiled politely back at everyone. There was no need to stop and exchange greetings and words. All cordiality with the villagers stopped short of conversation, except with the shop-keepers. That was the established order.

I followed Freddie to the end of the little village. The houses – cottages, rather – now were wide apart and straggled along the road; balanced on high thin stilts, top-heavy like the spindle-legged herons that fished in the paddy-fields. They looked ready to collapse at any moment, folding backwards at the knee. Some of them leaned precariously to one side. They had staircases with missing treads that led up to minute porches, open doorways, and empty window frames. They were of wood, but unpainted. They had gardens of unkempt bushes that reached over the broken-down palings and up the banisters, sometimes brilliant with bougainvillea or hibiscus. Houses as tiny almost as dolls' houses. I had seen them before but never noticed them. I realised now that people lived in them. Whole families. I saw faces at the windows: women, children, old men, babies in arms. Small dark hands waving. I waved back.

Presently, Freddie turned left into a lane between two houses. I followed. Soon we were in the fields: a cow paddock here, a vegetable patch there, a hut, a shack. On we walked. By now it was mid-morning. It was the first day in weeks that the sky was cloudless – which I thought a good omen – and by now the sun had risen high enough to warm the land. Steam rose up from the moist earth and from the flooded paddy-fields that now bordered the path, brilliant green from the young emerald shoots rising up through the water. The recent rains had obviously brought forth new life. A few East Indian women stood bent double in the fields, weeding. Freddie walked on.

'How far is it now, Freddie?' I asked after we had walked for some twenty minutes. Freddie only shrugged and pointed to a group of trees in the distance before us, and indeed, as we approached I saw a large white house hidden in the greenery. We approached the gate and I saw it more clearly: a two-storey white Dutch colonial house on grand white pillars that looked as if it had been uprooted from Main Street in Georgetown and plonked down here in the middle of this wilderness. Its Demerara windows were all painted green, as was the banister of the stairs leading up to the front porch and wide door, which, like all the other doors hereabouts, stood wide open.

The house stood in a garden of bounties. Flowering shrubs lined a pathway to the front stairs that led through a garden teeming with colour – all the flowers in our own garden. Yet, because it was so much smaller and compact, this one seemed much more profuse in its celebration of nature's abundance, and less immaculate. Hibiscus in all hues vied with red frangipani for attention,

and marigolds trailed all over the ground. Beyond, the same com-
pactness held true for the orchard. I identified at a glance at least
five fruit trees: mango, guava, sapodilla and paw-paw, and two
huge genip trees laden with bunches of plump ripe genips just
waiting to be plucked. A ladder leant against one of the trees. As
for the mango tree, it was a child's delight; its branches forked
low enough for small scrambling limbs to climb up, and a rudimentary swing hung from one of the sturdier horizontal boughs.
A blue-and-yellow macaw, unfettered, flapped and flew towards
the front garden; it landed on the bottom banister post where
it fluttered its wings in great excitement and called out 'Robert!
Robert!' Just gazing into that garden made me want to be a child
again; I felt strangely at home, glad to be here, welcome. But we
could not yet enter.

A white paling fence surrounded the house, and the gate, unlike the front door, was closed against the road, chained to the
gatepost, and locked with a mighty padlock. Several dogs rushed
up barking, and flung their bodies against the gate. They raised
the alarm, for immediately a woman appeared at a first-floor window and a man came hurrying out from under the house, calling
to the dogs to 'Get back!' Which they did, cringing around his
feet with their tails tucked in, and then disappearing behind a
lattice-work screen behind the front stairs.

The man was Mad Jim. He walked up to the gate, smiling and
waving at me.

'Hello, hello, hello,' he said as he pulled a key out of his pocket
and turned it in the padlock. He unwound the chain from the
gate and swung it open. He held out his hand. 'I've been wondering if you would make it – glad you could come so quickly.
Welcome, Miss Cox, welcome!'

I was more confused than ever. Instead of entering or returning his greeting with a smile and stretching out my hand to shake
his, I stood rooted to the spot, frowning.

'George …?' I managed to say. 'Is he …?'

'Yes, yes, I'll explain everything. Come on in. Freddie, you come too – you can wait for Miss Cox and take her back to the village later. Auntie will give you some genips.'

I followed Mad Jim back to the house. As we approached, a man slunk out from underneath, a tall thin coolie in an unbuttoned shirt and worn-out long trousers; quite young. He looked somehow familiar – and then I recognised him. The man from the post office, the man who had so rudely stopped my Morse lesson – I couldn't recall his name. As he passed by he glowered at me; such scorn was in that look that I flinched. What was he doing here?

'All right, Uncle, ah gone!' he said to Mad Jim, who simply raised his hand and said,

'See you tomorrow, Bhim. Close the gate when you leave – don't bother with the chain. Come, Miss Cox, come on upstairs. My wife will make you some lime juice – you must be thirsty after that walk in the sun. You too, Freddie!'

We all trooped up the stairs, with Mad Jim leading the way and Freddie bringing up the rear. We entered the house and I looked around, expecting George to emerge from the shadows and take me in his arms. No such thing happened. Instead, a coolie woman with a baby on her hip came forward. She was smiling.

'Welcome,' she said, almost in a whisper. She took my hand and led me to a group of rattan chairs in the front gallery. I sat down. I wondered who she was – not his wife, certainly. The woman I had seen with him, so many years ago, had been black as coal, African. This woman was Indian.

This was all wrong. A lump rose in my throat. I swallowed it, and said again, 'I don't understand! Tell me … Mr – Mr …' I didn't even know what to call him. I could hardly address him as Mad Jim, and Jim would be too casual. He was, after all, a stranger. I was in a stranger's house and I had no idea what was going on.

'Booker,' he said, 'Jim Booker. Me wife, Bhoomie. But you can call me Uncle Jim, if you like. Everyone 'round these parts call me that.'

He spoke Creole. It was the first time I'd ever heard a white person speak in that lilting, broken English; it seemed incongruous. Ludicrous, even. The huge bush of his beard shook as he laughed. Bhoomie, by this time, had placed a glass of lime juice in my hands. I sipped and waited. Silently, she handed Freddie, who had plonked himself down on the polished floor near the window, a bowl full of plump green genips, which he grabbed and placed before him on the ground, and set to work at the business of eating them: cracking open the firm outer skin with his teeth, plopping the golden fruit into his mouth, sucking off the tart-sweet flesh, and spitting the stone into his hand. The woman, who had disappeared for a moment, returned and handed him a saucer, for the sucked-out stones. She placed a plate of biscuits on the glass-topped table before me. She slid away again, noiselessly.

I watched all this in a sort of daze. Nothing made sense. Why had George lured me here, only not to be here himself? What had this man, this Mad Jim, this … suddenly, the name clicked.

'Mr … Booker?' I said with a start. 'You mean …THE Bookers? Booker Brothers? You're one of *them*?'

He laughed again. 'Yeh – I got the Booker blood all right, and the name. But that's all. Black sheep; the one the family don't want to know. Mad as a hatter, they say.'

'Oh,' is all I could say. So, then, the rumours were true, and even more scandalous than I had thought. Mad Jim, a member of the most prestigious family in BG – a pariah for marrying a darkie woman – it was all beginning to make sense. One thing I was sure of now was that he was not mad. Not in the least. The calm and humour in those blue eyes of his were anything but mad.

Mad Jim, Mr Booker, Uncle Jim, whatever I would eventually call him, had a soothing effect on my confusion. I instinctively trusted him.

'George,' I began, 'The note he sent – I thought …'

'You thought he'd be here. But he ain't. George gone back to Georgetown. He can't see you again. He wrote you a letter and he asked me to give you it. It's here. Read it – now. And when you finish readin', if you still don't understand, I'll explain.'

He handed me a small white envelope. I took it, hand shaking. Mad Jim stepped away and left me alone in the gallery to read. Not quite alone – Freddie still sat there, munching on the genips, a pile of sucked-out stones growing on the saucer.

Slowly, dreading what was to come, I removed a sheet of paper from the envelope, unfolded it, and read it.

*Dear Miss Winnie,*

*I apologize deeply for the liberties I took with you. I am very sorry and I should not have done it. I promise not to bother you again.*

*Yours truly,*

*George Theodore Quint*

※ ※ ※

## Mama's Diary: Norfolk, 1891

*Liebes Tagebuch*

*Archie writes to me often, and his letters are full of enthusiasm. A lovely big house, made of wood, is waiting for me. Fields of green, and a vast blue sky! It seems there is little else to recommend the place beside these two things: green fields and blue skies. Oh, and sun, of course! And rain! These four elements of nature are the components of my new home: fields, sky, sun and rain. It sounds rather dull, but of course Archie will be there. And Kathleen is growing bigger by the day, a little person in her own right! She is so droll! I can hardly wait for her to be with her Papa.*

*And that will be soon: our vessel leaves in less than a month! Oh, what an adventure. I look forward to it with all my heart. The lack of distractions will only forge Archie and me closer together. In his letters he tells me how much he misses me – that I am the backbone of his life, and without me he is lost. Imagine that! My big strong husband, complaining that he has no backbone! That his little wife, she who has accomplished nothing apart from a little skill at the piano and the violin, and giving birth to a daughter, should be the mainstay of his life! I am happy to play that role. It gives me worth and value.*

*I confess that I am a little frightened about the long sea voyage. But not as frightened as I was when Archie left me. But God is with me and prayer shall sustain me.*

# Chapter Twelve

I cried out in anguish. My fingers closed into a fist around the paper, and crushed the note into a ball. With blurred eyes I looked up and around – where was Mad Jim? He was nowhere to be seen; only little Freddie still sat on the floor diligently cracking, opening, sucking and spitting. 'Mr Booker!' I called as I leapt to my feet. 'Mr Booker!' Mad Jim emerged from a room at the back, presumably the kitchen. I rushed up to him.

'Why?' I cried, my voice shrill with panic. 'Why did he do this? Where is he? Why? *Why?*' My fists, still clasping the crushed note, rose up as if to pummel his chest. He placed steady hands around them.

'Hol' on, Miss Cox. Come, leh' we go and sit down and talk.'

He led me back to the gallery and to the chair I'd been sitting on. I dropped into it, suddenly limp. He sat down on the chair opposite, and leaned forward. His eyes gazed into mine. They were as calm as a rock. He seemed to see into my soul, and by the very act of seeing brought back a sense of ground within me. The abyss closed up. My breath returned to normal.

'Why?' I said again. My voice seemed far away, to me, like the voice of another. The red-hot panic had left me, to be replaced by grey despair. I slumped in my chair. I dropped the note to the floor and pressed my face into my hands. Mad Jim waited a while before speaking. I finally lowered my hands and looked at him, ready to hear what he had to say.

'First of all, this: he had to go. His work in Berbice done. He went back because Mr Perkins returned from New Amsterdam sprightly as a young goat and wanted his job back – bored with retirement. So George had to go back to his old job. George wrote you the note and asked me to get it to you. He's an old, old friend – me first wife Gladys and he distantly related.'

His first wife? Ah, that explained what I had wondered about. His first wife had been a darkie. Bhoomie, his new wife, was Indian. I wondered what had happened to Gladys.

'But he didn't have to write that horrible note! We love each other! Why does he think he insulted me? Even if he's in Georgetown, we could ...'

'If he's in Georgetown and you up here it's easier for you to forget each other.'

'But I don't want to forget him! I love him! I'll wait forever for him!'

Mad Jim shook his head, slowly. 'I told him to go,' he said. 'Blame me. I told him he got to put an end to it. I told him I'd talk to you, explain.'

'I just don't understand,' I said weakly. 'I thought – I thought ...'

'You thought he loved you?'

I nodded.

'And it's true,' said Mad Jim. Gradually his language changed as he spoke – I felt he was making the effort to speak in King's English, just for me. 'But George is a dreamer. And so are you. You need to nip this thing in the bud. Before it's too late. For both of you, it's puppy love. It will pass.'

'No,' I said. 'Never.'

'Miss Cox,' he said, his voice slow with contrived patience, 'I know what you feel. Your face, Miss Cox! Your eyes! You remember the day, before the rains, when you met him in the post office, and you ran out and bumped into me? Your face was radiant! Your eyes! The eyes of a young girl in love. The same the other day, when I found you at the table in the post office. Such shining eyes! I'm an old man, Miss Cox, and I've seen a lot. I know the signs. But any fool could read your face and know you're in love.'

'My sister Yoyo can't!'

'Ah, but she's too young, too involved in herself. It would-a have to be written all over you in bold letters for her to know.'

'Well then! If that is so, you know we belong together.'

He sighed. 'You're so naïve!'

'Mr Booker! I'm not naïve! I know about love! I …'

'Call me Jim, Uncle Jim. I don' like that Mr Booker title too much.'

I swallowed, and tried it out. In spite of everything I liked him; he was kind, and seemed to truly care.

'Uncle Jim …'

'That's better.'

'We love each other. I know it will be difficult, because he's a darkie, but … '

'Do you know how patronizing that word is?'

'Oh! I didn't … '

'See? That's just a small example of how ignorant you are. How completely unaware of the great harm you do – we do, we whites – in this country. You live in a dream world, Miss Cox. This love of yours can't survive in the real world. You have no idea!'

Tears pricked my eyes. 'But it can! If we are strong and hold on to it and …'

He reached out and grasped my upper arms; I thought he was going to shake me, and maybe that was his intention; but he thought better of it and let go, and sighed.

'Anyway, George understands. He's gone, Miss Cox. Grasp that, and get over it. George knows it's impossible, even if you don't.'

The tears escaped and ran down my cheeks. I wiped them away with my sleeve, furiously.

'I can't believe he gave up so easily! That he just ran away from me like that!' I clicked my fingers and glared at Uncle Jim. 'I thought his love was real, and true! But he's so fickle! He just runs away because you tell him it's too difficult! I wouldn't run away! I would fight for him, wait for him, anything!'

He buried his face in his palms for a silent few seconds, as if gathering patience to deal with my stubbornness. Then he looked up. 'George isn't fickle, Miss Cox. He was in agony. But he knows there's no other way. There's no future for this love of yours.'

'There is! Why not? If we stay strong and wait … I don't want him to …'

Uncle Jim leaned forward and took my two hands; his huge paws closed around them. He looked down and mused.

'Like two li'l birds, these hands!' he said, then raised his head and, now serious as ever, gazed into my eyes. I held his gaze. 'Because he got to,' he said. 'He got to forget you, just as you got to forget him.'

I pulled my hands from his and leapt to my feet again. 'Never!' I cried. 'How dare you say that? He told me he loves me and if it is true then I must find him and *tell* him I was not insulted! I must tell him I love him! He has to know! He *has* to!' I ran to the window and glared back at him. I wanted to pummel him; and yes, he really was mad or something similar. How could he play with me this way? First reassuring me that George loved me, explaining why he had written the note, filling my heart with hope and confidence – only to shatter it again with words of such finality? Even now, he seemed unmoved by my outburst.

'Sit down, Miss Cox,' he said, and there was not a single note of sympathy or understanding in his voice. Yet I obeyed.

'You don't understand,' I said. 'We love each other. I know we do. I have to tell him I love him – he has to know!'

'What do you know of love!'

'What do *you* know!' I cried. 'You don't know what I feel! Who are *you* to judge!'

'Ha!' he said, and his chuckle once again was most unfeeling. He produced a large handkerchief and passed it to me. I patted my eyes dry. 'See, Miss Cox, what you call love ain't nothing but sentimental mush. And the same goes for him. I had to hear it from him, too, this nonsense of *I-will-love-her-forever* and *she's-the-only-one.*'

I looked up. 'He said that?'

He nodded. 'Yes. And I told him the same like I'm goin' to tell you now: get over it. What you call love might feel like the real thing now, but it isn't. True, it could *grow* into the real thing but you must not let it. *You can't afford to let it.* You need to root it out now, while it's small and young. A little plant. Before it grows too big and strong to handle. Before it grows roots and takes over you whole life and destroys you both.'

'But it's *not* tiny! It's strong already! And grand and wonderful and …' I looked at him and did my best to put some authority into my voice. 'Love is … the grandest, strongest thing there is. I know we'll have problems but our love will give us the strength to overcome them. Love is all we need; it will see us through.'

Uncle Jim only rolled his eyes. 'Heard it all before,' he said. 'Rose petals floating down from heaven, violins in the sky, a whole orchestra. Oh, I know. Don't think I don't know. But I know something else too.' He leaned forward and looked at me steadily and earnestly. There was no mocking in that gaze now, no scorn or pity. I met it as calmly as I could, and nodded.

'It cannot be, Miss Cox. This love, if it's real, is doomed from the start. You cannot encourage it. You cannot let it grow. You need to pluck it out by the roots. Now, while it is still young and fresh. Anything else is sheer madness. How can you ever marry George! Do you know what would happen, were you to ever make this infatuation of yours public?'

'I don't *care!*' I cried. 'I know it's going to be difficult. But I don't care! I know I can do it. I know my love is strong enough. I'm ready for anything. I can face all hardship. I know I can. Just because I'm young, you can't just dismiss me like that!'

'How do you know? You can't know till you been there; till you walked through the fire and come out the other side intact and your love stronger than ever. You can't know when the fire is still in front of you. Nobody can know. See, you don't even know George. You don't know if his love is of that calibre. All you both can really know is that you've fallen in love and it's wonderful and beautiful but is it enough?'

'I know it! I feel it!'

'Excuse me, Miss Cox. You don't. You feel the *emotion* but you don't know the reality of what you would face if you do not uproot this thing right now, while you still have the opportunity. You're too young.'

'How can you know how strong my love is? How can you judge me? And George? You don't know!'

He chuckled. 'True enough, I don't know if *your* love – if that's what it is – can survive the trials ahead of you, if you pursue it. But don't tell me I don't know the trials, because I do. I was young once too, you know. Young and in love. And I do know this much: you can't judge the quality of love by the strength of that first hurricane.'

'But it's not just a hurricane!' I cried. 'It's deep, and true, and lasting!'

'There's only one way to know if it is lasting,' he replied, 'and that's for it to last. To last the test of time. To outlast the battering. The hammering. The insults. The humiliation. The rejection … child, you have no idea.'

'Don't call me child!'

'Then stop behaving like a child, and *listen*.'

'I've heard everything you said.'

'Hearing is not the same as listening. And I'm not finished. I haven't told you what I brought you here to tell you. I haven't even *started*. And that's because you're not listening.'

'I *am* listening.'

'No, you're not. You've put up a wall, and you're hiding behind it.'

'How do you know that? You can't see into me.'

'I can see more than you think. You don't speak only with words, you know. You're easy to read.'

That's what Papa always said about me. And Yoyo. They said my face was an open book. These last few weeks I thought I had changed; that I had learned the art of keeping secrets and subterfuge. Mad Jim – Mr Booker – Uncle Jim – whatever his name was, he seemed to think differently. But then, he had information the others didn't.

His own face, which till now had revealed a touch of mocking, teasing humour, turned strict and serious. He stood up and walked to the window, where he stood looking out. His back still turned to me, he said, 'You don't know. You can't know. I don't want you to find out – at your age – no. And not George either. You're too young, too naïve – it would break you. Spoil you for your whole life. Ruin you for love. Wreck your soul. Miss Cox …' He swung round then, and his eyes seemed to blaze with some violent passion as he spoke.

'They'll kick you, spit on you, call you the most despicable names. They'll drag you through the mud. They'll tar and feather you. They'll put you in the stocks, brand you. They'll skin you alive. The way they used to do with the slaves. You know about slavery, of course.'

His outburst had come out of nowhere and laid me flat. So much vehemence in those words, so much rage!

'And always, it's the women they go after. Somehow, the women are the ones they hang up to dry. My first wife Gladys – do you know the names they called her? The so-called civilized race, I mean. *Your* race, and mine. I won't repeat those words. They say sticks and stone can break your bones but words don't hurt. But they do. They tried to break her. They tried to break *us*. They kicked us out of their world, threw us to the wolves. And then they killed her. Burned down our Georgetown house while she was in it. Luckily the children were at school, except one. The youngest one died too. Oh, I won't go into the details. That's not the point. But I'll say this much: what they did was criminal. Criminal, criminal. Gladys and I, we tried. We braved the storm and only one of us came out on the other side alive and intact. That's why I can only laugh at your use of the word *love*. You have no idea. You think love is a walk through a garden. A dance on the beach. It's not! It's only when you've walked over the burning coals and you're still holding hands on the other side; it's only when you can look into each other's eyes and know and say, 'we have survived it', that it's worthy of the name. Through thick and through thin. That's love. It's an *after* state. The *before* state is still infatuation.'

'I … ' I couldn't find the words to continue. Jim was still staring at me, staring into me, as if he could read every single thought passing through my mind.

'And for you, it will be worse. It's always worse the other way around. A white man with a black woman – well, that's allowed as long as he's just her whore – excuse my language. The trouble only starts when he marries her, elevates her to his status, as they like to put it. Because the black person and the woman are down there.' He pointed to the ground. 'The man elevates the woman, the white man elevates the black. According to their way of thinking, that is.

'In your case – I can't even begin to imagine it. I can't think of another example in this whole country – if it ever happened, then it was kept secret. But if you were to marry George. Do you know what the consequences would be?'

I shook my head. There was a lump in my throat. My eyes bristled with unshed tears. My face must have been red as a tomato. I felt sick.

'Your family: they'll disown you. Your own father will throw you out. Your sister will turn away. Your mother – well, your mother's different. A gentle lady, a real lady. And she's gone, so I'll leave her out. But your people, your friends: they'll cast you out. White society will treat you like a leper. You'll be on your own, with only George as a companion, because black people won't accept you either. You'll make them uncomfortable. They might not insult you to your face, but they'll turn away from you. Because they know you're not really one of them. You're still from that *other* world, the world of privilege and status, and you cannot know, you cannot possibly know, what it is to live in another's skin. As for what they'll do to George ...'

He paused. The silence grew long. When he spoke again his voice was quieter, and the fire in his eyes had abated.

'But that's why, Miss Cox, I'm advising you, just like I advised George, to put this thing away. Don't let it grow. I know what you're going through and I know you think it's impossible but it's not. You can do it. You're young, and resilient, and there are so many young men your age and rank just waiting for a pretty girl like you. Forget George.'

Now it was my turn to be silent. My breath grew still as I listened to what my heart would say, and when the words came it seemed as if it was not I that was speaking them, but another being deep within me. 'Mr Booker,' I said, for I could no longer call him Uncle, 'If someone – someone well-meaning, like yourself, had told you this at the beginning of your love of Gladys, would you have backed away from it?' He did not answer, and that was my answer. I stood up.

'Thank you, Mr Booker, for your concern. I will think about what you said. But for now, I need to get back home. Freddie ...'

We all three stood up. My composure had returned to me. And so I said the thing that had been preying on me right from the beginning. 'Mr Booker – that little speech of yours was really quite unnecessary. I don't know why you brought me here. I don't know why you're interfering in my affairs. You're quite the busybody, aren't you, to lecture me about my private life at our very first meeting. It's not terribly polite, is it!'

He laughed out loud. 'Politeness was never a quality I've been known for. Straight talking, honesty, truth – that's my way.'

'Well, then, you've made a mistake with me. You don't know me at all!'

He shrugged. 'I know you got mettle. I know you don't fold at the first obstacle. I like that.'

'Unlike George, who ran back to town the moment you gave him the same treatment. The coward!'

He stopped laughing immediately. 'Don't you – don't you *dare* call George a coward!' His eyes were fiercely glaring, and for a moment I even felt fear. 'You little, white, pampered, cosseted princess! Do you know what it cost him to give you up! He did it for *you*! He did it because he would not put you through the ordeal he *knows* would follow if you should pursue this – this *madness*! He did it because giving you up is the only way to protect you. George is anything but a coward – but you could not possibly know about real courage, could you? How could you, living in your fairy palace!'

We glared at each other. Then, as suddenly as he had flared up, he relaxed, smiled, shrugged.

We did not speak again. We trooped down the front stairs, and walked in silence to the gate. He opened it and let us out. We stood facing one another over the gate.

'Goodbye, Miss Cox.'

'Goodbye, Mr Booker.' Still I did not turn to walk away, and neither did he. Finally, reluctantly, I said it, '… And thank you.'

He nodded then, and turned away. So did I.

✸ ✸ ✸

On my walk back to the village I noticed a woman and a little child walking towards me, hand in hand. Even from a distance, the woman looked familiar, and as she drew near I recognised her. I ran forward to embrace her.

'Iris!' I cried. 'Oh, it's so good to see you again! Where've you been? Why don't you visit?'

For years, Iris had been the nearest thing to a best friend, not counting Yoyo. She was Mildred's granddaughter, just two years older than me, and we had played together as children in the yard. When I was ten, Iris, only twelve, had been appointed as personal maid to Yoyo and me; I had enjoyed that, as it meant that Iris could come upstairs, into my room, and we could chat while she worked. I'd never been much of a chatterbox myself, but with Iris I could say exactly what was on my mind, for I knew she was discreet and trustworthy. She never told me much about herself, but I always supposed it was because she didn't have much to tell me; I knew all about her life. She lived with Mildred and her father – one of the yard boys – in a sweet little wooden cottage at the back of our compound. Her mother was dead.

Three years later, when Iris was nearly fifteen, she had simply disappeared. One day she was with me, the next day she was gone. I never saw her again, and neither Mildred nor Papa would tell me where she had gone. And now, here she was.

'What have you been doing with yourself?' I said, taking her hand. I looked down at the little boy at her side. Clinging to her hand, he sucked his thumb and stared up at me. He was very light skinned. 'Oh, did you get a job as a nursemaid?'

That must be it: she had found steady work with one of the coloured families living in the village. In the past, in her free time Iris had often taken care of the younger children in the senior staff compound while their parents worked.

But Iris shook her head vigorously. She did not return my smile, or my embrace. In fact, she was quite unfriendly. 'No,' she said. 'That my own li'l boy.'

'Oh! You had a child? But – oh, so you got married?'

She did not answer. She only shook her head, pulled her hand free from mine, and strode off, dragging the little boy away. He did not want to go. He walked backwards, stumbling as she dragged him, staring at me. Finally she turned around and swept him into her arms. He continued to stare at me over her shoulder as she marched away.

❋ ❋ ❋

## Mama's Diary: Plantation Promised Land, British Guiana, 1892

*Liebes Tagebuch,*

*And now I am in my new home. I am discovering that Archie did not exaggerate when he spoke of a dearth of distractions. He was right: cane fields, endless miles of them, flat and green, their fronds waving as the breeze sweeps over them like a gentle hand. The sky, vaster than I have ever seen it in Europe, for there are no hills, no mountains, no houses even to break its endlessness. Clouds drift across, and sometimes over, that vast sky, and it turns grey. Sometimes it rains, and then the rain stops and the clouds disperse and there is only that endless blue again. And the sun. Merciless, hot, all day, all year, for there are only two seasons, the dry and the rainy. I almost look forward to the latter.*

*As you can guess, I do not like this place, but my liking or disliking is irrelevant. I have a role to play and I will do so to the best of my ability. I have no time to indulge my sense of being an alien in this hot wasteland. That would be so selfish, so weak! Instead, it is up to me to provide the entertainment so lacking. If only I had some kind of task; but servants run after us and take care of our every need. Imagine: Archie even has a boy to remove his riding boots! Papa would laugh at such a pampered life as I now live, but I have married Archie and this is where I am. I refuse to complain – how can one as privileged as I am complain!*

*And of course, my resource is music! I must fill this house with mu-sic! Happy music! I have my violin, and dear Archie has bought a piano and had it transported all the way here from Georgetown. It is not a very good piano, only an upright, but it is good enough for me. Beggars can't be choosers! I am making the most of what I have. I provide music, and laughter, and dance. Yes, Archie and I dance! Obviously it is difficult as we have no music to dance to, since I am the only musician near and far! It is rather droll! But I sing the tunes and we dance to them, and it is so funny we laugh, and we have made our happiness here.*

*I suspect that another child is on the way. I have not yet told him, but he will be delighted. He is the born father.*

*Sometimes I am lonely. But I push those feelings away. Sometimes we visit Georgetown, the capital, which is a day's journey away, and there I have made a few lady friends, but I do not like them very much and they do not like me. They are such snobs. I have the feeling they look down on me, because I am not English. So I have only my husband, my daughter, and you, dear diary. You three will have to suffice. Even though I seem to neglect you, writing in you only occasionally, I talk to you all the time. There is a running commentary in my head as I tell you all the news, and all the things that have happened. Though there is not much happening from day to day! Ah, the torpid languor of a sugar plantation!*

*PS: I can't believe I forgot to tell you that I survived the fearful Atlantic Crossing! How droll! As you can see, I am alive and well, though I was seasick for most of the journey!*

# Chapter Thirteen

If Mr Booker thought that his little lecture would discourage me and diminish my love, he had misjudged me. The effect was the opposite: it spurred me into action. It seemed to me, in the days of rumination that followed, that Mr Booker had been far too interfering. It was perhaps entirely *his* fault that George had written the letter he had, and run back to Georgetown with his tail between his legs. Perhaps Mr Booker had put the fear of God into his heart, and talked him into desertion; convinced him that he had insulted me, and that to love me was to ruin me forever. He may have meant well; but finally it was none of his business. And it was even *less* his business to summon me to his home only to give me a ticking-off for loving George, and to harangue me into giving him up. What a dreadful busybody. The more I thought about his words, the more they seemed to me a challenge. Far from deterring me, they were to me a gauntlet, and I had to pick it up. *I* would win this challenge! Or rather, *love* would win!

I never had a single doubt as to my next move. It was as clear as daylight to me. My only doubt concerned the means, not the goal. Once again I was called upon to use wiles, and trickery, and lies. It stood me in good stead that I was known as the quiet, innocent, undemanding one among us three sisters. It is that very reputation that had always misled Yoyo into regarding me as lacking in initiative; as needing her lead in all matters; when in fact all I had needed in life was *a worthy cause*. Still waters run deep, it's said. I was not one to waste energy on trivialities, and only of late had our lives spiralled into realms of serious consideration.

I had to get to Georgetown. I had to get to George. I had to declare myself to him. More than ever, George needed to know my heart. That I loved him; that he had not insulted me; that I was not afraid of the obstacles that might lie ahead; that I would wait for him until I was of age. Beyond that disclosure, I had no plan. I would cross each bridge as I came to it. The future was vague, but our love would give us the strength and the courage to face whatever came, just as Mr Booker had defined it. This was no passing fancy; it was real, and I would prove it so. I was not so foolish as to believe we could marry now; I was only sixteen, after all, and even had I not needed Papa's permission, I was not ready. But in five years I would be 21, a grown woman, legally free, and would need no one's permission. And though it seemed a lifetime away, time itself was one of the crucial tests, just as Mr Booker had said. This was one I would pass with ease.

Declare myself to George, that was the first step. Everything else would follow on from that. I had to go to Georgetown. Once there, George and I would find a way. It would take a great deal of planning. It would take money, and timing, and subterfuge. *Money* I could come up with. We each of us kept a stone jug on our dressing tables, into which we dropped our spare pennies after we had spent whatever we wanted in the village.

*Timing* would take more thought. I decided to wait. Papa had planned a trip to Barbados in June, two weeks from now; our uncle Don lived there, on Enterprise, another family plantation. Papa and he exchanged visits on alternate years, and this was Papa's year. He would be gone for a month. Perfect.

*Subterfuge* would be my greatest challenge. The longer my own absence from Promised Land remained undetected, the better my plan would work. I thought it over again and again, and finally wrote it down on paper, so I would not forget. It seemed foolproof.

Who would have ever guessed that dear, sweet Winnie Cox was so good at concocting lies! I was myself astonished at this new-found ability: I who had never told a single lie in all her life, calmly developing a master plan of deceit, while all the while pretending that nothing, nothing in the world, had changed! If it were not all so deadly serious I would have laughed out loud. In the meantime, I had to bear the excruciating wait until Papa left. But finally, leave he did. Poole drove him all the way to Georgetown and returned with the empty motor car. The thought of the motor car inspired me no end. It kept me awake at night. I waited three more days before rolling out my plan. It needed to start on a Friday.

That day, I came down to breakfast holding my jaw. Miss Wright immediately asked, as I knew she would, 'What's the matter, Winnie? Have you got a toothache?'

I nodded. 'It's awful; I hardly slept at all last night.'

So far, no lies; at least, none in words. Indeed, I had not slept the night before.

Miss Wright frowned. 'Oh, you poor thing! Let me run up and get you an aspirin.'

I made as unhappy a face as I possibly could and told my first lie of the day. 'I took one last night, Miss Wright, before I went to bed. It hasn't helped a bit. In fact, the pain is even worse today!'

'You probably need an extraction,' said Miss Wright.

'You poor thing!' said Yoyo.

'It's off to the dentist with you!' said Miss Wright briskly. 'Yoyo, you and Maggie will have to manage on your own for today's lessons. You can catch up on your French and write me an essay on Julius Caesar. I'll inform Mr Poole to get the motor car ready. I'm sure Dr Hodgkin can arrange an emergency appointment. We'll just turn up at his surgery.'

'Oh, Miss Wright, *please* don't trouble yourself!' That, of course, was kind, thoughtful me, always accommodating to others, never wanting to put anyone out of their way for my sake. I continued. 'You see, I thought – as it's Friday – I'd like to spend the weekend with Emily Stewart. You know Emily, my friend?'

That was a bit of a stretch. Emily wasn't exactly a friend; she was a girl my age, the daughter of one of the Scottish overseers.

Like almost all the older girls in the senior staff compound, she spent the term in New Amsterdam in order to attend secondary school there. Her parents rented a second home there, where Emily and her older sister lived with their mother during term time.

'Emily has always been begging me to come and visit for a day or two, and I think I will – if only I can get rid of this pain! Why don't I just kill two birds with one stone: get the tooth extracted, and then pop over to Emily's? Poole can pick me up again on Sunday afternoon.'

Emily had indeed invited me to stay; several times, in fact. I had accepted the invitation but never taken her up on it.

'You can't just arrive at the Stewarts unannounced!' said Miss Wright.

'Oh, but I can! Mrs Stewart said so quite expressly! She said I can come to stay any time I wanted. Just knock on the door, she said. I have the address, upstairs!'

That much, at least, was perfectly true. Mrs Stewart was one of those people who fawned over those of higher rank, and wanted her daughters to move in more elevated circles. I also suspect she hoped to marry me off to her son Roland, who was presently in his first year at university in England. Mrs Stewart would not only have no objection to find me standing on her doorstep, suitcase in hand, she would be delighted.

'Oh, but I want to go too! Do let me go too, Miss Wright!'

It was quite typical of Yoyo to ask Miss Wright for permission to accompany me, but not even to consider asking *me* if I wanted her to come; much less, to ask herself if Mrs Stewart's invitation included her at all. It was true that for years we had been inseparable, but we had grown apart recently, and it was most trying of her to take my compliance for granted. Thank goodness for Miss Wright's sense of responsibility.

'No, Yoyo,' she said firmly. 'I think this time, you stay behind and we can catch up on your French – you do need extra time.'

'I hate French! Why do I need to learn it?' Yoyo grumbled.

'And anyway, what about Maggie? She'll be here in a short while.'

Yoyo made a face; she'd obviously forgotten about Maggie. She shrugged, finally accepting her fate.

Miss Wright turned to me. 'Well, Winnie, that sounds like a reasonable plan. Very well. You may spend a couple of days in New Amsterdam. It will be good for you to cultivate a friendship with Emily – your social life is so restricted. After breakfast you can go upstairs and pack. Do you need any help?'

I smiled at her. 'No, Miss Wright. I'll be fine.'

I had almost forgotten about my toothache. I screwed up my face in pretended agony and buried my jaw in my hand once more. The first stage of my little scheme had worked.

✳ ✳ ✳

I was astonished at how good I was at this new art of subterfuge. I played my part so convincingly that neither of them had the slightest suspicion that all was not as it seemed. In a way, I suppose, it was simple: I did not have to play a part. Just by being myself I was able to convince them. I lied only when I had to, and the lies came easily. I had told the truth all my life, worn my heart on my sleeve, never told an untruth, and now the fibs rolled off my tongue as if lying was second nature. I did not even have a guilty conscience; I reasoned to myself that it was not *I* who was in the wrong, but *they;* they would reject George out of hand for despicable reasons. They would call him names, and be cruel, if they knew; whereas I quite simply loved him. As long as I caused no harm to anyone it was *right* to fight for love, right and good and noble. I was on the side of humanity, and if that demanded stratagems that included bending the truth, well, God would forgive me. I know that I forgave myself, and instantly.

All of this went through my mind as I packed my suitcase after breakfast. Miss Wright had suggested that Nora pack for me, but I had rejected this offer, and nobody was the wiser as to why. Of course I needed to pack myself! I'd be gone far longer than a weekend. I packed as much as I could to last a while and as little as needed to prevent suspicion. And then there was the jug of coins. I delighted at the flow and tinkle of copper as I emptied this into a separate cloth bag. There was no time to count the money, of course, but I was sure it would last me quite a while. And if not – perhaps I could get a job in Georgetown. I was certainly willing – but would my age be a handicap? Would I need Papa's permission to do so? An unpleasant shadow passed over my elevated spirits. Papa. What would he do, what could he do? He'd search for me. Would he find me? Bring me back? Enough of that. That was future, this was now. First I had to get to Georgetown. Declare myself to George.

And then? Where would I live, since we could not yet marry? I had heard of a boarding house for young women in Georgetown. For girls, rather. Some of the girls around my age from the senior staff compound stayed there in order to attend school in Town. Bishops' High School was the girls' school. It was a good school. Why couldn't I go there? Would I be able to stay at the boarding house if I were not a pupil, but a working girl? Surely there were other boarding houses? George would help me. But it was futile to think of these things at this stage. I would take this one step at a time, cross each bridge as I got to it, buoyed by confidence. Love would see me through and give me strength. It was time to go.

I picked up my little suitcase. It was unevenly heavy, due to the coins. I needed to ensure that nobody else handled it; it was far too heavy for a two-night stay, and would raise undue suspicions. I managed to slip down both flights of stairs unseen. Poole had already driven the motor car around to the front and was waiting in the driver's seat; before he could climb out and open the door for me I did so myself, and threw in my suitcase. Immediately, Poole was at my side, tipping his hat hurriedly.

'Oh, Missy, I sorry, I didn't see you come – lemme put the suitcase on the luggage rack,' he said.

'Oh, no, don't bother,' I replied. 'It's only a small one. It's not worth it.'

'If you say so, Miss.' He looked doubtful, but accepted my words.

'I'll just run back up to say goodbye and then we can be off,' I said to him. 'You can start the motor car.'

'Very well, Miss.' He walked around to the front and began to crank the motor.

I turned to go back upstairs, but Miss Wright and Yoyo, and Maggie, who had arrived by now, had come down to see me off. How kind everyone was, how unsuspecting! And how underhand of me, to trick them all like this! But, I reminded myself, it was all for a good cause. I smiled, and at the last moment remembered to cradle my jaw and wince in pain.

'Oh, you poor dear!' said Miss Wright. 'There's nothing worse than toothache, is there! But Dr Hodgson will soon put you right. Poole will wait for you and drive you to the Stewarts. Oh dear! It just occurred to me that I should send something as a gift – how can I let you go empty-handed! Let me just look in the larder, perhaps Cookie has some nice treat I can send, guava jelly maybe – or perhaps …'

'Oh, I'm sure Mrs Stewart won't mind!' I said. 'And it might be insulting for you to send some of Cookie's guava jelly.'

'Do you really think so?' She was frowning, obviously confused as to the correct etiquette for sending a young girl to stay at a friend's house unannounced. Miss Wright was often out of her depth when it came to our more casual way of doing things in the colony, having learnt the art of governessing in a formal home in London.

'Yes,' I said. 'We just turn up whenever we want. We're always welcome.'

That at least was true. If I had really been going to stay with the Stewarts I would not have needed guava jelly.

'Winnie! I just had an idea!' exclaimed Miss Wright. I frowned. Hopefully her new idea would not call for new explanations, lies, and manipulations. I need not have worried.

'Poole!' she called next. He came forward, tipping his hat again. 'Yes Miss Wright?'

'You're from New Amsterdam, aren't you?'

'Yes, Miss Wright.'

'So your family lives there. Well, I was just thinking. We won't need you this weekend so why don't you take the two days off and stay with your family, then collect Miss Winnie on Sunday afternoon? It would save you two empty journeys.' Poole looked simultaneously pleased and doubtful. 'I don't know, Miss Wright – what Massa gon' say?'

'The Master has given me complete authority to make such decisions on my own,' said Miss Wright. 'If it is convenient to you, you may do so.'

'Very well, Miss.'

Miss Wright took me in her arms. 'Goodbye, dear. Do have a good trip. You'll feel so much better once the tooth is out.'

I hugged her back. I felt sick to think of how deceived she'd be when Poole returned with an empty car on Sunday. But it had to be. I hardened my heart and turned to Yoyo.

'Bye, Yoyo,' I said, and the twinge of conscience this time was sharp and painful. I was deceiving her, as well, my sister, my best friend and closest ally. I had never held even a small secret from her, but now I was withholding – well, there would be an explosion when the bombshell finally dropped. For the past several weeks, I had treated her as a stranger, and she, distracted by Maggie's presence, had noticed nothing. It was as if the chain of events, starting with our visit to the *logies*, had driven a wedge between us; after the first deep shock and the grief, she had recovered quickly and reverted to her usual high spirits. Whereas I – I had changed forever. I could no longer be happy at Promised Land. That one day had thrown up dark stains impossible to efface; if I could not remove them I must flee them. But to the outer world I remained the same, because who would understand? If anything, I had grown yet quieter, keeping my secrets and my love locked up. Yoyo's trust in me was absolute, and now I was betraying it. Now she, too, clasped me in her arms and said,

'You lucky thing – about visiting Emily, I mean, not about the dentist. Ugh, I do hate dentists! But I hate toothache more. Get that beastly tooth out, and have a wonderful time!'

I slapped my hand to my jaw at the reminder, and hugged her back.

'Bye, Yoyo,' is all I said. It was indeed a betrayal. But she noticed nothing.

✷ ✷ ✷

### Mama's Diary: Plantation Promised Land, British Guiana, 1894

*Liebes Tagebuch,*

*Another daughter! This one we have called Winifred, after Archie's favourite aunt. She (the aunt!) is my favourite, too, quite unlike her vapid sister, my mother-in-law. (I refused to name the child after her, for fear she might take on those unpleasant qualities I told you about!) Aunt Winifred is unmarried, and such a character! So I was happy to name my daughter after her. Aunt Winifred is also very musical, which meant that we had a close connection, so much in common. But she is so far away, as is everyone else. I miss Father so much! I do wish they could all come to visit, but they can't. We are on our own. Oh dear diary, I am so very lonely at times, and it seems not even my beloved Archie and my beloved daughters can dispel that loneliness!*

*I wish I could tell you more, but honestly, there is nothing to tell. One day is very much like the other here. We see the same people, and for the most part I do not like them.*

*For instance, Mr McInnes, Archie's estate manager – I cannot stand him and I wish Archie did not drink in his every word. He sometimes comes over for dinner and then he and Archie shut themselves away in the study and drink their rum swizzles and chat about whatever it is men chat about when they are on their own. And I play my violin, or my piano, and pour my loneliness into that. Oh, how I miss Papa, my brothers, the cobbled streets of Salzburg, the opera, the balls, the concerts! The mere tuning of an orchestra now would be the sweetest music on earth!*

*Here, we have servants to fulfil our every desire. Archie even lets his boots be removed by someone he calls Boy. I found out that Boy actually has a name, and it is Wilfred. I call him Wilfred.*

*There are other people on the estate: a whole community of English and Scottish people right next door, the senior staff and their wives. I find I cannot talk to these ladies. Something must be wrong with me but I just don't know what to talk about – I cannot chat the way they can. And they too disdain me, because I am a foreigner. They laugh at my imperfect English. What would they say if they knew I was born Jewish!*

*Then there are the coolies, who work in the fields. But I have nothing at all to do with them. They do their jobs, and are part of the landscape. Once Archie said to me that they are like animals, and I flinched. How can he say that, I wonder? Where is his Christian heart, to describe other humans as such? I am sure he got it from Mr McInnes. I truly loathe that man. But enough. Archie does not like me to think about business, and he is right.*

# Chapter Fourteen

The sun was already half-way up the sky when we reached the East Coast Road. This was my first real drive in the car. I had been out with Papa a few times on the plantation in the last few weeks, just to try it out, but only Yoyo had been on a proper excursion, and as the East Coast Road was the only properly paved road in the district, Poole was able to drive at full speed. Rice fields and villages popped into my window and disappeared again, racing past us, though of course it was we who were racing. I leaned forward.

'How fast are we going, Poole?' I asked.

'Thirty miles an hour, Miss Winnie. Top speed!'

'Goodness! Why, we'll be in New Amsterdam in no time!'

'Yes, Miss.'

I regarded Poole with interest. He was tall and thin and very black indeed. He wore white gloves and a white shirt, and in contrast his face and neck glistened as if polished. He glanced back at me.

'Are you comfortable, Miss? You want me to drive slower?'

'Oh, no, of course not! The sooner we get there the better. I dare say you'll be happy to get to your family sooner, as well!'

He smiled. 'Yes, Miss.'

'You're married?'

'Yes, Miss. I got a wife and three li'l chirren.'

'Really! I wouldn't have thought ...' I stopped, not sure if it would be polite to say he looked too young for such a large family. Instead, I said, 'You must miss them when you're up at Promised Land!'

'Yes, Miss, I do. But Massa generous wit' holidays an' I get to go down once a month.'

'That doesn't seem very often!'

'Better than other men in me family that does work on the estates, Miss. Me brother …'

He stopped suddenly.

I waited, and when he didn't continue, I asked, 'What about your brother?'

'Never mind, Miss. I only want to say I ain't got nothin' to complain about.'

Soon we were in quintessential Booker territory, if such a thing could be claimed in a country that belonged to Bookers lock stock and barrel. We passed Albion, a Campbell estate; Papa was friends with the manager, Mr Bee. The Campbells themselves being absentee owners, and we had often exchanged visits with these families. I recalled those days as of a bygone age, as far from my present reality as the moon. If they could see me now, those ladies in their prim frocks, looking over us girls as if we were so much cattle. We were prizes on the marriage market, that we knew. And here I was, off to meet my darkie sweetheart. I smiled at the irony of it all. If they could see me now!

We were nearly there. Conversation drew to a halt. Poole had by now told me not only about his close family but his cousins, aunts and uncles in Georgetown. There was nothing left for him to say, and nothing for me to say to him because by now I was going over the plan again and again in my thoughts. It had to work. I had to make it work. I unfolded the note and read the plan again, to make sure there were no loopholes:

a) go to the dentist. Leave suitcase in car. Go in and make appointment for later.

b) return to car, get Poole to drive me to Emily's house.

c) take suitcase into Emily's yard, but hide it in the garden, under a bush (Emily's garden is full of bougainvilleas!) So her mother doesn't ask difficult questions.

d) ring the doorbell. When the maid answers, ask to see Emily. Greet Mrs Stewart politely. Tell her I just came for a few hours, until my dentist appointment.

e) confide in Emily. Don't let her know that George is who he is. Let her think he is white.

f) (I need to convince Emily! But she loves a good romance. I'm sure she will help.)

g) Give Emily the note for Miss Wright, letting her know I'm safe and in Georgetown.

h) go to the dock, buy ticket, and catch ferry to Rosignol

i) buy ticket for train to Georgetown, get on train

j) arrive in Georgetown, and FIND GEORGE!!! (Go to the Post Office and ask for him.)

❊ ❊ ❊

The nearer we drew to New Amsterdam, the more crowded the houses, the more people on the road. We drove past a large market where portly women sat or stood behind stalls piled with fruit and vegetables. The car slowed to a crawl, for it was the only one and people swarmed over the street. Some of them peered into the car, and stared at me as if I were a foreign artefact intruding into their world. I felt alien, as if I was on a strange new planet. It was a feeling I would have to get used to; in running away to George I'd be leaving my old familiar world behind and jumping head-first into another. My heart began to thump audibly, and for the first time I felt panic. I remembered Mad Jim's lecture. He had meant it well. What if he was right? What if I could not face the backlash that would come? I steeled myself against that doubt. No. I would. I could.

It was approaching midday when we finally drew up at Dr Hodgkin's surgery, and I was already worried; I had not calculated time into my plan at all. Poole came round to my door and opened it. I stepped out into the sunshine. I left my suitcase on my seat and said to Poole, 'Wait here a moment. I'll just go and make an appointment for this afternoon.'

'Lemme come in wit' you, Miss!' said Poole.

'No,' I said.

'Miss Wright said I gotta look after you!' Anxiety veiled Poole's eyes. 'NO!' I cried and glared at him. 'I'm NOT a child! I don't need looking after! Wait here!'

I strode off before he could reply, marched through the gate and into the receptionist's office.

They knew me here, of course. Mama had brought us girls for regular check-ups all through our childhood, and in our later years it had been Miss Wright. The receptionist was a plump, older darkie woman whom I had known for several years.

'Miss Cox!' she exclaimed when she saw me! 'Eheh! But is good to see you again! You come for a check-up? Where you sisters?'

I placed my hand on my jaw. 'No check-up,' I said. 'Tooth-ache! I think I need an extraction. Can you give me an appoint-ment for this afternoon?'

'I can give you an appointment right away!' She looked at her ledger and picked up her pen.

'No, that's not necessary!' I said. 'You have all these people waiting.' I gestured around the room, which was lined with chairs, all of them occupied by darkies and a few coolies.

'Don't worry about them!' said the receptionist, embarrass-ingly loudly. 'I can get you in now. Won't be ten minutes. You can wait in the office, we got a nice comfy chair there.'

'No,' I said. 'I can't stay now. I'll come back later. Maybe at two o'clock?'

'You quite sure? You can stand the pain that long?'

'It's not that bad,' I said truthfully. 'That's settled then. I'll see you at two.'

I gave a sweeping and rather nervous smile to everyone in the room as I turned to go. None of them smiled back.

Poole leaped out of the motor car and held open the door as I approached.

'All done!' I said. 'I've got an appointment for two o'clock. Now let's go to the Stewarts.'

He nodded as I stepped into the car. 'I shall come and pick you up at two, Miss.'

'Don't be silly, Poole! I can walk over easily. It's not that far. Just drive.'

'Yes Miss.' He cranked up the car and we drove off.

❀ ❀ ❀

Sly. That's the word. Almost overnight I had turned into a sly, conniving young woman and I didn't much like this new person. But I could no more stop the momentum than I could pull out a bad tooth on my own. It had to be. George Theodore Quint was a giant horseshoe magnet and I was a piece of iron drawn to Georgetown by a power I could neither explain nor resist. The steps I had to take to get there might be underhand and reprehensible by the principles of morality, but they were just that: single steps that didn't matter in the long run. All that mattered was getting there. *Your family will be hurt!* Said a quiet voice within me. But I refused to listen. I had my plan, and I would follow it through to the end.

But already the original plan was in shambles. It was so late! And I would arrive at Emily's at lunchtime, and surely Mrs Stewart would invite me for lunch, and I would have to be polite and nod and make small talk and then talk to Emily and that would all take an hour, or more. I calculated mentally. If I had a quick lunch – for I was indeed hungry – I could get to the ferry by one o'clock; cross the Berbice River to Rosignol; get the two-o'clock train to town, and I'd be there by four. Would there be time to find George? I feared not. When did he finish work? I had to devise an alternative. Quite probably I would not find him today, which would leave me stranded in Georgetown.

Worse yet: I had not once considered *how* I would find George. I had vaguely imagined turning up at the main post office and asking for him by name; as if Georgetown's post office was anything like our little one in the village, with only one clerk. That was my entire plan. But Georgetown was huge! The post office would be huge! And anyway, George delivered letters; he might be anywhere in town. And if I arrived too late the post office would be closed and I would be in a strange town without my family and with only a bag-full of coins to my name.

Well then, I'd go to the Park Hotel. That's where Papa always took us when we stayed in town. They knew us. They knew me. I could ask them to put the charge on Papa's bill. Papa never paid cash anyway, that much I knew. Papa was an important man. They'd never turn me away. Or else – I knew people. We had friends in town, the Dalgliesh's and the Turners, I knew where they lived. I was good at lying by now. I'd tell them some story, I'd think it up on the journey down, and ask to spend the night. They'd let me, and I knew they would believe me, because everyone knew what a good, quiet, honest girl I was. Now, if it were Yoyo – people would suspect Yoyo of mischief right away. Not me. Yes. I would think of something. I would find George, and he would help.

✷ ✷ ✷

Emily Stewart's home was on Pope Street, less than five minutes away. New Amsterdam was not a large town. I knew the house well, and I knew that the front garden was full of shrubs and bushes. This time when I left the car I grabbed the suitcase. Poole reached for it.

'I'll carry that for you, Miss!'

'Oh, don't bother. I'll be fine. You go off to your family. They'll be so happy to see you!'

Poole looked unconvinced. 'I shouldn't just leave you like this. Lemme carry the bag and walk you to the door.'

'No!' I said it firmly, and clasped the little suitcase to my chest as if it were a treasure.

'Just go!'

My voice must have sounded harsher than I intended, for he looked at me with confusion in his eyes before looking down and apologizing. 'Very well, Miss. What time I should pick you up?'

'At four on Sunday afternoon.'

'Very well, Miss. Goodbye.'

'Goodbye, Poole. And thank you. Enjoy your holiday. .'

I opened the gate to the Stewarts' garden and turned around to wave goodbye. The motor car still stood on the curb, the motor running; Poole waved back. It seemed he would not budge until I had arrived safely at the door, which was a problem since I had to hide the suitcase. In the end I shrugged and marched off. Let him see me at the door without the case. He might not notice, and if he did, well, let him think what he wanted. What could he do anyway? No plan is completely perfect.

High bougainvilleas hid me from sight as I walked towards the house, and I shoved the suitcase out of sight, in among the bushy base. I walked on, and up the stairs to the front door. I lifted the rapper, and knocked three times. I waved again to Poole down in the motor car; he waved back, but still did not drive off. The door opened; it was a maid, and at last Poole drove away. Only then did I relax.

The maid knew me. 'Come in, come in,' she said. 'Missy Emily gon' be home soon! Come in. She gon' be happy to see you!'

I'd quite forgotten that Emily'd be at school. Another big hole in my carefully laid-out plan. I began to panic. Why had I started out so late? Why had I included Emily in the plan? The morning was almost over and I was only in New Amsterdam, and now even more delays. Foolish, foolish, foolish.

'Who is it, Ivy?' called Mrs Stewart from the drawing room.

'Is Miss Cox, Ma'am!'

Mrs Stewart came bustling out, a wide smile stretched across her face. 'Winnie! Oh, Winnie, dear! How lovely to see you! Emily will be delighted – she'll be home for lunch in a minute! Have you come for the weekend?' She looked around. 'No luggage? Oh what a pity! Is this just a flying visit, then? But you will stay for luncheon, won't you?'

'I-I have a dentist appointment,' I said. 'At two. So I just thought I'd drop in and say hello.'

'And you're all on your own? Goodness, you are getting grown up! I thought your governess – what's her name now – ah yes, Miss Wright – usually brought you girls down?'

'Yes, when we have a check-up. But I had a toothache so I came down by myself, with the chauffeur. I'm quite old enough!'

'Oh yes, I heard your dear Papa now had a motor car. How exciting for you! But do you mean to say you couldn't get an emergency appointment right away? How dreadful of the receptionist! These people are really getting so uppity these days – why not try Dr Thompson, he's our dentist and he's …'

'Winnie! Oh, how lovely to see you!'

Emily, a pigtailed girl in the New Amsterdam Girls' School uniform, came flying into the gallery through the still open front door. I allowed her arms to fold me into a bear hug that was most definitely genuine.

Yes, I thought to myself. I can trust Emily. Definitely. No slyness required here.

❊ ❊ ❊

'The thing is,' I said to Emily once we were alone. 'The thing is, I've got a secret and I need you to know, but you've got to promise to keep it.'

We were up in her bedroom, where her mother insisted I change into one of Emily's dresses; my travelling clothes were already limp with sweat, heat and dust. I should have thought of that and brought a change for town along with me; but one can't think of everything. Now, though, I was glad I was here, in spite of the delay. It was good to have an ally.

'Ooh, a secret!' Emily knocked her knuckles, clenched her shoulders and giggled. 'Go on! I won't tell a soul!'

'Promise?'

''Course I promise! Is it a love secret?'

I nodded.

'Ooh! Really? Who is he? Do I know him? Go on, tell!'

I shook my head. 'I don't think you know him. But I can't tell. Really I can't. It's someone Papa would never approve of and – well, that's why it's a secret.'

'Oh, go on! I promise not to tell!'

'No. It's for your own protection. See, if you don't know you don't have to lie when it comes to the crunch. I don't want you to lie for me. Lying is horrible! But this way, you can tell them everything you know and I'll still be safe.'

'You make it sound like a conspiracy! *When it comes to the crunch* – whatever do you mean by that?' Emily had relaxed by now. She took my hands in hers and shuffled closer to me. We sat on her bed, on its edge, just as we were both on edge with the drama of it all. We lowered our voices to a whisper, though there was nobody listening. I leaned in closer yet.

'I'm running away!' I declared.

She immediately bounced back, letting go of my hands. 'No! Not really! How? When?'

'Today, and you've got to help me, cover for me. You know I said I've got a dentist's appointment? Well, I haven't. At least I have, but I'm not going to keep it. I'm going to take the ferry instead and then the train to Georgetown and I'm going to meet him there.'

'Winnie! You don't mean you're *eloping*, do you? But you can't! You're far too young, you need your Papa's permission, and there isn't a Gretna Green in BG! You know that! You …'

'Ssh! Not so loud!' I looked around at the door. Emily's voice had risen in her shock and I didn't know who might be hovering outside. 'No, I'm not eloping. But we need to talk, to be near each other, and – I need to tell him something important, and – I need to get away from Promised Land, from Papa. Oh Emily, my life is so topsy-turvy right now and I've just got to get away. He's the only one I want to see, to be with. The only one.' My voice trembled and rose with emotion, and my determination not to cry.

'So that's why you're here!' She leapt to her feet, and stood on the carpet facing me. 'You're just using me, so you can get to the *only one* you want to see? Well, thank you very much!'

I stood up too, took her hand, and drew her back to the bed. She let it happen but slipped her hand from mine. I was losing her.

'Oh Emily, don't be so silly! I didn't mean it like that. I just mean I'm in *love*. You've been in love, a million times. You know what it's like!'

'Yes, but I didn't ever run away to be with the boy!'

'You didn't *have* to because they were always in the compound in the school hols, and if he *did* go away, you knew he'd be back in the next hols.'

'Wait a minute, it hasn't been *that* often! There was just Edward McDonald, and – and Andrew Clark …'

'And Percy Whippet, and …'

I held up my hand to count them off on my fingers. Emily fell in love every two or three weeks of the summer holidays, and each time it was *forever*. This had been going on since she was thirteen. Sometimes, her loves lasted a whole year, while the boy in question was at school in England. They would write each other fevered letters. Then he would return for the summer and she would fall in love with someone else.

'Oh, all right! But even if they weren't I would never run away. I *never* would. When I marry I want to do it properly with a big wedding and – oh Winnie! You're not going to *do* it, are you?'

'Yes, of course I am! I'll be off to the ferry right after lunch!'

'No, No.' Giggling, through raised palms, she whispered: '*It!*'

'What, it? Oh, you mean *that*. Well, no, of course not – don't be silly!'

'Oh.' She sounded disappointed. 'Well I suppose you don't want a bairn yet.'

'Goodness, Emily, just because I have to run away it doesn't mean I've lost *all* my morals! I just need to run away because otherwise I won't be able to see him again *ever,* and I haven't told him I love him yet, and he needs to know; he thinks I don't, so I just want to tell him.'

'But has he told you he loves you?'

'Yes! He loves me desperately! And I him! And I'm not like you, Emily. I won't be over it in a few weeks and loving someone else. I've never loved anyone before. You know that. And when I do love it will be forever. Just one, and it's him. For always!'

'Oh *Winnie*! That's so *romantic!*'

She clasped my hands again, closed her eyes. 'So you'll wait for each other? But what will you do in Georgetown? Why can't you just tell him you love him, promise to wait for him, and he'll promise too, and then go back home? Nobody will know the difference and then you can have a proper wedding and everything. I'll help you run away but you've got to promise to come back.'

'No. No, I can't. It's someone Papa would never approve of. Not ever.'

'I wish you'd tell me who! Just give me a hint. Or let me guess. Someone your Papa wouldn't approve of – but where did you meet him, then? Go on – just give me a little hint. A tiny hint. Where did you meet him?'

I thought for a moment, and decided to lay her a red herring. I couldn't tell her about George. Not yet. She'd be far too shocked. But I had to stop her pestering me for clues. 'At – at one of the big houses.'

'Ah! Thank you. That's a great help. So let me guess. You don't have to say you told me because you didn't, so I won't have to lie but now it makes sense. He's a Booker! Am I right? No, don't answer because that would mean you told me. But how exciting! You, marrying a Booker! Your Papa will have a fit! I do understand now. If you marry a Booker that will be the end of Promised Land, won't it? It will get swallowed up and won't be in your family anymore and everyone knows how your Papa feels about that.'

'Do they?' Emily had been successfully diverted, and I wanted to keep it that way. Her believing George was a Booker would help keep the truth hidden – even if she did ever let it slip, it wouldn't matter. So I let her talk, and guess around *which* Booker boy it might be – there were several to choose from, as he might not be a Booker in name but only from a Booker plantation – and kept my lips sealed from then on. No more lies were necessary. But before we went down to lunch I wrote a few lines of explanation to Miss Wright. I folded the letter, put it in an envelope, and handed it to Emily.

'Give that to Poole when he comes to collect me on Sunday.'

After an excruciating lunch through which I struggled to keep up the small talk and an innocent face with Mrs Stewart, it was time for Emily to return to school and for me to catch the ferry. We left together, collecting my suitcase from the bushes on the way out.

Emily, still excited at being part of the conspiracy, skipped and danced along beside me as we made our way to the town centre; Pope Street was a leafy, shady boulevard not far from the town centre, and it was only a few minutes' walk to the bustling main street; there, our ways parted. Emily pointed out the way to the ferry. We hugged.

'Take care!' she said. 'And good luck.'

'Thanks. I'll need it. And Emily …'

'Yes?'

'Thanks so much. I'm so grateful for your help. I can't even begin …'

'It's all right! I'm so glad you turned to me! I'll keep your secret – and now we can be real friends, can't we?'

I nodded. 'Yes. We are. I'll write to you as soon as I can.'

We hugged again, and parted. I stood for a while watching her she walked away. I was on my own. And not at all sure I was ready. For a brief moment I wanted to call out: '*Come back! Take me with you! I can't do this!*'

But I didn't. I pushed away the lump of panic rising through my being and strode off towards the wharf.

❋ ❋ ❋

### Mama's Diary: Plantation Promised Land, British Guiana, 1895

*Liebes Tagebuch,*

*I have developed what the English call a Stiff Upper Lip. Not literally of course, my lips are far too curved for that! But I am stalwart and stoic; Archie once called me his backbone, and that is how I define my role. I am the backbone of our life here. It is nothing but my faith that keeps me going, and I have faith because I love my husband and my daughters. All are thriving. I am thriving too, in my own way. If I am the backbone of the family, well then, music is* my *backbone, my strength! The house resonates with the sound of music! Alive with the sound of music! What joy I derive from music! I am determined to spread that joy, to place joy at the heart of my family. That is my role in this godforsaken place. I will NOT let it pull me down!*

*The children are well; Kathleen is beginning to talk and Winifred – we call her Winnie – to crawl.*

*But behind the music, life goes on, as monotonous as ever. I look forward for months to our visits to Georgetown, even though I am still not well accepted. It's the same when we are invited to the neighbouring plantations, Dieu Merci and Glasgow. I am a misfit in this country. But I am strong, if silent; I am the backbone! I will conjure happiness into my family! As ever, I fill the house with music. The children love it! Winnie, though she is so small, definitely has a musical vein – she keeps the beat with her little waving hands! So sweet!*

*The only drop of wormwood is that Mr McInnes. I loathe him more than ever. I have the distinct impression he is poisoning my husband. Not literally, of course, but poisoning his mind. Archie is changing right under my nose. Sometimes I don't understand him at all. He is becoming more and more like his mother. Where is that kindness and gallantry I so loved in him! But never mind. I love HIM, and he loves me, and I will fill this house with love and gaiety if it's the last thing I do!*

# Chapter Fifteen

I had not imagined the crowds. In the past, whenever we had taken the ferry I had been with the family and one of the servants had bought the tickets for us and we had made our way with ease past the bustling, jostling horde making its way to the wharf – the *hoi-polloi*, as Papa called it. Market women with bundles on their heads, long men bent double under bulging sacks on their backs, families with bawling babies and everyone, it seemed, calling to each other at the tops of their voices. I asked an older woman, a plump darkie with a full-to-bursting bag in each hand, the way to the ticket office. She stared at me for a moment as in wonderment, and pointed with her chin.

'That buildin' over there!' she said.

I joined what seemed to be a straggling queue four or five people wide. Everyone turned to stare as I came; then, as if waking from a trance, quickly looked away again. And, it soon became clear that they edged away at my coming. It was as if I had a contagious disease: me with my little suitcase in a bubble of air, melting the crowd as I came amongst them. Over the next half-hour I slowly inched forward with it. I turned left and right and tried to speak to people, but they only muttered a few words and turned away.

I approached one of the women standing nearby. 'What time is the next ferry?' I asked.

She shrugged and pointed to a blackboard on the building, on which some numbers were scribbled in chalk. 'Two o'clock,' she said. She wore a scarf brightly coloured in reds and yellows tied under her chin, and a blue dress with a faded flowery pattern. In her arms was a toddler of about two, and clinging to her hand a little girl who stared up at me unabashedly. Two suitcases stood at her feet. The woman stood to one side as if waiting for something or someone; and I was right, for almost as soon as she had spoken a man walked up, tickets fanned in his hand.

'Come leh we go,' he said, slipping the tickets into the breast pocket of his shirt. He bent to pick up the suitcases, then followed the woman's gaze and saw me. He frowned.

'Wha' you want?' he asked brusquely, and walked away, gesturing to his wife to follow. She flung me a half-smile and walked off behind him, dragging the little girl behind her, twisted backwards as she continued to stare at me.

After about twenty minutes I was at the ticket-office cage.

'A ticket to Rosignol,' I said with as much confidence as I could muster.

'Single or return?' The voice was listless, bored.

'Single.'

'First class?'

'No! No.'

'Second?'

'No – do you have third? The cheapest. If not, second.'

'One shillin', Miss.'

I laid my suitcase on the ground, opened it, and removed the bag of coins swollen and heavy with ha'penny and penny bits. I stood up with the bag and emptied a handful of coins on to the counter.

'I'm sorry,' I said, 'I need to count a bit.'

'Miss, you holdin' up the line!' said the cashier. 'Why you don't go 'way and count out the fare and come back.'

'Oh, please, please, no! I'm sorry – I didn't think! It's only twelve pence – I'll be quick.'

I counted out six pennies and twelve ha'pennies, pushed them over to him. He handed me a ticket. I thanked him and took it. I slipped it into my skirt pocket and then moved away to let the next person forward. I crouched down to put the coin bag back in the suitcase, closed it, and then stood up. The people in the haphazard queue were staring at me with some distaste. I smiled at them, but no one smiled back.

'I looked around. People were milling about everywhere. There was a donkey and a net full of chickens, and piles of plantains and coconuts, which men were packing into sacks. Chaos and noise, dust and heat. My head began to swirl. What was the time now? Would I make the two o'clock ferry? Again, panic rose in me. I couldn't miss the ferry! According to the timetable the next boat after that was at four. If I took that boat I wouldn't get a train till five, probably, and not arrive in Georgetown till seven. It would be dark. I'd have to go straight to the Park Hotel; but how would that look, a young girl, even one of my standing, arriving so late? I had to get to the ferry.

Hurrying forward, I finally arrived at the pale wooden planks of the wharf and to my great relief there stood the ferry. People were crossing the gangplank that led to its deck. I joined the queue and before long I found myself on board.

I had made the crossing many times before with the family, and always first class. I knew where the first-class lounge was but that was no use to me. I followed the line of people who had boarded with me and they took me to a large open area filled with wooden benches. The benches were crammed full. Indeed, there was no sitting space anywhere so I placed my suitcase on the ground and sat on that.

A few minutes later the steam engines began to rumble and the crew and wharf workers began to shout and the boat moved away from the dock. I ought to have been feeling elation, joy, relief by this time; not this nibbling anxiety! I had escaped! I was leaving the Courantyne! Crossing the Berbice River into the County of Demerara, and on my own! There was no going back! I was well and truly on my way to George.

❊ ❊ ❊

I used the time spent crossing the river counting my coins into shillings and tying the little piles up into the corners of my cotton shawl. I did not want to repeat the embarrassment of counting ha'pennies before a crowd of impatient passengers at the train station. It was bad enough, when the time came, that the ticket seller had to re-count the heap of coins I shoved at him for the fare to Georgetown, but at last I had my ticket in my hand. I passed the turnstile, handed the conductor my ticket, and boarded the train.

Once again, all my previous journeys had been in the first-class compartment and once again, the third class was filled to bursting, with all the wooden benches occupied. But this time it was different. For a reason I could not explain, the two men sitting on the foremost carriage bench both stood up and offered me their seat. I looked from one to the other, not sure which one to accept, and finally chose the older of the two. I sat down. But instead of sitting down again, the other man remained standing.

'Do sit down!' I said to him, and pointed to the empty seat. He shook his head, mumbled something undecipherable, and moved away down the aisle. A fat woman with a bundle under her arms entered the carriage. I smiled at her and pointed to the empty seat. She looked at me and frowned, seemed to consider my offer, and reluctantly sat down next to me. She was so fat I was pushed against the window.

By now the doubts were tumbling through my mind. This was all a big mistake. A huge mistake! But it was too late now; no going back. I was on my way. The stationmaster's whistle pierced the babble of muted noise in the carriage, followed by a gasp of steam from the engine and a series of jerks and squeals and clanks, metal scraping on metal. Faces at the open windows, raised voices, hands reaching in as relatives said their last good-byes. Slowly, creakingly, we juddered into movement. Straining like an old man whose joints refuse to comply, puffing as if out of breath, the train crept through the outskirts of Rosignol. As the last houses gave way to open fields, we gathered momentum. The train's whistle screeched joyously, and losing its last restraints, the engine huffed and puffed and plunged forward, our carriage rattled along behind it, swaying and rumbling and throwing me alternately against the fat woman and the wall. I gazed through the window, seeing nothing. My vision was blurred by unshed tears. I held my breath in the effort not to cry. All my pluck, all my confidence seemed washed away in a flood of memories: of Papa, Mama, childhood joys, Promised Land, waving cane, big skies, home. Goodbye to all that! I buried my face in my palms and shook with a dry sob as it truly dawned on me what I had done.

'Here, Miss,' said the fat woman. 'A kerchief for you. It's clean!' She waved a piece of off-white cloth at me.

'Thanks,' I said, and took it, blew my nose and handed it back.

'Keep it,' she said, and smiled at me. I managed to smile back. 'You goin' to Georgetown?'

I nodded.

'I saw you on the steamer. Is a long way for a young girl like you to be travellin' alone. You goin' to join family?'

Tears rushed to my eyes and spilled out. It was the word family that did it. I had no family now. Unless, unless I truly got out and turned back. Gave up. Like the coward that I was. The woman's voice interrupted the torrent of self-incriminations.

'Darlin', don' cry! Come sweetheart, what's the matter? Tell Auntie!'

The voice was so warm, so soothing, I looked at her and through my tears I actually *saw* her for the first time. Up to now, she had been just a fat darkie woman who took up more than her fair share of space on the much too narrow wooden railway seat. Now I saw all the things that had escaped me through the shroud of self-concern that closed me in. She wore a faded blue skirt stretched tight over her thighs and coming apart at the hem, and a similarly washed-out floral blouse with a collar edged in lace, strained tight over an enormous bosom. Like me, she had removed her bonnet, and it lay across her knees, a miserable brown thing that looked like a hen's carcass. But her pitiful attire faded into insignificance beside the deep concern that rang through that voice and now, as I looked up and met her gaze, shone in her eyes. Her clothes may have been dull and drained of life but not the eyes that met mine above the smooth plumpness of her cheeks, they shone like black diamonds, and in them was a spirit so acute, so sharp, it startled me right out of the spiral of self-abasement.

My fingers fumbled with the cloth she had given me, twisting and untwisting it. I found I could not speak, for a lump in my throat converted the sound I tried to make into a croak. I bowed my head and more tears came. I dabbed them away. Finally, the words came out.

'I don't know what to do! I don't know where to go! I don't know anything!'

She laughed then, a cascade of gurgles that came right up from her belly so that her bosom shook like jelly.

'Chile! Which of we really know what to do an' who we is or anyt'ing at all! We think we does know but we don't know nothin'. Nobody know anything. We just do what we got to do. So what *you* got to do?'

'I want to go to Georgetown but I don't know where to go when I get there because I planned this journey all wrong and it will be too late when I get there and I just don't know!'

'Jus' a minute. Start at the beginning. First of all tell me where is home. New Amsterdam?'

I shook my head in misery. 'No. Much further away. Promised Land Plantation, up the coast.'

'So your family live there?'

I nodded, miserably.

'You daddy does work on the plantation, then.' It was a statement rather than a question, but I corrected her.

'No, he owns it. He owns it and I hate that he owns it and that's why I have to leave.'

Now it was her turn to be startled – she even drew away from me. 'You daddy own the plantation? Promised Land? Oh Lordy! An me thinkin' you was some pore-white girl!'

I knew what she meant – the daughter of one of the lesser employees on the plantation, a man from England or Scotland who had come here to better his lot only to find himself and his family on the lowest rung of the highest strata.

I shook my head. She was silent for a while, perhaps gathering her thoughts as she reconsidered her attitude towards me, for when she spoke again it was with far more formality.

'But what you doin' in a third-class carriage, Miss, and all alone?'

The words 'all alone' were enough to make my face crumple as I fought back another torrent of tears. Maybe that's what melted her because all of a sudden she was all tenderness and comfort again.

If we had been standing she would surely have hugged me; as it was, she took both my hands in her huge ones and pulled me gently sideways so that I sat side-ways on the seat, and, looking earnestly into my eyes, said, 'So you is a rich girl in trouble. I think you better tell Auntie Dolly everything.'

To hear those words, suffused with kindness, was all I needed. 'You see,' I began, 'I met this young man …'

❊ ❊ ❊

I told her everything. Telling the truth for the first time in days was more healing than a bowl of steaming chicken soup. 'So,' I finished off, my voice breaking, 'I'm going to Town to find George … but … but I won't get there till late and I won't able to find him … and, and it's such a nightmare! Do you … do you know of a cheap hotel where I could stay tonight, because we usually stay at the Park, and maybe I can charge it to Papa's account, but I look so scruffy they would turn me away and I don't know where to go and what to DO!'

The last word was a wail: drawn-out and desperate, containing all the hopelessness and helplessness, all the yearning and the aching of a child caught up in a self-made plight too huge for her to handle.

'Righty-ho,' said Auntie Dolly after a while. 'Lemme get this straight. All you know about this young man is he name and where he work.'

I nodded. My face must have looked as miserable as I felt for she squeezed my hands – which she had been holding all this time – and crooned, 'Oh Lord, have mercy upon this chile. Dear Lord have mercy.'

She let go of my hands then and flopped back into her seat. She sighed audibly. She picked up her bonnet and began to fan herself with it. Indeed, it was hotter than ever, as was usual in the hours past midday. Even the breeze fluttering in through the open window was hot – hot and dusty, and blowing my hair out of the careful coif Nora had created that morning.

All of a sudden Auntie Dolly turned back to me.

'I know what you should do,' she said.

'What?'

'Get off at the next station and go back home. The train will pass back in about two hours. Go back home. Forget this Georgie-boy. You never thought about it? How it goin' to work out – you a white girl an' all?'

'But … but …' And then I flopped back into my seat and began to cry in earnest. Because I saw that she was right and what she said was true. There was no question – I had to go back.

It was a full-blown disaster. How could I have ever *thought* it would work, me running away to Georgetown with such a badly drawn-up plan? What would I do once I got there? Once I had met George and told him I loved him? What then? I knew we couldn't marry – not yet – and sooner or later Papa would come and set the police on my track and find me and drag me home in disgrace and that would be the end of it. I just hadn't thought that far ahead. That's what comes from being a mollycoddled little princess who never had to think for herself. Idiot. I couldn't do it. This great plan of mine – a failure. I had to get out. Get out at the next station. Get back home. Get into the next train travelling east to Rosignol, take the steamer back to New Amsterdam. Walk to the Stewarts. No one at home would ever know the truth. It was over. I'd never see George again.

❊ ❊ ❊

Auntie Dolly had fallen asleep, her head thrown back against the wall of the train. I shouldn't have told her my story. That was stupid. Yet it had done me good to talk. It had helped to calm me down, to put things into perspective, to dry my tears. So what if it had put her to sleep with boredom. I could see clearly now. The adventure was over.

The train creaked into a station and drew to a juddering halt. I tied on my bonnet, got up, and stood on tiptoe to lift my suitcase down from the luggage rack. Auntie Dolly turned to me. Her hands flapped in the air as she shooed me away as if I were a nasty smell.

'What you waitin' for? Go. The train gon' start up again in a minute.'

But I didn't go. I just stood there staring at her. New passengers left the train, easing themselves down the crowded aisle, and new ones boarded. It was high time for me to leave. But I didn't. I placed my suitcase back on the rack, sat down next to her, and untied my bonnet.

'I can't,' I said to her, calmly and firmly. 'I can't go home. I have to see George. I have to talk to him. It can't end like this.'

On the platform, the stationmaster's whistle screeched and the engine belched steam; the train trembled and huffed and juddered into creaking movement, and I was still on it. And I would stay on it, all the way to Georgetown.

'I'm going to George,' I repeated. 'To Georgetown. To George. I have to see this through. I can't give up.

Auntie Dolly almost exploded at the words.

'You crazy lil' girl! You lost you mind or what? You know what, you *can't*! You can't do this! You white people! You think whatever you want you can get! All you gon' do is bring down trouble on George head! Crazy, crazy, crazy!'

On and on went the tirade. Her voice grew louder, angrier. People peered, and turned to stare, to smirk. What a scene! But it was of no use. With every word of reproach I only grew more and more determined. I would not give up so easily! I would find a way! I had to speak to George, and I would find him. Somehow. So I simply smiled politely at Auntie Dolly as she raged. And finally she was spent. She threw herself back against the seat, pulled another handkerchief out of her bosom, wiped her face with it, and fanned herself with her bonnet.

When she had finished speaking, I said, quietly and firmly, 'You see, I love him.'

She glared at me. 'You don't know what love is. You much too young.'

'No, I'm not. I know.'

She fell silent then, closed her eyes and I thought she was asleep. But after a long while she spoke again.

'Very well. I gon' help you.'

'Help me? Really? How?'

'Take you to me house for the night and go with you in the morning to the Post Office. Help you find he.'

'Auntie Dolly! Really! That would be so – so wonderful of you! Thank you!'

She muttered grumpily. 'What else I gon' do? Let you go to Georgetown all on you own, a stranger, a young white girl, and walk the streets lookin' for a place to stay? At evenin' time? You know what would happen to you? I can't let you do that.'

'Thank you! Thank you so much!' I grabbed her hand and kissed it. She pulled it away with a snort.

'Don't thank me. Thank the Lord. I say a prayer and that is what he tell me to do. I don't know if is right to help you. Maybe is wrong. Maybe is right. What do I know? Only the good Lord know what is right an' wrong so I did pray to he and he did say I got to help.'

'I'm so grateful. I'm sure I would have found a hotel or something, or maybe friends of my father's to put me up, but this is much better! Much!'

'Well of course if you Daddy got friends in one of them big mansions in Main Street you welcome to go there! I only got a small-small house in Kitty. It not going to be good enough for the likes of you ...'

'Oh, Auntie Dolly, that's not what I meant at all! I'd *love* to come to your house!'

She looked me up and down and seemed satisfied that I was sincere.

'Very well. So you can spend the night at me place in Kitty, and tomorrow I gon' go with you to town, an' we gon' to find this George together. But only on one condition.'

'A condition? What condition?'

'I only gon' help if you promise me to go back home after that, Sunday morning, and not to run away again. So you see George and tell him what you want to tell him. And see what he says. And then go back home and wait.'

'Wait – for what?'

'Till you get old enough to know you mind better. Wait to see if the love hold out. Five years at least. You much too young to face the troubles now.'

'All right.'

'You'll do that?'

I nodded.

Auntie Dolly frowned sternly as she looked at me, trying, it seemed, to probe into the depths of my mind, to extract that promise that was the price of her help.

Of course, she couldn't see my hands, which I had subtly slipped behind my back. She couldn't see the crossed fingers. Back to Promised Land, that sullied paradise? Back to Papa? Never! By promising to help find George, Auntie Dolly had also restored my confidence in our future together, my faith in a love so strong it would sustain us through thick and through thin. How could I go home and *wait* for five years? Five years! That was an eternity!

'Yes,' I said. 'I promise.'

She was not satisfied.

'Say it!' she insisted. 'Say it out loud. Say I promise to go home and not run away again.'

This time I hesitated. But then I said it. 'I promise to go home and not run away again.'

I pressed my crossed fingers tightly together. It felt terrible to lie to Auntie Dolly, she who had only just relieved me of a terrible burden of falsehoods. But actually, only half of it was a lie, wasn't it – the part about going home. Because if I didn't go home, I could not run away again.

'Good girl!' she said, and patted me on the thigh.

❀ ❀ ❀

After that she fell asleep, her head lolling to one side. I too was exhausted – putting your burdens on someone else's shoulders must be almost as exhausting as being the one so burdened, but for me the exhaustion came more as a kind of nervous restlessness: I could not sleep. If there had been enough space I would have walked up and down the aisle of the crowded carriage. As it was I stayed seated and gazed out of the window, wide awake.

By now we were halfway to Georgetown. The train rattled on in a pleasantly clanking rhythm, swaying merrily along in beat to the steam, and stopping every now and then at rural stations for passengers to get on and off. At every stop women strolled past the window calling out their wares: pine-tart, bananas, small bunches of genips, bread-and-fish.

I counted out some coins and bought a bread-and-fish. It was a slice of fried fish in a tennis roll with a sliver of tomato. Eating helped calm my nerves. I was thirsty, too, and bought a water coconut which a vendor passed through the window, its top sliced off. I put my mouth around the hole, tipped back my head, and drank. Delicious!

My hunger stilled and thirst quenched, a new sense of adventure crept through my being. Of anticipation – a sense of living in the moment not knowing what the future might bring, but trusting it would be good. Auntie Dolly's offer of help had brought order into the chaos that had gathered momentum since the morning. I took a deep breath. Here I was on a Demerara train hurtling towards a great big question mark, and yet I felt the strength to face whatever might be waiting round the next corner. And tomorrow, if all went well, I would see George. At the mere thought of his name warmth and joy and courage welled up in me. I saw his face in my mind's eyes and felt the rain on my cheeks, heard his voice, the tremble of emotion in it: 'I love you so much.'

The countryside rolled by. Flooded fields of emerald green paddies with coolie women bent double in the water, weeding. Miles and miles of cane, not yet at its full height. Fishing villages with black nets spread over the bare ground and fishing boats upside-down beside the seawall. The seawall itself – that long brick structure stretching from Georgetown to Rosignol as a bar-

ricade against the ocean. Papa had told us that the coastal plain
was six feet below sea level and the Dutch had built this wall as
a protection; that it was Dutch expertise that had made these
lowlands fit for farming; that most of the plantations along the
coast had once been in Dutch hands, hence some of the names:
Beterverwagting, Niewkerie, Uitgtveldt. And French names, like
Non Pareil, La Bonne Intention and Mon Repos, and of course
our own neighbour, Dieu Merci, because the French too had been
part of our colonial past; but mostly English names, names that
sometimes reflected the spirit that had brought these pioneers
here: Adventure. Land of Canaan. Promised Land.

The train rolled metallically along the rails in a clattering,
comforting rhythm into which my own heartbeat settled. The
wind, cool and salty from the ocean, swept in through the open
window, brushed my cheeks, whipped my hair against my cheeks.
I yawned, and closed my eyes.

* * *

**Mama's Diary: Plantation Promised Land, British Guiana,
1897**

*Liebes Tagebuch,*

*I can't believe that this time, not months but years have passed
by since I last wrote to you! I may have neglected you by touch,
but never in my mind. You are the one I talk to in the stillness
of the night, as I cannot talk to Archie, my daughters are too
young, and I have not a single friend here. I fight against a certain
despondency. Writing to you takes a distinct effort to lift myself
out of that sense of being buried under a great weight. I shall try
to do it more often. But I cannot promise. Sometimes the effort is
just too great.*

*We have a third daughter! We have called her Johanna, and this
time I chose the name, and it had to be German, pronounced, too,*

*the German way. She is named after Father – Johann. How I miss Father! My brothers! My friends from Salzburg! The snow-capped mountains! The walls in this house are plastered with paintings of those mountains. Sometimes I close my eyes and imagine myself there. Boating on the Wolfgang Lake! Sledding with father and my brothers on the hills outside the city! Operas and balls in Vienna! Will I ever see my home again! Because this place is not my home. But I must make it my home, for the sake of my daughters. For the sake of my husband.*

*I love Archie. I always will. I must wrench him from the clutches of that Mr McInnes. I must, I will! I will seduce him with music and dance! With love! I will not allow him to be poisoned! I am his backbone – I must keep him upright!*

# Chapter Sixteen

'Miss Winnie! Miss Winnie, wake up! We done get there! Kitty! We got to get out!'

'What?' I shook my head to dispel the sleep and it took a good few seconds before I could recall where I was and catch up with real life. The train had stopped. All around there was bustle and noise, voices raised and people pushing down the aisle. Auntie Dolly was on her feet, reaching up into the luggage rack. She pulled my suitcase down and dropped it to the ground at my feet, reached up again for her own luggage. I rose slowly to my feet on weak and wobbly legs, adjusted my hair and pushed my blouse back into my waistband.

'Girl, we int got time for that sorta thing. Come, let we go – before the train drive off an' we still standin' here – hurry, hurry – push you way through!'

I grabbed my suitcase and did as she said, pushing my way into the line of humanity creeping down the aisle to the carriage door.

'Excuse me,' I mumbled as I edged myself in. 'Excuse me, please.'

A man stood still to let me in, but not without a look of blatant astonishment which at first I did not understand. Auntie Dolly soon cleared up that bewilderment.

'Eh-eh!' she said, in voice high with sarcasm. 'You never see a white girl in you life before? Lemme in behind she before she get lost.' And she pushed in behind me.

I edged forward and reached the door, where I stepped out onto the platform. It was bustling with people: people waiting impatiently to board the train, people waving and calling as they waited for their relatives, people with bags and bundles rushing to and fro – sheer pandemonium. Auntie Dolly got out behind me, hoisted a large cloth bundle on to her head, and, taking hold of my elbow, guided me towards the simple station building made of wood painted white and edged with green. A large sign read Kitty Village. I had seen that sign so many times when we stopped here on the way to Georgetown; it was the sign that said we were just one stop away from the capital. I had never, though, left the train here before. Why should I? Archie Cox's family had no business in Kitty, a darkie village on the outskirts of Georgetown.

That a Cox had no business here was made abundantly clear as we walked out into the street beyond the station. Just like the man on the train, everyone stared; eyebrows raised in astonishment, heads turned, children giggled and pointed. Auntie Dolly pursed her lips and, still clasping my elbow, pushed me onto the pavement and nudged me forward. Her other hand was raised to steady the bundle precariously balanced on her head.

'Is what all-you staring at? We is some animal in a zoo? You never see white skin in you life?' So she called out to the various on-lookers, forcing them to look away. Auntie Dolly sucked her teeth.

'Them people stupidy bad. Them in't got no manners. Don't worry, girl, Auntie Dolly gon' take care of you. Come, this way, this way, cross the street! Mind that donkey cart! Hey, driver! Watch where you goin'! Keep you eye on the road! Is a girl I got here, not a circus clown! That suitcase not too heavy for you? Why not put it on you head, like me?'

We stopped then; she carefully set her bundle on the ground and helped me lift my suitcase to my head. It had indeed become too heavy for one hand, and my fingers hurt. Together we steadied it on my head, and I held on with both hands.

'Good, good. Now come this way. Is not too far. Jus'a few blocks down. Don't bother with them people, let them stare. They only ignorant. Come dear, you got it good? Walk straight and you gon' find it easy. Chin up! Head high! Hold on tight!'

Auntie Dolly set a brisk pace. We walked along a cracked pavement, so narrow that I stepped back and let her lead. We crossed several streets, passed the market closed down for the day, and plunged ever deeper into the heart of Kitty. The streets themselves held little traffic; just the occasional dray cart or donkey cart loaded with wooden planks, or plantains, or coconuts. People still turned to stare. We must have indeed been a strange sight, a fat darkie with an even fatter cloth-bundle on her head, followed by a dishevelled white girl with a suitcase on her head hurrying to keep up. I really couldn't blame them for looking and, well, *wondering*. But the closer we got to home the more belligerent Auntie Dolly became in her scolding, shouting at them from across the road, calling them out by name, even stopping at garden-gates to holler at some poor lad peering at us from the safety of his own home:

'Get you stinkin' eyes off a we, yes, is you I talkin' to Errol Johnson! Go home an' mine you own business or I gon' come roun' an whip you backside!'

'You, Daisy! Is what you tink you lookin' at! Get you little rass back in you house or I gon' come roun' an' quarrel wit' you Mammy this very evenin', you tink I don't know 'bout you an' that boy from de wharf?'

She bellowed at them with the wrath of God. Her swearing was worse than a cane cutter's at harvest time, but I was used to their curses and so I kept my head straight ahead and walked on, trying hard, sometimes, not to smile:

'Bertie Williams, you backside gon' turn so raw by the time I finish wid you it gon be worse than if red-ants did eat you down to de bone! You gon' be sittin' in a pan a coconut oil for a week! You never see a white girl in you life before? You Mammy din' teach you no manners?'

We left the commercial section of the village with its quaint little shops – a haberdashers, an ironmonger, a baker, not to mention the closing-down fruit-and-vegetable stalls of the market – and walked down a street lined on both sides by little houses on stilts. Children played in the yards and on the stairs to the front doors. They resembled the village houses at Promised Land, and once again I felt that old sense of shame – that in these houses smaller than our lounge entire families lived, while we Coxes rattled around in our sprawling mansion. I supposed it wasn't my fault; I didn't choose to be born into that family, after all. But still. I felt that shame.

I was weary, and lagged behind. Auntie Dolly would have none of it. She stopped, turned around and now I was the object of her bellowing:

'Move those legs! You think you is out on the plantation with a crowd a servants runnin' behind you? Move you li'l white backside!'

No darkie had ever spoken, no *shouted*, to me in that tone ever before. It had always been simpering, grovelling obeisance, demanded by Papa, accepted by me. I had taken it for granted, taken it, in fact, as natural law, the way things had to be and ought to be, and now involuntarily a heat-wave of indignation rose to my head; I must have turned scarlet, as her next words indicated:

'My my, I see you really got red blood runnin' in you veins; I did tink' with you people it was gold!' She cackled with laughter but her voice turned mild. 'We nearly there. Only five more minutes.'

It was actually more like fifteen, but eventually we turned into a yet narrower road with a potholed tarmac enclosed between grassy verges badly in need of a trim. There was no pavement here, but also little traffic; only a donkey-cart laden high with cut grass plodding towards us. We edged past, then Auntie Dolly waited for me and I walked on beside her. The houses here were smaller still, but set farther back from the road. As ever, gutters ran along both sides of the road. A group of half-naked boys sat on one of the bridges, exclaiming excitedly as one of them lowered a fishing-net into the water. A couple of guppies swam in a jar beside them. The boys looked up to stare in silence – at me, not at Auntie Dolly – as we passed, but she, this time, reprimanded them with only an impatient gesture. A cow, so skinny you could almost count her ribs, grazed by the wayside. Eventually, Aunt Dolly turned on to one of the bridges and opened a rusty creaking gate.

'Me house,' she said simply and with a modicum of pride. 'Bought and paid for by the sweat of me own brow.'

A bell attached to the gate jangled as we entered the yard. Immediately a host of ragged children swarmed around her, jumping up at her and pulling on her arms, and calling her grandma. She, smiling fondly, admonished them mildly.

'Jack, Molly, Winston – where you-all manners? You don't see we got a visitor?'

They all turned around then and stared at me in silence. This vexed Auntie Dolly.

'Is where you-all think you is, in the zoo? Where you manners? I will have you know that this is Miss Winnie Cox from Plantation Promised Land and she will be our guest tonight.'

And then they all came forward, one by one, holding out their little hands and shaking mine and saying 'good evening'; the little girls held out their skirts as they curtsied and the little boys bowed slightly. Aunt Dolly nodded sternly and led me up the rickety front staircase and the jabbering children trailed behind.

The front door stood open; we entered. It was the first time I had even been in a darkie house, discounting the staff cottages in our compound at Promised Land. To say it was tiny would be an exaggeration. The front gallery was little more than a strip of space lined with windows. At its far end, in pride of place, stood a Singer sewing machine. Neat little piles of fabric lay on the machine itself, on a small table next to it, and on the floor. A half-finished cotton dress, its hem, armholes and neck lined with pins, hung on a coat-hanger on a cord suspended across the room. A group of cane chairs was squashed into the remaining space in the room.

Before us, extending into the house itself, was another narrow room, in which stood a long wooden dining table alongside the right wall, with several wooden chairs and stools pushed up against it. On the wall to our left, two half-open doors. Beyond the table, another door opened into what was obviously the kitchen, for the smell of something mysteriously spicy and deliciously inviting emerged from its innards. I realised that I was ravenous.

'Mummy, is you?' called a female voice from that source of mouth-watering delight, and a younger woman bearing a strong resemblance to Auntie Dolly though far less corpulent emerged, a cooking ladle in one hand. 'Them Winston too hard-ears – I send he to Mr Godfrey and ...' She stopped mid-sentence. She had seen me.

'Is who that?'

'Is a girl I meet 'pon the train. Don't stare like that. Is a nice girl. She got a bit a trouble so I bring she home. She gon' spend the night. She hungry bad. Miss Winnie, this is me daughter Myrtle. Myrtle, this is Miss Winnie Cox.'

Myrtle ignored the formal introduction. She glared at her mother.

'Eh-eh! Since when wehn is a hotel fuh white people!'

'Is a nice girl, a good girl, Myrtle. Don't be rude. Is I invite she. She need help.'

Myrtle stood now arms akimbo, staring at me. I trembled under her wrath.

'An' where pray this Miss Princess gon' sleep? In the four-poster bed or in the hammock in the bottom house?'

'Don't be like that, Myrtle. I sorry for she. I gon' give she me bed, an I gon' sleep with you'all in de big bed. Is plenty a room for one more. Winston could sleep on the floor.'

Winston, a boy of about nine, had something to say about that. All the children – five in all, aged from about three up to him, had been giggling and shuffling behind us up to now, obviously intrigued by the drama.

'I not gon' sleep 'pon no floor!' cried this Winston. 'You not gon' make me sleep 'pon no floor!'

'You shut you mouth, boy! You eye pass me or what! You gon' sleep where I tell you to sleep! We got a guest for the night an' we got to offer she a bed!'

'But Granny …'

'You hard-ears? You in't hear what I say? Now, Myrtle, get back in de kitchen an' finish the dinner an' remember to cook for one extra – two a-we hungry bad. Miss Winnie, come lemme show you where you gon' sleep. Here. Your room. I gon' put clean sheets on the bed and you gon' sleep like on roses.'

While speaking she pushed open the first of the two bedroom doors. I entered behind her. The room was as small as to be expected – about as big as our bathroom at Promised Land. There was a narrow bed pushed into a corner and a single wardrobe occupying another corner. There was a cord spanned across the room from which hung various garments on coat-hangers: dresses, shirts, blouses, trousers. The rest of the floor space was filled with piles of folded fabric, as in the front room. A heavy pair of black scissors lay on top of one of the piles. It was not hard to guess Auntie Dolly's profession with all this evidence, and, in fact, throwing the bundle she had brought onto the bed, she declared proudly:

'I's a seamstress!' She opened the bundle and more fabric spilled out: brilliantly coloured parcels of cotton, tied up with string and each with a piece of paper pinned to it.

'Orders from New Amsterdam!' she said. 'Me son does live there – a stevedore. He does get plenty orders for me. He wife an' all she friends. They like to have a seamstress from the City.

We know more 'bout fashion than them New Amsterdam seamstresses.'

I nodded. I had not spoken a word since we had left the train. I was too dazed to properly register what was going on, much less react appropriately and politely to events, to act as a guest should act. My throat was parched, and my head throbbed. My stomach growled.

Auntie Dolly may have heard it, for she said, 'Put down you suitcase in here' – for I still clutched it in my right hand – 'and then let we have some food. You must be thirsty – Marlene, run an' get she a glass a water.'

A little girl ran off and returned with the glass, which I drank gratefully. I even managed a smile and a faint thank you. Marlene stared up at me with huge black eyes. She was about seven or eight, a waif of a girl with shiny black skin and hair pulled back from her scalp into several small plaits, each one tied with a scrap of red ribbon. Perhaps encouraged by my smile, she reached up and touched the tendril of my hair that dangled over my shoulder.

'Is so soft!' she exclaimed, twirling it between her fingers. All the children – till now gathered in the doorway staring in silence – scrambled forward exclaiming about 'white-people-hair' and wanting to feel, and would have without Auntie Dolly's boisterous intervention.

'Shoo! Scram you chirren! You 'int got no manners? Since when you does go about touchin' people hair? Myrtle, food ready yet?'

This last called out on her way out of the room. I followed, as did the children. Auntie Dolly led me down to the yard where she showed me the water vat and a dripping tap where I washed my face and hands. We returned upstairs. Myrtle, with Marlene's help, had laid the table. Auntie Dolly pointed to a chair. I sat down and ate. I had never in my life eaten with such gusto. Never in my life had food tasted so delicious.

❈ ❈ ❈

The rest of the waning day, the night, and the following morning passed as in a dream. After a visit to the lavatory – a ramshackle hut in the backyard – I went to bed and fell asleep to the sound of a violent argument between Auntie Dolly and Myrtle, an argument that started in the dining room where I could hear every word, as the rooms had no ceiling. Eventually they withdrew to the kitchen and the row grew more muted. Vaguely, disinterestedly I took note of Myrtle's aggrieved voice haranguing her mother for harbouring white people in her house, and Auntie Dolly murmuring stoically back on my behalf. I fell asleep to the muted hubbub of their spat.

❈ ❈ ❈

I woke up in the middle of the night to a backdrop of sound: frogs croaking from the yard, and a dog barking in the distance, followed by a return volley of barks from nearer at hand. In the next room somebody snored. The room was filled with a half-light from the swelling moon outside the open window. A mosquito net enclosed me like a ghostly tent. Mosquitoes swirled around both inside and out of it, as it had several holes and was little more than a nod to convention, and their buzz seemed the loudest sound of all, and the most annoying. But louder than all of these scattered noises were my thoughts. They descended on me like a swarm of locusts. Yesterday, passing events had taken over my life and I had moved from one adventure to the next almost in a daze, my internal life an emotional roller-coaster that kept any semblance of serious reflection at bay. Now, in the semi-silence of night, I allowed thoughts to come, to parade before me and deliver their conflicting messages.

Only one thing was certain: I had plunged into a world so entirely different to my own I might as well have been on a different continent.

*So this was how darkies lived.*

I had no idea.

George was a darkie. He would live like this too, no doubt. *This was my future.* A cramped room and a mosquito net full of holes and a latrine and rain-water vat in the yard. Somewhere inside me a little voice was calling: *Are you completely out of your mind?*

❋ ❋ ❋

## Mama's Diary Plantation Promised Land, British Guiana, 1899

*Liebes Tagebuch,*

*The girls are growing; no longer babies but children, each with her own distinct personality! Kathleen is very English, quite a prim and proper little lady, and a little vain, I'm afraid. She is now seven.*

*Winnie is five, and takes after me: she loves music and dance! She already plays the piano vey skilfully for her age, and is eager to learn the violin, so I have written to Father to ask him to send a child-sized instrument for her. I so look forward to teaching her! She is also perfectly bi-lingual, unlike Kathleen, who refuses to speak a word of German.*

*Johanna, though only three, is turning out to be quite a wild little thing. She is such fun! We call her Yoyo, as that is what she calls herself, and it suits her – she is just like a yoyo, bouncing up and down with energy, with her moods; a tantrum one minute, the next, bubbling over with some new enthusiasm, and the tantrum forgotten!*

*What a little trio we have! Archie adores them all, though he has longed for a son ever since I was expecting Winnie. He says it's not that he loves the girls less; it's just that we do need a boy to inherit the plantation, to learn the ropes, as it were, from a young age. It seems there are some business troubles – the Bookers company which dominate this country is threatening to do us harm. Sometimes I do wonder about these matters but I must leave that to Archie. He probably knows best. I do wonder, though.*

*I am no longer pining away with loneliness. It is as if I have turned a corner, found my strength. In not giving in to those feelings of despondency, I have grown into my true personality and now I really am the backbone of this family. I recognise Archie's weaknesses, though he does not do so himself. He truly thinks himself the master here, not recognizing that he is just like a creeper, limp and weak without its support. And that is me. I am slowly but surely easing him out of the grasp of Mr McInnes. Not an easy task, but I will do it. I have to, for my own sanity.*

*I have to say, dearest diary, that you have helped me through all this. I talk to you all the time. I tell you everything, even if I don't actually write it down. I speak to you in my thoughts, as if you are a living friend. I know you are there, somewhere, listening, and holding my metaphorical hand. You are my lifeline! So there's no need to feel neglected. You are my constant companion! The twin sister I never had! You know it, don't you? You are always listening! Always reading!*

# Chapter Seventeen

In the morning a great commotion shook me out of my sleep. Dazed, I wondered where I was and what great disaster was upon me. Then I remembered the night before and the sounds identified themselves as simple morning sounds balled into a tangle: children squabbling, pots and pans banging, water rushing down in the yard, a bicycle bell ringing, and behind it all the inevitable dogs barking. At Promised Land we no doubt also had all these noises but they were spread over a vast space, some of them behind closed doors. And, I noted by a glance out of the window, it was much, much too early. I pressed the pillow over my ears. But it was no good. This was the day.

I felt stiff and still exhausted; the very thought of the coming day filled me with both excitement and dread. It is extraordinary how even a little injection of doubt can pull down a sky-high edifice of hope. Extraordinary, too, how that dread, though immaterial, can manifest in such very physical symptoms. My whole body felt heavy and dark, and it was all I could do to drag myself to a sitting and then standing position. It was as if I had not slept a wink – but I had. It was the doubt creeping through me that pressed me down, earthwards, made me want to creep back into bed and cover myself with a sheet and wake up back in Promised Land.

I supposed I still could. I had the choice. I could go to the station, count out my fare in pennies once more, board a train and make my way back to Rosignol and New Amsterdam. I would turn up at Emily Stewart's house and invent some excuse, some lie to explain to her mother my reappearance. On Sunday, tomorrow, Poole would come and pick me up as arranged. No one who mattered would ever know of my foolishness. It would be so very easy. It was so very inviting.

What was it, then, who was it that cried, 'Yes, I'm up!' to Auntie Dolly's rap on the door and wake-up call, 'Winnie! Get up! Time to get ready!'

Why were they up this early? It was Saturday, after all; there would be no school. I soon learned why, for Auntie Dolly told me over breakfast: Myrtle ran a stall in Kitty Market where she sold clothes that her mother made. It was, it seemed, quite a successful venture. Normally Auntie Dolly would stay at home to do some more sewing and look after the children. Today, the children would be going to the market with their mother, a source of some subdued grumbling on Myrtle's part, but not of a quarrel. It seemed that she had relented somewhat in her opposition to me. Auntie Dolly herself, of course, would be accompanying me to Georgetown to hunt down George Theodore Quint. The quest was on! It was here, today, happening! The next thing I knew I was seated in a chair in the cramped front room and Auntie Dolly was brushing my hair free of knots and dressing it into an elaborate style. As she fiddled with my hair she talked, and I learned some of her story.

'I use to work for a white lady,' she said. 'When I was young. Young like you! I was a maid in a big house in Georgetown. And then I get to be lady's maid. I know how to dress-up white people hair – the daughter, Dorothy – my, that was a vain one: "*No Dolly, I want it* so, *no Dolly, I want a chignon today. No, Dolly, the part in't straight.*" She marry a big boss from Bookers. Livin' now in one-a them big houses in Main Street – I gon' show you the house when we pass it today. My, them was fancy days! I did serve at big dinners an' clean rooms an' all kind-a-thing. That lady did have a seamstress who did come in the house to make she clothes. I use to help wit' de pinnin' an' de tackin'. De seamstress did make a lot-a money an' when she buy a new fancy Singer machine she did give me the old one – this one right here in de corner. That's how I did learn seamstressing an' get me machine an' build up me own business. I save up me money an' one day I buy this house.'

She spoke with great pride. And slowly I realised: this place I had turned up my nose at, this little cottage where the rooms were so small you could stand in the middle and touch opposite walls, was for her, a great achievement. A success story. The result of diligence and ambition, of a lifetime of scrimping and saving for an end result that I, in my immeasurable arrogance, deigned to criticize and disdain. What had I done in my life that came even close? I was born into privilege. I had not earned my position. I had no real right to it. And here I was sneering, albeit silently, at Auntie Dolly's great life achievement, and flirting with the thought of flight just to avoid a similar future.

I straightened my spine. No. There would be no flight. This was, indeed, the day.

Auntie Dolly pulled and prodded and tweaked at my hair. Her fingers wove expertly between the strands, and when she finished she showed me the result in a tiny mirror, and borrowed a second tiny mirror from Myrtle to show me the back. I gasped: she had done a beautiful job; two long plaits arranged like garlands around my head, with a smooth crown at the top.

'Lovely!' she said. 'You look lovely! Now go and put on some nice clean clothes; come let me help you.'

Auntie Dolly and I looked through the clothes in my suitcase and chose the prettiest blouse, white sprinkled with blue flowers and a high laced neck, and a smart blue skirt. Again, I looked at myself in the two tiny mirrors, but it was Aunty Dolly's word that convinced me the most.

'Beautiful' she said this time. 'Just beautiful!'

She conjured a box of Pond's Face Powder from somewhere and patted me all over my face with a powder-puff. Another look in the mirror: who was that wide-eyed girl staring back at me? A princess about to set off to find her prince, that's who!

There was a little hullabaloo concerning my suitcase. I wanted to take it with me. Auntie Dolly insisted I leave it behind; after all, wasn't I going straight back to the Courantyne tomorrow? Wasn't I spending a second night with her? How would it look, my turning up in George's life with a packed suitcase? I was loathe to leave it, but I had to concede she was right, and so, removing only the bag full of coins, we set off together.

It was strange to see that this time, nobody stared. They glanced, and looked away.

'Is because, today you look like a lady,' explained Auntie Dolly when I remarked on this.

'You look like a lady, an' I look like you servant. That's the way they expect things to be. Yesterday, you was lookin' more like the servant, an' carryin' you own suitcase too.'

❊ ❊ ❊

We walked to the station, where a crowd of people was waiting for a hackney carriage, and queued quietly under a rain shelter. The carriage arrived as we did, the two horses' hooves clattering on the tarmac as they passed us. 'Whoa!' cried the driver, and they slowed to a walk and then came to a standstill. Several people emerged from the coach; those waiting clambered in. The driver descended from his seat, removed his cap, and turned to me with a polite bow. 'You wantin' to go to town, Miss? Plenty of room for you!'

It wasn't true. The coach was already full, and more people waited. I shook my head. 'No, thank you.'

He ignored me. 'Don't worry 'bout them people – they can get down and wait for the next coach.' Without waiting for a response, he turned to the people already seated. 'You-all don' see the lady waitin' to go to town? Get down all-a you!'

And indeed, some of the passengers obediently stood up and made to descend back into the street.

'No – no! Please don't get out! Please sit down! Stay where you are!' I called out, flustered. I turned to Auntie Dolly.

'Do we have to take the coach? Can't we go by train?'

She shrugged. 'In't no train comin' this whole mornin'', she replied. 'The Rosignol don't get in till midday. You want wait so long?'

'No, but …'

'You is a lady. You can't travel with common people.'

'But I can! Of course I can! We'll just wait for the next coach!' And I walked off and joined the back of the waiting queue. Heads turned, brows raised, lips whispered.

'Miss Winnie, you can't …' She tugged at my elbow.

'Yes, I very well *can*!' I said firmly, and loud enough for everyone to hear. I shook her hands off my arm. 'We will wait here just like everyone else and sit in the carriage with everyone else. I don't need a private coach. It's just not right. It's not right, Auntie, don't you see it's not right? It's just *wrong*!'

By the time I had finished speaking my voice had risen and I could myself hear the note of hysteria in it, the hysteria of sheer helplessness. What was this thing I was up against? This huge nameless, shapeless *thing* that put me at the head of queues and into empty carriages while others waited and caused heads to bow deferentially at my coming? What was it, what caused it? Why? It made me feel bad: shoddy, wicked, crooked, tearful.

The driver climbed back into the carriage, flicked his whip; the horses nodded, swished their tails, and lumbered off.

Auntie Dolly pursed her lips, and shrugged. 'If you say so, Miss Winnie. If that's what you want.' She drew nearer and whispered: 'You don't see people gon' get confuse? Why you got to be so different?'

'Because I'm *not* different!' I said, quite loudly. 'I'm just like everyone else. Don't you see?' I pinched my arm. 'It's just skin! That's all! Inside I feel just like everyone else. No different!' I looked around, at the faces fixed on me. 'Don't stare! It's nothing! Just let me be! Please, just let me be!'

They all turned away then, as if embarrassed at my outburst, the outcry of a spoiled child, because that's exactly how I felt. As if I'd had a tantrum and got my way, and yet still burned with frustration.

The next carriage came after fifteen minutes. Again, the driver invited me for a private drive but I shook my head and Auntie Dolly explained and we climbed in and took our seats. There was room for six in the carriage and there had definitely been more than six passengers waiting, but several had mysteriously melted away so that I was able to embark without displacing another. The seats were arranged along the sides of the carriage with an aisle in the middle. Auntie Dolly made me take one of the front seats. I shrugged and took it, though again I felt some kind of symbolism in this position. But by now the fight had gone out of me.

The driver collected our fares. I counted out my coins and handed them to him. I wanted to pay for Auntie Dolly as well, but she refused: 'I is not you servant!' She said quite loudly, embarrassing me further.

Once everyone was seated we drove off, hoof-iron clip-clopping along the middle of the road. I felt rotten and sulky for half of the journey to Georgetown; but then my spirits lifted, and I remembered what this day was all about: this was the day I would see George.

❊ ❊ ❊

### Mama's Diary: Plantation Promised Land, British Guiana, 1900

*Liebes Tagebuch,*

*So much has happened. I now have a friend. In Georgetown. Someone I can speak to intelligently, and divulge my cares and worries to, just as I do to you. I cannot be more precise. It is too dangerous. The thing is, he is a man. He speaks to me of things Archie has always hidden from me; rather, things I did not wish to know, for they are far too painful. They cause me great grief and great guilt. If I had known these things before, well I would never have come.*

*Slavery has always been an abomination to me. I now know that this place, this Promised Land, was built on the backs of slaves. That the cane fields have been nurtured by the blood of slaves.*

*I honestly don't know what to say, what to think, what to do. I only know I am sick to my stomach. It seems that even though slavery has been abolished, the slaves replaced with indentured servants from India, things are not much better. This friend – I dare not even name him – has given me literature on the subject.*

*All I can say is that I feel despondency creeping up on me again, and this time I feel defenceless against it. Not even music is helping. Not even my joy in my children. Nothing is helping. I wish I could say more but I can't. Though I know you are discreet, I feel that everything I say or do is under surveillance. I know it isn't but I feel that way. I cannot even mention his name. It is like a lump at the back of my throat.*

*Archie, oh Archie. What is happening to us? Where has the love flown to, the love we swore was eternal? Most of all, what have you become? Where is that wonderful young man I fell in love with, the man so full of dreams, the man I laughed and danced with?*

# Chapter Eighteen

The horses kept up a brisk trot all the way through the fields to Georgetown. We turned down Camp Road and drove past Queen's College, a one-story, cream-coloured long wooden building set back from the road. My heart beat faster – this was where George had gone to school! I imagined him as a schoolboy, sailing through those wide open gates on his bicycle, school bag slung across his shoulder just as his post-bag had been that first day we met, grinning his huge wide infectious grin; I saw his face, rich-brown in a sea of pale English faces, and felt inordinately proud of him. My George.

We turned right into Lamaha Street and headed west towards Main Street. Auntie Dolly had said it was best to go to the main post office in the centre of town, for there he would be known and we could seek further directions. It might take us some time to find him, she had said; it was a bit of a wild goose chase.

'But everybody know everybody in Town,' she had concluded. 'We gon' find him. Don't worry.' And I didn't. I knew we'd find him. A second sense, a feeling of joy and immanent fulfilment, made me heady, tingling all over. This was the day!

The coach stopped just past the junction of Camp and Waterloo. A man and a woman stepped down on to the street. The driver flicked his whip and we set off again. We turned south into the shaded avenue of Main Street, stopped again for another passenger. I looked around me in appreciation: this was one of the loveliest streets in town, with its white wooden mansions set in gardens overflowing with colour. A walkway ran up the middle of the street, lined on both sides with flamboyant trees – now in full flower, flaming red. Set between two wide grass verges, the path was strewn with fallen blossoms – a red carpet set in green.

Here lived the high and mighty: government dignitaries, Booker managers, friends of Papa. I had been in a few of these houses, met their inhabitants, in my other life. If one of those fine ladies should step out into the street right now, and see me in a carriage full of darkies – I smiled to myself at the thought. She'd fall over in a faint, most likely.

It was then that I saw him. On the other side of the walkway, just coming out of one of those very mansions, closing the gate, stepping out into the street, turning to head for the next house. In his dark blue postman's livery, his postman's bag at his side, its wide strap slanted across his back as he turned to walk away.

The coachman flicked his whip to urge the horses on, but I shouted to him. 'No! Stop! Stay! Let me out!'

'Miss Winnie …'

'Auntie Dolly! Look! There! Over there – between the trees – oh, you can't see him now, he's gone through the gate – but it's him! George! It's him, it really is! Come on, come down, let's *go*!'

I got up, grabbed her hand, tugged her to her feet; almost fell over my own feet in my haste to descend. Huffing and puffing and raising her skirt to climb down the steps, Auntie Dolly followed. The carriage drove off, its inhabitants peering at us through the open windows.

I rushed across the street, hardly looking out for traffic. Auntie Dolly called after me to *wait*, to *take care*, to *stop*, but I did not heed her. I ran across the first grass verge on the walkway, leaped the gutter, across the brick path and the second verge and second gutter. I had to stop for a moment then, for a coach came clip-clopping past. And then I darted across the street, towards the gate I had seen George enter. There I stood, looking up. He had climbed the staircase to the front door. There he was, pushing a handful of letters through the letter-box. It was him. It was truly him.

'George!' I shouted. 'George! It's me!'

He turned at the sound of his name. Looked down. Saw me at the gate. I entered the yard, ran towards the staircase. He flew down it two at a time. He gathered me into his arms. He squeezed me as if he would never let me go. He sobbed into my hair.

'George. Oh, George! I love you so. I love you, I love you, I love you!' The words came out in great blubbering gasps. I was sobbing and laughing and gasping for breath all at once, hugging him and feeling his arms around me and flying as he raised me up and swung me around and around and around. For the first time since that day in the rain I knew the meaning of perfect joy.

And then it all came crashing down. George placed me on my feet. He took a step back, the joyful smile melted from his lips, from his eyes. He looked up at the window and then at me.

'We – we can't do this – not here – not now. What you doin' here? Why you come? I don't understand – come.'

I followed his glance upwards – was that a shadow I saw reflected in the window-pane – a shadow retreating backwards into the darkness of the house? I shuddered, and tried to answer George's questions, but the words came out in an incoherent jumble.

'I had to come – Uncle Jim told me – I couldn't bear it any more, George! I just wanted you to know, to tell you – and then Papa was so beastly, and I saw the *logies* and I can't bear Promised Land, I don't want to live there, I want to be with you, I love you, and I ran away and, and, that letter you wrote me, it broke my heart and I had to come, I just had to! And then …'

George had grabbed hold of my hand and was pulling me out of the yard, all the time glancing up fearfully at the window.

'Miss, Miss …'

'Don't call me Miss, please don't, I can't bear it! Winnie! Call me Winnie!'

By this time we were out on the road. Auntie Dolly material-ized, pushing her round body between us. She grabbed George's wrist and mine and separated our hands. There was a wet stain beneath one of her eyes, as if she had been crying.

But suddenly she stopped, and stared at George. 'It's you? *You're* George?'

George's face turned to stone. 'Say nothing,' he said, and there was a warning in his voice I didn't understand. So, Auntie Dolly recognized him? From where, exactly? But Auntie Dolly had immediately pulled herself together, and launched into her stern-protective-mama role once more.

'This won't do. Y'all can't behave like this in public. You George should know that. You in't got no sense in you head? I should never-a bring the girl here. I should-a know you can't control youself. Young people these days! In full public view!'

George stared at her. 'And who are you?'

So Auntie Dolly knew him, but he didn't know her? A thousand questions crowded my mind, but all I did was answer his question.

'She's Auntie Dolly!' I said. 'I met her on the train – she knows the whole story – I told her. I spent the night with her, and …'

'Young man, you better get back to you work. People up in the house lookin'. Come, we gon' walk with you.'

We walked together to the next house. We stopped in a cluster before it, and George turned to me.

'We got to talk, Miss …'

I interrupted him again. 'I just told you … don't call me Miss anything. Winnie!'

'Winnie. We got to talk! But I can't talk now, people gon' see, it gon' cause big trouble. Can you wait till I got lunch break?'

'Of course! And then where shall we meet?'

'In the Promenade Gardens. We could find a private place there. You know where that is? Corner of Middle and Carmichael Streets?'

'I know where!' said Auntie Dolly firmly. 'I gon' bring she. But now you got to come wid' me, Miss Winnie.' She turned to

George. 'She don't understand. She don't understand one thing 'bout this. All she know is love. Ah me. Why I is such a weak-hearted ole lady?' She swiped her eyes, almost viciously, and I knew she had shed tears. For me? Tears of sadness? Tears of joy? I was on the verge of them myself, and I didn't know their reason either. In me was a jumble of emotions – that initial joy, so pure, so beautiful, was now alloyed with something dark and ugly, a kind of sticky, hollow dread; a sense of fear and insecurity, put there by the alarm I saw in George's eyes.

Did I really not understand, as Auntie Dolly had said? But I *did*! I knew very well that we white people did not usually marry darkies. I remembered Uncle Jim's warning; I remembered too the scorn with which Papa had spoken of him, Uncle Jim, so long ago. I know it was against the grain. But surely love would conquer all of that? What else mattered? Yes, I was too young right now but I would grow older, wouldn't I? Wasn't it important to declare our love now, while it was fresh and new and strong? Wouldn't it give us strength and courage to face the future? I was disappointed in George. I knew he had written that letter under Uncle Jim's persuasion, but there was no such force here now, and still he looked afraid. Even though he knew now that I loved him, that I had left home and hearth to be with him. Wasn't that enough? Why this cowardice?

George took both my hands in his now, and looked me straight in the eye. 'We'll talk about it,' he said. 'But not now. People watchin'. Come to the gardens at twelve o'clock – meet me at the Round House. You gon' bring her?' He let go of my hands and turned to Auntie Dolly, a plea in his eyes.

'Yes, I gon' bring she. Go back to you work. I gon' look after she till then.'

And then it was over. George turned away and entered the gate to that new mansion – bigger and better than the one next door. Mansions where 'my people' lived. The people I no longer felt a part of.

'George!' I called after him. 'I love you!' He turned only slightly, made a little wave of his hand as if to quieten me, and marched away, up the stairs to the front door.

I had never felt so lonely, so abandoned, in all my life. It was worse, even, than the day Mama sailed over the ocean. Something was very wrong about this love of mine and I didn't really understand what. Wasn't love meant to overcome all obstacles? Didn't it even say so in the Bible? Hadn't Mama drummed it into me since day one of my life? Yet I had lost her – my first great love. I could not, would not, lose this one too. Auntie Dolly took hold of my elbow and gently drew me away, across the street and into the walkway. We stepped onto the carpet of fallen red flowers and walked slowly on, towards the town centre. Auntie Dolly produced from somewhere another huge hanky, like the one she had given me on the train. She stopped me and dabbed my eyes with it.

'Don't cry, sweetheart. You got to be strong. Is not easy, but Mr George gon' find a solution. He look like a sensible young man. You can' do nothin' foolish. Remember what I tell you yesterday? All you got to do now is promise to wait for each other, and then you gon' see is much, much better. Tomorrow you gon' go home, to you people, an' …'

'But I don't *want* to go home! I want to stay here! I don't even have a home! I don't have any people! I hate it all! I can't go there! I want …'

Immediately her tone turned from comforting to stern, bordering on angry. 'What dis I hearin? 'I want, I want, I want.' When me own chirren come to me wit' '*I want*' I does tell them, '*I want never gets*'. An' is true. Only babies get to cry '*I want*'. You is almost a grown up girl. So stop this '*I want*' and '*I don't want*'! I know all-you white people think you could get everything you want, that you only got to say the words '*I want*' and it fall into you lap like in the Bible manna from heaven, like Moses in the

Promised Land. That is white-people thinkin'! An' it *wrong*! You got to think, what is *possible* an' what is *right*. That's the grown-up way. '*I want*' is for babies. An' lil chirren. An' white people. For them in them white Main Street mansions. So make up you mind right now, is which way you goin'. If '*I want*' gon' be you new gospel than we might as well go home an' let me pack you on the train today today. Cause I not gon' be helpin' no '*I want, I want*' white lady. No sirree.'

While speaking she stalked away from me now, at full speed down the red-carpet walkway. I scurried to catch up. I tried to butt in, to put in a defence, but she wouldn't let me.

'An' here me, thinkin' you gon' be sensible an' what you go an' do? Huggin' an' kissin' right there in white-people yard! An' that boy too! No sense in y'all head. No sense at all. I should never-a bring you here. I should never-a interfere. Oh me oh my. An them white people did see, I tell you! I see them at the window – one white lady peepin' down at y'all huggin' an kissin' in she yard. What was you thinkin'! You mad crazy out-a you mind, or what! 'An with him, of all people. Of all people. Like it wasn't bad enough, you white and he black.'

Chin in the air, she marched on, berating me all the time. It was all I could do to keep up. I grabbed her arm, but she flung me away.

'Auntie Dolly, please! Tell me! Who is he? How come you recognized him but he didn't know you? What …'

'Don't *Auntie Dolly please* me! You promise! You promise! You promise to behave youself an' then this You trick me into helpin' you to find him, an' then what you do, huggin' an kissin' in the middle of the road with the whole town watchin'! No, no, that's not what I bring you here for! I bring you here for a respectable and sensible discussion! That's what! Not this shameless behaviour! Middle of the road! I tell you!'

A woman pushing a pram, a darkie in a blue uniform and white apron, was walking towards us. She stared, frowning, at Auntie Dolly, who charged on, grumbling to herself. I took a step back to allow the woman to pass. I glanced into the pram; it was a white baby; the woman was a nanny. She looked at me as she passed, slightly askance, as if afraid to look me in the eyes. She gave her head a slight shake, as in puzzled disapproval. It's only then I realised what I had done: under the normal rules of etiquette, it would have been Auntie Dolly's role to step aside to make room, not mine. Anyone seeing the two of us together would assume I was the Young Lady and Auntie Dolly my servant; in which case I should be in charge, perhaps giving *her* a scolding for some transgression. Instead, the roles were reversed: the servant reprimanding the mistress, the mistress meekly stepping aside to make room for a darkie. I flushed, and hurried back to Auntie Dolly's side. I cried out:

'Auntie, I'm sorry, I wasn't thinking. Can you please *stop* because *you're* the one making a scene now!'

She did stop then. She turned and looked at me. 'Very well. I not gon' say one more word on the matter. But, young lady, I don't care if you is white or blue or green or golden: you got to obey me now. None-a this rushin' off to hug and kiss negro men. You understand?'

I flushed again. She had said The Word. I knew The Word. It contained a universe of contempt, scorn, and sheer revulsion. It was the second ugliest word I knew. Papa used it often, with palpable disdain in his voice.

Was I really that naïve? For me, George had always been a *darkie*. That was different. A darkie was a *good* person. Many of them were like family members. We girls grew up playing with darkies; they were our friends, our confidantes, people we grew fond of and cared about. Lovely smiley-faced people whose skin just happened to be dark. Darkies were respectful and respectable, well-behaved members of decent society. I had just happened to fall in love with one of them. You can't help who you fall in love with, can you?

*Negroes* were different. They were uppity troublemakers who made newspaper headlines. Sometimes when Papa opened his *Echo* at the breakfast table – it would have been delivered with the previous day's post, but he always saved it for breakfast – he would exclaim in annoyance. 'Those uppity negros!' he would say. 'That Brewster – who does he think he is? That's why they should never be given an education. When you give a negro a law degree you're asking for trouble.'

Negro, of course, was the polite word for those Georgetown troublemakers. There was another word, dirty, ugly, forbidden by Mama, though I had heard Papa utter it once or twice in agitation, long ago; she had rebuked him, but we had heard.

'Girls, you are never to use it!' Mama had warned us 'Papa made a mistake and that's that.' But we weren't stupid. We got the gist of it. Compared to that *other* forbidden word, negro was polite, yet bad enough, and we put the pieces together: down in Georgetown there were negros, who, unlike darkies, were not on Our Side. They were dangerous, rebellious, demanding; contemptible, vile and evil. Of course we had asked questions. 'Why?' we had asked, Yoyo and I, and 'What have they done?' But always Papa changed the subject. 'Don't bother your pretty little heads,' he would say, and turn the newspaper page.

And now here was Auntie Dolly, a darkie herself, calling my George, another darkie, by That Name. How could it be? I had to defend my George.

'He's not a Negro!' I cried. 'Don't call him that!'

We stood there, glaring at each other. It's a good thing the walkway was sheltered from the houses by those red flamboyants and the bushes between; it meant we couldn't be seen from the houses. But if anyone had passed by at that moment and seen us they would have stopped to stare. A young Englishwoman and her servant, blocking the path, glowering at each other; the servant arms akimbo, head pushed forward, frowning; the Mistress – for that is what I'd appear trying to look stern with a wagging forefinger, but failing desperately. It was a farce, and Auntie Dolly recognised it right away. She burst out laughing. Then she turned around, grabbed my elbow, and led me onward toward the Town Centre.

'So he in't a negro?' she said, in a friendly voice, as if truly interested in my opinion.

'What he is then?'

'A – a darkie!' I said, still belligerent. 'Darkies are *good!* They're just like us! They're not violent or – rude like negros. They're …' But then … I remembered now that Uncle Jim had reprimanded me for using the word 'darkie'. He'd called me patronizing. And now Auntie Dolly was lecturing me too.

'Stop right there!' She commanded, and I did. It was extraordinary, what authority she held in her voice. I found myself obeying her every order, bowing to her every wish. It had been that way almost since the moment we met.

'One thing you gotta learn, my dear, is that they in't no difference between darkie, Negro, nigger, coolie, buck, coloured, Mulatto, Quadroon, dougla, African, East Indian: whatever y'all want to call we. Because when you get down to the bottom of everything we is all in the same boat and, an' y'all is all in de other boat. In't no difference there far as I can see. Some-a we got education, some-a we got money, some-a we does own we own house an' we own business and some-a we is even lawyer an' doctor. But that don't make one lil pea-a difference. Because all a-we, every last one, light-skin-dark-skin, all a-we is down here, and all a-you is up there. An' the first thing you gotta learn, lil' Miss Lady Winnie, if you think you gon' love one a-we, is to get down off you high horse and come right down here wit' we. Because when you up there lookin' down you can't never ever even begin to understand. How can you love what you don't understand?'

What could I say to that? Not a word. Her little speech burned inside me. It churned inside me. I was blushing, and it started in my belly and spread all over my body – a deep red burning sense of shame and mortification, and a sudden glaring bright sense of realization, the knowledge of what she had said and what we had done and how wrong everything was and how right her words were and how guilty I was, we all were, and how horrible it was and how evil. I felt like sinking into the earth. Crawling on the ground. Prostrating myself before her and begging for forgiveness, on behalf of all my people, and for her absolution, on behalf of all her people. Instead I kept silence.

After a while I said, meekly and softly: 'Where are we going?'
'Peter Rose Street.'
'W-what's in Peter Rose Street?'
'Me daughter.'

❊ ❊ ❊

It was a half-hour's walk to Peter Rose Street. It seemed we had called a truce, because Auntie Dolly no longer lectured or scolded me; she chatted all the way there, telling me about her daughter Maybelle, married to a minor clerk at the Office of Lands, Mines and Forests (he doin' well for heself) and her son Jasper, a stevedore on the Georgetown wharf (if he didn't-a been so damn lazy in school he could-a get a better job.) She told me about their families, their worries, their daily lives. She spoke to me as if I were at last, a friend, an equal, and not just a spoiled runaway child she had to bend into shape. And mercy, I was grateful for that treatment. I had behaved badly enough for the day. And not wanting to spoil the mood, I didn't insist on her answering my question: *who was George?*

I understood now what I had done. I realised now that I had ventured onto treacherous land. I had plunged headfirst and eyes closed into a world of which I knew nothing, following only my passions and my headstrong will, without regard for the silent invisible currents of taboo and prejudice; I had broken rules built up over centuries, fiddled with an edifice of convention that at any moment could come toppling down on my head. I vowed to tread more carefully in future.

Her daughter Maybelle lived in a pretty wooden cottage behind a larger, more imposing mansion in a delightful garden. The cottage was as small as Auntie Dolly's, and young children played in the garden, just as they did at hers. Auntie Dolly introduced me to Maybelle and offered no further explanation as to my presence. She sat me down in a corner, and Maybelle offered me tea and biscuits, which I gratefully accepted.

Auntie Dolly followed Maybelle into the kitchen. I immediately stood up and followed them on tiptoe to the kitchen door, where I stepped aside so as to remain hidden. I knew, I just knew, Auntie Dolly would talk. And talk she did. Or at least, she whispered. They both whispered. And I listened.

'Is what going on?' Maybelle asked, her voice lowered. 'What you doin' wit' a white girl?'

'Shhh! Keep you voice down! Is some girl from a Berbice plantation – I meet she on the train. She got a sweetheart here in town and you never guess is who.'

'Who?'

'Theo X!'

'What! Mr X heself?'

'No other!'

Maybelle whistled, a long drawn out whistle. Then she said, 'I gone get some water from de vat – you comin'? Bring that bucket and help me, nah.'

I heard the creak of a door opening, and then diminishing footsteps on the back door steps.

My ears were burning, and I pressed my hand to my heart to calm it down as I returned to my seat to wait for them. Theo X? Mr X? So George had a secret identity in Georgetown? I remembered that his middle name was Theobald, so it made sense. Who was he? Obviously, he was well known … and even so obviously, I was not allowed to know more. I decided to play innocent for the time being. But I would find out more. At the very least, from Uncle Jim. For now, though, I had to behave.

Auntie Dolly and Maybelle spent a few hours exchanging news and gossiping. They both ignored me. I was no longer of interest. I was not the centre of attention. I was no more than a piece of furniture. I bore it as stoically as I could. My time would come.

After a while, Auntie Dolly, glancing at the clock, stood up, straightened her clothes, and said, 'Well, sweetheart, we gotta go. I gotta take this chile to the Promenade Gardens, an' I don't want be late. Was lovely talkin' to you. Bye-bye sweetheart.' They hugged and kissed. Then she turned to me.

'So, Miss Winnie. Is time to go. You ready?'

✳ ✳ ✳

## Mama's Diary: Plantation Promised Land, British Guiana, 1903

*Liebes Tagebuch,*

*We have had a most dreadful row. The first I have ever had with Archie – for mostly I hide my feelings, my thoughts, from him – and it was all so very public. Even the girls were present. I cannot forgive myself for opening my mouth – it was very indiscreet of me – but somehow I had to and the words of protest, of rebuke against my own husband, emerged. At the dinner table, in front of guests! So very wrong. And then, after the guests had left, we quarrelled deep into the night, and the girls heard. It is a disaster, an unmitigated disaster. Now it is all out in the open, though he does not know the whole truth, the truth of my 'friendship'. I cannot even confide in you, dear Diary. It seems too secret, so ultimately* verboten. *And yet – I feel no shame. Perhaps it was inevitable.*

*My life is crumbling into pieces. Music does not help. Nothing helps. Darkness is encroaching on me, and I do not know how to dispel it. That darkness I thought I had dispelled. Now it is back but a thousand times worse than before. No light anywhere. Not even a spark.*

*Before I am lost to the darkness I must instruct my daughters. They must know of the evil man commits against man. I have read to them the stories of slaves in America, and told them how evil this thing is. I have not told them that their beloved father is guilty of something very similar. I cannot break their illusion of him as the epitome of perfection, a Sugar King radiant in his glory, for that is how they see him. They adore him. How can I spoil it for them? I am in despair. What can I do?*

# Chapter Nineteen

There are two public gardens in Georgetown: the Botanic Gardens and the Promenade Gardens. Papa had often taken us to the Botanic Gardens, a sprawling haven in Georgetown's south-east corner. Green clipped lawns and sandy paths lined by beautiful palms, here and there a magnificent island of vivid colour; the brilliant reds and yellows of canna lilies, and of course roses galore. Still silent ponds on which floated the giant pads of the Victoria Regia lily; the Kissing Bridge humped over a stream, where, when we were small, Mama and Papa would inevitably lift us up and kiss us all, laughing. Then the Zoo near the entrance, which we always saved for last; the pond with the manatee. We always took bread for the manatee. If you stood at the edge of the pond and whistled he would rise out of the deep like some subterranean monster, and we girls would clap and scream in glee. What carefree, glorious days those were!

I had never been to the Promenade Gardens, located in the town centre, and much, much smaller than the Botanic Gardens. They occupied a neighbourhood block quite near to where we had first met George, with entrances on all the four streets surrounding it. Being smaller they were also more intimate – a warren of weaving sandy paths between islands bursting with colour, towering shrubs in full flower and tall trees strategically placed providing shade for people strolling by. Butterflies flitted from bush to bloom, and birds warbled overhead, serenading one another. A few people ambled through the garden; others sat on the wrought-iron benches enjoying a rest. It was an oasis of peace and calm.

In the centre of it all, in a large clearing, stood the Round House. Not really a house: it was obviously a band-stand, similar to the one on the Sea Wall where we often went as a family when we were in Town; but this one was bigger. Round, or almost round, it was like a pavilion, raised a few steps above the ground, with only an ornate wrought-iron balustrade around the sides. I could well imagine the brass bands that would play here in the early evening, drawing in the people who lived nearby. Good, decent, respectable people who knew the rules and kept to them. Not people like me, like us, who broke them.

George was already there. He sat on one of the benches around the clearing, nibbling at a sandwich. A glass bottle half-full with water stood on the ground at his feet. He sprang to his feet as he saw us, and, with a hasty look around to make sure no-one was watching – they weren't – rushed up to meet us, leaving his sandwich on the bench.

Auntie Dolly was on high alert. With one arm hooked into my elbow she clasped me to her side; the other arm she raised, palm outwards, warning him to slow down. He did; but she need not have worried. Though I longed to rush forward into his arms I now knew better, and he, not ambushed by surprise as on the earlier occasion, slowed down of his own accord as he drew near. My heart thumped palpably. My face felt as if it were just one huge smile. His certainly was, though his eyes were veiled by anxiety.

He came to me, and stood before me, and all that unease melted from the gaze that now seemed to swallow me up. Oh, how I longed to just let go, to fling myself at him, to be consumed by the love I saw there! I could only hope that my own eyes mirrored that love, and perhaps they did, because now it was Auntie Dolly who grew anxious.

'Two a-you, stop that! Stop it right now, you hear me?'

Stop what? We had not even touched! But Auntie Dolly was looking around in great agitation and whispering to us conspiratorially.

'Y'all can't behave like this. You can't. Somebody gon' see an' then all three a-we gon' be in trouble. Behave youself.'

George, then, came to his senses. He looked from me to her and his face lost that exhilarated expression – I was sad to see it go – and he said, 'All right Auntie. I promise to behave. But I need to talk to her. We need to talk. Maybe …'

Auntie Dolly pointed. 'There!' she said. 'Go down that way with she. Sit down on the bench and talk. I gon' stay here and keep guard. But only talkin, you here? No lovey-dovey?'

'I promise, Auntie!' said George. She turned to look at me.

'Well, Miss Winnie?' She frowned, and wagged a warning finger.

'I promise, Auntie.'

We walked off. 'And remember: you goin' right back home tomorrow!' she called after us. I said nothing to that.

We sat down on one of the benches, a foot apart. I folded my hands primly on my lap. I did not look at George. All of a sudden I felt shy. I had no idea what to say. The memory of rushing across the road, flying into his arms, made me blush – what had I been thinking? Not thinking at all, according to Auntie Dolly, or thinking stupidly. Maybe he thought so too, Maybe he thought I was brazen. Maybe he thought …

'Winnie,' he said, in a low soft voice. I turned to look at him.

'Yes?' We gazed at each other over a gap that seemed so much wider than a foot of garden bench. I realised that he was just as tongue-tied as I was, struggling to find words.

'I don't know what to say,' he said, and it came out almost as a wail. 'I – I was so happy to see you this mornin'. So happy. And yet, and yet … Winnie – I think about you all the time. I tried to forget you, I really did, but it didn't work and then you was there, were there, standin' at the bottom of the stairs. I'm sorry. I'm so sorry.'

'You're always saying you're sorry,' I replied. 'That's all you ever say. Are you sorry you love me, then?'

'No,' he said at once. 'No, Of course not! Lovin' you – is the most wonderful thing in the world but also I'm broken-hearted because …'

'But I love you too, George! I told you that! That's why I came to town, to tell you that because that letter you wrote me, it was so wrong! So very wrong! How could you even think of saying such horrible things to me? Do you know how you broke my heart?'

'Uncle Jim told me to write.' His voice contained a world of desolation. 'Uncle Jim said there was no hope for us in the world. He said I would only get you into trouble, bad trouble. He said I would ruin you with my love. He said your father …'

'Oh, fiddlesticks! That Uncle Jim – an interfering old man!'

'He's not! He's very wise and he knows what he's speakin' of. He and his wife …'

'But that's them and this is us! I don't care, you see. I don't care! I don't care what my father or anybody says! I hate my father! I know what he does! He's an evil, evil man!'

'Why you say that, Winnie? You got to love you parents! You is their child!'

'They don't own me! They don't own my heart! I'll love who I want to love! And now that I know what Papa is like I just don't care if he approves or not! In fact, all the more reason to disobey him and shock him and – and slap him in the face!'

'I don't understand. What he done to you, to make you hate him so?'

'Oh, nothing. Not to me, personally. But I saw – I saw what he does, what he did, to our coolies. I saw how they live. I saw him whip them, George! I saw it with my own two eyes and I couldn't bear it! And since then all I can think of escaping him, and you, and coming to Georgetown, and …'

'Winnie!' He spoke sharply now, which I was not expecting. 'Did you come to me to punish you Daddy? Is that all this is about?'

'No! No, of course not. I love you! I love you with all my heart, with all my soul and I wanted to tell you that. I had to tell you, and that's why I came. After I got your letter it's all I wanted, to tell you I love you, you see, I couldn't let you go on believing I was insulted. Loving you makes me so happy, George. It's the only thing in the world that makes me happy. You're the only one I want to be with. That's why I came – to tell you that and to be near you. I don't care what Papa does or what anybody thinks. And I'm not going back! I told Auntie Dolly I would but it was a lie. I only told her so she would help me find you, because I was late yesterday, you see, and didn't know what to do, and I almost gave up, and then I told her everything and she offered to help but only if I promised to go home, so I promised, but it's not true. I can't go home, George. I don't have a home!'

'Wait, stop.' He held up a hand to brake the avalanche of words. It was as if I needed to tell him my whole life story right there and then. I had not only found my voice, I had found my very spirit, and he needed to know. Know everything.

'I'm so miserable, George! I had to come. Being with you is all that makes me happy. I

want …'

'You can't always get what you want!'

He said it so sharply, almost belligerently, that I stopped right there. It was exactly what Auntie Dolly had said. About my expecting to get everything I wanted, just because I was white and privileged. To hear the exact words from George's lips – well, all of a sudden I felt a deep shame. It rose up in my being like a deep red blush that must have turned my face as red as a tomato. It silenced me completely. It was George's turn to speak.

'You can't,' he said. 'You can't just run away from home like that. You're how old? Fifteen? Sixteen?' I nodded. 'Well then. You're a minor. You can't do what you want for five or six more years. Your father has to give permission to anything you do. You can't just come to town and be with me!"

Oh, the embarrassment! To hear him put it like that – as if I made an indecent proposal! I shook my head in misery.

'I thought – I thought, I would get a job. Live in a hostel – there's a hostel for English girls, you know! And – and I could work, maybe in a bank.'

Lots of English girls worked in banks. Girls I knew – the elder sisters of my friends from the senior staff compound. They worked in banks until they got married. Barclays Bank, the Royal Bank of Scotland – those were good, decent girls. I could do that. Except that I was hopeless with numbers. But George didn't know that.

'You'd still need your father's permission, Winnie. You'll need it until you're twenty-one. Haven't you thought of that?'

I shook my head. Despondency brought tears to my eyes. I wiped them away with the back of my hand, and looked up at George.

'Please, George. Please! Let me stay! I love you so much!' More tears came. George produced a huge handkerchief from his pocket and handed it to me. I wiped my cheeks with it. It was wet not only with tears but with sweat: the sun was now high overhead, and though the bench stood in the shade my clothes felt like hot damp rags. Why did we women have to walk around in so many yards of clothing? I envied George his open-necked, short-sleeved shirt. I pulled at the high lace collar of my own blouse, and pushed the sleeves up my wrists. Auntie Dolly's dresses all had short sleeves. When I came to live in Georgetown I too would wear short-sleeved dresses and blouses. And no corsets and long underwear. And it was *when*, not *if* I came to Georgetown.

'I love you too,' he said, and his voice was gentle again. 'And that's why we really have to be sensible about this. And mature.

Uncle Jim is right. You much too young. It's too difficult. Winnie – I want you to go back home. You can't stay here.'

Another gush of tears. 'I hate my home!'

'But you have to go. Go back tomorrow. Promise me?'

I shook my head. 'No. I want to stay.'

'You with your 'I wants!' This time he really exploded. 'You don't see, Winnie, you behaving like a spoiled li'l girl – a spoiled li'l *white* girl! All-you think you can just decide things you want for yourself and then you can get them, just like that.' He snapped his fingers. 'But it's not that way at all! You want to get us both into trouble?'

I looked up at that. 'You'd get into trouble too?'

'But of course! What you think? A black man interfering with a white girl? You know in America, black men does get *hanged* for that? You don't read the newspapers, or what? You never heard of *lynchings*?'

'Oh!' is all I could say to that. No, I didn't know. All at once I felt stupid and childish. A long deep silence fell between us, a silence in which I felt like a piece of dirty clothing in a wash-tub, pounded and scrubbed by a pair of strong black hands. I edged nearer to him. One of my hands fell from my lap on to the boards of the bench. A few moments later the side of his hand touched mine. And then his hand was covering mine, then closed around mine.

Those clasped hands became to me an anchor in the sea of my tossing emotions. All at once I felt calm. The tossing ceased, and though I can't say I felt strong, I suddenly *understood*. I understood the full extent of the madness I had set out to accomplish. I understood the magnitude of my own utter stupidity. The magnitude of the risk and the danger and the divide between us. The fullness of the love that would close that divide, but which must remain hidden.

I squeezed George's hand to tell him I understood. He squeezed mine back. As at an invisible signal we both turned so that we sat slanting on the bench, facing each other; he raised a tentative hand and touched my chin, as faintly as if it were a butterfly's wing brushing past. He pushed a loose lock of my hair behind my ear. He gazed into my eyes, and I into his.

Footsteps scrunched on the path before us; it was Auntie Dolly, marching towards us with a thunder-darkened face. Hastily we drew apart; she stood now directly before us, looked from one of us to the other. Her frown faded. She too understood.. I had admitted defeat. The little girl that had been me had grown up in the space of a lunchtime break.

George looked at his watch, as if Auntie Dolly's approach had pulled him back into the real world.

'I got to go,' he said.

'Can't we – can't we meet again?'

He frowned, an odd expression in his eyes. I continued, stuttering a little.

'I mean – I mean, I know you have to go back to work but after work? I mean, can't we meet this evening, tonight, maybe? I only have to go back tomorrow. I've lots of time …'

*And it seems a shame to waste it*,' I wanted to say, but he interrupted.

'I don't have any free time,' he said. 'After work I got to mind my parents' shop, in Albouystoun. And … and tonight I got to … see some people.' I nodded, accepting. He stood up. He held out a hand; I took it and he pulled me up so that we stood facing one another. Simultaneously we glanced at Auntie Dolly, as if asking for permission. She snorted, looked around for possible danger, nodded slightly, and turned her back. Then George's arms closed around me, and he drew me to him. We embraced; a quick hug that said it all, then we pulled apart, smiling both. He kissed me on the forehead.

'I'll write,' he whispered. 'I'll write to you care of Uncle Jim. Go there whenever you can. You can write back to me through him.'

I nodded. There was a lump in my throat. No words came; not even goodbye. Now that it was happening, now that he was really leaving, I wanted to cry but I wouldn't. I would be strong. No longer a spoilt little girl who couldn't get her own way. I watched him walk away.

'You must be hungry,' said Auntie Dolly. Her voice was gentle and full of understanding, comfort even. I nodded. I only noticed it now, the hunger. It wasn't important, though, for it was nothing next to the emptiness now that George had gone. But I had to be strong. I had to remember.

'Come,' said Auntie Dolly. 'Let's go home.' She took her parasol from under her arm, pushed it open with a whoosh, and held it over our heads as we left the Promenade Gardens.

❄ ❄ ❄

Myrtle had cooked enough to feed an army: a huge pot full of cook-up rice, and a little chicken to go with it, and fried plantain, crispy golden on the outside. The walk back home had only increased my appetite and I ate ravenously, all the more because the food was truly delicious, quite unlike the English meals Mildred had been instructed to cook at home. Myrtle gave me second helpings, and seeing me enjoy her cooking must have melted her a little towards me, because when she spoke again there was no more hostility in her voice.

'You mus' be tired after all that walkin',' she said. 'Lie down and take a rest.'

I thanked her. I was indeed tired, and I did retire to my room – Auntie Dolly's room – to lie down, but the last thing I could do was sleep. It wasn't just the noises in my head that kept slumber away; it was the sounds that came in through the open window. Most of all, the murmur of Auntie Dolly and Myrtle as they conversed down in the yard. I immediately got up and walked to the window. I could not see them but I could hear them; they were at the tap next to the vat just below my window, washing dishes. Auntie Dolly was doing the talking. I could not hear what she was saying above the splashing of water and the clatter of crockery, yet I knew that once again she was sharing the news of me and my mysterious sweetheart.

More frustrated than ever, I returned to the bed, lay down, and tried to sleep. I couldn't. After a while, the whirr of Auntie Dolly's sewing machine in the gallery took over from the racket downstairs, and what with the squeals of children playing in the yard and my own chaotic thoughts, I could not even dream of sleeping. I got up and got dressed.

I was thirsty, and walked towards the minute kitchen. In passing a sideboard my eyes caught on a word written on a piece of paper, weighed down with a small wooden statue. The word that caught my eye was – *Theo.*

I looked around, listened. Auntie Dolly was busy sewing, Myrtle was in the yard. I picked up the paper, and read it. It was a notice:

*MEETING.*
*Saturday 20th July, 9.30 pm*
*Kitty Foreshore*
*Speakers: Dr Night, Theo X, Brother K, Boatman.*

I replaced the paper, entered the kitchen, drank my water, and went downstairs.

Myrtle had finished the washing-up and all the pots and dishes were on the back stairs, drying in the sun. She was now filling a huge wooden tub with water from the vat. She glanced up. I smiled. She smiled back, turned off the tap, and dumped an armful of clothes into the tub. I walked away, sat down on the front steps, and watched the children playing hopscotch for a while. The two older children were not present. I had heard their mother telling them to 'run off and help ole' Granny Rose with she cleanin'.' So they were working, like their mother and grandmother. George was working too. Only I wasn't. I was like the children, free to do what I wanted.

There was a hammock under the house. I settled into it and once again tried to doze off, but once again couldn't. This time it was not noise, internal or external, that kept me awake. It was the sense of uselessness, and restlessness that went with it.

I got up and walked over to Myrtle.

'Can I help?' I asked. She looked up, astonishment written so clearly across her face I wanted to giggle. And then she said, 'Yes, of course.' She rose to her feet and pulled a length of off-white cotton, dripping water, out of the tub.

'You can help me wring this sheet,' she said.

So together we wrung out the sheet, twisting and turning it this way and that until every last drop was squeezed out of it. As we worked we laughed – 'One more drop!' cried Myrtle, and we'd give one more big heave till several more drops fell to the ground; and then again, and again, until we truly could not extract one more drop out of that twisted snake of sheet. And Myrtle patted me on the back and told me I'd done a good job, and my heart swelled with gladness and lo and behold, the noises in my head had stopped.

We hung the sheet on the line together, still laughing together like a couple of schoolgirls. And then I helped Myrtle with the rest of the laundry – it turned out she was a washerwoman for Kitty's wealthier inhabitants – wringing out all the smaller pieces of laundry once they were rinsed, and hanging them on the line. And then I ironed some finished pieces for Auntie Dolly, using a huge heavy iron filled with red-hot embers, on a table under the house. And then I helped Myrtle to 'ketch a fowl for dinner' at the back of the yard, chasing squawking fluttering chickens back and forth. Watched as Auntie Dolly wrung its neck and plucked it. And then I bathed three squirming, squealing brown toddlers at the vat, using a sliver of Palmolive soap no bigger than a lime leaf.

'Them chirren more slippery than fish!' Myrtle called from the kitchen window, and I looked up and called back that I agreed; just as naked little Patsy slipped her arm out of my grasp for the fourth time. I couldn't very well confess I had never held a real live fish in my hands. And then the six-o'clock bee announced the endofday, reminding us that it was suppertime, and we ate together at the cramped but happy dinner table. I helped put the little ones to bed; they all, mother and five children, slept together in a bed that completely filled the second room except for a narrow passage between it and a built-in wall cupboard. Each one of the children hugged and kissed me and called me Auntie.

I had never been called Auntie before.

And then it was dusk and the *crapauds* began their chant of dissonant croaks, joined by the crickets and a myriad invisible bugs, reminding me of home. What was Yoyo doing right now, I wondered? Was she sitting on our veranda all alone, listening to similar sounds? And I realised I somehow did not care. She, and Papa, and everything at Promised Land, lived and moved in a different world to this, and somehow I had slipped into this alternate hemisphere as foreign to me as fish from fruit; and the strangest thing of all was the sense, deep and complete and immensely satisfying, of being perfectly at home, here, now.

Auntie Dolly, Myrtle and I settled into cracked wicker chairs in the tiny front gallery. The day's work was done. The sewing machine at rest, neatly folded pieces of half-finished garments arranged around it in anticipation of the next day's work. The noises in my head had stopped entirely – that permanent snivelling and wailing that for the last few months had been my constant companion. Auntie Dolly, it turned out, had a gift for telling stories, and tell them she did. I heard of Granny Rose and her pet monkey who was terrified of cows, and would screech in terror and hide up Granny's skirt as soon as one passed by. I heard of Uncle Arnold who gambled away every last bit of clothing at cards and came home naked one night to an incensed Auntie Jean, who hit him over the head with a wooden cooking spoon harder than she meant to, so that she thought he was dead and screamed down the village, till the neighbours came running and declared him only drunk and lugged him into her bed. I heard of the fearsome Old Maid Dorothy, once Most Beautiful Woman in Kitty, who had rejected one hundred offers of marriage and allowed no man to cross her threshold. Swell-Belly Bungo, a homeless old man with a club foot who slept under bridges and begged from door to door. Dr Danger, the village rogue, who had been in jail sixteen times. And a host of other Kitty characters who came to life that night for my entertainment. But engaging, and sometimes hilarious, as the stories were, as time passed by I started to disengage as I wondered what the time was. Somewhere nearby, a church clock chimed; I counted eight. Auntie Dolly said, 'Well, me dear, I better get up and do some more work. I got three dresses to hem this weekend and with all the galivantin' through

Georgetown …'

She moved over to a rocking-chair by the sewing machine and lit the kerosene lamp hanging on the wall, and in that dim light took up her work. She hummed to herself as she worked; I recognised many of the hymns we sang in church. I was left with Myrtle, who wasn't as entertaining a talker as her mother but did her best, asking me polite questions about Promised Land and telling me a little about her own life.

After a while Myrtle, too grew fidgety. I knew exactly why, and when the church clock chimed nine I wasn't surprised when she stopped speaking abruptly and stood up.

'Well, it's off to bed for me,' she said with an exaggerated yawn, 'Tomorrow more work waitin.'

'I'm tired too,' I said innocently. 'That was a long hard day!'

She raised her eyebrows, as if surprised. 'Really?' is all she said. I said goodnight, lit another kerosene lamp, and withdrew with it into my room.

❊ ❊ ❊

I had it all planned out. Yes, I felt guilty looking through Auntie Dolly's wardrobe but I did it all the same; I was, after all, an experienced spy. I found it; a back church hat with a veil. Cradling it on my lap, I sat on the bed and listened. A murmured conversation between Myrtle and Auntie Dolly drifted in through the open ceiling, but I could not understand a word. A few minutes later, I heard the click of the front door. That was my cue. I waited a few minutes, and then I was on my feet, tiptoeing through to the back door, slipping down the stairs to the yard, out the gate and down the road. Running, as fast as I could. I had to catch up with Myrtle.

I raced to Alexander Street and turned north towards the Atlantic. The street was quiet at this time, but I noticed that a few other people were walking in the same direction. I continued to run. Yes, it would draw attention but at this moment I didn't care, and finally I saw her ahead of me. Breathless, I drew up next to her.

'Hello, Myrtle!' I said.

She swung around, eyes open wide. 'Winnie! What you doin' here?'

'I'm coming with you – to the meeting!'

'The hell you comin' – pardon me!'

'I am too! Come on – don't stop!' I grabbed her forearm and tried to pull her forward, but she refused to move on.'

'Winnie, go back home, immediately! I ain't takin' you!'

'All right, then I'll go on my own!' I let go of her and marched away.

'Wait, wait!' She hurried behind me and, catching up, said, 'How you know about this?'

'You think I can't read? If you leave announcements lying around the house what do you expect?'

She groaned. 'Winnie, you can't come! People will notice you – you with you white skin gon' stand out like a ghost!'

'I already thought of that,' I said, and waved the hat in her face. 'See! It has a black veil. Nobody will notice me.' We were now walking briskly northwards, side by side.

'Mummy gon't kill you tomorrow,' she said. 'Why you can't just keep quiet and do as she says?'

'Because I need to know!' I cried. 'I saw that George – you call him Theo X, right? – is one of the speakers. What is he speaking about? Why all the secrecy?'

'You gon' find out soon enough,' she said grimly. 'You just better pray that hat protect you. People not gon't like to see you there. The situation precarious enough as it is.'

'I'll be invisible,' I promised. 'I just need to *know*.'

'White people!' Myrtle sighed in frustration, but at least she seemed to have accepted the fact that I would not be chased away. 'Put on that hat now!' she insisted, and I did as I was told. She pulled down the black veil, made sure it was in place, tucked the ends into the high neck of my blouse. 'Keep you hands in you pockets!' She ordered, and again I complied. 'All right. let's go.'

We walked on in silence. As we neared the coast more and more people appeared on the gloomy street, all making their way northwards. The street was dim, lit only by an occasional gas lamp, and the figures looked like sceptres as they made their way silently forward. As for me, I was tingling with excitement. I would be seeing George again! George, in a secret identity as Theo X! I was thrilled beyond words. What would he be speaking about? A lecture on Telegraphy, perhaps? But why hadn't he invited me, when we spoke that morning? I was determined to get close to him and reveal myself. How surprised he'd be!

By the time we reached the Sea Wall we were many. In single file we climbed the stairs to the Wall and down the stairs on the other side, to the beach. The moon was full, a glowing ball above the Atlantic that seemed near enough to touch. The tide was out, far, far away, and along the horizon a strip of ocean glittered silver. The entire world was cast in a ghostly pale light. A cool, gentle breeze wafted in from the Atlantic. Dark figures like silent shadows descended the wall and spread out across the hard undulating stretch of baked sand, each finding a place to sit, bending over to spread pieces of cloth on the beach, dropping cross-legged to the ground. In spite of the half-light I could make out that was a mixed crowd: men and women, old and young, Africans and East Indians.

I was the only white person, and I felt conspicuous, in spite of my veil, and the masking cover of night. I was also the only person wearing a veil, though many of the women wore hats or head-scarves. One or two people glanced curiously at me, but looked away again. As for Myrtle – she was now pointedly ignoring me. She had brought a small cotton square of cloth which she placed on the ground and signalled for me to sit down. I shook my head; it was hers. But she stamped her feet and raised a fist as if she wanted to cuff me and I hastily dropped to the ground and sat on the cloth. Myrtle herself sat on the bare sand.

The atmosphere tingled with suppressed excitement. People murmured among themselves, but Myrtle said nothing. I tried to listen to the conversation of a couple right next to us, but they spoke a very fast Creole and I couldn't understand a word. I did, now and again, decipher the word *Theo*. I wished Myrtle would speak to me. I had so many questions. But she remained stubbornly silent, her face turned away from me as if in protest, and I didn't dare provoke her further.

At last, the four speakers arrived, stepping gingerly through the seated crowd. The hum of conversation rose to an animated buzz; one or two people clapped, a few called out names: *Theo!* and *Bravo, Brother T!* My George was right there, dressed all in black. I felt a swelling of pride. My George! I glued my eyes to his beloved form.

The speakers made their way to the front, where the first one climbed up onto a raised platform of some kind. The crowd clapped, and some voices called out: *Dr Night!* We sat near the front, and I could make out that Dr Night was an East Indian, perhaps in his forties, though I never could guess the ages of adults much older than myself. But his hair was smooth, black and long, and shone in the moonlight. The clapping died down and he began to speak.

'Brothers and Sisters!' he began, 'We have once again gathered here to fearlessly proclaim our solidarity. The struggle is underway. We are the ones who will herald in change. We are the ones who will end the centuries of oppression in British Guiana. We are the ones who will put an end to the white man's domination …'

On he went. His voice boomed out, angry, aggressive. Dr Night was a gifted speaker, drawing out the crowd. Now and again he called for responses: Are you ready? *YES!* The crowd cheered. Will you put up with white domination? *NO!* It cried.

And as he spoke a dark cloak pulled itself around my heart and at last, at long last, I *understood.* I understood the rage and the frustration and the helplessness of these people. And I felt a smothering, overwhelming, agonizing sense of guilt. I realized that this society was divided cleanly into two; that there were two clear-cut sides, and that I, through no fault of my own, fell clearly on the wrong side. I was that oppressor of which Dr Night spoke! I was the *enemy!* Dr Night's speech was laced through with hostility, hatred even. He described the acts that had called forth that hatred: the injustice, the deprivation, the oppression of the people who worked in the cane fields and, here in town, in the dockyards and factories. 'My brothers and sisters, Indians and Africans,' he finished off, 'We are together in this fight, and we must link together, arm in arm. The white man has had his chance, and he has failed. The day of Massa must come to an end! *Massa day done!*'

*Massa day done! Massa day done!* The crowd took up the chant, jubilant as it clapped to the rhythm, contagious in its confidence. I felt my lips forming the words, my hands itching to clap – yet I couldn't.

How naïve I had been! What kind of meeting had I expected? A friendly cultural exchange? Shouldn't I have known it would be political? Did I live so outside the beating heart of my homeland that I was so unaware of this swell of protest? Had I not seen enough in Promised Land to know that there was more at stake than just a few hundred disgruntled sugar workers? Shouldn't I have felt, seen, sensed, known that the entire country was in revolt against us, a little white bubble at the top? And George, my George, my beloved – how idiotic he must think me, how silly and childish! Was he, too, full of hatred for my race? How, then, could he love me? What would he say? My heart began to thump almost audibly as the chant died down and Dr Night stepped down from his box and handed the megaphone to George – and George stepped on to the box raised it to his lips.

'My beloved friends, brothers and sisters,' he began, and a cheer went up, louder than any reaction Dr Night had brought forth. And I realised: this crowd knew and loved my George.

But what a difference! George's speech was not angry. There was no hatred in it. It was cool, calm, and reasonable. It was historical, yet laced through with humour and goodwill. He told the story of the absentee European planters exploiting British Guiana's resources, both human and economic. Wealthy men with, George said, enough rum to turn all the water of the Thames into rum punch. 'All Londoners could get drunk on our sugar!' he laughed, and the crowd laughed with him. George spoke calmly of the slave trade, which was followed by indenture. He painted word-pictures of Africans brought over in overcrowded ships, bent low in the fields, whipped and abused. Contract workers, lured from their villages in India to what they thought was a Promised Land, only to find themselves under the boots of their masters, unable to escape, unable to return home.

'While my brother Dr Night represents the sugar workers up and down the coast,' said George, 'I am here to speak for the dock workers, the factory workers, Georgetowners. You can all, every one of you, come to me with your troubles; any time of day or night. I am yours.'

*Yours,* he had said. The proverbial penny finally dropped. And at last I knew George, knew the secret side of him that had till now been veiled from me, because I would not see it, ensconced as I was in my sweet little bubble of privilege. I saw, now, what drove George, and it was not love for me, no matter how much he loved me – and I knew he did, but I also knew that that love would always, must always, come second behind this other, greater, more serious love. Young as he was, George had a Calling, and this was it. His voice vibrated with it. In that voice was a greatness, a grandeur, a mission. This was the real George. I could not divert him away from that. This was why, back in Promised Land, he had seemed so ambivalent. It was not through lack of love for me, or cowardice, but through the knowledge of how deeply, how incorrigibly, our paths fell apart from each other. We were on two sides of a wall. My choice was to give him up, or join him on the other side of that wall.

'Brothers and sisters, I'd like to finish off with a song,' he said then, and a muted cheer went up – it seemed the crowd knew what that meant. George bent over and someone handed him an instrument, a banjo. He held it to his chest, plucked a few strings. Someone held a megaphone to his lips, and he began:

*I believe, the darkest night will turn to day,*

*I believe, that we below, will find a way,*

*Every time I take a breath I know our prayers will see us through,*
*will make us free, there will be joy, for me and you,*

*I believe, I believe ...*

By the time George had finished the three verses of his song I was in tears, rivers of tears, silent tears that flowed unhindered, the tangible melting of every last frozen piece of my soul. His voice was exquisite. Deep and true and resonating with such warmth and strength it caused my whole being to sing too, to be caught up with his and sing with him, if silently. George was musical! Why had I not guessed that before! As the final chords of his song died away a deep sadness replaced the jubilation that had swept me into a private heaven. I wiped away my tears. My childish dreams crashed to the ground, I felt lost, abandoned.

But I had to see him. I would see him, speak to him. He had to know – know what I now knew.

George was speaking again. 'I'm afraid I must leave you now; enjoy the rest of the evening,' he said. 'Brother K and Boatman have important things to say.' He placed the strap of the banjo over his head, pushed the instrument around to his back, stepped down from the box and handed on the megaphone, and to a storm of applause stepped through the seated crowd back towards the sea wall. This was my chance. I leapt to my feet. Startled, Myrtle pulled at my skirt but I snatched it away and stumbled more than ran towards George.

He and I arrived at the wall simultaneously.

'George!' I cried, and lifted my veil. He stared. 'Winnie!' he said. 'What on earth ...' 'George,' I repeated, 'You were wonderful! Marvellous! And George, I want you to know, you're right, about everything, and I believe you and understand. I truly understand. I won't stand in your way. I'm with you!'

'Winnie, you can't ...' he began but he stopped and turned, his features frozen as if listening intensely. From faraway down the beach, the muted sound of Brother K speaking. But that wasn't it. I listened too, and then I heard it. The unmistakable clatter of horses' hooves, far away yet, down the Sea Wall road.

But even before that thought had registered, George had grabbed my arm and was running, dragging me along with him. 'Run, Winnie, run!' he cried, letting go of me, and I lifted my skirts and ran as fast as I could behind him. He was heading towards a group of fishing boats moored on the beach about thirty yards away from where we stood. We arrived, and before I could even gather my breath he lifted me into his arms and heaved me up and over the side of one of the boats. He too was breathless, and his words came in gasped groups: 'Winnie, you're just the most exasperating, the most stubborn, headstrong – I don't have words! What made you do this? Come here?'

'I love you!' I bleated.

'Love! I don't *care*! Winnie, there's no time for love. Children are starving! This is *serious*!'

'I know! That's what I wanted to …'

'No time to discuss now. Get down. Hide under that seat. Keep your head down and be quiet. You understand?'

'Yes, yes.'

George, mild, sweet-natured George, was a different man tonight: strong, commanding, in charge. I ducked down, crawled into the space under one of the boat's seats as George ran off.

But not for long. I couldn't resist: cautiously I emerged again and peeped over the edge of the boat. George was a black shadow racing towards the crowd. He reached the edge of the seated group, stopped. He seemed to be shouting something, and gesticulating, shooing the people away. Immediately the people sprang to their feet and began running, some to the west towards Georgetown, some eastwards. Scattering, fleeing, dissolving into the night. By this time, the mounted police – for that was what the clattering hooves had been – had arrived, jumped from their horses, and policemen were swarming over the wall, racing behind the scattering hordes, calling out 'Halt! Come back!' One policeman fired shots into the air, but no one stopped. A few policemen raced after the fleeing shadows, but they were too late, too far behind.

Only George did not flee. They caught him. Both arms held by two officers, he walked back towards the Wall. There they stopped, and, it seemed, interviewed him. I saw him clearly. He appeared so calm. I could even see that he was smiling. At one point he twisted around to retrieve the banjo, held it up, and even, plucked a few strings. How courteous, how confident he looked, standing straight and tall, chatting with the policemen as if just minutes ago he had not taken part in an obviously forbidden political rally! My heart swelled with pride. He was so young, and yet already a leader. A great leader.

But all his words seemed to have no effect, for a minute later the handcuffs came out and George was being led away. As I cautiously watched from the rim of the boat, a hard lump rose to my throat. Was this my fault? Was I, through that irrepressible ardour that seemed to always run away with me, somehow, responsible for the trouble George was in? And though reason told me no, that I had nothing to do with George's arrest, I knew without a doubt that the guilt I now felt was visceral, instinctive, based on far more than tonight's events. It was a collective guilt, and it would follow me for the rest of my days. When all was quiet I made my way back to Auntie Dolly's. I could not tell if Myrtle was back yet, and I did not check to see. I threw myself, clothed as I was, onto the bed, buried my head in the pillow, and sobbed.

That was the night when everything within me shifted, rearranged itself. When I finally *grasped* what my life was about, which course it had to take. Life could never be the same. I grasped the thing that George had hinted at, that Uncle Jim had warned me of, that Auntie Dolly had spelled out to me in crystal clear letters.

The wall between me and George was so high it was insurmountable. Not even the greatest love could cross that barrier.

❋ ❋ ❋

The next day I returned to Promised Land without incident. I travelled First Class at Auntie Dolly's insistence, caught the steamer, and arrived at Emily Stewart's house just in time to be picked up by Poole. I stepped into the motor car and back into my old life.

❋ ❋ ❋

## Mama's Diary: Plantation Promised Land, British Guiana, 1902

*Liebes Tagebuch,*

*From bad to worse. I have taken now to exploring the plantation and I have seen the evil with my own eyes. I have seen those dreadful logies. I have seen even worse. I followed my husband into the fields, on foot. He could not see me coming as the canes were high, above my head, and he did not look back.*

*There is a place, not too far into the fields, a clearing with a few coconut trees, breaking the monotony of the flat endless fields. I heard a commotion there and I crept up on them, hidden by the canes. I saw it all. A man, a coolie, stripped naked, tied to the trunk of a tree. My husband, my Archie, whip in hand, lashing and lashing and lashing. The man's back was striped with bloody welts, and still my husband lashed on. I could not watch for more than a few seconds. I turned and ran, coward that I am, and once I had gone a little way I stopped to vomit, and then I threw myself to the earth and wept.*

# Chapter Twenty

Back at Promised Land no one noticed a thing. Perhaps I was an excellent actress – me, who Papa had always accused of 'wearing her heart on her sleeve'. Perhaps we were all too wrapped up in our own little worlds to notice any change in each other. As for me – I worried about George. Was he in prison? If so, on what charge? Had he lost his job? Or had they let him go in time? I worried for days, waiting for my chance to get news. At last, that chance came: one day when Miss Wright was away and Yoyo was out riding with Maggie I seized the moment: grabbed my bicycle and sailed down the road to Uncle Jim's.

There was a gathering of workers under the house, a meeting of some kind. One of them, a young, bare-chested Indian, stood talking to others sitting on the ground, gesticulating. He looked familiar. From the gate I could not hear what he was saying, but I could tell he was agitated. No-one had seen me yet. Then the dogs stormed the gate barking and they all turned around to stare and the speaker fell silent. Uncle Jim, who had been sitting on a bench carving a piece of wood, walked over to hush the dogs and to open the gate, and even as I walked in, all the Indians stood up and walked out. And as they passed by me each one threw me a look of such hostility I wanted to sink into the ground.

I recognised the speaker: it was the man called Bhim who had harangued George that day at the post office. And now I realised one more thing: it was the very man Papa had whipped. His bare back was marred by scars, black stripes where Papa's whip had slashed it. No wonder he was hostile towards me! I flushed with guilt. It was as if I, personally, had delivered those welts.

Uncle Jim had already received news. George was fine. He had been released from police custody early on Monday morning with no charges. He had been late for work and reprimanded, but otherwise his life was back to normal.

'So now you see,' said Uncle Jim, 'why I wouldn't let you call him a coward.'

'Yes,' I whispered. I felt two inches tall. 'I understand ... you must have thought me so silly and arrogant!'

'Not at all,' he said, and patted me on the shoulder. 'Just young.'

❊ ❊ ❊

In the following months I wrote to George as frequently as I could. I poured out my heart to him. I exposed myself completely. 'I'm sorry,' I wrote in my first letter. 'What a silly little girl I must have appeared to you! I didn't understand, George, and my only excuse is that I've lived under my father's protection and influence all my life and I could never even begin to feel what life is like on the other side. It was a life of ignorance, and I am ashamed of it.

'It's that ignorance that drove me to run away to Georgetown – I blush now at the very thought of what I did, how ridiculous, how childish! And yet so much took place in that short time – so much! My eyes were opened, finally, George. Forgive me! I do love you, but in just a few days I have grown up and grown into a new understanding – one that will give me the patience and the endurance to survive my life on Promised Land, as well as prepare for whatever the future holds in store for me. You have changed my life around, George. My love for you has reached a deeper, more solid foundation. I have become a woman.'

I signed the letter Winnie X. How could I be a Cox, now that I knew what that name meant? Now that I knew the cruelty, the oppression, and the tyranny associated with that name? No, it had to be reduced to X. X was the real me, the real Winnie. Besides, George too, had a secret life. The real George was Theo X: we already shared a surname! Besides – X was a kiss – just one.

I brought the letter to Uncle Jim, and let him read it; it was important that he, too understand the change in me. He nodded, folded it, nodded at me in approval, and replaced it in its envelope. 'I'll make sure he gets it,' he said.

Ten days later, I collected a reply from George.

'Winnie, I do love you, and I'm glad you see now the hurdles in our way. It's more, far more than the fact of our disparate worlds: you saw what I am doing in Georgetown. You saw that I am bound up in something I cannot turn my back on. Can our love overcome this? Can it last? Is it strong enough? Everything in my heart screams yes; yet the reality of my role, and yours, screams no. That you now understand speaks volumes, and I am glad; had you remained that innocent, naïve and reckless girl I knew from the plantation we would not have had a chance. All I can say is this: write to me, Winnie! Let me know you through your words. If I cannot see you, hold you, at least I can meet you in the freedom of mind, reach out to you in spirit, and feel your response between the lines of your letters. I don't know where this will take us; I only know I cannot let you go. Not yet. Just one thing I beg of you: destroy my letters once you have read them.'

And that is what I did. More letters came; I read them at Uncle Jim's, and immediately burned them, and I watched the flames devour each one while the flame in my own heart grew stronger and steadier. I lived for George's letters, and I lived to reply to them. I lived for this back and forth in which we poured out our hearts to each other in a way we had never done in speech, for we had never had the chance, the time. Paper is patient, they say, and on paper I bared my soul to George. I told him of my happy childhood, of my closeness to mama, of my music and my ultimate disillusion, the crashing down of the idyll. George's letters, too, were long; he told me of his family, of his childhood in Georgetown, and finally of his Calling. George had a gift for words, both spoken and written, and on paper used them with the same eloquence that had won me on the Kitty foreshore. He signed his letters George X. That X was our secret code, our lives joined. Those letters kept me alive.

❊ ❊ ❊

Yet how I languished in isolation on Promised Land! How I longed to actively move my life forward! So when the chance came to pull some weight of my own – why, I jumped at it.It happened a few weeks later. Uncle Jim and I were sitting, as we had at my first visit, in the gallery. All the windows fronting the room were wide open, so it was as if we sat in the open air, but the high trees outside the windows kept the sun out and the breeze sweeping through held a fragrance of some sweet blossom. Aunt Bhoomie – for that's what I called her later, once I got to know her and understood that her silence was one of intimacy, not of distance – brought out a tray on which stood two long glasses of passion-fruit juice. I took one and looked up at her, smiling in gratitude. With Aunt Bhoomie words seemed superfluous; she emitted a sense of comforting self-sufficiency that made me feel I had known her forever, that all that had to be said had been said. I sipped at the juice and turned to Uncle Jim.

'Five years! Five whole years. It is as if I have to hold my breath for this time. The suffering is almost *unbearable*,' I complained. 'This endless waiting, hiding my true self away, playing a role in my own home.' When he did not reply, I muttered on.

'Pah!' he said. 'You really call that suffering? *Unbearable* suffering? Really?'

I pulled myself together immediately. 'No. I'm sorry. I shouldn't have said it's unbearable. I can bear it. I *will* bear it.'

'I'm on your side, Winnie. Bhoomie too. I understand: you're impatient an' frustrated. But you got to learn to wait.' He chuckled. Aunt Bhoomie drifted back to the kitchen.

'Five years seems like eternity when you're young,' he said. 'When you get ol' like me is quick like this.' He snapped his fingers. 'An' you goin' be a changed person at the end.'

'But I don't want to change!' I cried. 'I can't love him any more than I do now!.'

'Pah!' Uncle Jim scoffed. 'At your age, nobody knows what love is. Love changes, and grows. Who knows. You might find someone else.'

'I won't! I know I won't!'

'Give someone other boy a chance, Winnie. Don't shut down all the doors. What 'bout them young men in the senior staff compound?'

For the August holidays had broken. The August Holidays! Year after year we sisters had looked forward to those weeks with the excitement of children waiting for Christmas. The August Holidays meant days and evenings spent in the senior staff compound, where all our friends were finally back from school: one or two from their boarding schools in England, some from their boarding houses in Georgetown, some, like Emily Stewart, from their term-time homes in New Amsterdam. In the past these were days of fun and laughter. We had the freedom of the compound all to ourselves; deep friendships formed one year, only to dissolve over the months of separation, and new alliances formed the next year. We girls met boys; always under the well-chaperoned auspices of each others' parents, of course, yet still, we fell in and out of love, exchanged knowing glances, giggled and tittered and wondered who we would marry. .

Not so that August. That August, Emily Stewart appointed herself my very best friend, and I let it happen. It was a protection. Emily alone knew of my excursion to Georgetown, and of course she longed to know the details. I told her only that it was unsuccessful; that my love was impossible, and that I must forget him. But our shared secret drew us together, and frankly I enjoyed having one friend on earth of my age and my background who knew even a little of my heart. Emily knew why I was indifferent to the flirting approaches of some of the more eligible boys. She knew why I acted shyer than ever before. She took me under her wing, and I was glad to be there. I longed to confess fully to her; but some instinct held me back.

❊ ❊ ❊

Otherwise, life went its old boring way, with a few changes. Yoyo and I drifted further apart. She seemed determined to put the past behind her, to forget the shocking scenes we had witnessed in the blinding light of our awakening. She, who had been most passionately affected by the squalor of the *logies,* who had been ready to tear the whip from Papa's hands herself, had to all appearances forgiven him all and returned to being the carefree, headstrong youngest daughter who bantered and argued with him at the dinner table, laughed at his weak jokes, and teased him for the shape of his moustache. I could not understand it.

Between us, too, everything had changed. There was now a barrier. A barrier I had placed by keeping the greatest thing in my life a secret from her. How could I ever tell her about George? How could I tell her about the roller-coaster ride between euphoria and despair I had travelled along since that day at the post office? How would she ever begin to understand, she who scoffed at the very idea of romance, and dismissed my love-story novels as drivel? I couldn't. To do so would be to dishonour that love by dragging it through the mud of her scorn. As the days and weeks passed I learned to play the part of myself: of Winnie, the dear quiet elder sister, reticent, always smiling, always supportive. But beneath the surface of that Winnie, a thousand feelings, insights and perceptions struggled for a final form. The real Winnie, the woman I was meant to be, was taking shape just as a caterpillar becomes a butterfly within the concealing hull of its cocoon, out of sight from the world.

But the biggest change to life at Promised Land was the arrival of Clarence Smedley.

❀ ❀ ❀

I loathed Clarence Smedley at first sight. I loathed those beady blue eyes that inspected me up and down as if I were a prize cow at auction. That self-satisfied guffawing at his own weak jokes. The way he strutted through Promised Land as if it already belonged to him, with us, Yoyo and me, as its appendages, up for grabs. His slimy ingratiating voice when he and Papa conversed at dinner. His oily smirk whenever Papa mentioned *future developments*. His unctuous assumption that he was the prize bridegroom; that our politeness was veiled attraction; that our reserve towards him was a 'feminine game of hide-and-seek.'

For of course Yoyo detested him too. 'He's worse than I ever imagined!' she whispered to me the first evening, and in that at least we again found common ground: an alliance of abhorrence. We no longer joked about marrying him. That dismal prospect was too near to home; how could we giggle about an outcome that everyone treated as a finished deal?

Uncle Jim liked to tease me about Clarence Smedley. 'Sounds like a good match!' he said, with a playful twinkle in his eye.

'Don't joke about it!' I said, 'Papa really believes I should marry him!'

'So you gon' let he marry some other girl,' said Uncle Jim, 'and allow your inheritance to slip through you fingers?'

'What do I care? I can't wait to turn my back on Promised Land. I hate it. I hate everything it stands for. I don't care about any inheritance. And anyway, Yoyo and I've already inherited – when our grandfather in England died he left us both a trust fund which we come into when we're twenty-one. Mr Smedley can have Promised Land. All I want is George. All I'm afraid to lose is – is George's love.'

'That might happen,' Uncle Jim conceded. 'It *could* happen. Just like *you* might stop loving *him* ... No, don't bother to protest ...' I had opened my mouth to say that *that* would never ever happen. I shut it again.

'Is better to face reality than to run from it. When you're young emotions can be as strong as a hurricane. While they're there you think that's all there is in the world, that nothing else can ever exist, and you want to hurl yourself into its vortex and be swept away in your euphoria. But hurricanes pass by, Winnie. They're as fleeting like they strong.'

Suddenly he dropped his stick, grabbed my shoulders. He shook me, and cried, 'Winnie, wake up! Come to your senses! Jus' wake up – oh, damn it!'

I let myself be shaken. I simply hung limp and looked at him without speaking. He let go of me, almost flung me aside. Then he spoke again.

'Waiting might sound boring to you. But it's the only thing that'll work. If after five years, you both have found your feet again and stand up straight and look each other in the eye and still say *I love you*, then I'd say you've got something real there. Real love is quiet. It's what remains when the storm pass. And it's strong; and trust me, you goin' to need strength. Because if the day comes that you can be together, that's the day the real storm will come and it will be from outside, not from inside, and if you want to survive it you'll need to be able to stand straight and steady. Or else it'll destroy you.'

'How can I bear it – out there with Papa and knowing – knowing ...'

❊ ❊ ❊

Papa! How can I even begin to describe the collapse of every daughterly affection I had ever held for him! The pain of discovery, as I realised that what I had once adored had been only a mask, one he had worn at home for our appreciation and applause. Oh, I did not doubt his love for us was genuine: Papa was a family man, and we were the centre of his world. But the face he presented to us was not the real one, and the image he had cultivated for our benefit was little more than a role played on a stage. The guilt I felt at being his daughter consumed me.

'You can't help the circumstances of your birth,' said Uncle Jim. 'You can't help being his daughter. You're not responsible for the things that go on there.'

'But …'

'I know it's not fair. The East Indians see you as their enemy, even though you've done nothing yourself. You can't change that.' He must have been reading my thoughts. I was about to remind him that the Indians *did* hold me somehow responsible. To them, I was on *the other side,* the wrong side.

'I don't want them to hate me! I want to help them! I'm on their side! Really I am!'

'That's a good place to be,' said Uncle Jim. 'But you can't expect them to fold you into their hearts. You'd have to prove yourself in order to that.'

'How can I prove myself? How can I help?'

'Winnie, you're …'

'Don't say I'm too young! Don't treat me like a child! Yes, I know it was childish to run away like that but I learned my lesson and I grew up so much when I was in Georgetown and I've thought about it a lot and I want to help. I truly want to *help*. There must be something I can do? Some little thing – so that people, Indians, can trust me and know, and not look at me like that, as if I were some, some white devil or something.'

Uncle Jim didn't reply right away. He just looked at me. He looked at me in a thoughtful, quiet way, as if sinking into himself and not really thinking about me at all but listening to some other voice, not mine; almost as if he hadn't heard. Then he stood up and walked to the window and stood with his back to me. The minutes ticked by. I thought he had forgotten me. Perhaps I had said something of such extraordinary stupidity he was lost for words. I began to get nervous. I reached out and grabbed myself a handful of peanuts from the bowl Aunt Bhoomie had left on the table. I cracked open the shells and ate the nuts one by one, still waiting for Uncle Jim to come back and sit with me and talk.

At last he returned. He sat himself down opposite me and reached for a handful of nuts himself. He casually cracked open the first one.

'There *is* something you can do, Winnie. If you really mean it. His voice rose with the question. My heart gave a little spring.

'Yes, yes of course! Tell me! What?'

'Is just a little thing. Is not at all dangerous for you. I wouldn't-a put you into any danger; you know that. It's a small thing. But still – it'll be a solid proof of your loyalty. Whether it's there or here. Can you do it?'

'Well, just tell me what it is and you'll see!'

'Listen,' said Uncle Jim. 'Just listen.' He stopped there. I didn't understand. I waited for him to continue but he didn't.

'I'm listening,' I said. 'Go on!'

'No. That's it. I want you to listen. When you're at home, keep you ears open and listen. Let us know what your father is thinking. If he planning repercussions to – to any of the actions – let us know. Can you do that?'

'Of course I can! Why, that's the easiest thing on earth!'

'I don't think you understand,' said Uncle Jim slowly. 'It will mean disloyalty to your own father, your own blood. It goes against your own interests. Because if the labourers get what they want – well it's not exactly what your father wants, which is more and more profit. You'll be turning against him. It's a question of family loyalty. It will make of you a sneak. It's – no. No, I can't ask that of you. Forget I ever asked. I'm sorry. I wasn't thinking.'

'No, no wait! Of course I can do it! Of course I will! I understand! I know what you mean! You want me to be a spy! A spy, not a sneak! Why, that's the most exciting thing I've ever done! I'd love to, if it will help!'

'You will? Really? That would be excellent! Just excellent! Brave girl!'

'No, not brave at all, just a little less cowardly! I'd love to do so much more and I would if I could!'

'You can't.' Uncle Jim's voice was firm and absolutely final. 'But that's already a lot. And I want you to know, Winnie: the Indians mean no harm – no physical harm, I mean, to your father or his property. They don't want to overthrow him or destroy the plantation. This is their livelihood. Their work. They came here to work and that's what they want. All they want is better conditions. Better wages – wages they can live from and support their families. Better housing. You've seen the *logies,* I've heard, so you know. They want medical care, and education for their children. If those demands are met there will be peace. Until then – there's a big fight ahead. And if you want to show whose side you're on …'

'I do! I will! I'd love to! Thank you! Oh, I don't know what to say – thanks for giving me the chance, for trusting me!'

❋ ❋ ❋

And that was how I became a spy against my own father. There are people who will point at me and curse me; blood is thicker than water, they'll say, and what I did was despicable. Sneaky. To them I say: there is a relationship of the heart, and that is thicker yet than blood. My heart cannot be with those who are cruel, who oppress, who whip and kick at helpless people. Rather, my heart must be with the underdog. They are my brothers and sisters. To them, I must be loyal. That was the reasoning behind what I did.

And truly, it wasn't much. As ever, Papa never brought business to the dining table. He and Miss Wright discussed mostly foreign politics: the worsening situation in Europe was the topic of the day and Yoyo and I listened, but Europe's politics were hardly of interest to me. Europe was on the other side of the world. I cared only of what was going on right here, under our very noses. That, now, was my job.

The only time I was able to report to Uncle Jim on anything of substance was when Papa had guests, owners and senior staff from Promised Land or the other Courantyne plantations, and occasionally even from Demerara and Essequibo. After dinner Papa would take the men to his library and then the serious talk began, and my job. It was easy, so easy. The front veranda could be accessed from any of the downstairs rooms; all I had to do was draw one of the wicker chairs near to the library, whose windows and veranda doors stood always open. All I had to do was sit there, as if enjoying the evening breeze. Just as Yoyo and I used to do, when we were younger.

How could Papa ever suspect anything? I was that docile, introverted, romantic girl who took no interest whatsoever in business or politics. I was that harmless daughter who dreamed away her days. If ever the men came out with their rum-swizzles and cigars to stand on the veranda and talk, they would merely glance at me and smile or remark on the lovely evening or the beautiful moon, and sip their drinks and puff on their cigars … and talk.

Up to now I had always shunned the politics of the sugar industry. It had indeed been men's business – boring talk of labourers and profit margin and export and grinding charges. It had nothing to do with me. I'd basked in my persona of romantic dreamer who cared only for the beautiful things in life: poetry, and art, music and flowers, novels and love. Now all those things dropped away and I listened. I listened carefully and secretly. In listening my awareness grew. The more I learned of the sugar industry and the history of its workers the more I understood that only a man of no conscience could stay at its helm. It was as if the Papa I had loved had been a mere coating made of some fragile substance. Truth had cracked that outer coating and it had fallen away to reveal the real man behind it; a man of cruelty and hardness whose only care was for profit; a man lacking in all the sensibilities that were the essence of humanity. I judged his morals, and found them deficient. In my heart I turned from him in disgust. Yet on the surface I continued to play the part of the Sugar Princess, the role he had assigned me. And behind it all I plotted.

I would play this role. I would play it to the best of my ability. No-one must suspect the truth. Not Papa, not Miss Wright, not Yoyo, not Emily Stewart. I would go through all the motions expected and required of me. I would play their shallow games and join in their false laughter. It was a waiting game, dictated by necessity, and by my youth. It was a life in abeyance. I played croquet on the lawns of the Senior Staff Compound and all the while I yearned to catch a Demerara fowl. One day, I would.

❊ ❊ ❊

But between my stolen visits to Uncle Jim and the occasional nights listening to Papa and his fellow planters on the veranda and days splashing about in the senior staff pool or playing tennis with my would-be friends and being friends with Emily Stewart there was the sheer emptiness of life at Promised Land. Of course, in these August holidays there were no lessons to fill the days. Papa had sent Miss Wright to stay with family in Barbados, for a holiday, and Yoyo and I were set free to do as we wished. Yoyo, very much at home with Maggie McInnes and the other young people in the senior staff compound, led her own social life.. I read books, practised the violin, and dreamed of the future. I made simple, inconspicuous changes to my life, such as never again calling the Africans darkies or the Indians coolies or the house servants 'boys' and 'girls'. I was slowly, gradually, becoming a new person. But I was bored.

❄ ❄ ❄

Then one day, I remembered the paper with the Morse code that George had given me so many months ago. It seemed an age since I had brought it back home from the post office, still flushed with exhilaration. Then, I had been so caught in the throes of emotion I had completely forgotten it. I'd put it at the back of one of my drawers, where it languished unseen.

One day that August I remembered it. I brought it out, and unfolded it. I sat at my table and tapped out a few words, just my finger on wood. George's name. My own name. '*I love you,*' '*Wait for me.*' And many such silly things. Just trying it out, getting back into practice. After a while I got up and searched for Mama's sewing basket. I found her silver thimble and slipped it on. Then I searched for a suitable hard surface, and came upon the china plate beneath the jug of water standing next to the basin on my wash-hand stand. I experimentally tapped my thimbled finger against the plate: instead of the dull thud of flesh on wood, the satisfactory *clackety-clack* of metal on china. I smiled, and took the plate to my desk. I had created my own Morse key.

Before the holidays were over, I not only knew all the letters of the Code by heart, I could tap them out with some speed. I wished there was someone I could send messages to and receive them from! I closed my eyes as I tapped, and learned to 'read' the tapping sounds as easily as I could read written language. Learning all this somehow brought me closer to George. It was my link to him, however tenuous; it was our secret language, and even though we could not actually speak in it, just knowing that we shared this language was enough.

❄ ❄ ❄

And so it came to pass that one October evening, I was sitting on the veranda as usual, all on my own, sipping at a sundown swizzle, listening to the silver chorus of night insects and the soothing rhythm of faraway drums when a strange thing happened. I could *understand* the drums, the faint throbbing that came from Dieu Merci. Involuntarily, heir thump-thump-thumping made sense to me, formed words I could hear as easily as I could read a book.

'STRIKE ON PLANTATION ROSE HALL MONDAY,' said the drums. 'EVERY DAY PLANTATION STRIKES EAST UP THE COURANTYNE COAST.'

I sat up straight. The hair on the back of my neck stood on end. Was I hearing right? Yes. I was. The message repeated itself, again and again. There was no mistake. And then the same message, louder, this time coming out of our own *logies,* was carried on the Atlantic breeze drifting over the cane fronds, to be heard by anyone who could read this language. Fifteen minutes of that, and then, faint again, another set of drums took up the same rhythm, further down coast. Glasgow Plantation. The message had passed on to the next plantation.

And then I laughed. I laughed so much I almost fell off the chair. So this was the big secret! Papa and his friends had always wondered at how well coordinated the strikes and demonstrations and even riots were that plagued the Courantyne Coast. Sometimes the strikes would move swiftly along the coast from one plantation to the within two hours of each other; the Indians would simply lay down their tools and not work for a few hours on one plantation; no sooner had they started work again, than the next plantation, miles away, would stop work. Or sometimes, the entire coast would stand still and the workers would march to the owner's house, chanting their demands, using the same words down in Albion at one end, as in Skeldon on the other. How did they communicate, Papa and his cronies had wondered. Now I knew!

✳ ✳ ✳

'I know,' I said to Uncle Jim the next time I saw him. 'It's the drums.'

He looked at me suspiciously. 'Drums? What you mean.'

'You know what I mean. The drums, at night. The Indians – that's how they communicate. Isn't it? It's Morse code.'

When Uncle Jim smiled his whole beard tilted upwards at the sides. He said nothing at first.

Then. 'All right. If you clever enough to figure that out you deserve to know the rest. Who you think teach them?'

I didn't have to think for very long. 'George.'

'Right. Your George. Why you think he came up here in the first place?'

'Because Mr Perkins retired?'

'And why you think Mr Perkins retired? Just so we could get George up here for a couple months. It wasn't too easy – we had to find representatives from all the plantations who could read and write English, to teach them the code, and then we had to get expert tabla players from all the plantations up and down the Courantyne, and teach them to drum the code, so that it sound natural.'

'Isn't it risky? What if someone from plantation management knew the code, and figured it out, just like I did?'

'A risk we had to take. Not too many people know the code. And not too many English people clever enough to sit down when night fall and listen to the drumming. To them is just coolie noise. It would-a been safer to send the messages in Hindi or Urdu but we'd-a had to figure out some whole new code since is a different alphabet. So it had to be Morse.'

'Anyway, it's brilliant,' I said. 'Papa and his friends just don't understand how well coordinated the protests are. And to think that George – George …'

'And that's another reason why George so confused 'bout you. You're not only on the wrong side of the racial divide, you're a Cox. You belong to them up there. The Sugar Kings. Them in those big plantation houses with they English lawns. The Bookers and the Coxes and the Davsons and the Campbells – all-a them Sugar Kings. You understand a little better now?'

I nodded. I did. 'But *you're* a Booker.'

'Right. But a black-sheep Booker. I got a long history of pro-testing Booker politics. Standin' up for the workers. Marryin' a black woman. Not playin' the Booker game. I already show whose side I on. You, now ...'

'All I ever did is run away to Georgetown like some foolish love-sick schoolgirl,' I said, and I had the grace to blush at the memory. 'But I'll prove myself, Uncle Jim! I will; I promise! I know I haven't produced much useful information yet. But may-be one day I will. I mean it. I really mean it.'

Uncle Jim patted me on the shoulder. 'You'se a good girl,' he said. 'You take after you mother.'

'You knew my mother?'

'Met she once or twice. But anyway, everyone know 'bout she. People does talk, you know. She was good to the servants. For a white woman, she was good. Got a good reputation with the Africans and Indians. A good woman; got a good heart. I was sorry to hear what happen. About the lil' boy.'

'She never got over it. And then she abandoned us.'

'It must-a been hard for she, to know what goin' on here, and not bein' able to change anything. Just like you. Or, you jus' like her.'

'Except that I *will* do something, Uncle Jim. I *will* take a stand. For George. I'll prove myself to him.'

He patted me again. For a moment I even thought he was go-ing to hug me, but he must have changed his mind. But certainly, he was moved.

'Do the Indians know? Do they know I'm on their side?'

'I told them you support their cause. I din't tell them the other thing. Spyin' is secret business and got to stay secret. But they trust me an' if I say you is all right then is all right. But you is the Massa daughter, Winnie. That's a hard thing to overcome.'

'I'll overcome it,' I said.

✳ ✳ ✳

One day I was able, at last, to deliver some news: useful, but devastating.

'Uncle Jim,' I said, 'They've got a spy. An Indian spy. I don't know who he is; they refer to him as *our boy* and never mention his name. I believe he lives in the *logies;* he's not one of the inner circle. But there's definitely a spy.'

'Hmm.' Uncle Jim said. 'Keep listening. Keep watching.'

But for all my listening and watching I could not find out the identity of the spy.

By this time I felt more at home than ever with Uncle Jim. He was certainly more a father to me than Papa, and a girl does need a strong old man in her life; a man who can guide her and help her find her way. Uncle Jim was my support, the only one I had in those empty years. His home became my home. His family, my family. I met his adult children over time, Gladys's children: Rose and Amy, Peter, Michael and David, all of them living in Georgetown. One son, Andrew, was studying in London. All of them accepted me, and even the Indians, who came and went, people who worked on the plantation, now sometimes smiled and waved when they saw me. I was earning their trust.

Not Bhim, though. Bhim, I eventually learned, was not a labourer. He was an educated Indian whose parents were labourers on our Promised Land; he had no apparent source of income but, I learned, he wrote for and edited a small protest newspaper that was circulated in Georgetown and on the plantations, which was strictly forbidden by the colonial authorities. Bhim continued to hate me. I could see it in his eyeswhenever he saw me. No matter what I did, Bhim would always hate me for no other reason than the accident of my birth.

Bhim's motherthough, liked me. I met her several times at Uncle Jim's: a thin, tired woman who looked twice her age. So proud of her eldest son: he who had escaped the drudge and the struggle and the sweat of indenture by winning a scholarship and climbing the ladder of education. Bhim had attended Queen's College, just like George. George had probably known him; they looked the same age. In fact, George *must* know him, as both were friends of Uncle Jim. Once I was married to George, Bhim would accept me. He would have to.

❋ ❋ ❋

## Mama's Diary: Plantation Promised Land, British Guiana, 1906

*Liebes Tagebuch,*

*I am pregnant! I have made some calculations and it is all wrong – on the other hand, it is all right. I only hope this child will be born early, as the others were. If not, if it is full term, there will be a lot of explaining to do – when actually there is no explana-tion. It is all so simple. Yes, I am guilty of the most shameful sin and yet I feel no shame. Perhaps this child will be my salvation. I feel a spark of hope. Maybe he will pull me out of the darkness. Maybe he will give me the courage to start a new life. That 'he' slipped out voluntarily – Archie has longed for an heir for so long, I automatically think of my next child as a boy. How ironical, if it is a boy, at last, the heir Archie longed for, and yet not!*

*Whatever it is, boy or girl – it means change. I must find courage: the courage to leave this place of darkness, even if it will cause scandal. Will I take my daughters with me – move to George-town, buy a house with the money I have inherited? I don't know – I only know I cannot stay here. I must start a new life, a new family! I will teach my son to be a good man. That is all I can do. That is all a mother can do – raise the next generation to be better than the last. A noble task indeed! All my hopes are now pinned to this child. He will save me, save us. What will Archie say, what will he do when he finds out? Right now, I do not care. I only know that I have found hope. It is over.*

# Chapter Twenty-one

I survived those two years as in a waking dream. It wasn't real, this life; I could not be real! It was not for me! I was only playing a part, and one day it would all be over and I would sail off into the horizon to be the one I was meant to be. People are entitled to their dreams, I suppose. But then they need not complain when they are given such a pinch they wake up to find everything crumbling around them into small pieces and they know not where to turn. In my case, it was Yoyo who delivered that pinch. I did not see it coming.

Yoyo and I had drifted completely apart, each of us living in a world of her own, locked away from the other. I was aware that she had secrets, but really, I wasn't interested. Nothing about Promised Land interested me anymore, except for the work that I did to undermine its existence. It was a tainted paradise, and I lived only for the day I could escape. But all this time Yoyo was growing up, changing, developing her own ideas, cultivating her own future in her own way. She was now sixteen, a beautiful young woman who in a different life would have been the darling of the London season, coming out to a flurry of flirtations and marriage proposals. But here on Promised Land everything was different. She could have had her pick of any of the young men coming of age in the senior staff compound, but Yoyo was clever and ambitious had always looked down her nose on romance.

I might even have seen it coming, if the very notion of it had not been such an atrocity.

It happened on one of those occasions when Clarence Smedley had come over for dinner. This happened on a regular basis, now. In spite of his dissolute ways – for he was as much a drinker, a gambler, and as louche here as he had been in London – he had over time learned the basics of plantation management, and Papa was pleased enough. I suppose he provided male company for Papa: serious conversation, the discussion of politics, cigars, drinks, cards; the kind of after-dinner entertainment that makes men feel like real men. It is very possible that I was the last to know, because surely Mr Smedley had dropped hints along the way. Be that as it may,

on this specific evening, Yoyo, who had been particularly quiet all through the meal, suddenly spoke up.

'Papa!' she said, during a pause in the conversation. 'I have an announcement to make.'

Papa, who had just told a rather silly joke, looked up at once. Yoyo was still his favourite, and when she spoke he listened.

'Yes, dear? What is it?'

'Rather,' said Yoyo, '*We* have an announcement. Clarence and I. We're engaged to be married!'

I almost fell off my chair. My jaw dropped and I sat there staring at her in stupefaction.

'Darling! Wonderful! Congratulations! Congratulations to you both! Oh, that *is* marvellous news – though I can't say it wasn't to be expected. Smedley, you rascal, I knew you were up to something! Yes, I knew. Oh, well done, well done. I thought it would never happen, and you did too, didn't you, at first? But didn't I tell you? 'Girls like to play hard to get,' I told you, didn't I, over and over again. 'Persevere,' I said. 'Try harder'.'

He turned to me at that moment. 'I hope you aren't too disappointed, Winnie. By rights it's your turn to marry first. But you have only yourself to blame – if I remember rightly you were not particularly welcoming – well, let's not talk about that. Yoyo it is, and nothing could please me more. This calls for celebration! Mildred! Mildred!'

He rang his little brass bell and Mildred came bustling out of the kitchen.

'Yes, sah?'

'I believe we must still have a bottle of champagne. Go down into the store-room and have a look. Bring out the champagne glasses!'

Miss Wright had turned to Yoyo – who was sitting next to her – and was warmly shaking her hand and whispering some congratulatory words; their two blonde heads were bowed together, and Yoyo was smiling and nodding.

Mr Smedley sat next to me, chest thrust forward, grinning smugly about the room, inordinately pleased with himself. I sat there like a statue, stiff and speechless. I stared at Yoyo, trying to catch her eye, but she was still preoccupied with Miss Wright. Bile rose in my throat. I wanted to scream, to storm, to pummel Mr Smedley with my fists to wipe that smirk form his face. It could not be! It could never be!

'Winnie!' It was like a whiplash. I turned to Papa and finally closed my mouth. 'Your manners, Winnie!'

'Oh,' I said. I raised my hand and turned to Mr Smedley.

'Congratulations,' I said. My voice was as listless as a damp floor cloth. My hand hung limp in his as he pumped it. I met his eyes. They were beadier than ever, lit up by a self-satisfied leer.

'Sorry to spring this on you,' he whispered hoarsely. His breath smelt of stale rum. 'Yoyo thought it was best. You looked shocked; but you did have first choice, you know. I wasn't going to wait around forever.'

My stomach twisted into a knot. I jumped to my feet; my chair fell over and crashed to the floor. I ran to the door, flew out into the hall, vaguely aware for a split second of three pale faces staring at me in shock. I was never the one to create scenes; that was more Yoyo's forte. But she had had her little scene, and it was too much for me to bear. I raced up to my room. Footsteps clattered behind me: Yoyo was hard on my heels. Reaching my room I slammed the door in her face, but she pushed it open and barged in. I flung myself on to the bed, face down.

'But why? Why, why, why? *Why?*'

With every 'why' I pummelled the pillow. I had to punch something, preferably someone. Yoyo, or Papa, but best of all, Mr Smedley. Him, I longed to punch until he was black and blue all over, a walking bruise. I had never, in all my life, hit anybody, or had even wanted to do so; Mr Smedley had pushed me to a level of exasperation beyond anything I'd ever known before.

She, the author of all this rage, sat calmly on the rocking-chair next to the window, facing the bed.

'Let me explain,' she said for the fourth time. 'Winnie, just listen …' But I wouldn't. I wouldn't let her speak. Winnie, the quiet, paragon of virtue (or so they thought), was beside herself with rage. Yoyo was now the meek one, pleading for my ear.

'Nothing,' I glared at her as I spoke and I hoped my eyes were every bit as fierce as my voice. 'Nothing in the world could excuse such a thing. Mr Smedley! Mr Smedley, of all people, Mr Smedley! You know what he's like. You detest him! And you're going to marry him? Him? How could you, Yoyo. How could you?'

'I'll explain,' she said for the fifth time, and this time I didn't interrupt. I was breathing heavily now but my ire had exhausted itself. I still could not imagine any good reason to marry the detestable Mr Smedley, but I was just too tired to protest further.

'It's to save Promised Land,' said Yoyo. 'We always knew, didn't we, that one of us would have to.'

'Well, of course I know Papa's plan,' I replied. 'That's obvious. Marry the heir so that the plantation stays in the family. I just didn't realise how much you wanted to be Queen Sugar. That's you'd whore yourself to get there.'

'Winnie! That's not fair! You still haven't heard me out! You're jumping to conclusions! Just listen, will you!'

'You don't love him, do you? You can't love him!'

'Of course I don't! Don't be silly! You know what I think of love! I think he's just as horrible as I always did. But ...'

'His hands on you! His lips on yours! Revolting!'

I shuddered, shaking my head vehemently to rid it of the ghastly image.

'I'm strong,' said Yoyo. 'I can take it. It's worth it. See, I want sons – two of them, at the very least. And then Promised Land will be ours again. Winnie, don't you understand? It's all a plan. It's a good plan. Listen!'

Something in the gleam in her eyes as she leant forward to take my hands cut off the caustic comment I was about to make. Sons! Heirs! It was like one of those awful history lessons Miss Wright was always pushing down our throats, where the only point of marriage was to continue the bloodline. We had always scoffed at such marriages. And now this. But I let her talk.

'You see, Mr Smedley has no backbone. He's a slithering, spoiled weakling. He has no guts, no character, and no ideas. My plan is to marry him and then hold him in the palm of my hand. He's besotted with me; he won't even see what's happening. I can do it, Winnie. I can. Then I'll take control of Promised Land. I'll encourage Papa to return to England, to retire. You know he wants to. And when he's gone I'll run it. And once I run it, well, I can do everything we said we'd do. I can change things, Winnie. I know I can! I can run the estate!'

'You! But – but you're just a ...'

'Just a girl. I know it. But I'll be a woman one day, and who says women can't run an estate? I know Papa would never teach me himself but you see, my plan is big, Winnie. Really big. I'm going to learn everything. I'm going to go to Georgetown and take a course in Business Management at the Government College and …'

'Georgetown! You want to go to Georgetown?'

'Yes – for a year, till we get married. I'll take a course, and … '

'They'll never let you. Papa will never let you. And only boys study Business.'

'I can deal with Papa. As for the course, I've made enquiries. That is, Miss Wright has – she supports my plan entirely, you know – and they have accepted one girl already. So why not me?'

'So, you told Miss Wright, but not me?'

'I had to tell her. I needed her help. And why I didn't tell you – well, I knew how you'd react. And I was right. Winnie – forgive me for keeping secrets from you. It's just that – I knew you'd disapprove. I know your thoughts on love, and marriage, and all that …'

She was going to say 'all that rubbish' but I wouldn't let her.

'Because love and marriage are wonderful, beautiful things! And what if you do meet someone and fall in love? It could happen, you know. What then?'

'Oh, you mean a *grande passion*! I wouldn't mind having one of those, one of these days. But I won't let it upset my life. I'll take him as a lover, that's all.'

I shook my head. This was, to my ears, almost blasphemy.

'What about Mama! Didn't she always, always teach us about the power of love? That love was the highest, the greatest, the most wonderful thing on earth? I mean, everything I believe about love, I got from her. Those beautiful stories: she and Papa, in Vienna …'

'If anything, it's Mama and her example that showed me what nonsense all that is!'

Yoyo's voice was hard now, and grating. Her eyes, so warm just a minute ago, were now cold as a glacier.

'All those lovey-dovey stories of how she and Papa met and fell in love and defied their parents in order to marry. All that dancing to the Blue Danube – remember? Like a fairy tale. And that's all it was. There was never any love. It was just some kind of sentimental emotion and it fled at the first opportunity. Where's love in that, Winnie? Where's love, when a mother can stop loving her daughters just because one little baby dies – stop loving them to the point of actually *deserting* them and running back home to her own mummy and daddy? All that talk about the power or love – just empty talk. Sentiment. Stupid. I swore long ago never to let love influence my decisions and I'm keeping to that. I swore never to marry for love. A marriage is nothing more than a business arrangement. That's what I'm doing, Winnie. My wedding to Mr Smedley – actually, I call him Clarence, now – is just a contract. Once I sign it, I'll be working myself to the bone to be head of this plantation. And there'll be some sweeping reforms, I can tell you! I still can't believe what Papa did to Nanny. Because if anyone taught me about love, it was her.'

I could say nothing to that.

'But he's such a – such – I mean, haven't you heard? He runs after all the African and Indian women. He's got bastards with them. He's …'

'So what? All the senior staff men have darkie bastards. Papa's got a few, for that matter.'

'Don't be ridiculous!'

'Oh Winnie! You're so – so utterly naïve! You're such a child! I can't believe you're two years older than me! You live in some perfect little dream world – you've no idea! Of course Papa has his fun with the servants and labourers! They all do! Don't you know what men are like? How do you think he's managed all these years without Mama? Do you think he's some kind of a – a monk, or something? You're the ridiculous one. You really should grow up.'

I bit my tongue so as not to say what was on my mind. Instead, I took a deep breath. 'In some ways, maybe,' I said instead. 'But at least I have enough self-respect not to marry a man for profit.'

She turned on me then, eyes blazing. 'You, with your romantic dreams! Your stupid sentimental dreamy ideas of love! You don't even begin to understand. This is about *change*. It's a plan. You've probably forgotten everything we talked of that day, that day when Papa whipped the coolie. You've forgotten, haven't you? Remember how we said we'd change the whole plantation? Well, I haven't forgotten. One of us *has* to sacrifice herself. And it *has* to be me. It couldn't ever be you. Maybe you hate what's going on with the coolies as much as I do but you've just put it to the back of your mind and one of these days you'll fall in love with and marry one of those Booker boys and close your eyes to what's going on and raise a horde of children and nothing will ever change. You were never one for action, Winnie, and I don't mean it as a criticism. People are different, and you're a soft feminine woman who will always fit in and goodness knows, there's nothing wrong with that. You'll make some man a wonderful wife, a wonderful mother to his children. But I'm different, Winnie! I've always been different. I want to change things. I want to help the coolies. I want to make a name for myself in British Guiana. Women can do great things just as well as men, and I want to be that woman. I want to change history! I don't suppose you'll ever understand that, but it's just the way I am.'

'Yoyo, I …' I was bursting to tell her. Everything. To refute her condescending judgment of me. To let her know that I too, in my own way, could be an agent for change; that I too had secrets and plans and that marrying some Booker boy and settling into a life of placid convention was the last thing on my mind. I was a spy, against my own father! I was part of a brewing revolution that came from the coolies themselves! I was aiding and abetting that revolution because they trusted me! I was harbouring secret plans to drop out of all the privilege granted me by the accident of my birth and to start again from the very beginning – that I loved and was loved outside of my race and my class and that that was as revolutionary a thing as anything she would ever do through this repugnant marriage.

But I held back the words. Betraying even a small portion of the task would be to play with fire. Yoyo was unpredictable – as evidenced by this whole Clarence Smedley development! – and I had learned through cruel experience that the wrong knowledge in her hands, coupled with her volatile nature, could be disastrous. So I swallowed my pride and her insults and instead picked up another of the bombs she had dropped.

'Where will you live in Georgetown? I mean, have you talked it over with Papa? Does he agree to it? He was always so against the two of us going to school in town!'

'Yes, but we're older now. Grown up, almost. I haven't told him yet, but I will soon. And trust me, he'll let me go. I'll make him.'

Oh, I trusted her to make him, certainly.

'And I'll come with you!'

'*You?* What'll you do in Georgetown?'

I smiled to myself. If only she knew! 'There must be some course I could take, too. Maybe not business, but history, or French, or something.'

'There's that finishing school some of the senior staff girls go to,' Said Yoyo. 'Miss Yorke's. They learn things like etiquette and running a household and art and music. That sounds good for you. I'd love you to come! I didn't think you'd want to – you have seemed so – satisfied these last couple of years. As if you'd made your peace with the way things are and you're just waiting to get married. I never thought …'

More insults, but I put them behind me; from her perspective she was right, and from mine as well. These last few months my waiting, waiting, waiting for the age of maturity had become a mere passive counting off of the days till I was 21, and legally able to marry whom I wanted. I had made up my mind to wait, and it had never occurred to me that there might come a time and an opportunity to leap ahead of myself. Georgetown! To live there, with Papa's permission; to see George now and then! He would still have to be a secret of course, until the time was right, but oh, how much happier the waiting would be!

'Of course I want to go! I'd like nothing better than to get away from this – this …'

Yoyo leapt to her feet then, reached for my hands, pulled me to my feet.

'We're going to Georgetown, Georgetown, Georgetown, to start a new life, life, life!'

She threw back her head, delirious with laughter, caught hold of my waist and danced a jolly polka round the room, I laughed too as I swirled with her, but all I could think as she sang was, '*I'm going to George, George, George!*'

❊ ❊ ❊

## Mama's Diary: Plantation Promised Land, British Guiana, 1906

*Liebes Tagebuch,*

*It was indeed a boy. I use the past tense because he did not stay with us. He was born early and from that aspect my secret was safe, but he was weak and after a week he died in his sleep. And with his passing every last sliver of hope has departed my soul. The darkness has taken over completely. Nothing but black. It is like being in a deep dark pit where I cannot see, and however much I scratch at the walls to escape I cannot. I know I need to live on for the sake of my daughters and that is the only thing that prevents me from jumping from the top window of our home. I am no longer a mother to them, trapped as I am in this darkness. I cannot even speak to you. I don't know when I will write to you again, if ever. I take refuge in music but it does not help. Nothing helps. I fear this is goodbye, forever. How melodramatic. But I have reached the end of everything.*

*All I have left are my daughters; but I can do nothing for them. The only thing I can claim is duty; I must stay with them for the sake of duty alone, and that is the only thing that keeps me going. They have my physical presence but nothing more. I know that my Winnie especially suffers from my withdrawal and yet there is nothing I can do to be the mother she needs. Kathleen and Yoyo are different, more independent somehow. Kathleen dreams only of England, and Archie will send her there one day. Yoyo has learnt to cling to Nanny. I am grateful for Nanny's presence – if I can even speak of gratitude in this state. But Winnie! The way she looks at me! The pain in her eyes! I can see it there but I can do nothing about it. I cannot come back to her. I am no longer her mother, but just a body that resembles her mother but without a soul.*

# Chapter Twenty-two

At the next opportunity, I slipped out of the house grabbed, my bicycle and flew down the path to Uncle Jim's. Breathlessly I told him the news – that not only would Yoyo be marrying the loathsome Clarence Smedley, but that she also had ambitions to be the manager and to make the required changes.

'So, you see,' I said, 'it's good news! The labourers will eventually get the changes they want. Yoyo is quite determined! She will be a kind mistress, Uncle Jim. I know it! Though I admire her immensely for the enormous sacrifice she is making in order to do so – I know I certainly couldn't! Marrying that lizard! But it means the labourers can hope for improvements. It will take a few years, of course, but change WILL happen.'

'Hmm,' is all Uncle Jim replied. I was disappointed; he seemed to doubt me.

'It's wonderful news, isn't it?'

'We shall see,' is all he had to say.

'Of course, it's only one plantation …'

'Exactly,' he said. 'And there's no telling what power will do to your sister.'

'Oh, you needn't worry about that!' I cried. 'She'll be a wonderful estate owner! After all, she's a woman – perhaps that's exactly what we need, more women at the helm! Women will be kinder!'

'Women can be just as cruel.'

'I don't believe it! At least, not Yoyo! She's sincere, I promise you! And she wants to see the labourers treated well. But the best thing is that we'll both be moving to Georgetown! Isn't that marvellous! Yoyo and I have already asked Papa's permission, and he has given it! So I'll be able to see George whenever I want to!'

'Winnie, no! No, no, no. Don't talk like that. Don't even think like that. Just because you'll be in Georgetown, it doesn't mean that anything has changed. You cannot see George whenever you want; you cannot be seen together. You cannot risk a scandal at this point!'

'I don't *care* about a scandal! Let people talk!'

He took a deep, audible breath, as if he was completely fed up with me. 'Do you care about putting George into danger?'

That silenced me. What a selfish, spoiled little girl I was, thinking only of myself! I vowed to improve. I vowed to be careful, to protect George. To put my own needs aside, and to wait.

But there was one more thing I needed to say. 'I'm sorry I won't be able to spy for you any more, Uncle Jim. Not that I produced much information.'

'Don't say that! You did. You were an enormous help. But you know, Winnie – there's one more thing you could do. Just one.' He paused.

'Go on!'

'Well, I don't like asking this of you … I asked you to just listen, and this requires a little more than just listening …'

'Yes?'

'A telegram was delivered to your father yesterday. Mr Perkins told me. We need to find out what it said. If important information about our plans has leaked to the estates. Especially now, when so much is at stake. We need to know …'

I smiled, and winked. 'I've been listening to the drums!' I said. 'I know what's going on!'

He put a finger on his lips. 'Shhh! Not a word more. Now, I wonder if you …'

'… can go into his study and find the telegram, read it and report? Of course I can! I'll do it!'

✽ ✽ ✽

Papa was still out in the fields, Miss Wright was in her room, Mrs Norton had gone to the village, and Yoyo and Maggie were out riding. The time was right.

Papa's study was sacrosanct; I had never in all my life been in there on my own before. This now, was proper spying; everything that had gone before was child's play. To actually go into his room, search his desk, read his papers! Because of course I wouldn't only look for that telegram – I'd keep my eyes open for anything else that could be of use to the protest movement.

My heart pounded audibly as I opened the door and crept into the study, tiptoed over to his grand purpleheart desk. There! I'd done it! I took a deep breath, and the panic subsided. I set to work.

I went about it methodically. First the papers on top of his desk, held in place against the sea breeze with a glass globe as paperweight. Then, one by one, the drawers. I glanced up: on the bookshelves there were files, all bearing letters to indicate their content: A-D, E-H, and so on. What a pity, I thought, that I had only now found the courage to take this step. My job of listening for information now seemed truly amateur. THIS was real spying.

*Spying against your own father.* I shook my head firmly, banning the bite of conscience. No! This was the right thing to do! My father was a cruel man, a despot, and he had to be stopped!

I found the telegram almost at once; it was right there under the paperweight. I read it, wrote down the content in the notebook I had brought with me. It seemed innocuous enough: notice of the Governor of Trinidad's impending visit and an invitation to a meeting in Georgetown. But I would let Uncle Jim decide. I continued my search, for something, anything, that might be of use.

One of the drawers in the desk, right at the bottom of the desk, was locked. That aroused my suspicion. Perhaps that was where he kept the truly important information. True, Uncle Jim only wanted to know the contents of that telegram, and I had that

– but what if there was something more, something vital to the movement, and he kept it in that drawer! I had to find the key.

I opened a smaller drawer at the top, one in which he kept smaller items such as pens, paperclips, and stamps – the obvious place for a key. And indeed, there it was, right before my eyes. A little key, a desk key. Did it fit? I tried it. Yes! It turned in the lock. I slid open the drawer.

The drawer contained just one item. A book. A book with a green fabric cover. Just one word graced the cover, embossed in great gold letters: **Tagebuch.**

The fact that the word was German told me everything, all at once. Mama's diary! What was Papa doing with Mama's diary? My hand trembled as I opened it to the first page. It was a terrible thing to read someone's diary, but if Papa had read it – and he surely had, having hidden it away in his desk; Papa would have had no scruples! – then I *had* to read it too. I had to know what he knew. My eyes, blurred now with unshed tears, read the first lines:

*Liebes Tagebuch,*

*I cannot contain it. I am simply bursting with it all but I have to tell someone or else I will explode! Oh, I will! How I wish I had a friend, a sister of my heart! Since I do not, dear diary, YOU must be that friend. I am in Love!*

I sobbed out loud and snapped the book shut. I slipped it into the waistband of my skirt, closed the drawer, locked it, replaced the key, and hurried down the hallway, up the stairs and into my room.

※ ※ ※

It was a short diary, and I read it, from front to back. Every word. I read it, heart hammering. Now and then a little cry escaped my lips; once, my hand flew to my mouth in horror to prevent an even louder cry. My eyes stung and I pressed them with the backs of my hands to hold back the tears. I closed them, breathed deeply, and read on. I came to the end. A sentence, unfinished – why?

Why had she broken off? Had she – but of course. The realization came: Papa must have entered the Seaview room and caught her in the act. I could well imagine the scene:

*'Ruth, what are you doing?'*

*Mama snapping the diary shut, trying to hide it.*

*'I – I was writing a letter.'*

*'To whom?'*

*'To – to Father.'*

*Papa striding up to her, invading her room. Looming above her as she sits at her dainty lady's desk, glaring down at her. Mama's hands fumbling as she tries to hide the book, in vain.*

*'That doesn't look like a letter! What is it!*

*'It's nothing – just a book – I was reading…'*

*'So you lied to me? What book is it? Let me see …'*

*Papa reaching out for the diary. Mama trying to hold it back. A struggle. Papa grabbing the book from her hands.*

*'What's this – Tagebuch? What does that mean?'*

*'It means – it means nothing. Please give me back my book, Archie!'*

*Papa recovering the little German he once knew. 'Tagebuch – day book? It's a diary?'*

*Mama reaching out for it, Papa pushing her away, opening it, turning to the first page.*

*'It's in German! Read it to me! Translate!'*

*'No! It's none of your business! It's private!'*

*'You're my wife! You have no privacy! All that is yours, is mine! So, I can't force you to translate. But luckily, Miss Wright knows German. I'm sure she'll oblige. Goodnight Ruth.'*

*Papa striding away to the door, Mama's diary and all her secret thoughts in his hand.*

Yes. That was what must have happened. Papa found her writing and grabbed the book, never gave it back. Kept it, and read it with Miss Wright as translator.

*And then sent Mama away.*

That, more than anything else, is what now filled me with both horror and relief. Horror, that Papa could exile his wife, the mother of his children, send her across the world and leave us deserted. But also relief, immense relief, that Mama in her own way had loved us to the end, and had never wanted to leave.

Yes, of course – it all made sense now. That scene on the ship that bore her away. It came back to me, even more vividly now that I understood: Mama finally waking out of her torpor, clasping me in her arms, her desperate cry: *Ich wollte es nicht, mein Schatz; ich wollte es nicht! I didn't want it, my treasure; I didn't want it!'*

Mama had not deserted us. It was Papa who had sent her away! Papa, who had *kept* her away. Papa, who had transformed from the gallant, kind and loving man she had once loved into the brutal despot he was today. Papa who had turned away from her from the start, and had let himself be drawn into the wicked web of Mr McInnes and company. Right under Mama's eyes, Papa had embraced cruelty, abused his power and become the hateful man he was today. I remembered Uncle Jim's words: *There's no telling what power will do to your sister.* Is that what power did? Change all that was good into all that was bad? It had certainly done so to Papa.

There was, of course, more, far more in the diary. Shocking things. Mama had had a love affair! Edward John was not Papa's son, but the son of this secret lover! Perhaps, for that reason, I should understand him for sending her away – but he could have sent her to Georgetown, couldn't he? Set her up in a house in town, so that at least we could have seen her from time to time? But no – he had to send her back to Salzburg, to the other side of the world!

I could not blame Mama for her infidelity. I understood it. Reading of her anguish, I could comprehend her finding solace in the arms of another. Solace, and even healing – but it was not to be. Edward John died, and that was the beginning of the end, for us all.

That night, I hid the diary under my pillow. The next day, if I could, I would go to Uncle Jim and discuss it all with him. Oh! I had even forgotten the telegram! I had to pass that information to Uncle Jim as well! But most of all – I needed to talk it all over, before I left for Georgetown. I couldn't wait – the secrets revealed by the diary were too much for me to digest on my own. Yes – tomorrow I would see Uncle Jim.

But *tomorrow* had other surprises in store for me. Tomorrow held the final falling of the axe.

❋ ❋ ❋

## Mama's Diary, Plantation Promised Land, 1910

*Liebes Tagebuch,*

*Many years have passed without me writing to you. I no longer even talk to you in thought. I am lost. Completely lost in the darkness. I don't even know if I love my daughters any more. I cannot find even the smallest spark of love for them, for God. The darkness has won. Not even music, my last refuge, can save me. My husband is a monster. I have married a monster. There is no escape. I am trapped in a cage. What can I do, where can I go? Just today, some little tendril of faith caught hold of me and I thought of you, dear Diary, and thus I am trying again. Yet I sit here with the pen in my hand and the words do not come.*

*Edward John's death was the final straw. Though many years have passed there is no recovering from my grief. Mourning has made everything so much worse. I reach out to you in my thoughts but you are absent. All that I find is a black thick vacuum. I am lost in this pit of darkness and if ever ...*

# Chapter Twenty-three

We were at dinner when the beginning of the end came. Miss Wright had returned from Barbados that day, and I had found no opportunity to visit Uncle Jim with my news. She had brought presents for us from our uncle and aunt in Barbados, and I'd been obliged to stay at home all day, unpacking them and making the appropriate sounds of gratitude. The six-o'clock bee had just launched into its screeching song; Papa and Miss Wright were, as usual, discussing the critical situation in Europe. I was dissecting a leg of chicken and absent-mindedly wondering who had plucked it.

Shouts outside the window stopped us all short in word and thought.

'Mr Cox!' someone called. 'Mr Cox!'

'That's Mr McInnes!' Papa sprang to his feet and reached the window in three long strides. By this time Mr McInnes had leaped up the stairs and was banging on the front door. Mrs Norton opened it. Mr McInnes burst in. His face was a bright and sweaty red, glowing in the lamp-light. He tore off his riding helmet. His eyes were wild, bulging out of their sockets; they scoured the room, and paused for a moment to rest on me; did I detect a shudder of sheer revulsion in that moment? But no, it was my imagination. Mr McInnes lunged towards Papa.

'Mr Cox – we have to talk. It's important.' His speech was clipped, breathless. I stared at the two of them as they hurried towards the library. They vanished into its seclusion and the door slammed shut.

A second later I was on my feet, lunging after them.

'Winnie! Stop! Where are you going? Come back!' I ignored Miss Wright's cry. I rushed out into the veranda and crouched beneath the open library window. Mr McInnes spoke loudly, un-restrainedly, and I could hear every word. I didn't need to hear much anyway, for the news was short and to the point, and really, only a few words stood out: *Jim Booker. Coolies. March. Fire. The factory. Your daughter Winifred.*

'Damn!' cried Papa. 'You can't mean it!'

'Every word! We have to stop it – now! They're at Mr Booker's place now.'

'Let's go.'

I sprang to my feet and ran back into the dining room, collid-ing with Yoyo on the way. She had rushed to follow me, appar-ently, and was still spluttering at me to come back to the table.

'No!' is all I said, and rushed forward, only to collide, this time, with Papa.

He grabbed my arm.

'You! You, young lady! Is it true? Are you friends with that, that scoundrel, that rascal Booker?'

A wave of relief swept through me. If all he knew was that I was 'friends' with Uncle Jim, then little harm had been done. It was the drums I worried about; my spying; George. Those were the *real* secrets.

'Papa, I …'

'I'll deal with you later.' He flung me away, so that I almost fell to the floor. Papa lunged towards the gun cabinet, in a corner of the dining room. He fumbled for his bunch of keys, unlocked the cabinet, removed a pistol and a holster. He lashed the holster around his shoulder and pushed the pistol into it.

'Papa! No! Don't! Please!'

'Winnie! Stay away! Do you hear me?'

He glared at me with such fury I would have turned to ash had I not myself been in the throes of an agitation powerful enough to overwhelm that flame of wrath and consume it.

'Papa, no, please, just *listen*!'

I was being foolish, and I knew it. Why should he listen to me, and what did I have to tell him that would make him change his mind? But I was not in my right mind. All I knew was that Papa could not go out there with a gun. I grabbed his arm. He tried to fling me away again, but I clung to him, crying out to him to stop, to stay.

Yoyo and Miss Wright screamed my name. Miss Wright tried to pry my hand from Papa's arm. I shook her off.

'Please, Papa, don't shoot anyone! Please! Listen to me! Just listen!'

I began to pound his chest with my free hand. Miss Wright tried to grab me but I pushed her away. Papa tried to fight me off, but I wouldn't let him. We struggled for a little while, I clinging to him like a monkey, begging him to listen; he trying his best to toss me away as if I were no more than an insect. Suddenly he managed to twist his arm free, and with the same movement grab hold of me again. He bent my arm backwards behind my back and marched me forward.

'Very well, young lady, if that's what you want, I'll listen. I'll not be held up by you a moment longer. You come along and on the way there you can explain whatever nonsense you think you have to say.'

The motor car was parked under the house. Papa pushed me into the back seat before striding to the front to crank up the motor. Mr McInnes got into the passenger seat. The engine coughed once, twice, three times, shuddered and sprang into life. Papa climbed into the driver's seat and slammed the door. His jaw was clenched, his gaze almost crazed as it brushed over me. Hunched over the steering wheel as if hugging it to his chest, he slowly drove forward on to the drive, turned towards the gate. The two watchmen opened both wings of the gate as we approached.

The car picked up speed once we had left the compound. Its headlamps flung a widening funnel of light over the road, framed on either side by the blackened stumps of the scorched cane fields. Tendrils of smoke gavetestimony to the last burning of the trash. The grumble of the grinding factory in the background was louder even than the motor's hum; all night long it rumbled away, Papa's precious factory, converting the cane into the brown gold of Demerara sugar. Mr Smedley's bride price.

'Very well. Explain yourself, young lady. I'm all ears.'

I leaned forward, resting my arms on the back of the front seat. 'Papa, you've got to understand. All the Indians want is fair treatment. Just give them better pay, and better houses, and clean water and sanitation. Let them live like humans and not like animals, Papa! That's all they want, truly! They mean no harm. All they want is humane treatment.'

'My word. Such big words. *Humane Treatment,* indeed. And you think you know what that is, do you? You, a girl hardly more than a child? '

'Yes I do, Papa. And I'm not a child any more. I know what's going on here. I know how the Indians live and it's disgraceful! It's cruel! It's …'

Papa interrupted with a roar.

'And that's why the bloody coolies are marching off to set fire to the factory, is it? For *Humane Treatment?* That's why they're going to burn down their own bloody livelihood, is it?'

My heart was thumping so loudly I could hear it. I wanted to scream at Papa but kept my voice calm.

'No, Papa,' I said quietly. 'That's not what they're going to do. They're going to occupy the factory. That's all. *Occupy* it. Take possession of it, halt the grinding, and not let you in until you agree to their demands.'

'Ah! You know that, do you? What a clever girl, up to her neck in coolie intrigues! And would you mind telling me how you know all this?'

Of course not. That was my secret. *Our* secret. The Revolution's secret. He would never know. About the messages pounded out all along the Courantyne Coast these last few nights. Night after night. *Occupy, Occupy, Occupy.* From Albion right up to Skeldon, the entire seaboard. Rose Hall. Belvedere. Hog Style. Comartry. Brighton. Good Banana Land. Gibraltar. Bachelor's Adventure. Whim. Dieu Merci and of course, bang in the middle of it all, Promised Land. The biggest protest there had ever been and the most damaging to the industry. The protest that would bring the Courantyne Sugar Kings to their knees. No, he'd never know how I knew.

'I just know, that's all.'

'It's that damn Jim Booker. He's been corrupting you too, has he? Putting all that communist nonsense about worker's rights into your head? Oh, I know. Mr McInnes told me everything. We have our sources too, not only you.'

I didn't answer.

'Little traitor. Despicable little traitor. I'll deal with you later. In the meantime, you'll see what happens to insubordinate coolies.'

'Papa – please. I beg you. Just – just talk to them. Just be reasonable. Maybe – maybe you can reach a peaceful settlement – if only – if only you'd …'

'Be quiet, you!' Papa turned to look at me as he bellowed the words. Never in all my life had I seen such rage. I wanted to curl up and die, withered down to nothing. Yet still I found the breath to continue.

'Papa – just don't shoot. Please don't shoot anyone.' Tears gathered in the sockets of my eyes, spilled out and ran down my cheeks.

'Crying for a pack of bloody coolies. My own daughter. As if I haven't got enough trouble on my hands – now a bloody traitor of a daughter.'

'I just want …'

'Quiet!' It was itself a gunshot of a command, cutting off what I was about to say. 'Not one more word! I've heard enough!'

It was useless. I slumped down into my seat, all my energy spent. I had done what I could. I knew now that the night would roll ahead as if in the throes of some mighty fate and that the end result would only be disaster. I turned away from Papa, faced the blackness of night outside the open window. The breeze that dried my cheeks and whipped my hair out of its molly was warm and smelled of smoke. Smoke and calamity. A great deep sorrow welled up in my chest and more tears swelled in my eyes and I blinked them away but still they came and I did not bother to stop them. I wiped my cheeks with my sleeve. The night was close and suffocating. I wanted to cry out to Papa to stop the car so I could get out and run away, run back home, away from whatever was about to happen because I knew with the sharpness of true instinct that it was going to be bad. *Stop the car, I want to get out,* I cried to Papa, but only in my mind. I was too paralyzed to say a word.

※ ※ ※

Just before the village, the car turned off into the lane that led to Uncle Jim's house. It did not take long before the headlamps caught the golden glow of fire, a bush burning in midair, moved towards us. Papa pulled at the handle to change gear and the car slowed down. It came to a stop, though the motor continued to hum; an animal in lurking position, ready to pounce. The fire too stopped moving. The headlamps now held the scene in perfect clarity in their glow. A crowd of people, men, Indians, across the width of the road and how many more behind them, we could not tell but for the fire, for many of them held torches aloft, and it was those flickering flames we had seen. They marched forward, towards us.

'Black devils!' mumbled Papa.

He set the car in motion again. It crept forward now, like a cat creeping up on a mouse. A mouse paralysed, held in an unearthly ban, caught in the glare of the headlamps. Dark skin, burning flames, here and there the glint of a cutlass. The horde of Indians too crept forward, towards us. The very atmosphere was charged with such menace my breath, my heart, the very world seemed to slow to a standstill.

About five yards from the crowd Papa stopped the car again. He opened his door and got out. Mr McInnes got out as well, from the passenger's seat. I stayed crouched in the back, watching, unable to move. The Indians stopped too. At the head of the crowd stood Bhim, a torch held high, legs apart, his hair as ever falling over his forehead and almost covering his eyes, one hand held high and holding the burning torch.

Papa strode forward, towards Bhim. Bhim scowled, and turned to the man beside him, said something I could not hear. He signalled with his free hand, and marched forward toward Papa. The mass of Indians surged forward behind him. A cry went up; many cries. Too many to understand the words they shouted. I only saw fists punching the air, the glint of blades, torches held aloft.

A shot cracked the night. Bhim's eyes opened wide in horror and realization. Then he slowly sank first to his knees before falling to the ground.

'No! No! No!' I screamed, but no-one heard. I collapsed into the back seat of the car, and darkness overwhelmed me.

# Chapter Twenty-four

Papa packed us off to Georgetown the very next day, Yoyo and I in the care of Miss Wright. Yoyo, who that whole week had been canvassing in vain for just such an outcome, was ecstatic. I was too numb with horror to feel any other emotion not even joy at my eminent reunion with George.

Yoyo had taken the news of Bhim's death with little more than a shrug.

'What do they expect?' she'd said the night before. 'The coolies have been acting up for years now; sooner or later it had to come to a head. There had to be a death. It's just a pity it had to happen on Promised Land.'

I was beyond consolation. 'But you don't understand!' I cried. 'Papa *murdered* him! Shot him in cold blood!'

'That's not what Papa said,' Yoyo replied coldly, for indeed, in Papa's rushed summary of the 'misadventure', as he called it, Bhim had wielded a cutlass and had been about to attack.

I shook my head in protest. 'No! No, it didn't happen like that! I saw, it Yoyo, I saw it! All Bhim had was a torch.'

'How on earth do you know the names of these people? They're nothing but a pack of hooligans. Rioting is not the way to implement change.'

'They weren't rioting! They were going to occupy the factory, that's all. Yoyo, have you forgotten? What happened back then, when Papa whipped that fellow? You know what he's capable of. Don't you *care* any more?'

'Of course I care; isn't that why I'm going to marry Clarence? But change has to come from above, Winnie. You can't have the coolies behaving this way, trying to twist our arms into doing what they want. *We're* in charge and the change has to come voluntarily: from us.'

I wasn't about to discuss politics with Yoyo. 'The police will be here again.'

'And Papa will get off again. It was clearly self-defence this time. Quite clearly. They won't be able to charge him with anything. Just wait and see.'

And for her that was that.

∗ ∗ ∗

Now, on the train down to Georgetown, she was chattering with Miss Wright as if nothing at all had happened. Miss Wright was unusually reticent; there was a line across her brow, which told me she was not quite as unconcerned as Yoyo, but nevertheless she made a good effort to keep up her side of the conversation. Perhaps, I thought, perhaps her worry was only self-concern, and not anything to do with our present trouble at all. After all, she'd be out of a job once Yoyo and I were in Georgetown. Where would she go next? But she had known this day would one day come. Perhaps she had made enquiries for a new job as governess in Barbados. As for me, I was too distraught for speech. Every now and then, a surge of emotion overtook me, and I burst into tears; Yoyo and Miss Wright seemed to think I was worried about Papa, for Miss Wright kept trying to assuage my distress with words to the effect that Papa would be fine, that he had everything under control, and such nonsense. I did nothing to persuade her otherwise.

Bhim, dead. Brave, fiery, intelligent Bhim! Though he had never overcome his mistrust of me I had grown to admire and even like him over time. Besides, he was George's friend – that much I had uncovered – and I would probably have to be the one to tell George of his death. Unless news of the uprising and murder had reached Georgetown ahead of me. Unless someone had sent a telegram … but there was no telegraph office in New Amsterdam, much less in Promised Land. I'd be among the first bringing the news to the capital.

Bhim, dead! What would happen now? If only I could talk to Uncle Jim. Uncle Jim would know. Uncle Jim would provide true comfort and good sense. Bhim's mother! I knew her quite well. She was, after all, Aunt Bhoomie's sister. She had been at Uncle Jim's a few times when I'd been there. A good woman. So proud of her youngest son. And now, what? I wept for Bhim, his mother, and the disaster that had broken upon us.

'Poor Winnie!' said Miss Wright, patting me on the back. 'Your eyes are quite red! Such a caring, sensitive nature! Don't cry, dear. Your Papa is a clever man. He'll sort everything out.'

I glared at her through my tears, and gritted my teeth. She was so condescending! The train stopped, as usual, at Kitty Station. I resisted the urge to rush to the door and leap down to the platform. Rush off to Auntie Dolly and lay the problem in her lap. I hadn't seen Auntie Dolly for over two years, but I knew where to find her and soon I would. I would see her and Myrtle and the children. And of course George. My George.

It was plain to see that last night had been the climax to a long, long stalemate. A bloodletting from which there would be no going back. Yoyo might pass it off blithely as simply another incident of self-defence against 'coolie insubordination' but I knew better. I knew the minds of the coolies. I knew that this would be more, much more, than Yoyo could even imagine. Their rage would erupt into something beyond imagination.

Yoyo had grown so callous. Two years ago, when we had first discovered the plantation's dark secret, she had been on our side, on the side of the coolies. Now she was firmly lodged on the planters' side. But then again, Yoyo's entire being was dedicated to the pushing away of all feelings she deemed weak, and to push ahead with those she considered strong. The planters' position was one of strength; the coolies' position one of weakness. Yoyo had simply grown up and found her rightful place. She would do things her way, and that was it.

The train's whistle screeched; we chugged away from Kitty. A few minutes later we pulled into Georgetown. Porters swarmed around us, loaded our luggage onto trolleys, and we emerged from the building into the hot midday sun. Several hansom cabs were waiting outside; Miss Wright hired one and soon we were clip-clopping down Main Street.

It was only a few minutes to the Park Hotel, a long low white wooden building like a bungalow on stilts, lined with dark green Demerara windows. It looked so cool, so welcoming. We walked beneath the green-and-white striped canopy above the entrance. It was like walking into an oasis of peace. Involuntarily a wave of quietude and harmony washed through me, conjured up by the greenery of the forecourt with its waving palms, the serenity of the hotel lobby with the smiling, bowing, liveried African staff. We were shown up to our rooms: a single for Miss Wright, a double for Yoyo and me, with a wide balcony facing the back of the building.

Later we descended to the open-aired dining room for our dinner. More palms and flowering bushes around a wide clipped lawn. A few guests sat at tables placed around the lawn; English guests, the ladies looking cool in their long white gowns, the gentlemen looking hot in their black suits. White-gloved black waiters glided back and forth, bearing trays of drinks. At the other tables sat other English guests. The hum of conversation, the clink of glasses and cutlery on china formed a muted backdrop of sound.

It was halfway through that meal that Miss Wright chose to drop the bomb that finally split apart whatever was left of our family.

'Girls,' she said, looking from one to the other of us, 'There's something I have to tell you.'

We both looked up. Something in her voice let us know that she was not simply going to announce her resignation.

'Your father and I are going to be married,' she said then, and smiled. A smile of such smug triumph I wanted to reach out and slap her. My face must have revealed that very unladylike thought, for she added quickly, 'I know this will come as a shock to you but as a matter of fact we have grown very fond of each other over the years and you can't expect him to live like a widower for the rest of his life.'

'But – Papa's still married! To Mama! And she'll be back!'

'Nonsense, Winnie. Your mother has deserted you and him, and has no intention of returning. That should be clear to you by now – it's been well over two years and not a sign of life from her in all this time. Desertion by the wife is grounds for divorce, as you might know; and your father plans to file for divorce.'

Yoyo, who had said nothing all this time, threw down her cutlery. 'I suppose that's what you planned from the start!' she jeered. 'Don't think I didn't notice. I know what you've been up to. I've seen you sneaking into his room at night. In fact, I've listened at his door when you've been in there. I should have known you were up to more than fornication!'

'Yoyo! How *dare* you!'

'You've always wanted to catch him as a husband, haven't you? Mama returning would have put an end to all your plans, wouldn't it? I've seen the looks you've given him. Batting your eyelashes at dinner while you discuss the crisis in Austria and all that rubbish. I should have known.'

'Yoyo, I will not have you speaking to me in this tone of voice! Go up to your room immediately!'

'I certainly *will*!' cried Yoyo, and rushed from the table. Several heads turned as she fled to the door. Miss Wright turned to me.

'I know it's a shock for you, Winnie, and I know how devoted you still are to your mother and how you always hoped she would return. All I ask is that you try to understand. Your father was extremely lonely and of course he turned to me for comfort. A man needs a woman to help him through difficult times. You're almost an adult now and you must understand that. You'll be marrying soon yourself, if all goes well. This is adult life and you need to know these things. And besides – besides …'

She had the grace to blush. I waited.

'Besides – your father is desperate for a child. A little boy! An heir! And I plan to give him just that. As soon as these troubles are over, he'll be filing for divorce and we shall be married.'

# Chapter Twenty-five

It was two days before I was able to meet George, and by that time the news of Bhim's death had hit Georgetown with gale force. The newspaper headlines screamed of it, and everyone we met seemed to be whispering of it, to repeat every detail and every rumour. At the hotel, people stared at us – they knew we were the killer's daughters. The killer. *My father was a killer.* At the thought of it, the memory of it, my knees gave way. But I fought, fought against the creeping sense of hopelessness and despair. When people stared, I stared back, which was very unlike me. Not in protection of Papa, for he was a stranger to me. Not in defiance. But to tell them: *You know nothing. Mind your own business!* They would then look away in shame. I was in fighting mood.

I had to see George.

※ ※ ※

The day after our arrival Miss Wright took us both to Miss Yorke's Institute for the Womanly Arts on Carmichael Street and arranged for our accommodation, supervision and education: not an easy task in mid-term, but Papa's name carried some weight – in spite of the present scandal – and Miss Yorke was no doubt eager to fill beds, and no amount of tut-tutting and lip-pursing and frowning could hide the gleam in her eyes as she finally brought out her ledger and entered our names, having accepted 'the little bonus' offered by Miss Wright.

Yoyo, still sulking and refusing to speak to Miss Wright, achieved her desire to attend courses in Economics, Accounting and Business at the Government College, while I would be studying violin with a Mr Greer, whom Miss Yorke claimed was the country's best music teacher. I would also be studying Advanced

French and Art in Miss Yorke's school. Both of us were to attend classes in Housekeeping, Needlework, and Culinary Arts, along with all the other boarders. There were twelve of us boarders – all upper-class daughters from the plantations or New Amsterdam – as well as several daygirls, who were daughters of English and Scottish businessmen settled in Georgetown. The boarders slept in dormitories of three or four girls. We all ate together at two long tables, headed by Miss Yorke and her second-in-command, Miss Humphries.

Having settled us in, Miss Wright skedaddled back to the Courantyne. We were on our own.

＊ ＊ ＊

*I had to see George.* I could not wait another day. It would require a certain amount of lying and subterfuge, but by this time I had no qualms and no conscience. That first morning at Miss Yorke's I complained quite brazenly of excruciating pains of a female nature, bending over double to demonstrate my agony. Miss Yorke sent me back to bed after breakfast. The moment the house was quiet I sneaked down the stairs, out the back door, down into the yard, and through the front gate.

Carmichael Street, to my great joy, was immediately parallel to Main Street. I had decided the best place to meet George would be on his delivery round. I had his home address, for I had been writing him there, but no idea whatsoever where Albouystoun was. Also, I knew that he was seldom at home, and I saw no point in confronting his parents on my own. And so, Main Street, just a block away, it had to be. I had worked out the approximate time we had met him here last time, and all I had to do was wait. I walked up and down the length of Main Street in my nervousness. I was not sure from which direction he would come, or which side of the street he would serve first: would he walk south from Lamaha Street, or north from the town centre? And so I prowled the avenue: up, down and up again, peering into the gardens of those splendid white mansions to catch a glimpse of the man I loved.

It was on that second walk up that I ran into Mrs Pennington, the wife of Papa's friend Brigadier Pennington. I didn't recognise her at first, as I hadn't seen her for at least four years. But she recognized me immediately. She was walking in the opposite direction, accompanied by an older woman with a pink-lace parasol.

'Why, Miss Cox! It is you, isn't it? Miss Winifred Cox? Yes, it is. My, how you've grown!'

I stared at her, not sure what to say. She took both my hands in hers and pulled me to her plump breast in a rudimentary embrace, pressing a dry powdered cheek to mine.

'Mrs Pennington. You do remember me, don't you? We met at the Governor's garden party some years ago – your mother was with you, and both your sisters – how are you all? I heard your mother is still in Europe? Oh, my manners – Mrs Dalton, this is Winifred Cox, the middle daughter of the Honourable Archie Cox, of Promised Land – in Berbice.'

Mrs Dalton, a tall, ramrod-backed woman held out a long thin arm ending in a white glove. I shook her hand; within the glove it felt like a dying bird.

I gave a little curtsy and managed to mumble, 'Pleased to meet you, Mrs Dalton.'

At that very moment I glimpsed a flash of khaki between the two women. I stepped aside to get a better look. Yes. It was him.

'Excuse me!' I cried to the two women, and fled.

I leaped across the parapet and out into the street. I raced behind the bicycle, crying at the top of my voice: 'George! George, come back! It's me! Wait! Stop!'

I must have been loud enough, for he braked, jumped off the bicycle, and turned around. Two seconds later I was in his arms. The bicycle clattered to the ground. We clung to each other. I could do no more than cry his name, again and again and again. He nuzzled his head into my hair. His arms held me so tightly I knew he would never let me go. Never. Never. But then he did.

'Winnie!' he said, pulling away from me and I saw that look on his face once more, the look I hated. The look of worry and fear, and his eyes unsteady, shifty, glancing left and right in suspicion.

'What you doin' here?' he gasped. 'Why? You can't do this, Winnie. In the middle of the street! Come, let's get away from here.'

He picked up his bicycle and wheeled it over the parapet to the avenue walkway. I glanced up: Mrs Pennington and Mrs Dalton stood exactly where I had left them about a hundred yards away, stock still and staring as if they'd seen a ghost. I didn't care. I didn't care one bit. In fact, to show I didn't care, I flung my arms once again around George and pulled him to me and kissed his cheek.

'Winnie, stop it! You can't do this!' He pushed me away; he too had seen the two ladies, staring unabashedly at us.

'Oh, fiddlesticks! I don't care! I don't care about anything anymore. I'm tired of hiding and sneaking and lying. I don't care who sees or what they say. I love you and if you love me still you won't care either. You do love me, don't you? You do George, don't you?'

I frowned as I gazed up at him, scouring his face for a hint of denial. He only squeezed my hand.

'Yes – but Winnie, it's *dangerous*. You don't know how dangerous – people watching. And after what happened …'

'Bhim died, George! Oh George … *Bhim*!'

His eyes grew moist at the name. 'That's what I mean, Winnie. Don't you realize – no, you don't. We can't, Winnie. Don't you realize – after this – we just can't – no matter what – it's just impossible – now …'

'Nothing's impossible, George! All I know is that I love you and I don't care who sees and what they think.'

But George had found some inner source of sense and strength, and he pulled away from my hands even as I tried to embrace him again.

'No, Winnie. You don't understand. You out of your mind, or what? How you could even think we could have a future after – this?'

'I just love you. That's all. And you love me too.'

'You don't understand'. All that don't matter. It don't matter one bit. We're jus' two li'l people and what we want don't count one li'l bit. This is bigger that both of us and what we want. So much bigger."

And then I opened my eyes truly and saw in his what he had been trying to say in words: grief and fury and desperation and emptiness. A deep pit of fear opened within me. I opened my mouth to speak but no words emerged.

'You got to go, Winnie. Go now. Don't walk past them ladies. Where you staying?'

I told him in a dull flat voice.

'Then go on down a bit and turn left at New Market Street. Walk for a block and then turn right into Carmichael Street.'

'When can I see you again?'

'You still don't understand? You can't! We can't meet ever again. Not ever – look how them ladies still starin'! They prob'ly gon' report me to the postmaster and then I gon' get the sack. And you …'

'They'll tell Papa but I don't care.'

'You're a silly, foolish little girl. And so reckless, so careless. I don't know what to do wit' you. I just wish I didn't – didn't have feelings for you.' He was crying, and trying not to.

'Just talk to me one more time. Please! Come outside my house tonight. I'll find a way out. Please!'

He stared at me, glanced at the ladies, back at me. 'All right then. One more time. Tonight. Nine o'clock. No, ten. Outside your house.'

And he walked off. I stared after him. He did not look back. He got on his bicycle and sailed away. I waved at Mrs Pennington and Mrs Dalton and went the way he'd said.

❊ ❊ ❊

I had not reckoned on the speed with which gossip flies in Georgetown. I managed to return to my room and my bed without being seen, and indeed, I came down for lunch, claiming my pains had disappeared. But by evening Mrs Yorke, and possibly every white adult female in the whole of Georgetown, knew. Well, I had known it was inevitable ... I had just misjudged the pace of passed whispers, and the morbid curiosity of bored English ladies.

Mrs Yorke removed me from my dormitory and locked me into a small room in a front corner of the house. 'I've telegrammed your father,' she said, 'And I expect he'll be here soon to deal with you. This is a home for decent young ladies, you realize. I cannot jeopardize its reputation with loose girls.'

And then the facade of calm dignity crumbled. Her face, up to now a stiff mask of perfect emotional indifference, collapsed, twisting into a grimace of sheer contempt.

'How could you,' she spat, 'how could you? Behaving like a common street girl with a – with a ...' She said it. She said that horrible ugly forbidden word, the word that not even Papa in his worst temper used in our presence, the word that would never pass my lips, that I would never write down or even think. She spat it out with such contempt, such hatred, such utter revulsion, I literally shrank into a corner.

'There's a chamber pot under the bed,' she said, regaining her countenance. 'Here's a lamp and your nightdress. You will be released when your father or your governess arrives.'

She thrust a roll of clothing and a small wicker lamp and matches at me. Slammed the door in my face and turned the key.

I inspected the room, but there wasn't much to see; a cot, a chair, a table. There was a water jug on the table with a basin for washing, a towel rack with a threadbare towel on it; and, as she had promised, a chamber pot under the bed. This was plainly some kind of a punishment room, a prison for naughty girls.

But the window was unbarred, and I lunged towards it. It was a tall Demerara window, with a little slatted shelf on the outside and a slanting, top-attached shutter, a pole to hold it open, and ornately carved triangular wooden sides. I leaned over the shelf to inspect the possibility of escape. The room was in a corner and a drainpipe ran down the side, but even in my state of agitated rashness I knew I would never be able to scale it; the drop was too sheer, and too high; the ground was three stories down.

I had hoped that the room was above the gallery; that I could somehow clamber down on to the gallery roof and from there, using a rope of bed-sheets, down to the ground. But the gallery did not run the entire length of the house. It stopped two windows away from mine, and beneath me was only a wooden wall. I was truly trapped.

The six o'clock bee announced the descent of dusk. The key turned in the lock and a servant entered with a tray: a glass of water, two slices of bread, a small pat of butter. But I was too wound up to eat. I drank the water, paced the room, thought and thought and thought. I had to get out. I had to speak to George. I could not let it end like this. George would be coming soon. In his present attitude of pessimism he would be glad when I didn't turn up. He didn't care for me. He didn't love me. What shame, to be chasing a man who repelled my every move! He could not love me, or he too would be willing to take every risk to rescue our love. But he did. I knew it. I saw it in his eyes. I saw everything in his eyes. I saw the love and the conflict and the misery and the desperation but he couldn't hide that small spark of hope. It was up to me to cultivate it. I had to do something. I could not give up.

Night fell. I lay down on my cot. It was hard, the mattress thin and lumpy. I was still in my clothes. Sleep – a ridiculous notion. What time was it? I lay in the dark and wished I had a watch. Where was the nearest church? There'd be a clock there and it would peal the hour. I listened to the town. The clip-clop of horses hooves outside, somewhere the beat of drums, dogs barking, the inevitable night orchestra of *crapauds* and crickets. I kept listening, and soon I was rewarded. A clock began to chime – possibly St George's Cathedral, a huge white wooden building at the top of the street. I counted the chimes. Eight.

I waited. The clock chimed again. Nine. A plan was beginning to hatch in my mind. I lit the lamp, and waited. Ten. I rose in my bed and walked to the window. I placed the lamp on the floor and looked out. Would he come? If I were not there, would he wait? Carmichael Street was black but for the circles of light thrown by the widely spaced lamps. All the houses were in darkness. Would he come? Would I see him?

As did Main Street, Carmichael Street had a central walkway shaded by trees. If he came at all it would be hard to see him. Possibly he would keep to the walkway, protected by the trees. What was that? A dark figure darted across one of the light pools thrown by a street lamp. Was it him? I could not tell. I wanted to shout, but did not dare. It was time to put my plan into action. I leaned over, picked up the lamp, placed it on the window ledge.

If he was watching the house he would see the light. It would be the only light in the house. He would surely see it, and know it was me. I turned the knob that lowered the wick. The lamp went out, I had lowered it too much. I muttered a little oath. I should have spent the last few hours practicing. I couldn't risk it going out again. I had to think. I needed something, an object, to hide the light. The wash-basin. I relit the lamp, replaced it on the window-ledge, held the basin in front of it. Lifted the basin, held it up, and lowered it. Quick and slow. Slow and quick. I soon found my rhythm. G-E-O-R-G-E. I spelled out the letters in short and long light flashes, over and over again. Calling his name in the only way I could. Our secret language.

There! That black shadow again! It was standing beneath one of the avenue trees. It was him. It had to be him. And there! The flutter of something white. Flutter, flutter, flutter: a white flag, now long, now short, now long again. My heart began to pound. He had heard! He understood! He had read the message! George and his handkerchief!

Y-E-S, said George. W-I-N-N-I-E.

I C-A-N-T C-O-M-E  L-O-C-K-E-D I-N  D-O-N-T G-I-V-E M-E U-P I L-O-V-E Y-O-U

The handkerchief flashed. I was self-defence. They say L-O-V-E Y-O-U  T-O-O B-U-T

I interrupted. N-O B-U-T-S  B-E-L-I-E-V-E I-N L-O-V-E I-L-O-V-E Y-O-U I L-O-V-E

Y-O-U

A pause. Then he too flashed goodnight. It had been a long conversation, thoroughly exhausting, but thoroughly satisfying as well. My heart swelled to almost bursting. I did not care that Papa, or possibly Miss Wright, was coming tomorrow. I did not care for whatever evil things lurked in our future. All I knew was the seed of hope in my heart. I belonged to him. He to me. That was a knowledge so complete, so certain, not even a flicker of doubt could displace it. Not ever.

❊ ❊ ❊

Papa himself came to pick me up the following evening. Miss Yorke had kept me imprisoned the whole day. A servant brought meals and took away the chamber pot. After lunch Yoyo appeared outside my door and called to me through the keyhole. I came and crouched beside the door, though she was the last person I wanted to talk to.

'I can't stay long. I've got to talk to you.'

'All right. I'm here.'

'Winnie, is it true? Tell me it's not true! You were making love to some darkie on Main Street?'

'I don't want to talk about it.'

'I don't believe it! I just don't. It's not like you at all! It's just some wicked rumour, isn't it?'

I shrugged, but of course she couldn't see me.

'Winnie! Just tell me it isn't true! Because I'm sticking up for you! Denying it! You would never do anything so barmy!'

I still said nothing.

'I don't understand. Who is it? How could you? What's got into your head?'

I stood up and walked to the window. I gazed out to the street, to the place he'd been standing the night before. All optimism, all faith in our future, gone, dissolved into nothing. Only despair remained.

❊ ❊ ❊

Papa stormed into my prison. His face was as red as a lobster, and the words spluttered on his tongue, and I learned the meaning of the word *apoplectic*. I did not, could not, look at him. I sat on my wooden chair with head hung low. I had to sit on my hands to stop them from covering my ears. He spluttered and hollered and glared and roared and I just sat there, looking down, silent. What was there to say?

'Do you realise? Can you even begin to realise how – *dastardly*, how entirely… ' He searched for a word but couldn't find it.

'Utterly atrocious behaviour, and at a time like this! It's bad enough as it is without you going berserk! Completely berserk!'

I said nothing. I gazed out of the window.

'*Look at me,* you – you vile creature!' I did as I was told. I looked at him, but my eyes glazed over at the sight. All I saw was a stranger in a terrible temper. I did not care. It did not affect me. The cruel words bounced off my body. I heard them without absorbing them.

'You don't care, do you? You aren't even listening. You don't care that your reputation is utterly and completely ruined. You don't care about the trouble you've created for me. You don't care about anything.'

I closed my eyes the better to form a shield against his shouting. He was marching up and down by now, bawling out the words. They were true. I didn't care. What could I say? There was nothing I could deny. Yes, I closed my eyes against them and took a deep breath.

'You *whore! Listen* to me!'

*WHAM!* My face exploded in red-hot pain. My eyes flew open as I cried out. Papa was standing right in front of me, rubbing the palm of his hand. His eyes were wild, his hair dishevelled. But striking me seemed to have provided an outlet for some of his rage. He shook his head in sheer perplexity and, without another word, strode out of the room, locking the door behind him.

Half an hour later he was back.

'Come with me, young lady. Your bags are packed. You can't stay here. You've brought disgrace to Miss Yorke's house. Do you know how I've had to beg and grovel to persuade her to keep Yoyo? We're leaving.'

Yoyo came too. She had been given leave to join Papa for dinner. As we walked out into the street she kept staring at me in wonder. I even detected a hint of admiration in her gaze. But I might have been mistaken.

We had dinner at the Georgetown Club, the three of us at a white-table-clothed table for four. Dark-skinned waiters in black-and-white livery like penguins glided to and fro bearing glasses and platters, bowing down to us as they served us. We had often eaten here in the past, as a family, with Mama and Kathleen. The room was filled with other guests at other tables; the Georgetown Club, though exclusive, was known as the best place for dining among the British community. The hush of muted conversation and the chink of glass and cutlery added to the atmosphere of dignified grandeur.

Papa's rage had now diminished into seething but quiet wrath. His eyes, when they glanced at me, were filled with disgust. Yoyo, too, kept looking at me.

'So it's really true, about Winnie! Golly, I would never have thought it of her!'

'Completely taken leave of her senses.'

So they talked about me as if I were invisible, as indeed I longed to be. I was aware of their conversation without taking any actual interest, though they spoke of me. I was past caring. I was also aware of the stares of several of our fellow diners at the neighbouring tables, the whispering behind upheld hands. My notoriety was drawing unwelcome attention. Papa ignored the ogling, though once he did look around, catching several gazes with silent belligerence. Faces turned red and eyes looked away.

'There's only one thing for it,' I heard Papa say from miles away. 'I have to send her away. I can't keep her in the colony; not after this. I'm sending her to England.'

Finally he'd caught my attention. I stared at him in wild horror.

'Don't look at me as if you're surprised. What did you expect? Who do you think will take you in after this? Do you think any decent English family wants someone like you?

'B-b-b-but …' I couldn't get the words out. They seemed all of a tangle within me. I didn't know what to say. My instinct was to spring to my feet and dash across the room and run into the street straight into George's arms. Luckily, a fraction of good sense remained in my addled brain. I had done far too many stupid things these last few days, things that, as I now realized, only hastened to put an end to all my hopes and dreams. England! I hung my head.

The conversation drifted on to Papa's situation. I hadn't really been thinking of that at all, too wrapped up in my own little drama as I was. It seemed he was as notorious, now, as I.

'It's not going the way I thought it would,' said Papa to Yoyo. 'Sergeant Jones came to take my statement yesterday and I told him the truth, of course. There really shouldn't be any problem but it seems there is. Those damned coolies are creating quite a stink.'

'But surely even they must realize that you had to defend yourself?'

'Yes. But now they're saying the scoundrel – the one who was killed, I mean – wasn't armed. They're saying I killed him in cold blood. That I had planned it, even. I don't understand why anyone even listens to them. Plainly, they are all in it together, with the lie.'

'But he had a cutlass. He did. Didn't he?'

'Of course he did! It was clearly self-defence. My goodness, the man was rushing me with the dammed thing! What was I supposed to do, stand there and let myself be slaughtered? Anyway, Mr McInnes is a witness and he will support me.'

By this time they had my full attention. I stared from one to the other, horrified. I gasped aloud, and my jaw fell open. They both turned to look at me.

'What is it you want to say, Winnie?' Papa's voice was quite calm now, friendly almost.

I struggled for words.

'But – but it's not true, Papa! Bhim *wasn't* armed! He *didn't* have a cutlass!'

Papa frowned. 'You seem to be very knowledgeable about the whole thing!'

'But I saw! I saw, Papa! I was there! *And he didn't have a cutlass.*'

'That's perfect nonsense and you know it. I don't want to hear you repeating such twaddle ever again, do you hear? Not ever again! Now, Yoyo, it's time for you to get back to Miss Yorke's. Poole will drive you there. Winnie, you stay with me. We're going to the Park. It's getting late. Bedtime for you girls.'

He raised a hand to draw our waiter's attention. He stroked his moustache and gazed at me. Worry veiled his eyes.

'Complete twaddle!' he muttered to himself.

# Chapter Twenty-six

Papa took me to the Park Hotel and deposited me in a room to which he held the key. There was a chamber pot in the room, and a jug of water and a basin. I was on my own, with only the Bible as companion. Papa had been extremely negligent in choosing this room, for it was at the back of the building and the next morning it didn't take me long to discover that the back windows opened up on to the fire-escape that serviced all the rooms at the hotel's rear. My plan was instantly made. I threw a few clothes into a pillowcase. I pushed up the sash window, climbed through onto the fire-escape, and scaled the steep metal stairs leading down to the ground. It didn't take me long to sneak around to the front of the hotel and exit the main gate. I was on Main Street now.

I walked north until I found a park bench; I sat on it to wait. It was still early; the church clock had only just chimed eight, and I knew that sooner or later he would pass by on his rounds. All I had to do was be patient. Papa would not miss me; his plan for today was to book me the earliest passage possible to England. That would surely take all morning. This was my last chance, our last chance.

The morning slipped by with the pace of a snail. I was terrified in case Papa were to return early and, going up to my room, find it empty; but what else could I do? I had to wait here for George. I contemplated other possibilities; I could, for instance, make my way to the Promenade Gardens and hide there, hide somewhere, anywhere, until nightfall and then find George's house. I could find a coach that would take me to Kitty, to Auntie Dolly. I could walk all the way to Peter Rose Street to Dolly's daughter Maybelle – I knew the way, after all. But I was loathe to involve either Auntie Dolly or her daughter in this escape plan. This was between

George and me. I had to see him – now. I could not wait until tonight. I could not just turn up on his parents' doorstep.

At last I saw him, making his way northwards up Main Street, his postbag slung over his shoulder. This time, I didn't call out. I simply ran. I ran towards him and threw myself into his arms. When he saw me hurtling towards him his eyes opened wide in shock and his arms opened wide to catch me. And then I was in his arms, and he was holding me close, rocking me, speaking my name, and I was safe.

When I could speak I gasped out my story. 'George – he's sending me away! To England! On the next ship! You can't let this happen! I can't go! I can't leave you!'

George came to his senses in a matter of seconds. 'Winnie!' he said, pushing me away and holding me at arms length. 'Winnie, how often have I said you can't do this. You can't ambush me on my rounds, in public! It's just – just not right!'

'Don't you love me?'

'Yes! Yes, you know I do! I love you with all my heart but we have to be sensible!'

'Sensible! How can I be sensible when he is sending me away! Away from you, forever!'

'Winnie, don't you see? Don't you realise? Things have changed. Everything has changed – with Bhim's death it's all over. There's no chance for us, no hope.' He pushed me away properly then, and turned his back on me, and then swung around and his eyes glistened with tears.

'We can't, Winnie! Don't you understand? Your father killed my best friend! It's no longer just about you and me! It's all over! We have to accept it's all over! It's best for you to go to England.'

'No! Don't say that!'

'But I am saying it!'

'You can hide me; let me stay with you!'

'What would I do with you, Winnie? They would find you and then – what?'

'Are you afraid of getting into trouble? Can't you fight for me, for us?'

He sighed deeply, and started again, calmly and slowly as if he were a parent trying to patiently talk good sense into a child. But I was desperate and wouldn't listen. And slowly I realized I could not win. I could not talk him into hiding me from my father.

'All right,' I said at last. 'I'll go. But I'll come back. You'll wait for me, won't you?'

He hesitated. 'Winnie. I love you and always will. But I can't promise anything. Everything has changed. I don't know what the future will bring. I might be dead by then. You see …'

'No! Don't say that!'

'Winnie …' He was growing anxious now, looking behind him and from side to side in case we were being watched.

'All right then. I'll go. I'll go because you don't want me now. But, George – George! I have an idea! Come to me tonight! To my room!'

'Winnie, are you out of your mind? How on earth …'

Breathlessly I told him about the fire escape and the open window.

'George, I'll go now and let you do your rounds. But come to me tonight. I'll be waiting. Come at ten. Just sneak into the hotel yard and come round the back and up the fire escape. I'll be there, waiting! I'll put a lamp in the window so you'll know!'

'Winnie – I …'

But I wouldn't let him finish. I wouldn't let him say no. I turned and ran, back to the hotel, back to my room. He would come. Tonight. I knew it. He would come to my room.

❀ ❀ ❀

When night fell I placed the glowing lamp on the window-sill and waited. Would he come? When? I hadn't given him a time. I hadn't waited for his answer. But he would come. He had to.

I lay down on my bed, still fully dressed, closed my eyes. Stood up, walked to the window, opened it, peered out into the darkness. Nothing. The seconds ticked away- The Sacred Heart church chimed eight, and then, an eternity later, nine. Now I stationed myself at the window. Outside, the night was pitch dark – it must have been new moon. I pushed open the sash and peered out. Nothing. Would he come?

I perched myself on the sill of the open window, lamp in hand. He had to come! He had to! If he loved me he would! But it was so dark. How would I know? My eyes strained to hear the sound of his coming: the scrunch of his feet on gravel, the creak of the fire-escape. But the night creatures were out in full force with their nightly serenade, and nothing out of the ordinary caught my attention.

And then it came. At first I thought I had imagined it – it was a whisper of the breeze, the swish of the tamarind tree in the back yard. But then it came again: an urgently whispered 'Winnie!'

Yes, it was him. My heart lurched and I leaned out of the window and whispered back, as loudly as I dared: 'George! Come up! I'm here!'

And then he was there. Outside my window, climbing in, standing in my room. Holding me,  clasping me to his chest, tighter and tighter, his lips nuzzling my cheek, my forehead, seeking, and finding, my lips.

I pulled away, but only for a few seconds. 'Wait!' I said and lowered the sash. And then I held out my hands to him and he took them and we gazed at each other in wonder for a second before a power stronger than both of us forced us together, into each others' arms.

We stood there in silence, kissing. He was mine, I his. I felt him hesitate, and I knew why. I pulled my lips away and spoke the words of permission:

'George – I love you. I want to be yours, all yours, in every way possible.'

He pulled away, as if the words had jerked him out of a spell. 'Winnie! I can't! We can't! Don't you understand!'

'Why not? Because we aren't married?'

'Because – because you and I – we can never – it's …'

'Let this be our marriage, George. Let this be our wedding night! Let it be between just you and me forever! George – my ship leaves tomorrow! To Barbados! There isn't a ship leaving for England for two weeks so he has packed me on the first vessel out! I'm going to my Uncle Don and Aunt Jane in Barbados! It's our very last chance! I need to be yours, George! Otherwise I will die! If I am yours nothing can ever separate us, not even the ocean. If we – then I will go in peace! I promise! And come back whenever …'

'Winnie! What if you get a baby!'

'There's nothing I would love more! Then you would *have* to marry me!'

'Oh Winnie!' He could not resist, for I was stroking him, his face, his chin, his back, pulling him towards me, towards the bed.

His protests were growing weaker. I pulled him down, down. I covered his face in kisses. In the lamplight's golden glow his face shone like polished bronze. He was beautiful, so beautiful he took my breath away.

'Winnie, you kill me!' he said, and started to unbutton my blouse, and I knew that I had won. We sank back onto the pillow.

\* \* \*

The next day I was on the HMS Amaryllis, Barbados-bound. And I was content. George had claimed me, sweetly, gently; I had melted into him, become a part of his body and his being. Nothing could separate us; neither time nor space. I had woken up that morning and found him gone, but a dent in the pillow next to me where his head had lain, and a delicious sense of calm filling my soul. I was content, and looking forward to whatever the future would bring.

I was fond of Uncle Donald and his wife Jane. They were much younger than Papa – Uncle Donald being the youngest of five children – and on the rare mutual visits between our families they had carved a place in my heart. Certainly, living with them until I came of age was the least of many evils, even if it meant a further three years of separation from George. At least it wasn't England, that cold dreary land so far across the seas.

Barbados! Uncle Donald had inherited the smallest and least profitable of the Cox West Indian plantations, but it was arguably the most desirable of all. Neatly tucked between rolling Barbadian hills and a private, palm-lined beach, it was a personal piece of heaven, and my first few days there I spent simply basking in pleasure, sloughing off the mental aches and pains of the last week. I locked it all behind an internal door. I could not bear to think of those final scenes on Promised Land. Bhim's look of horror as the blood spurted from his chest. Papa standing with a smoking gun. I could not bear to think of George, and what this would mean for our future. I could not bear to think of that last embrace. I laid my hand on my belly. If only – if only!

But enough of dreaming. I lived in the present, in the glorious, sunny, breeze-brushed gardens of Oleander Cottage. There I lounged with Aunt Jane on the fine white sandy strand just outside the garden gate; I frisked in laughter with the children in the clear warm turquoise waters of Caribbean Sea lapping practically at our doorstep. I lay on my back in that water and closed my eyes and basked in the glorious Now.

And then I talked. I talked and talked and talked. I told them everything and they listened sympathetically and without judgment. Sometimes I cried and Aunt Jane dried my tears. Uncle Donald nodded in empathy. No frowns of disapproval, no gasps of disgust when I said I had kissed George – more, of course, I could not confide. At least not yet; not until I must, if my dearest wish came to pass. But also: no encouragement.

'You see, Winnie, it really is an impossible situation. Marriage is best when the partners are from similar backgrounds. You and George: you may be madly in love now, but what will it be in a few years time, when the birds have stopped singing and the flowers have stopped blooming and you have to live through harsh reality together? For it will be harsh.'

'I know and I'm prepared for it. I believe that true love is also strength, and will carry us through.'

Uncle Don and Aunt Jane threw each other knowing glances. Then they both looked at me with loving smiles.

'He's your first love, isn't he?'

I nodded.

'First love always feels that way. It's so fresh, so pure, isn't it! It feels eternal. If only we could maintain it!'

'But I can! We can! I …'

Aunt Jane wouldn't let me finish. 'It always feels that way, Winnie. But you know what? It usually isn't eternal. Donald wasn't my first love, and I wasn't his. And yet, look at us! Aren't we the perfect pair!'

They laughed and hugged and snuggled up to each other. We were sitting on the veranda of Oleander Cottage on a mellow night about a week after my arrival. The younger children were all in bed, the two older ones playing a card game in the gallery. The stars were out in their full glory, scattered like silver jewels on a black velvet sky. On the table before us were long tumblers filled with golden rum punch. Several candles glowed in glasses, protected from the balmy breeze coming in from the sea. I looked at Uncle and Aunt and away again. I envied them. If only George and I – maybe one day. One day it had to be.

'And besides, you don't know him very well, do you?' Aunt Jane continued. 'How often have you seen him? How long have you been with him in total? How many hours? How many conversations have you had? How well do you know this man, Winnie?'

Towards the end of her little inquisition her voice grew stern and anxious. I knew she was genuinely concerned for me, but there were no words that could put her at ease. Thinking about her questions I realised, for the first time, how ridiculous this love of mine must look to an outsider,and  how very mismatched we were.

I remained silent.

Uncle Donald spoke next. 'What you need to do, Winnie, is meet some other nice young men. Who knows – maybe there is someone out there who is perfect for you in every way. Someone you can be happy with, someone who does not come with a burden.'

I looked at Uncle Donald and frowned. In the flickering candlelight his face was nothing but relaxed and friendly. His voice was calm and soothing, inviting me to listen and agree, almost hypnotic But I didn't trust it.

'Did Papa tell you to find a husband for me?'

He chuckled. 'Archie sent me a cable as long as a novel, and yes, part of his instructions were to make sure you were introduced to every single eligible young man on the Island. *English* young men, of course. Though even Scottish would do at a pinch.'

'I'm not interested,' I said at once.

'Let's not discuss that now, Donald,' said Aunt Jane quickly. 'There's lots of time. For the time being she should just think of enjoying herself. What would you like to do while you're here, dear? There's not very much to see and do apart from sea-bathing – it's a small island – but perhaps you've thought of something?'

I nodded. I had thought it all out while on the ship. 'I want to get a job,' I said. 'I want to work. In Bridgetown. There must be jobs available for girls like me? I've read in the English newspapers – lots of respectable young women are working in London. I'd like to do that here. And move out, into a boarding-house, or something like that. Rent a room with an English family, perhaps.'

They glanced at each other yet again, and this time I noticed a frown on both their brows.

'Are you quite sure, dear?' said Aunt Jane after a while. 'I mean – what would you do? What qualifications do you have?'

'Nothing much,' I admitted. 'But I was thinking of teaching. I could give violin lessons. Or I could teach French, and English, reading and writing to young children. And German! I could teach German!' I waited.

'Well, you'd need a teaching certificate for the best schools,' said Jane carefully after a while. 'I suppose you could give private violin lessons to children. But – well, I'm wondering how many pupils you'd get? Enough to live on?'

'And who on earth would want to learn German in Barbados?' scoffed Uncle Don. 'This isn't Europe, you know. French is about all you need – there are a few French islands dotted about the place, but there's not much exchange between us.' He paused. 'You see, Winnie, you do have to be sensible, and realistic. Yes, it's true that more and more women are working in England. But this isn't England. Girls from respectable families don't work in Barbados. Why should they? Why should you? You have everything you want. Your father arranged a generous allowance for you. When you come of age you'll have your trust fund. Why should you have to work?'

'Because – because of George,' I said, and my reasoning sounded lame even to me. How could he possibly understand? I had known for years now that, sooner or later, if George and I were to have a future, I would have to give up my pampered life. How could Uncle Don understand how spoilt I felt in the bosom of a family where everything was provided, where food appeared on the table as if by magic; where I never needed to pluck a fowl or boil an egg or even wash my own undies? Just one day in Auntie Dolly's care had changed my life forever; I could never be that mollycoddled English girl again.

'Well, in that case,' said Aunt Jane brightly and briskly, 'there's nothing like the present! Why don't you and I drove into Bridgetown tomorrow, and visit some schools? You can speak to the headmistresses and find out exactly how eager they are for your services.'

❄ ❄ ❄

'So that's that.' Aunt Jane slithered down the back seat next to me. Miller the chauffeur slammed the door, walked around the car, climbed into the driver's seat, and drove off, and headed back home. 'Well, dear, I did warn you.'

She certainly had. Just as she had predicted, none of the three primary and two secondary schools had been the least interested in my potential as a teacher. One or two headmistresses, in fact, had been quite scathing in their dismissal. But I wasn't ready to give up.

'Perhaps I can work as a governess,' I said. 'Or a nanny. In an English home, looking after young children. I do love children!'

Aunt Jane gave a yelp of horror. 'A nanny! What would your father say to that! Oh, he would murder us! We are responsible for you, you know! And a governess! Who do you think you are – Jane Eyre?'

I turned away from her, gazed out of the window. The last buildings dropped behind us and the glittering sea appeared past a field of palms. Tears pricked my eyes.

Aunt Jane reached out and squeezed my hand. 'I know you're disappointed, dear, but it was always going to be a long shot. I say – why don't you work for us? The nanny we have really isn't up to scratch and the children adore you. It wouldn't really be work as you spend so much time with them anyway and we could just pretend, and of course we'd pay you a generous salary. What do you say to that?'

I said nothing to that. Just shook my head and continued to gaze out of the window so she wouldn't see the tears I couldn't hold back. I bit my lip so it wouldn't quiver. *Little crybaby*! I scolded myself. *Take hold of yourself*!

And I did. I turned to Aunt Jane. 'Thanks, but no. I have to get a real job, and I will. I know I will. I need to move into Bridgetown, be independent. You see, it's important. It really is!'

She sighed audibly. 'Well, I don't know what your father will say to that – you living in some boarding house! He would think it quite common.'

'He doesn't have to know, does he? You don't have to tell him. Otherwise he'll just pack me off to England on the next ship. Please, Aunt Jane. Don't tell him.'

'Well, there isn't anything to tell yet, is there? And I don't suppose there will be. Who really wants a young girl without a single qualification or skill?'

I'd been asking myself the same question for days, which was why teaching had occurred to me as my only option. I had a sudden brainwave. 'I could take a course!' I said. 'Shorthand and typing! Then at least I'd be qualified as a secretary. I'd enjoy that – taking the course, I mean. And then I could *surely* get a good job.'

'A secretary! Really!' Aunt Jane's opinion of that suggestion was clear from her tone.

I said no more on the subject. But once we arrived home I grabbed the newspaper on the hall table and took it out to the veranda. There were several pages of advertisements near the back; perhaps I'd find what I was looking for there. And, it occurred to me now, why on earth had I not done this earlier? I always read the newspapers cover to cover – a habit I'd developed in my spying days – but never the advertisement pages. A serious omission.

'*Miss Kirby's Secretarial College*' I read now, and '*The Barbados School of Business*', offering courses in, among other things, shorthand and typing.

I circled those two advertisements. My eyes drifted down the page. And stopped. My jaw dropped. My breath stopped. I almost cried out.

'*Telegraph Operators Needed. Training Given. The Bridgetown Telegraph Office.*' I didn't circle that ad; I tore it out of the page. I ran into the kitchen where Aunt Jane was giving the cook instructions for tonight's dinner party.

'Aunt Jane! Aunt Jane!' I cried. 'I found just the job! I need to get back to Bridgetown – now! Can I borrow the car?'

'A job? What kind of a job?'

I told her. She raised her eyebrows. 'A Telegraph Operator? What an extraordinary idea! Why on earth …'

'Because I *can*! I know the Morse Code! I can work with a Morse machine! And I'm quick – really quick! I won't need much training! Oh, it's just the perfect job!'

She frowned. 'But I'm not sure if it's quite the done thing, dear. What would your father say?'

'He doesn't have to know! He doesn't! Please, Aunt Jane – just let me have the car! I know I can get this job!'

'Well, Miller can drive you back into town after lunch, but really – and where would you stay? You can't drive back and forth to Bridgetown every day.'

'I'll find a hostel, or something. I will. I'll get the job, and then I'll find a place to live!'

'I should really speak to your uncle. I can't come with you this time; I have this dinner-party to arrange; the Courtneys are coming. You'll have to go on your own. Are you sure …'

'Oh, yes, thank you, thank you!'

I lunged at her, grabbed her at the waist, hugged and kissed her, swung her around, and dashed off to find Miller.

✳ ✳ ✳

I got the job. Mr Clarkson, my future manager, was sceptical at first but then he let me demonstrate. I had never used a real Morse machine before, but I quickly mastered it.

'By George! You'll be our fastest operator!'

'I can have the job then?'

'Of course! Save us the trouble of training you. When can you start?'

'Just as soon as I can! As soon as you want me!'

'Right away. Tomorrow?'

'Yes, yes, tomorrow. But – oh, I need a place to stay – a women's hostel, or something. Do you know of anything?'

'Well – there's that place on Bird Street. Big white house with a sign. What's it called – *Miss Goode's Hostel for Young Women* or some such thing. The name's right though – Miss Goode. That's why I noticed it. Gives it a respectable touch, no doubt. Can't go wrong under Miss Goode's beady eye.'

Actually, it was *Miss Goode's Boarding House for Young Ladies*. Miss Goode was a plump Scotswoman with chestnut hair pinned on top of her head. She stared at me through large tortoiseshell spectacles.

'I've only got the one bed free at the moment,' she said doubtfully. 'But …'

She shook her head.

'But what?'

'I don't know if you realise this. Of course I couldn't put it on the sign. But this is a home for coloured women. Coloured middle-class women, working women, all very decent, of course. Secretaries, teachers, and so on. All coloured. There's a hostel for English women on Parade Street. You'd fit in there better.'

'No – no! Of course not! I – I don't mind at all. I'm happy to stay here. I'll take the bed.'

'It's in a double room,' she warned. 'No vacant single rooms.'

'A double room is fine. How much is it?'

She told me; I gulped, but agreed. I wasn't working for the money but for the independence.

She looked me up and down. 'You're very young. I hope you're not a runaway! We don't take runaways. If you're a minor we'll need your parents' permission.'

'No! No I'm not running away. I've got a job! I'm a telegraph operator – look, here's my contract!'

I whipped out the paper I'd just signed. She glanced at it.

'Parents' permission? Your parents have to act as guarantors.'

'My guardian. My aunt – she's my guardian; she'll be my guarantor.'

'Then welcome. You'll be sharing with Miss Hart – Sibille Hart. When do you want to move in?'

'Right away! No, wait – I have to go home and pack. But tomorrow! I'll come right after work.'

'Very well then. So – come into my office and I'll get your details down. And tell you aunt to come and sign.'

❊ ❊ ❊

'A *telegraph* operator? What a very peculiar thing!' Mrs Courtney looked me up and down as if I had a bad skin disease, and passed me the sauce.

'It's not really peculiar,' I said. 'Lots of people do it. If you have telegraphs you have to have people operating them.

'Not a terribly *ladylike* occupation, I dare say,' she replied. 'Jane, dear, I do congratulate you on your beef. Your cook is a pearl. May I steal her from you?'

'Certainly not!' laughed Aunt Jane.

'And you taught yourself the Morse Code, you say?' said Mr Courtney, across the table from me.

'Yes,' I said. 'Someone gave me a leaflet with the code and I practised and practised until I could do it.'

'Goodness gracious! Why ever would it even *occur* to you to do such a thing?' Mrs Courtney wrinkled her nose as she spoke. I shrugged.

'I had a lot of time on my hands on the plantation. I was bored, I suppose. But it's also terribly interesting. Like learning a new language. I'm good at languages.'

'Winnie's quite the little linguist,' put in Aunt Jane. 'She achieved top marks in French in her School Certificate, and she's fluent in German. Bilingual, in fact. Her mother's Austrian and the two of them used to chatter away in German.'

'Austrian! Well, that's not a very nice thing to be in this day and age, is it, Henry? Or German, for that matter. Henry's always going on about those dangerous Huns. He's convinced there's going to be a war.'

'Take my word for it,' said Mr Courtney. 'War is inevitable. My prediction: give it another year. Two at the most.'

'That's the reason we've persuaded Thomas to come back home,' said Mrs Courtney to Aunt Jane.

Aunt Jane looked at me. 'Thomas is their son,' she explained. 'Their second son. He's just finished his Law studies in London . A lovely boy.'

'We're very proud of him,' said Mrs Courtney. 'Of course, he could have had a far better career in London. He would have ended up in Whitehall, I should think. But London isn't a safe place at the moment. Come home, we told him. Come home until the war's over, at least.'

'I think he should settle here,' said Mr Courtney. 'He can have quite a brisk business in Bridgetown. Who wouldn't want to live in Barbados?'

'He can't have the plantation, of course. That goes to Richard. But we're going to give him the Sunset Bay property. The beach there is perfectly delightful, and near enough to Bridgetown for him to travel to town quite easily for work.'

'I'm sorry to hear Miss Cartwright broke off her engagement,' said Aunt Jane. She threw me a significant look. I had long caught on to her tactics. This was not the first eligible young man she had manoeuvred into conversation in the three weeks I'd been here. I had even met one or two of them – Barbadian versions of the spoilt brats of the senior staff compound.

Mrs Courtney snorted. 'I'm not sorry at all. The truth will out – that young lady was a fortune hunter right down to the tips of her toenails. The moment she found a better prospect, off she trotted. The Governor's son, no less. A pompous fool twice her age.'

Aunt Jane smiled brightly at me. 'You must all come to dinner with Thomas once he's back, and you too, Winnie. It's time you met some young people your own age.'

Mrs Courtney grasped what Aunt Jane was hinting at. She swung around to stare at me again.

'I really don't understand why a girl like you needs to work, Winnie. A telegraph operator – my word! You say her father owns a British Guiana plantation?' She turned to Aunt Jane to ask the question, who nodded in reply.

'One of the last privately owned ones. You must have heard of him – the Honourable Archie Cox, second son of Lord Cox of Camberley?'

Mrs Courtney grew quite flustered. 'Oh – oh really? Oh, how very interesting! Very interesting indeed! And you say, dear ...' she turned to me again, and in a much more affable tone of voice, 'I suppose that this Morse Code business is really a sort of hobby? You're not working because you have to – but just as a sort of pastime?'

And so it continued. I fled the table as soon as I could do so politely, and vowed never to dine with the Courtneys again, Thomas or no Thomas.

# Chapter Twenty-seven

I had lived 18 years on earth without ever having had a best friend. A *real* best friend, not a bossyboots of a younger sister, and Emily Stewart didn't count, being an *only* rather than a *best* friend. The moment I met Sibille Hart I knew what I'd been missing.

She was in our room when I returned from my first day at work, exhausted but contented.

She was sitting before the vanity mirror, unplaiting her hair, and swung around as I entered. She sprang to her feet; tall, thin, gawky, she stood there with one plait hanging over her shoulder and the other half-undone, ending in a copper fan of frizz. Her face was perfectly oval, its silky sapodilla-brown skin splattered with freckles. Big brown eyes, and a smile so wide and welcoming I could not but return it.

'Hello! You're Winnie! I'm Sibille!'

She stretched out a hand and came towards me; I took that hand and met her eyes and smiled back. I had no choice but to embrace her; it was involuntary, two pairs of arms opening up to each other. It was like meeting a long-lost sister. She spoke easily and freely, in a clipped up-and-down Barbadian accent and a rich dark voice. Soon I was helping to brush out her hair. That hair! A glorious mane that sprang outwards as if alive to frame her face. I loved it; it drove her to the edge of insanity.

'I got to comb it twice a day!' she complained, 'evenin' an' mornin', mornin' an' evenin', nicht an' day. I don't know why I don't jus' cut the whole thing off. Run around like a boy.'

'Oh, no! It's beautiful!' I said, pulling a brush through it. 'You should just wear it loose, like this.'

'Eh-heh, and then they throw me in the loony-bin,' she replied. 'An' you know how much it tangle if it loose? Nah. Got to tie it down. You plait that side, I plait this.'

Later, we went down to the kitchen and she cooked me a meal. She had bought a fish on her way home from work.

'Is enough for two,' she said as she cleaned it.

'What can I do?' I asked.

'You can fry them plantain. And boil the rice.'

'Oh – yes, of course – ah – how do I do it?'

'You never fry a plantain before? Never boil rice?'

I shook my head. 'I can peel the plantain I suppose; just like a banana. But then?'

She left the fish and moved over to me and showed me what to do. Cut a slice of plantain to show me the width, and measured out the water for the rice.

'The rice don't need pickin',' she said. 'I always pick it on Sunday for the whole week. Just rinse it out and throw it in the water once it boil.'

We ate on the back veranda. Other young women had joined us in the kitchen, cooking their own meals, laughing and joking together and discussing their day. Their initial formality towards me soon melted; they seemed to sense my reticence was shyness rather than conceit. They reached out to me, asked me questions, told me about themselves: Janette, a clerk in the Ministry of Health. Babsy, a nurse. Antoinette, a secretary in a shipping company.

Sibille herself was a primary school teacher. I told her of my efforts to find a teaching job, and she laughed.

'You're not going to find any violin pupils in the local schools,' she said. 'Where the parents going to find money to buy the instruments? You would need to find private English pupils.'

She squinted at me. 'Violin. My, my! You must come from some high-class family. So what you doing working, living in a house full a coloured girls? You parents throw you out, or what?'

And so, later, as we lay in bed, I told her my story. It came out easily, but not necessarily in sequence, for Sibille listened carefully and with both ears, and asked questions; questions that made me jump back and forth in my story, to Mama, and Yoyo, and the Indian problem, and Uncle Jim, and Aunt Dolly. To Bhim and the strikes and riots, and my conflict with Papa. But most of all I told her about George. George was the golden thread that held my story together. George was the beginning and the middle and the end of my story. George was everything.

'You got it bad, girl!' she said at one point.

'Have you ever been in love, Sibille?'

She nodded. 'Sure. I still am. In fact, I'm engaged to be married!'

'Oh!' I glanced at her hands, those long slim fingers that would have looked beautiful on the keys of a piano or holding a paintbrush.

'No ring,' she laughed. 'Actually, it's a secret engagement. Because my parents wouldn't be too pleased.'

'Why not? What's wrong with him?'

'Nothin'. Nothin' at all. Everythin's right. But he got the wrong job. He's a house-painter by day, an artist by night. My parents wanted something better for me. A senior civil servant, or a businessman. Good coloured middle class, preferably light-skinned. Not black like my Max.'

'Oh!' I said again.

'See, not only you white people is racist. We's racist too. We got it ingrained in we heads that white skin better, white skin more beautiful, white skin more valuable. We girls got to marry up, into white skin. We can't marry down. So basically, I got the same problem as you. But you got it worse, of course. Much worse.'

'But if you're actually engaged to him it means that you believe, like me, that we can get over it. We can overcome the prejudice and marry the man we love!'

If I was hoping for encouragement from her, I was to be disappointed. She shook her head.

'Is different between you and me, Winnie. See, once I'm married and settled and once Max and I manage to get recognition for his painting – and he will get it one day, because he's good, really, really good – my parents will come around. I'm not really marrying outside my class, outside my clan. Max's parents are poor, but he's intelligent and had a good education and all he wants to do is be an artist. When he finally finds recognition he'll end up middle-class, like me.

'See – my parents ain't got no reason to be high-and-mighty. Their parents were poor, and struggled, to give them a better life. He's just a generation behind, that's all. As for me being brown, he black: all it means is that in my family some poor slave-gals got raped by some arse of white slave-drivers. I don't see that's something to be proud of. So you see, between me and he is not too much difference. All my family got to overcome is a bit of snobbishness, a bit of artificial pride, a bit of prejudice. When I get my first baby all of that going to vanish like mist.

'You, though. That's a different story. That's like – like trying to span the Atlantic with a piece of string. The gap too wide. Your people will never, ever accept your George. Never. You and you babies going to be outcasts. You got to make that clear in your mind.'

I shook my head in defiance. 'I don't care. We love each other. That's enough.'

'Love! Hah! A bit of emotion. You think that's really enough? Chile, you don't got no idea what you lettin' youself in for. Sounds to me that he got a better idea than you. That's why you is the one runnin' after he, when he should be the one courtin' *you*. He knows you can't manage. This thing too big for you, girl.'

'No! I …'

But she wouldn't let me have my say. 'You say he keep tellin' you it can't work, it can't work, it can't work. Why you don't listen to him? For once? What you don't understand is this: if you marry George, you ain't just marrying one man. You marrying his people, his people's past, his whole history. You marrying one huge burden. You jus' ain't got the shoulders for it.'

'How can you tell that? You don't know me!'

She chuckled, and picked up my hand. 'That's how I know. This hand today cut a plantain for the very first time. It throw rice in a pot-a boilin' water for the very first time. It never hold a mop. It never pluck a fowl.'

'I did! I did pluck a fowl! And I caught it myself, too!'

'Ha! Once! And you mighty proud of that one-time pluckin', right?"

She stroked the back of my hand, held it up, inspected it in the lamplight's glow. 'Soft, delicate, precious. That's you. You can't help you past, but you can't live in George's world with those hands.'

She chucked the hand back into my lap, and sucked her teeth. 'Listen, girl: I giving' you a piece of free advice: find some nice uncomplicated white Bajan boy and settle down here an' forget George. That's the best thing you could do. Everything else is looking for trouble. There ain't going to be no happily ever after with Georgie-boy.'

'And what if I'm carrying George's baby?' I patted my tummy. I hoped and hoped.

She stared at me, frowning. 'That's a possibility?'

I nodded, smug in my anarchy, certain she'd be impressed.

She wasn't. 'Well, girl, you better get down on your knees and pray it ain't so. Because if you think you got troubles now … 'She shook her head slowly in a blatant expression of utter disdain at my foolishness.

※ ※ ※

I wasn't carrying George's child, and I grew to be relieved. Over the next few weeks, Sibille took me in hand. She brought me into her circle of friends: an eclectic group of writers, artists, musicians, teachers, politicians, would-be revolutionaries, male and female, young and old. We met mostly at Oskar Greene's big, rambling, slightly ramshackle house near the seafront; there he lived with his one-legged mother, his sister Viola, and his friend Ivan.

Oskar was in his early forties; he worked in one of the ministries, though I never found out which one, and wrote poetry in his spare time. As his mother was black as ebony, and he was light brown, I assumed his father – long deceased – had been white, and rich; whatever the case, Oskar was a lawyer, trained in London, and up to his ears in politics, and when the subject turned to politics it was Oskar who kept us all riveted.

It was Oskar who told me gave me some very interesting information. We had been talking about George, one evening. Oskar and Ivan and all my new friends, of course, knew the story of George; all were sympathetic, but basically pessimistic. But that night Oskar said, 'You do know, don't you, that it might be possible for you to be appointed a ward of court. Then you could possibly get permission to marry without your father's permission.'

I sat up. 'No, I didn't know. What's a ward of court?'

'Well, put simply, it means you must prove to the court that you are mature enough to make your own decisions regarding marriage – which you obviously are, with a job and living on your own, earning your own keep. That you and your father are estranged. Which you are. In that case, the court can grant you permission to be married before you have reached maturity.'

I flushed with pleasure. 'Really! No, I didn't know that. Thanks, Oskar. I think that's what I'll do.'

'Don't rush back home, Winnie!' Valerie, a colleague of Sibille's warned. 'Take your time.'

'I will,' I said.

'We don't want to lose you yet,' said Johnnie, a journalist at the Barbados Star. 'And anyway, why don't you ask George to come here? We'd love to have him.'

'And he could stay here, with us. We've lots of room,' said Ivan. 'Haven't we dear?'

He looked at Oskar, who nodded, squeezed his hand, and smiled. 'Of course,' he said. 'He's welcome.'

Ivan was sitting next to Oskar on a wicker settee on the sea-facing veranda. They were holding hands. Ivan was a tall, gangly, very handsome man who tried to make a living as a musician, but otherwise seemed to fill the role of housekeeper and cook to Oskar, and more.

'Oskar and Ivan behave like a married couple,' I said to Sibille one day. 'Isn't that strange?'

She only laughed and shrugged. 'Not for them,' is all she said.

It was Ivan who played the upright piano in Oskar's living room, Ivan who sang the songs of his own composition that fuelled our parties, and Ivan who told ribald jokes that made me blush.

In an upstairs corner room Sibille's fiancé, Max, had his studio. It seemed that Max, too, was sponsored by Oskar. Oskar bought his paints and his canvasses, arranged his exhibitions, and managed his career. Max's paintings were as wonderful as Sibille had said. He painted everyday scenes on enormous canvasses, his subjects almost – but not quite – in full height. A fisherman mending a net. Two market-woman arguing behind a stall of pineapples, one with her finger raised in admonishment, the other glaring back, arms akimbo. Boys playing cricket in a field of goats. Sibille was right: one day, Max DeVere would, must, find the recognition he deserved.

I listened and I learned and as the days and weeks crept by I relaxed into carefree, buoyant island living, a melange of gravity

and nonchalance, hedonism and political fervour. My new-found
friends were kind to me, yet at the same time distant. They accepted me, yet kept me at   arm's length. I was with them, yet
apart from them. They loved me, but locked me out. And yet,
slowly but surely, what felt like an invisible wall began to crumble.
Gradually I morphed into another – into a truer, more genuine
version of myself, the person I was meant to be. Not through an
actual change of character, but through shedding one layer after
the other of the person I had once been, to discover she who
had always lived in the shadows. I loved it here. I felt at home. I
even relaxed enough to adopt, just a little, the melodic Barbadian
dialect they spoke among themselves.

Maybe, just maybe, Ivan was right: George and I could make
our home here. He could come and join us, join this happy
carefree community, free of the troubles and travails of British
Guiana. Hope sent its rays through my being. My spirits lifted.
I wrote to George to tell him of this new version of our future.
'Come,' I said to him. 'Come to Barbados! We can make a life
together here.'

And then came the letter that burst my little bubble of contentment. It was from Yoyo.

*Dear Winnie,*

*I don't know if the news has reached you over there, but Papa's in
great trouble. Do you remember that bother with the coolie who
got killed? Well, it's not going the way we thought; things are coming to a boil. For a start, Papa wasn't able to convince the Police
Chief in New Amsterdam that it was self-defence; it's a new chap,
who seemed to believe the coolies more than he does Papa! Can you
believe it? They're all denying it was self-defence. They say that the
dead coolie was unarmed. So it's Papa's word against theirs – and
Mr McInnes, of course, confirms that the fellow was attacking Papa
with a cutlass. And so the matter was taken up in Georgetown and*

*there have been all sorts of demonstrations and even riots, negroes and coolies picketing the Law Courts for 'Justice'. And worst of all, they've put the case in the hands of a new Crown Prosecutor, a Mr Bhattacharya, and he's an Indian! Can you imagine it! So of course he's terribly biased against Papa and is out to get him. Papa was even in jail for a day or two but his friends got him released on bail. He's now staying in Town at Government House. All our friends support us, of course. Everyone is horrified at the lies these coolies are spreading, just to make the whole thing political. The trial is in a few weeks time – in the New Year …*

The rest of the letter was filled with her own news – the trivialities of life at Miss Yorke's, her studies, little titbits of gossip. I skimmed over the words, hardly reading them. I wished I had not read this letter. It brought me back down to earth with a heartshattering thud. It dropped to the floor. I bent over, burying my face in my hands; I wanted to cry, but no tears came, only a deep dry sob. I wanted to shout, but I had lost my voice.

The door opened and Sibille entered. 'Winnie, aren't you coming down for breakf …oh, what's the matter?' She rushed to my side and sat beside me on the bed, and put an arm around me. I pointed to the letter on the floor; she picked it up and read it.

'Oh dear. That sounds bad for your father. Must be so worrying for you.'

Worrying! What an understatement! I was devastated. But what could I do, so far away? I was lucky to be out of it. Papa and Mr McInnes knew I'd been in the car, knew I'd seen it all, but obviously had refrained from mentioning my name. I was not to be called as a witness, and I could only thank God for that. And Papa, of course. Papa was protecting me. Or maybe, came a niggling thought, *maybe he was protecting himself? Maybe he had deliberately sent me away, not because of George, but because I was a danger to him?* I pushed that thought away. Firmly away. No, I was out of it. Far away. I would not think of it.

So I pushed the whole nasty business into a little box in my mind and locked the mental door. I wrote a letter to George, gushing with love. I told him I would wait. Three years. I had waited two; three more would be easy, so easy. 'If necessary,' I said, 'I'll wait forever.'

❊ ❊ ❊

Just a few days later, another letter arrived, and was waiting for me in the front hall. I recognized the writing at once. I grabbed it and rushed up to my room, tore open the envelope, threw myself onto my bed, and read it.

*Dear Winnie,*

*Waiting is not the problem. My love for you is deep and lasting. The separation from you only forces me closer to you; as if love is something waiting in my heart, so comforting and so beautiful, and so perfect. The fact that I cannot <u>have</u> you, cannot marry you, cannot ever be with you, only pushes me deeper into a love that is not bound by physical presence; a love that does not depend on <u>having</u> or <u>wanting</u> or <u>getting</u> you. A love that is independent of your presence, and all the stronger for that reason. Do you understand? Do you also understand what I am saying?*

*I cannot come to Barbados. That is another of your innocent dreams. It can never be, you and I. No, I don't think you can possibly understand, shielded as you have always been from the dark side of life. For you, love is always perfect, always right, will always conquer, and I love you all the more for that innocence, and that's why I won't ever discuss with you the reasons why it cannot be. I do not say this without guilt; I took liberties with you I perhaps should not have ... liberties only a husband may have. Yet I have no regrets, and I hope you too have none; I am only glad there are no consequences because of what I must say next.*

*You and I: it cannot be.*

*We are from two different worlds. Worlds that cannot meet, not ever. Not in our lifetime. Maybe in some wonderful different future. Maybe a hundred years from now, those two separate worlds will cease to exist.*

*My friend Bhim was a Hindu: Hindus believe in reincarnation. If reincarnation is true, my darling Winnie, then you and I are destined to be together in such a wonderful future. But in our lifetime? No. It cannot be.*

*That is why, and it breaks my heart to say this, I want you to be free. I want you to be happy. Find someone else, Winnie. Find someone from your own world, someone who loves you. I want you to find someone suitable, so that you can move on and find a life where you can be fulfilled as a woman. Do not worry about me. I have my task in life, and I will do what I have to do.. There will be no pleasure in that life, for it is one of constant struggle; and yet there will be fulfilment. Did you know that pleasure and fulfilment are not the same thing? Pleasure does not necessarily bring fulfilment; it can leave a person empty and hungry for more. But fulfilment: it sinks right down to the bones, through body and soul, and it comes from doing the right thing. I cannot do otherwise. It's a calling.*

*But you: you must move on. It is for the best. And you will forget me.*

*Yours,*

*George*

George without an X. That is what broke my heart the most.

❀ ❀ ❀

That night I cried myself to sleep, and nothing Sibille could say would make me stop. She read the letter; she tried to comfort me;

but I would not be comforted. In the morning I woke up and there was only one word on my mind: *Never*.

Three weeks later, another letter lay on the hall sideboard: addressed to me, no stamp, hand delivered. I opened it in my room. It was from Aunt Jane.

*Dear Winnie,*

*It's been simply <u>ages</u> since we've seen you and I take it that that's a good sign. I hope you're enjoying your work and your life in the big city. But I feel guilty; as your guardians we do need to keep a better eye on you. We do need to talk to you occasionally! Why don't you come up for the day on Sunday? I'll send Miller down with the car in the morning to pick you up – you can spend the night, and Miller will bring you back to town the next morning for you to go to work. We'll have a really lovely lunch, a picnic on the beach at teatime, and a cosy chat on theveranda under the stars at night. I can't wait to hear what you've been up to!*

*Aunt Jane*

*PS the Courtneys are coming to lunch. Their son Thomas is back and I'd love you to meet him!*

I groaned as I crumpled the letter into a ball. Between the lines the message was clear.

'She's playing go-between for me and this Courtney boy,' I said to Sibille later. I un-crumpled the letter and let her read it. She only laughed.

'I think it's a good idea, in principle. Maybe he's *the one*.'

'*The one* is here. Right here,' I said, a hand on my heart.

# Chapter Twenty-eight

Aunt Jane looked up at the sound of wheels crunching the gravel, and a short sharp toot of a horn. 'They're here,' she said. She jumped up from her chair and rushed to the window, gesturing to me to follow. Reluctantly I did; I was curious, in spite of myself.

The motor car had parked in the drive just a few yards from the window. Miller got out of the driver's seat, walked around the bonnet to the front passenger seat, and opened it. Mrs Courtney emerged, brushing at the lap of her dress. The two back doors opened simultaneously and two men emerged on either side, one old, one young. The young one looked up, as if he knew he was being watched. In spite of myself, I caught my breath.

'He's so good-looking,' sighed Aunt Jane. 'Isn't he? You have to admit it, Winnie; he's really handsome, isn't he? Such a lovely smile!'

She waved and smiled back; Thomas had seen us standing at the open window. He waved both arms above his head and walked around the car towards us. He walked with a casual but firm gait and a lithe swing to his long legs. He wore white long trousers and a white short-sleeved shirt open at the neck, dressed as if for cricket. His hair was blonde and a little too long, and flopped over his forehead as he walked. He pushed it back impatiently. He looked around for his mother, whose arm had been taken by Mr Courtney, and, not being needed by her, strode forward to climb the stairs to the front door. The maid, Rosie, had already opened it for him and a minute later he was with us, Aunt Jane in his arms.

'Auntie! So good to see you again! How are you!'

'Is this my little boy, my little adopted son? That little spotty teenage boy I sent away four years ago? I can't believe it! Let me look at you, boy!'

She held him at arm's length and looked him up and down. He let himself be inspected, grinning amiably, his hands held firmly in hers. Then she started, and turned to me. 'Oh! Where are my manners? This is my niece, Winnie, from British Guiana.'

His eyes rested on me. I sensed the approval in them and dropped my gaze to the floor.

'Mother has told me about you, Winnie. How do you do?' He held out his hand, and I took it. We shook hands.

'Pleased to meet you,' I murmured, looking up again. I wished he wouldn't stare so; it made me nervous. And shy. And tongue-tied.

By this time Mr and Mrs Courtney had entered the room and Aunt Jane was busy greeting them; and then it was my turn to say hello and Uncle Donald emerged from his study and the children came running down the stairs followed by Nanny and everyone was exclaiming over this and that, except Thomas, who was still looking at me and seemed hardly to notice Uncle Don's greeting, or the older children crowding round him and calling out his name. It seemed he was a well-loved member of this household, the four-year absence merely increasing his popularity.

'Come, let's go out to the veranda and have some drinks. Mayleen has this wonderful new rum punch recipe and I'd like you to try it – it's made with passion-fruit and is simply heaven!'

We all walked out to the veranda, Thomas and I bringing up the rear. I felt his eyes on me. I kept mine averted. We – the adults – all sat down around the table; the children were sent away to amuse themselves till lunchtime. At first, Thomas was the centre of attention, cajoled by Aunt Jane into giving a summary of his last four years in London. He spoke easily, saying neither too much nor too little, with just the right mixture of friendliness and politeness, answering questions, telling funny little anecdotes that made everyone laugh out loud. I took note with only one ear, hearing without listening. I was far too busy trying to deal with that look in his eyes whenever his gaze scanned mine – which was far too often for comfort.

To my dismay, I was the next object of conversation. Mrs Courtney insisted on a reiteration of my family credentials, and I knew very well it was all for Thomas's sake. And then the talk turned to my life in Bridgetown, which brought about an instant diminishment of her approval.

'I still don't understand how a girl of your upbringing could possibly want to work at all, much less in a *telegraph* office. A telegraph office! Gracious, it sounds so very common! Sending telegram here and there!'

'Well, *someone* has to do it!' said Thomas. 'Think of all the telegrams you've sent me over the years! Do you think they got to me by magic?'

'Yes, but it doesn't have to be a young lady whose grandfather is an Earl! If *we* don't keep up the standards then who will? Surely …'

'Oh, Mother, what a lot of twaddle! The world is changing, and so quickly! What does it *matter* who her grandfather is? Lots of young women are working in London these days, and I say, jolly good for them! They're far more interesting than those spoilt brats mollycoddled in Papa's mansion in Surrey, fishing for titled husbands in ballrooms!'

Mrs Courtney gave a little gasp but Thomas had turned his attention to me. 'So you had to do a training course in Morse code, I expect. Is it hard to learn?'

I shook my head and spoke a full sentence for the first time since his arrival.

'No – I already knew it. That's how I got the job. I didn't need any training.'

'Really? How on earth did you learn it?'

'A – a friend gave me the code,' I said. 'But I taught myself.'

'You could work as a spy in the war!' said Mr Courtney with a loud guffaw. 'They'll need people who know codes and things!'

'Oh, do be quiet, Henry, there isn't *going* to be a war!'

'There is, there most certainly is!' said Mr Courtney. 'If Germany doesn't …'

But Mrs Courtney wouldn't let him continue. 'You don't mean to say, Thomas dear, that you're in favour of those horrid suffragettes?'

'I certainly do think women should have the vote,' replied Thomas. 'Why ever not?'

Mrs Courtney spluttered something about husbands, and Thomas took the opportunity to turn to me again.

'What do you think about women and the vote, Winnie? Are you interested in politics? Would you vote if you had the chance?'

I actually had never thought of such a thing, but I did now. It was as if a light went on in my head and I thought of British Guiana and the plantations and the situation of the Indians and what would happen if there was a party that stood up for them and if women could vote and, being more compassionate by nature than men, how we could change the world.

I nodded vigorously, instantly making up my mind. 'Oh, yes, indeed! I'd vote if I had to, and if there were a party that supported my views!'

'See, mother? You can't roll back time. Things are changing!'

Mrs Courtney snorted and brushed back her hair and made a new start with me, but on the same track. I focused on my meal. It was a typical Sunday lunch of roast beef and potatoes. At Promised Land, Mildred had even tried, but failed, to reproduce Yorkshire pudding. What is it about the English that makes them want to live exactly the same everywhere, no matter what country they are in?

'And where are you living, Winnie dear? In a boarding house, or with a private family?'

'In a boarding house.'

'Ah yes; I heard there's a hostel for English women in Bridgetown. I suppose it's quite respectable.'

I raised my eyes head, looked her straight in the eyes. I shook my head and said, loudly and clearly. 'No. I'm in the other boarding house. The one for coloured women.'

A stunned silence fell over the table. Even Mr Courtney, who had been involved in war talk with a nodding Uncle Ronald, looked up, brow creased in puzzlement. Then Thomas roared with laughter.

Aunt Jane stuttered, 'Really, Winnie, I don't think …'

Mrs Courtney exclaimed: 'Goodness Gracious!'

Back to Thomas, who stopped laughing and said, 'I like that, I like that. The one for coloured women! Hysterical, just hysterical. Mother, I think you've met your match.'

Aunt Jane said quickly, 'You see, Mrs Courtney, there was no room available at the English home …'

'But that's not true, Aunt Jane. I didn't even know if there was room or not. I didn't ask. I went to the home for coloured women first – I didn't even know it was that – and they had a room available and I took it. A bed, I mean. It's a double room. I share with a woman called Sibille Hart and she's my best friend.'

The thing is, I was sick and tired of lies and subterfuge. Sick and tired of sneaking around hiding the truth from everyone. Sick and tired of feeling shame for liking or loving people my people disapproved of. Sick and tired of *my* people and *your* people. It may have been necessary – or opportunistic – in British Guiana, but it wasn't here. What did I care of Mrs Courtney's opinion? What did I care if Aunt Jane reported back to Papa? I straightened my back, looked from Aunt Jane to Mrs Courtney and back and said,

'She's a fine person, a teacher. I'm learning a lot from her. She's a Barbadian, a *real* Barbadian. You English, you're really just like pot-plants in a greenhouse – you don't belong here. You may have lived here all your lives but you live apart in your own little bubble, just like I used to do back in BG. And it's not a good thing, not a real thing. I used to live that way and I wasn't *real*. Now I am. Or at least, I'm beginning to be. I was shy and confused and selfish and now I'm trying to change. There's nothing wrong with that and I just wanted you to know, and if you don't like me because of that – well, you don't have to. I don't really care.'

Aunt Jane leaned towards me and said, 'Dear, that was very rude. Apologize immediately!'

'But why should I apologize? It's the truth!'

'Quite right! If it's the truth she wasn't rude!' And I looked up then and met Thomas's eyes as boldly as can be.

Thomas chuckled and clapped. 'Bravo!' he said.

Aunt Jane changed the subject, and the meal eventually came to a welcome end.


There's a natural tiredness that sets in after lunch when the sun is directly overhead and the day is at its hottest. After lunch we retired to our rooms for a midday rest. The Courtneys were offered lounge chairs on the veranda, which the elders accepted gratefully. Mrs Courtney, especially, seemed exhausted. She had avoided any direct conversation with me for the rest of the meal, and seemed happy to retire for a while.

My foot was on the first step of the stairs when Thomas appeared out of nowhere. He placed a hand on mine, which was resting on the banister.

'Winnie,' he said, 'would you come for a walk with me?'

'A walk? At this time of day?'

'It won't be far. Just to that tree over there; it's nice and shady underneath. Or to the rose arbour. Or we can just stay in the house if you prefer.'

I slipped my hand neatly from under his. 'I'm sorry – I really am tired. Maybe later on.'

He nodded and drew away his hand. I walked up the stairs, fully aware of his gaze on my back. I reached the top landing and walked on to my room. I did not look down. But I knew he was watching.

❀ ❀ ❀

For the rest of the day I stubbornly avoided any time alone with Thomas. We had a picnic on the beach later in the day when the sun had lost its fierceness, and everyone except me went into the sea for a bathe. Thomas tried to persuade me but I resisted adamantly; my bathing costume, in spite of the high neck and long arms, was embarrassingly revealing with its waist-length skirt, and even more so when it was wet. It just would not do to encourage that penetrating gaze of his.

So I sat on one of the beach chairs the servants had brought down for us and watched. And though I resisted as much as I can, it was Thomas who seemed to overshadow everyone else; playing with the children, throwing them into the air and letting them fall, screaming, into the water; letting them climb onto his back and swimming with them there, ducking them and chasing them and splashing them and laughing, laughing, laughing.

In a random thought it occurred to me that I had not seen George laugh once since that first day when he had sailed into our compound on his bicycle, weaving to and fro, waving an arm through the air as if he had not a care in the world.

It occurred to me that I had made George miserable.

It occurred to me that George bore not a laughing child on his back but an enormous burden – the burden of his race, his race's history, his race's future. And how much I had complicated a life that was complicated enough already.

A deep, wretched sadness opened up in me, an abyss that had no floor. A melancholy and sense of hopelessness that rose up and moistened my eyes, leaving a veil of tears that blurred my sight. Thomas and the rest of the company disappeared from my sight, from my mind. I thought only of George, and the happiness denied us.

'What's the matter?' said a voice beside me and I looked up, and through my tears I saw Thomas's smiling face, his concerned eyes, his hair, dark and wet now, clinging to his forehead.

I shook my head. 'It's nothing,' I said, but he saw through the lie.

'It's something,' he said, 'but I don't want to pry.'

Then all the children came running up the beach to smother him with their wet young bodies, and he laughed and threw them off and ran away with them to play with a ball.

I got my wish that day: I did not have a conversation alone with Thomas. But that did not lift my despondency.

\* \* \*

'Actually, he sounds perfect for you,' said Sibille the next day after work. 'I think you should take your time and let things take their course. If he can prise George from your mind, so much the better. You obviously like him, so what's the problem? It's not as if he's some horrible suitor your people are forcing on you.'

'But I don't want him to prise George from my mind!' I wailed. 'I love George! I promised George I'll wait!'

'A promise he has not returned,' said Sibille. At times she could be so cruel with her love of showing me the things I did not want to see.

'George loves me. I love him. Together we can face everything.'

'Oh, twaddle!' said Sibille. 'You have no idea. You're looking at this whole romance through rose tinted glasses. You think you know what you're letting yourself into with George but you don't know a thing. You've got some kind of a God complex. You're looking *down* at him and his life from your high horse and you're thinking you can somehow spread some magic and wash away the problems, wash away all the obstacles. You have no idea. Girl, you have no idea whatsoever. George may love you but he can see right through your ideal vision of the future and he knows it is non-sense. That's why he tries to push you away. You're not fit for him.'

'What do you mean, I'm not fit for him?'

'I mean exactly what I said,' she answered, and refused to say a single word more on the subject.

❊ ❊ ❊

Two days later, I looked up as a customer entered the Telegraph Office. It was late afternoon; soon I would be tidying my desk in time for my nightshift colleague. The customer approached the counter, and I looked up. It was Thomas.

'Hello!' he said, removing his hat.

'Oh! Hello!'

'I want to send a telegram,' he continued, 'to a good friend in London.'

'Yes, of course.' I got up and walked towards him, handed him a pencil and a message form. 'Each letter in capitals, please, and in a square. But I expect you know that.'

'Oh yes; I've sent many telegrams in my life. But this one is special.' He bent over the counter, carefully pencilling in the message. He pushed the form towards me. 'Finished!'

'Thanks.' I told him the price, he paid. I took the piece of paper over to the machine and sat down to start tapping. I finished tapping in the address and got to the message itself.

'Oh!' I said again, and looked up – Thomas was still waiting, and watching, a cocky smile across his face.

I flushed, and looked down at what he had written, and my hand shook a little as I tapped in the message:

'MET THE MOST WONDERFUL GIRL IN THE
WORLD STOP THOMAS'

I looked up again; the smile had left his lips and he had the
grace to look slightly worried.

'Sorry. It's just a bit of a joke. I needed an excuse to see you
again, and, well …' the sentence petered off; a new customer had
entered the office and I turned away. There was a wooden bench
along the wall of the customer section of the office; Thomas sat
down and waited patiently till I had dealt with the new message.
The moment the customer left Thomas leapt to his feet and returned to the counter.

'What time do you finish work, Winnie?'

I looked up at the wall clock. 'In about ten minutes.'

'I thought so. Do you mind if I wait for you, and walk you
home? I'd like to talk to you.'

'Oh, well – yes of course you can wait, but …'

'I won't be a nuisance. Just go ahead with your work. We'll talk
afterwards.'

Fifteen minutes later we were walking in the direction of Miss
Goode's house.

'I came into town today to do some investigations,' said
Thomas. 'I'm looking for a job as a junior in a solicitor's office
and have been making the rounds. I've found a few possibilities,
had a few interviews. It shouldn't take long.'

'So you – you're moving to Bridgetown? Soon?'

'Well, it will take a while till I'm settled, even after I've found
a job. I'm with family friends in the meantime and then I'll look
for a place of my own, a flat or a house.'

'Oh.'

I genuinely could not find anything else to say. It didn't seem
to matter, for Thomas seemed happy to chatter away all the way
home without requiring any response from me beyond a nod or a
smile or an occasional *really?*

'I know of a place where there's a magnificent view of the sunset,' said Thomas suddenly. 'Would you like to watch it with me? Sit down for half an hour?'

He was altogether so charming, so polite, so solicitous – how could I possibly refuse?

'Yes – why not?' I said, and so he lured me towards the shorefront of Bridgetown. There was indeed a magnificent view of rooftops before a vista of vivid blue sea sparkling in the waning sun. Several boats were moored in their docks, their sails lowered, bobbing gently on the water. Some were obviously fishing boats; they looked old, tired, their paint peeling away. Others were bigger, better, white and smart. Thomas pointed.

'One of those sailing boats belongs to a friend of mine, Walter,' he said. 'He's a member of the Yacht Club. Perhaps you'd like to come when we go out sailing one day? It's great fun. You'd enjoy it. And you'll make some new friends.'

'Oh, I'd love to!' I said before I could stop myself. How often had I watched the boats out at sea, their white sails furling in the wind! Just looking at them skidding along on the water brought to me a feeling of immense freedom and space. How glorious, I had thought, to be aboard one of those! And now I had a chance.

That enthusiastic response was an invitation to yet more suggestions: a trip around the island, a visit to the old Fort, an invitation to the Barbados Yacht Club New Year's Eve Ball.

I agreed to all. I met his eyes and thrilled at the admiration in them. I laughed at his jokes. I relaxed. I completely forgot the time slipping away. Perhaps Sibille was right after all.

❊ ❊ ❊

'Well, where've *you* been, Miss Sparkly-Eyes?' said Sibille the moment I walked into the door. 'Left me to do all the cooking by myself – anyway, food's ready.'

Over dinner I told her, and as I spoke the sparkle left my spirit and no doubt my eyes.

'And now I feel so guilty!' I wailed. 'I feel as if I've betrayed George!'

'Interesting,' said Sibille. 'And now you have two choices. One is to take that sense of guilt as a sign from your conscience that you did wrong, and to let Thomas know at the earliest opportunity that no, you can't do all these wonderful things with him. Your other choice is to brush away that guilt and just enjoy yourself. You're only young once and Thomas sounds perfect for you. Why not? You'll never get the chance to go sailing and attend the Yacht Club New Year's Ball with George. Give Thomas a chance. Maybe this is life offering you a hand to climb out of all your problems. Why listen to a boring sense of guilt? Why not? Go ahead, I say.'

'Really? You really think it's all right? Do you think George would be angry, if he knew?'

'Maybe not angry, but hurt, for sure. But you know what? To hell with George. For one, he'll never know unless you tell him. Second, George himself told you to find someone suitable. Here's someone. You have George's permission.'

'True,' I agreed. Secretly, I basked in her encouragement. She was validating my acceptance of Thomas's courtship.

'The thing is,' I said, 'it just feels so good to be actually *courted* by a young man, a young man who obviously admires me and seeks my company and wants to be with me and making the effort to please me and, and, well, just to be *wooed* for a change, instead of having to do all the wooing, all the persuasion myself. George is so, so … *reluctant.*'

'Every girl likes to be wooed,' said Sibille, 'still, I want to stick up for George. He really doesn't have a choice than to be reluctant. He knows, far better than you, how little you fit into his world. He knows the problems that lie ahead should you marry. How can he ever court you, woo you, propose to you, when all he can offer you is a life of humiliation and struggle and hardship? How can he ask you to step down from your privilege into that life? I don't doubt he loves you – but the fact that he's trying to protect you, to warn you off – well, it works in his favour.'

There it was again – this tremendous sense of guilt, descending on me like a big black cloud from the sky, spoiling all the pleasure of anticipation. I wished Sibille had not explained about George. I wished she'd continued to encourage me, to persuade me that yes, it was fine to enjoy Thomas and all he could offer.

'I'm only young once,' I reminded myself firmly, and with a hefty shove cleared my mind of all guilt, all sense of disloyalty, all thought of George. I was here, now, and so was Thomas. I liked him, he liked me. In his presence all the burdens I carried melted away. And after all, going sailing with him and to dances didn't mean I had to *marry* him. I would live in the present, and enjoy my life.

❄ ❄ ❄

The New Year's Eve Ball was splendid. It recreated in real life all those stories Mama had told me about the dances and balls of Vienna and Salzburg – even if the setting was not a formal ballroom with chandeliers above and a marble floor beneath, but a spreading park with a wooden floor laid down for dancing, lined with waving palms, brushed by a balmy breeze, the stars twinkling above, the black sea glistening beyond the palms.

And above all, an orchestra. A real live orchestra! There were the violins, the cellos; the woodwinds, the brass, the percussion – everything Mama had once described with such longing – playing music that made my heart leap and swirl and swoon.

Thomas swung me around and we laughed, gazing into each other's eyes; it was the Blue Danube. *The Blue Danube*! Memories of childhood days, Mama and Papa dancing to this very music, played not by an orchestra but improvised by Mama singing,

Mama laughing and throwing back her head as she and Papa whirled around the room and we girls clapped. And further back yet, to a time before my existence, in a long-ago Viennese ballroom: Papa and Mama, young and beautiful, waltzing to this very music and falling in love.

'*If only you could hear a live orchestra,*' Mama used to say, and now I was, and it was better than a fairy tale. We laughed and waltzed and made the music our own, Thomas and I. It was Vienna in Barbados; my ancestors reaching across the ocean to claim me; my very blood surging within me to take wing. The magic of music and a warm breeze and the sea, and me swept away from earth in the arms of a weaver of a heart-capturing spell.

'There you are,' said Sibille when I described the ball to her, the music, and the dancing. 'There's your answer. Thomas is perfect for you. What more can you ask of a man, than music and dancing and nights under a moonlit sky?'

I looked at her suspiciously. 'Are you being sarcastic?'

'Not at all,' she replied. She sat at the vanity, plaiting her hair into one long rope over her shoulder. 'It's the truth, isn't it? He makes you happy, doesn't he? All George has brought you up to now is grief and problems, and more grief and problems are waiting for you if you choose him. There's no competition, really.'

'Yes, but ...'

'But what? Where do all these 'buts' come from? Maybe because you can't rescue Thomas like you want to rescue George? Maybe Thomas don't make you feel like God, high up in the sky?'

'Sibille, don't be horrible! You make me sound like a witch!'

'I just don't understand your problem. Why you still lookin' at me like that like if you're not sure about Thomas, after a night like last night? Lookin' at me with all that doubt in your eyes? Guilt? You don't need to feel guilt. George knows he can't marry you. You don't need to worry about him. Just go ahead. What on earth you waitin't for? My permission? You got it, girl. I not goin' to blame you at all if you choose the white man instead of the black. That's what you worried about, right? That you lettin' down the side you think you should be stickin' up for? That you not the heroine you thought you were? The great rebel?'

'You confuse me, that's all!'

'You confuse yourself! You had a magical night. You just told me that, your words. Magical. Wonderful. What more you want?'

What more did I want? I couldn't answer at first. I walked to the window and looked out over the back yard with its mango and coconut trees. They reminded me of home, of Promised Land, the land that wasn't as Promised as I'd thought. Could I return to that world? Because that was the world Thomas offered me. Back into the fold of my own people, my own race, yet free of the scourge that Promised Land held: no cane fields, no labourers to worry about. Well-treated housemaids and garden boys. And I would be the kind mistress they all spoke well of. Dinners with select company, waited on by black servants in white gloves. The tinkle of fine glass and china. Carefree picnics on a lovely white beach. Memories of last night swirled through my mind, the laughter, the fun. Sibille was right. Thomas was a gateway into such a life, an honourable escape from the problems I had created. I could go back into my own world. The door stood open. It was as easy as saying *yes*. Yet still ...

I turned around. 'Love!' I said.

'What?'

'You asked what more I want. And the answer is love. I know it now: I don't love Thomas. Yes, last night was full of laughter and pleasure but it wasn't full of love. Love is – something else. Deeper, more solid. Quiet. That's what I have with George. It's like a foundation, a rock that stabilizes my heart. Last night – yes, it was fun, but it was – a puff of magic. A mirage. Something that came and went, a puff. I don't want a puff, Sibille, or even a series of puffs. I want love. I want George.'

# Chapter Twenty-nine

On a Saturday morning two weeks after the New Year's Eve ball Thomas came to pick me up in the sparkling new car that had been his parents' Christmas present. I had seen nothing of him since the ball; he had gone back to his parents to spend some time before starting work in February, for he had indeed found work with Littleton and Field, one of Bridgetown's leading solicitor firms.

"You're looking very pensive today," he said as we drove southwards, out of town. "What's on your mind?"

"Oh nothing special," I lied. "Just a bit tired, that's all. I didn't sleep well last night."

It was true, yet the matter at hand was far more urgent. I could no longer see Thomas. I had to put an end to it, and I had to do so today.

"I'm not sleeping well myself, of late" he chuckled. He reached out and squeezed my hand. "Too many thoughts. Nice thoughts, though, and all about you. I hope you've got a similar problem!"

I didn't answer. Tears pricked my eyes and I looked away so he would not see, and a few minutes later he slowed the car and turned it right, driving into what looked like an empty field with a few cows grazing and a tangle of bushes at the further end. The field sloped gently down towards the sea. Beyond the bushes the sea sparkled, meeting the sky at the faraway horizon. A few clouds skittered across the sky, balls of white fluff against brilliant cobalt. A perfect day. He got out of the car, walked around to the passenger seat, opened it and held out a hand to help me out. Opening the back door of the car, he removed a canvas bag and slung it over his shoulder.

"Come," he said, taking my hand again. "I want to show you something."

He led me along a sandy path that cut through the bushes. He did not speak. The path was far too narrow to allow us to walk side by side, and the bushes were thorny, and so I walked behind him, holding my skirt close to my legs to avoid the brambles. Finally we emerged on the other side. I gasped. A magnificent vista opened before my eyes: a beach, perfectly white, stretching out along a softly curved bay and beyond it the serene aquamarine of the Caribbean. The water lapped, curled and frothed like a skirt of lace against the whiteness of the sand, making pleasant slapping and sucking sounds. Spellbound, I let my heart open in delight. I soared upwards in sweetness and light, in the pristine purity of it all, and I let out a laugh of utter joy.

"Take off your shoes," said Thomas, and I did, and so did he. We walked towards the sea, I holding on to my hat lest the breeze sweep it away. The sand was warm and as fine and soft as talcum powder beneath my bare feet. The wind played gently with my skirt blowing it against my legs, and puffed out my blouse so that I felt it cool against my skin. Thomas took my hand again and led me into the sea. The water, warmed by the sun, splashed ever so gently against my calves. I raised my skirt to protect it from the water, but I soon let it go, not caring how wet it would get. Not caring about anything. This was just too wonderful, too beautiful, too glorious to care. I laughed again and turned to Thomas.

"That's better!" he said, and took book my hands. "The sparkle's back in your eyes. You looked almost sad when I picked you up today. So you like it?"

"Oh Thomas! I've never seen anything so – so utterly breathtaking in my whole life! Oh, it's just glorious! Look! The water is so clear, it's like glass! It's even nicer than Uncle Ron's beach!"

"The best beach on the island," he said, "at least, the best one I've ever discovered. And it's all yours."

I stopped laughing and looked at him. I must have misheard. "Pardon?"

"You heard right. At least, almost right. It *could* be yours, because it's mine. This is the plot of land my parents gave me, as compensation for not being the eldest son and inheriting the plantation. But I don't want the plantation. This is better. Five acres, to build myself a home and create a piece of paradise. What do you think?"

My face must have looked as blank as the pristine sand.

"Can't you see it?" He went on. "A beautiful white mansion, made of wood, just like those lovely Georgetown ones everyone talks about. Lots of verandas and balconies. Red roses growing up the walls and a bougainvillea-shaded walkway down to the beach. Coconut palms dotted around the clipped lawns. All the windows facing out to the sea. Maybe a little jetty with a boat moored to it. Mother thinks I should put up a hotel here for people to escape the dreary English winters, but that would spoil everything. No – it's to be a family home. Children playing in the surf. Garden parties, picnics on the beach, evening strolls along the surf, gorgeous sunsets over the horizon." He spread his arms and turned around and around as if to claim the entire earth as his own.

"It's lovely, and that's nice, but I don't …"

"It's mine and it can be yours too."

He sank to his knees, fished in his pocket, and produced a little jeweller's box. He opened it.

"Winnie, I love you. You're the most lovely, enigmatic, interesting, mysterious, delightful, remarkable, smartest, most wonderful, bravest girl I've ever met. Will you be my wife?"

I looked at him, at those pleading blue eyes, the sun-kissed , straw-coloured hair, the face, so familiar now, looking up at me in anticipation. I looked at what he held in his hands: a ring with a solitaire diamond set in silver, reflecting the sun in a thousand shades of light. The breath caught in my throat. Something moved within me. My eyes grew moist and prickled with unshed tears.

"I – I don't know what to say," I said at last. I put my hands behind my back. "Oh Thomas! That's so lovely and so sweet of you! I – I'm so completely … I just don't know what to say. I'll have to think about it."

I didn't have to think about it. I knew my answer. But how could I say an outright no? I had to let him down gently.

He immediately stood up, snapped the little box shut and slipped it into his trouser pocket. His voice was sharp as he spoke again; I had never heard him use this tone.

"Think about it? I thought – I mean, I was sure you knew this was coming and were as excited as I am! Winnie! All this time, all these weeks – isn't this the whole point? I mean, you must have known I was going to propose! Girls *know* things like that!"

"But I didn't!" I wailed. "I mean, it's too early, I need time; there's so much to think about and to consider, and …"

"If two people love each other there's nothing to *consider!* I thought you *loved* me! You gave me every indication …"

"No, I didn't really – I mean, yes, I really like you and I've enjoyed all the things we did together, the sailing and the dancing but it was just pleasure; it was just enjoyment – I don't know if it was love. I just don't know! And …"

He was silent for a while. Then he walked over to the bag he had set down on the sand, opened it, removed a blanket and spread it on the beach. He gestured to me to sit down, and I did. I drew up my knees, wrapped my skirt around them, and burying my face against my thighs, hugged them. I felt rather than heard Thomas sit down next to me. Then he said:

"Winnie!"

I looked up.

"It's not someone else, is it?"

I didn't answer, just gave a sort of a shrug.

"It's not that chap in Georgetown is it?"

My jaw dropped. "How did you …"

He gave a wry, humourless chuckle. When he spoke again his voice was calm but restrained, as if he were holding back some great emotion. Now and then it cracked.

"Mother has good friends over there, in BG. When she first met you she wrote to them asking for information about your family – the reports were very good, excellent, in fact, which was why she approved of you in the first place. But then, just before Christmas, she got another letter with quite a different story. Seems you fled here in the midst of some scandal – some love affair with a darkie? And your father wrapped up in a murder investigation?"

I said nothing, my silence confirmed his words.

"See, I've known all of this for the last couple of weeks. Mother told me everything and strongly advised me against you. I went against her wishes. I was willing to forgive your past – we all make mistakes when we're young, and the way you flout convention is one of the things I love most about you. You're not like those silly fashionable girls in London who – well, never mind. I love the way you got a job and moved into a coloured women's hostel – I love your spunk. I admire everything about you. But sooner or later, we all have to grow up and find our place. I thought you'd realized that. I thought we were of one mind! I even stood up for you against Mother, told her that was all in the past and that you deserve a second chance. And you led me on. You played with me. I thought you were sincere – I – I can't believe – I just can't believe what a *fool* you've made of me!"

His voice was now loud and tinged with anger.

I glared at him. I could not argue with him. How could I? What defence did I have, except that I, not he, was the fool, the greatest fool on earth, naïve and stupid and immature. I should never have come here. I leaped to my feet.

"Well, then!" I said. "That makes it easy doesn't it! What would you say if I told you more? Oh, you would be so shocked!

Yes, Thomas, I love him, and what's more, I've been intimate with him and you would never, ever marry me after *that*, would you?"

I turned and ran back up the beach, towards the car.

'Winnie! Stop!' he ran behind me. I reached the brambles and stumbled – I had trodden on a thorn. He caught up with me.

'Your shoes,' he said, and handed them to me. I put them on, and he did the same.

'Wait and let me get the blanket. I'll take you home.'

We drove back to Bridgetown in silence. He stopped in front of Miss Goode's turquoise house and when he spoke his voice was calm once more.

'This isn't the end, Winnie. I still want you. I forgive you. Everything – even, even *that*. He seduced you didn't he? I forgive you. I want you as my wife. You said you'd think about it – please do. Think about it seriously. This is your future at stake. Don't make a huge mistake. You might never get as good a chance as this.'

He raised my hand to his lips and kissed it. I tried not to pull it away. I tried to meet his gaze above our clasped hands. I blinked back the tears, and nodded.

'I'll think about it,' I promised, but I already knew it was a lie.

❉ ❉ ❉

'You're probably the biggest fool who ever walked the earth,' said Sibille later that day. We had walked down to the harbour and sat watching the white yachts coming in, their sails billowing in the wind. 'You could have been on one of them boats a little while from now. Most girls would jump at the chance.'

'I'm not most girls and I've been on one,' I replied.

'I know. You said it was wonderful. I don't understand why you're turning down that sort of a life. I mean, I *know* why, but I just don't understand.'

'You sound disappointed.'

'Not really. Just surprised. I thought that's the direction you were drifting towards. You come home from these outings laughing as if it were Christmas, and then when it gets serious you throw it all away. For George? For hardship and struggle and humiliation all you life. And George hasn't even proposed!'

'He will!'

'He won't. Winnie – wake up! That last letter of his – you have to take it seriously!'

'No, I won't! He said he loves me! That's the most important thing! He loves me Sibille! He does! I know he does! He told me so! He'll never forget me'

'Maybe not. But deep inside you belong to another world. Thomas's world. Not George's. George's world is too tough for you, Winnie. And from what I know of him, he's trying to protect you from a life too hard for you to bear.'

'But I can! When …'

I looked at her more closely. There was something new in her eyes, something I hadn't ever seen before. A challenge? A goad? Something that told me to stop talking and listen to her.

'You're playing devil's advocate, aren't you?'

'I have to,' she replied. 'It's time to wake up, Winnie. This isn't a happily-ever-after love story. This is dead serious. George is dead serious, but you aren't taking him seriously. It's time you did.'

Something in her tone alerted to me. To – what? A sense of danger. A warning. 'What's the matter, Sibille?'

She slipped her hand into her pocket. 'Read this.' It was a newspaper page. 'This was today's Barbados Herald front page.'

The headline splashed across the front page screamed, in big, bold letters: **'BG SUGAR KING ON TRIAL FOR MURDER!'**

Right below the headline was a subtitle: 'VICTIM'S FRIEND LEADS PROTEST MARCH!', and below that, two photographs, portraits. One was a close-up of Papa. The other was a full length picture of George, my George, with his head tilted back and his eyes turned upwards as if to an absent God; his fist was raised to the sky, and he bore a placard across his shoulders, scrawled with the words: JUSTICE FOR BHIM!

My head swirled. My eyes swam, so much so that I could not read the words. I handed the clipping back. 'Read it to me!' I said. She took it and read aloud:

❊ ❊ ❊

*The murder trial of British Guiana Sugar King Archibald Cox, one of the few remaining independent sugar-cane planters left in the colony, starts next Monday under strong protest from the local population. Cox is accused of shooting in cold blood the leader of an East Indian labour uprising on his Berbice plantation, Promised Land. The trial is expected to last a month, since there are conflicting reports as to the crime: Cox claims self-defence, but the East Indian majority insist that that the victim, Bhim Persaud, was completely unarmed. Mr Persaud was himself not a labourer; educated at the prestigious Queen's College in Georgetown, a boys' secondary school whose pupils hail predominantly from the European upper class, he was however deeply involved in the recent wave of labour strikes and protest riots on the Berbice sugar plantations.*

*In Georgetown, a growing crowd has been picketing the Victoria Law Courts this past week and is expected to continue throughout the trial. The protest is led by the victim's best friend, George Quint, a former Queen's College schoolmate of African race …'*

'Stop!' I cried. 'That's enough. I get it.'

I got up and turned towards home, towards Bird Street and Miss Goode's Boarding House for Young Ladies. Sibille called for me to wait but I did not.

❊ ❊ ❊

Sibille organised an emergency meeting for that evening at Oskar's house. Everyone was there: Oskar and Ivan, of course, Max and Valerie, Johnnie and his girlfriend Amy, Richard and Paul, all laughing and horsing around and jostling. Oskar poured everyone a rum tonic while Sibille read out the newspaper article in full. Their laughter left their eyes and their bodies grew still as she read, and all eyes turned to me in the silence that followed.

'Tell them,' said Sibille. 'Tell them the truth.'

I told them. And I told them what I planned to do.

'I have to speak out. Bear witness, against him. Against my own father!'

Oskar let out a long drawn out whistle.

'Oh boy!' said Max.

'She's planned to go back to be a witness for the prosecution,' said Sibille.

'Very brave of you, Winnie,' said Valerie. She reached out and took my hand, squeezed it.

'No,' I said. 'It's not brave at all. It's horrible. My own father! I can't do it! But I have to!'

'It's a real dilemma,' said Sibille. 'Because if she doesn't she'll feel guilt, and if she does she'll also feel guilt.'

'Whichever way I turn, it's wrong!' I wailed. 'How can I turn in my own father! He'll get the death penalty!'

'Not necessarily,' said Oskar. 'Maybe they'll decide on second degree murder, and then it'll be life in prison.'

'That's bad enough,' I said.

'Better than the gallows,' said Max.

'Manslaughter?' asked Ivan.

'You say he took the pistol with him?' Oskar asked. 'From home?'

I nodded. 'Yes.'

'That sounds premeditated to me,' said Paul. Paul worked as a clerk in one of the Ministries.

'I thought you and your father were estranged?' asked Ivan.

'Yes, we are,' I replied. 'But he's still my father! I know he's a cruel bully, I know he's the worst kind of Englishman, I know what you think of that kind of person … and I agree with you. But he's still my father. And – and somehow, somewhere, I still love him. I do.'

Tears welled in my eyes and I brushed them away in anger. Anger at myself, for not being clear and decisive, and strong in my decision to do the right thing. I knew what the right thing was. I knew they all knew. It was as clear as day. Anyone of them, if asked, would say, 'You must give your statement. You must tell the truth.' I let my eyes wander from one of them to the other and I saw it there. They wanted Papa to face justice. It was only fair. To Bhim.

Oskar said: 'And this George, leading the protests … that's *your* George, isn't it.'

'Yes.'

'That's what makes it even worse. As if in making a statement, she's doing it for herself, to impress George. To win him back. I can tell them, can't I, Winnie?' Sibille looked at me and I nodded. I no longer cared what they all thought of me. Let them know the worst.

So she told them about George's letter. 'He loves her, but he's broken it off. He wants her to go her own way. With her own people. White people.'

'Whom she would betray, if she speaks the truth,' said Max, nodding as he understood the conundrum.

'But I have no *own people!*' I cried. 'I'm just a girl – just a person, a person who loves another person! But everyone will think I did it for him, for George – and it's not for him at all. It's because, because it's the truth, and I want justice for Bhim. I know his mother. I knew him, and even though he never trusted me, I liked him. I admired him. He was a good man, fighting for truth, and justice, and change, and my father killed him. My own father! How can I just keep silent, when I know what he did! How can I be such a coward, keeping the silence just because my father did it! But how can I send my father to the gallows! And by keeping silent – I mean, it won't bring Bhim back, will it!'

I stopped, and started again. 'But it will send a message. A message to all plantation owners, that they cannot do this. That they too are subject to the law of the land. They cannot do as they like to the labourers. Speaking out is right – but how can I!' 'The last words tailed off in a wail of despair. The only thing that broke the silence that followed this outburst was my own sniffing as I struggled to hold back the tears. Someone passed me a handkerchief, and I blotted my eyes and blew my nose. The silence remained. Then, at last, Oskar broke it.

'I think you should just do the right thing,' he said.

Max nodded. 'So do I.'

Everyone nodded and murmured agreement. I looked from face to face and I read there encouragement, hope, confidence in me. Confidence that I would, indeed, do the right thing. There was no doubt what the right thing was.

Then Ivan spoke again. 'Winnie, you and I need to talk. I'll give you some free legal advice. Let's go out to the veranda. There might be a way out for you.'

❀ ❀ ❀

The next day, my first telegram of the day was to George. It bore only three words:

'MARRY ME. WINNIEX.'

It was only after I'd sent it that I remembered George's words from long, long ago: 'You don't say *marry me* in a telegram – that's the best way to get a marriage refusal.' Well, it was too late now.

My second telegram of the day was to Mama in Salzburg, and it was a long one.


PAPA KILLED INDIAN LABOURER ON TRIAL FOR MURDER STOP I WAS WITNESS MUST TESTIFY

STOP HUGE COMMOTION IN BG STOP I LOVE
NEGRO MAN STOP NEED YOU DESPERATELY AT
HOME STOP IF PAPA CONVICTED YOYO AND I
ALONE STOP MAMA COME BACK WE NEED YOU
STOP PLEASE MAMA PLEASE COME HOME YOU
ARE OUR MOTHER COME HOME STOP WILL STAY
PARK HOTEL GEORGETOWN REPLY THERE STOP

In my lunch break I walked to the West Indian Line booking
office and booked my passage back to British Guiana, two weeks
hence. After my lunch break, I handed in my notice.

# Chapter Thirty

They all came to the dock to see me off: Sibille, Max, Oskar and Ivan, Valerie and Amy, Johnny, Richard and Paul. In the last two weeks it seemed to me that some major shift had taken place within the group; as if they had all made a collective internal shuffle to make room for me. As if I was now enclosed in one big shared heart belonging to them all. Without words, only with gestures and looks and smiles, I felt their support and their final acceptance. I was one of them. One by one they hugged me before I boarded. Sibille accompanied me on board, carrying my suitcase in one hand and my violin case in the other.

Uncle Don and Aunt Jane did not come to see me off; but then, I had not told them I was leaving. As my guardians they could have prevented my journey; but thank the Lord, the shipping company did not ask for signed parental permission. If they had I would have forged it.

Nobody in Georgetown knew I was coming, and so on arrival I took a hackney carriage out to Kitty, where I surprised Aunty Dolly in the process of hemming a frock. She frowned as she looked up.

'Eh-eh! Is what you doing here?' No smile of welcome, no hug for me. I did not care. I smiled and hugged her and asked if I could stay, at least for one night until I could find other accommodation. Myrtle had arrived on the scene by now. The two of them exchanged a covert look. Neither of them smiled, neither showed the least sign of pleasure on seeing me. Though I understood, my heart cramped as if in the grip of giant claws.

'It's all right,' I whispered. 'I'm on your side. I'll make it all good.' And they let me stay.

❋ ❋ ❋

Early, very early the next morning, I made my way to the Kitty Police Station. I spoke with an officer for a few minutes, after which he set me in a carriage that took me to a house in Kingston. I walked up the stairs and knocked on the door. After a while, an Indian woman, still in a nightgown but with a hastily thrown-over shawl across her shoulders, opened it.

'Mrs Bhattacharya?' I asked. She nodded. 'May I speak to your husband, please?'

Mr Bhattacharya, the Crown Prosecutor, came out in his dressing gown, and interviewed me just as he was. Afterwards, Mrs Bhattacharya offered me breakfast, and I accepted, though I felt little hunger and ate no more than half a slice of bread with a thin spread of butter. Mr Bhattacharya, now bathed and dressed, joined us, and very dapper he was too in his black trousers, crisp white shirt and dark blue tie. I had never seen an Indian dressed so smartly. To match his spruce outfit he spoke with an accent straight out of a London University, his enunciation cleaner than my own by far. A brown peer, who might have walked straight out of the House of Lords. He was tall and lanky, his hair jet black and shiny, thin lips beneath a neatly combed moustache, and sharp searching eyes that seemed to probe into the deepest corner of my mind. It wouldn't do to have this man on the other side. My poor Papa.

After breakfast, a hansom cab picked us up and carried us to the Victoria High Court. The crowd was already thick on High Street as we approached. People were chanting; an angry, passionate chant, but I could not make out the words. The signs people waved told me more: *Justice for Bhim!Down with racist trials!'Guilty! Murderer!* When I got out of the carriage someone recognised me.

'Is Cox daughter!' went the cry, and I was treated to a roar of fury. I bowed my head. Mr Bhattacharya held up his hand, put a protective arm around me; the crowd grew silent and parted to let us through, and then took up its chant again.

As we reached the other end a single voice reached me. 'Winnie?'

I looked up. George was standing right in front of me. I did not answer; I just stopped and we stared at each other for a while, and then I nodded slightly and Mr Bhattacharya and I walked on.

'Wait here until you're called,' said Mr Bhattacharya, gesturing to a bench in the corridor outside the courtroom. 'I'm going to speak to your father.' He walked away down the corridor, turned a corner, and disappeared.

I sat on the bench, stiff-backed and somehow very calm within. A man in uniform stood guard before the open courtroom door. People began to arrive. They all stopped to stare at me. Yoyo came, and Miss Wright, and Miss Yorke, and some of the ladies form the Main Street houses. They all stopped and stared and Yoyo tried to speak to me but the guard gestured to her to move on. Uncle Jim approached, and stopped when he saw me.

'Winnie?'

I looked up, and met his eyes.

'What's going on, Winnie? What you doin' sittin' here?'

I opened my mouth to speak but only a croak emerged, and the guard pushed him on too.

* * *

I waited. Time crept forward. A clock on the wall ticked far too loudly. The corridor had emptied long ago; everyone was in the courtroom, waiting. I could hear their breathing, their shuffling, their anxious murmuring, through the open door.

After what seemed an eternity, Mr Bhattacharya returned.

'Miss Cox,' he said to me, 'you may speak to him now. Come with me.'

'Oh!' I exclaimed, and the anxiety must have shown in his eyes. We had not planned this. I did not want to see my father face to face. What I was doing, what I had told Mr Bhattacharya was bad enough. Seeing him in the dock would be bad enough. But Mr Bhattacharya held out his hand, gesturing to me to get up. He even smiled, for the first time since we'd met.

'Don't worry!' he said, 'it will be fine.'

I rose to my feet and followed him back the way he'd come.

Another door, this one closed. Another guard. Mr Bhattacharya nodded to him and he opened the door. He made a gesture towards me, rather, towards the handbag and I handed it over immediately.

'Please raise your ...' but Mr Bhattarachrya stopped him mid-sentence.

'No need to search her,' he said. 'She's unarmed.'

I entered the room. It was a small, shabby and sordid enclosure, its wooden walls covered in scuffed and peeling grey paint, and divided into two by a wall of metal bars with a padlocked door set into it, making a jail of the far portion. Inside that jail sat Papa, slumped on a chair drawn up to the bars. A broken man. A caged man.

Pictures ran through my mind. I saw us all, Mama, Papa, we three girls, in the drawing room at Promised Land; we girls clapping while Mama and Papa swirled laughing to the *Blue Danube* sung by Mama. There was Papa, a younger, kinder Papa, sitting on his favourite chair and we three little girls climbing all over him, giggling and pulling his moustache; he tickling us and hugging us and being all a Papa should be. Papa, dancing with us one by one, teaching us all to waltz while Mama played the piano. Papa, my hero, my god, my father. Reduced to this: a prisoner in a cage.

Papa looked up as I entered, and a half-smile moved his lips. His moustache was turned down, limp and unkempt as was his hair, which had obviously not been cut in months and hung over his forehead and onto his collar. He wore prison clothes: a weary blue-grey ensemble with a number stitched into the shirt pocket. Papa, an abject soul, lost. Involuntarily, a lump rose to my throat. I stood looking at him, unsure of what to do, what to say.

Another man, on my side of the cage, stood up as I entered and introduced himself now as Mr Harper, Papa's lawyer. He offered me his chair, the only chair on this side, and I sat down.

'You may leave now, Mr Harper' said Papa to him, and he tried to protest, but Papa only roared at him. 'This is my daughter! Leave, I tell you!'

He left, and silence followed. Papa and I sat looking at each other.

'Papa,' I said eventually.

'Winnie,' he replied, and stood up. For a few seconds we simply stood, staring at each other, and then I sat down and so did he. I could not find words to speak, but at last he did.

'So it is true,' he said. 'You are on their side. You will tell your story.'

Something in me that had been turning soft hardened. 'I will tell the truth,' I said. 'Papa, you know it is the truth.'

More pictures flooded my mind. A different Papa. His face distorted with hatred, whipping an Indian labourer. Papa, using ugly forbidden words to speak of the man I loved. Papa, drawing a pistol and pointing it at Bhim. And Bhim. One hand raised and holding a flame. Bhim's face, wide-eyed with fear, screaming words I could not hear. His other hand, empty, an open palm, held out towards Papa.

Papa slumped forward, resting his elbows on his knees, his head on his hands.

'Yes, he said eventually. 'I know you speak the truth. I cannot blame you for that. You always spoke the truth. Always, always. It was what I always loved most about you: so candid. Never devious, as Yoyo was. And your kind heart. Always for the Poor Unfortunate. Just like your mother.'

'Yes,' I said. 'Like Mama. That's what she taught me, Papa. The best person I have ever known. The best person, probably, that *you* have ever known. A kind, compassionate woman, full of light and joy, full of love for all of us, until you destroyed her. You turned her against yourself, didn't you. You turned her away. With your cruelty. And then you sent her away. Even though you knew we needed her, you sent her away.'

Papa hammered his thigh and glared at me. 'I sent her away because she was a tramp! Your mother is no saint! You have no idea!'

'Yes, I do, Papa. I read her diary. I know – I know everything! I know about Edward John! But still you should not have sent her away! She was our mother! We needed her! At the very least you could have let her stay in Georgetown. But no – she had to go so that you could keep on being the monster you turned into!'

Papa leapt to his feet, grabbed the rails of cage. I was glad they were there – would he have attacked me in his rage?

'Monster! How dare you! How – how …'

And then, as suddenly as he had leapt up, he fell back into his chair, a broken man. Broken with sobs, sobs that horrified me as much as, somehow, they moved me. How is it possible to keep a hardened heart when the object of that hardness is weeping in contrition?

'Yes. I sent her away. I could not have her in my house, knowing what she had done. She begged to stay, because of you, Winnie, and Yoyo. Begged on bended knees. She'd given him up, years before, she said; it was over, over at Edward John's death. She promised to change, to wake out of her darkness, if only she could stay. Promised even to leave Promised Land and live in Georgetown if I could not have her in my house. But no. I could not have her in the country. How could I bear it? I sent her away, Winnie. Ostensibely to accompany Kathleen, to avoid scandal – but she had no choice. She had to go. I threw her out in my rage and jealousy. Yes. You have me to blame for that as well, for sending your mother away. You can hate me even more. Go on. Just hate me. I deserve it. I am a cruel man. A bad man. She was good, too good for me, and I drove her into his arms and then I drove her away. She was all I ever loved. I was a broken man, Winnie; I couldn't take losing her love. I *am* a broken man. A criminal. A – a murderer. But it was her fault! She betrayed me! Adultery! How could I keep her after that! She had to go, Winnie. I had to do it. I banished her. Sent her into exile … I lost her. My most precious …'

On and on he rambled. The words tumbled out from his lips in a torrent, confession following accusation, blame riding on the back of self-reproach; recriminations, excuses, explanations, all spilling from his lips in an uncontrolled frenzy, a temporary madness, Perhaps, too, a release. My own mind reeled as I listened in stunned silence, but at those last words I broke in.

'You didn't have to lose her!' I cried. I was parched inside. I longed for a glass of water. 'You could have changed. You could have forgiven her and changed – because you know very well why she did what she did! You could have put things right – loved her again, become a good man again! Let her show you a way of love, and kindness.'

'Love! Kindness! You're a dreamer, Winnie, you always were! I had an estate to run!' Papa roared. 'You cannot run an estate on kindness! That was the first thing Mr McInnes told me! You have to show the coolies who is master! But once you start, it takes hold of you – drives you to do things – terrible things – brings out the worst in you … the evil … I …'

And then, once again, he switched. Fury flared again in his eyes, and he pointed a finger at me. 'You, Winnie, you! You betrayed me too! You! You little sneaky slut! Throwing yourself at a nigger! You ran to that rat, that Booker rat, that mad Booker traitor! You took sides against your own father! Him, of all people!

Him! That rat! That bloody nigger-lover! Him of all people! Just like your mother! Yes, just like her – nigger-lover!'

I stared. I couldn't believe what I was hearing. Not the shocking words so much, but the meaning behind them. The hidden meaning. Could it be true? Or was I misinterpreting?

'Papa – Jim Booker – Mama – was he the – the man who …'

'YES!' Papa roared. 'Of course he was! Who else! Who else would she run to but a nigger-lover like herself! You both – both of you! Behind my back! Traitors both!'

Now I was the one to slump. I tried to say something but nothing came; I could not say a word for the lump in my throat blocked all speech. Uncle Jim! He was the man Mama had loved! The father of Edward John! No wonder – no wonder … my mind stumbled through the past, trying to fit together the jigsaw pieces, but I couldn't. A thousand questions rose into my mind, all needing answers I could not find. Uncle Jim! It must have happened between wives; after Gladys's death, before Bhoomie. Uncle Jim seemed to favour women of all races. But of all people, Uncle Jim! I had assumed Mama's lover was the Troublemaker. Uncle Jim! That explained so much! My mind reeled. Meanwhile, Papa raged on.

'Of all people, him! Him and her, and then him and you! What about me! What about me! Her husband, your father! Why, why, why!'

That's when I finally found the words. 'Because, Papa, you were no longer that man we loved. You became a monster. You drove us away. You drove us to him. Uncle Jim is a father to me, the father you weren't.'

Papa stared at me, and than, for the second time, he broke.

'Yes. I drove you away. I lost you. I lost you both. Two of the four people I love most in the world. I lost you, and I have only myself to blame. You are right. I became a monster. How could she love me. How could she love a monster? My fault. I drove her away.'

'That was it, wasn't it?' I said. 'The reason for her darkness..
She discovered, just as I did, what sort of man you were. A cruel,
ruthless man. A monster. What sort of man you *are*.'

'No. Past tense, Winnie. I am no longer that man. You are
right. There *was* a monster living in me. You saw. You know.
*She* saw, and she knew, and yes, you are right, it drove her away,
turned her against me. Destroyed her love. Turned it into hatred.
Drove her away. Drove her to *him*. I could not take it. I couldn't
take the reproach in her eyes. I could not take her knowing I was
a monster. I could not take her infidelity; that she could find a
better man than me.'

He stopped speaking. Papa sat upright again, looking straight
into my eyes. 'Winnie,' he said. 'Ah, Winnie. My little girl. You
are so like your mother. That's why I love you so much. Yes, I still
love you. Even though you betray me.'

'Then, Papa, if you still love me – don't make me do this! Don't
make me stand up there in court! Please, Papa! We both know the
truth. We both know what happened. For Mama's sake, Papa –
tell the truth! It will save you. It will save us all.'

Right on cue, there was a sharp rap on the door, and it opened
slightly. I looked around; Mr Bhattacharya stood just outside. He
pointed at his watch.

'Miss Cox? Are you nearly finished? Time's running – the
court is waiting …'

'We're nearly finished,' I said, though in fact we had only just
begun. So much still unsaid. A lifetime of errors to be put right,
here and now.

'Papa,' I said. 'What now?'

'I am a broken man,' he said simply. 'It is all over. I have lost
everything – everything of any value to me. I lost her, and you,
my daughter. Winnie, I – I …' He stopped. And then he said,
'Winnie, call in Mr Bhattacharya.'

I stood up, and stepped to the door, slightly lightheaded and still unstable from the distress of the conversation. I opened it. Mr Bhattacharya, sitting on a chair just outside, jumped to his feet.

'Please come in,' I said to him. He entered the room. Papa was standing in his cage.

'Mr Bhattacharya,' he said. 'I wish to make a confession.'

❈ ❈ ❈

An usher escorted me into the packed courtroom. There were no seats left, just standing room at the back. Black people stood there. Several faces turned as I entered, white faces, black faces, frowning faces, puzzled faces. A hum of murmuring filled the room as people nudged each other and looked at me and looked away. Was I a friend, an enemy? No one could tell; what they did know was that I had held up the process and was thus, in some way, significant.

The room was divided into two; on one side sat the people who looked like me. On the other side sat those who looked like George. White people, black people. My people, his people; but to me, just people, and I belonged nowhere. Where was George? I scanned the backs of heads, looking for him, and in that moment he turned around and our eyes met across the room. He was on a bench near the front, as I had guessed, but even at that great distance I could feel it, that spark of *connection* that never failed when I was in his presence. I quietly moved to stand at the back, with the black people. I knew my place.

The judge entered, everyone stood up, and I lost sight of George. He sat down again. I could see the back of George's head, Papa in the dock.

My head was spinning by this time and I found I could not pay attention. Too full was I with my conversation with Papa, this new Papa full of regret and self-accusation, full of blame and jealousy and distress. This new small Papa who bore no resemblance to the Papa I had once known. The things he had told me! Shocking things, and things that made everything fall into place. I understood now, everything. Mama had not deserted us! And Mama – Mama and Uncle Jim – the two of them – Edward John …

The world turned fuzzy and my knees gave way. It seemed to happen in slow motion, for the last thing I remember is a man, a stranger, crying out as he reached out to grasp me as I sank to the floor. And then everything turned black.

When I came to I was once again in the private room, lying on a cot, and George was there sitting on a chair next to my head and holding my hand. I sat up immediately.

'What happened?'

'You fainted. They brought you here.'

'No, I mean to Papa. The verdict?'

'Second degree murder. They said he deliberately took the gun as self-protection, but that he had no intention to kill originally, but he genuinely believed Bhim was armed and he reacted out of fear. It wasn't intentional, the judge said. And because he confessed, he'll get a lighter sentence. Ten years in prison, Winnie.'

I sobbed aloud.

'But he'll get off early,' George said. 'And they'll probably send him back to England. It would be too dangerous for him, prison in BG. The other prisoners – they'll be furious and might harm him.'

That was a relief, but only a minor one. I collapsed into his arms, convulsed with sobs.

'Papa! Oh, my Papa! I made him do this! Oh, I hate myself! I loathe myself!'

George rubbed my back and murmured comforting words.

'You did the right thing, Winnie. The courageous thing. You made him confess.'

'I had to! I couldn't keep silent! I didn't realise – I couldn't ...'

'You did the right thing,' he repeated.

'I don't know what's going to happen now. To us both, Yoyo and me. Yoyo will hate me now! And what is to become of her? She's so young, and now she has neither mother nor father. And what will I do, where will I go? Everyone will hate me. Everyone knows what I did. Everyone knows it was me. That I somehow changed the outcome; they saw me arrive with Mr Bhattacharya. They know, and they'll hate me for it.'

'Not everyone, Winnie. Don't you realise? To us you're a hero!'

'Am I?'

'Of course you are. How could you not be?'

And yet, being a hero seemed not to matter. It was a minor thing. A very minor thing. Only one thing mattered, now.

'I sent you a telegram. A silly telegram. You don't say things like that in a telegram.'

'No. It's not a thing for a telegram.'

'Then ...'

'Winnie ... you haven't thought it out properly. You don't know. I can't offer you anything. Only hardship and struggle.'

'I want to struggle at your side, with you. Isn't that what marriage is about? For better, for worse?' I could feel my lips quivering. I bit the bottom one, to stop it.

'You're so young. So innocent.'

Now it was my voice that quivered as I spoke. 'Not so innocent any more, George. I've dug deep inside myself. It's not just some sentimental fairy tale. Not any more. I've been tried and tested. I've been lured into a better life and I almost took the bait. I've been forced to grow up. I'm not a little girl any more and I know life isn't going to be all roses and violins, life with you.'

The words sounded so false; true on the surface, and yet …
I had rehearsed them so often to myself. It was what I wanted
to say, what I felt I should say, and they were true but only to a
degree.

'You don't understand, Winnie. It's not personal any more. It's
political. I have to step into Bhim's shoes. I have to follow in his
footsteps, fight for his sake, so that his death was not in vain. Up
to now I've been covert, an underground fighter. I have to come
out, Winnie, and speak up openly and fight openly. It's bigger
than just you and me. Any woman at my side would have to take
second place to that fight.'

Now, both lips and voice quivered. But I had known he would
say that, and I knew the answer I had to give. 'Your fight is my
fight. I will be there. I can do it. I know it.'

'Winnie – are you sure? Quite sure?' His eyes were fully of
worry, full of hope; surely they saw the tendrils of doubt in mine.
I was wearing a mask, a mask of bravery I did not fully feel. Surely
George knew that I was not yet ready. Not yet capable. Not yet
strong. That I still had knots to untie, matters to put right.

A vision rose in my mind's eye of a beautiful house on a white
powder beach lapped by sparking turquoise waters, roses growing
up the walls, and, yes, from somewhere in the sky an orchestra
playing the Blue Danube. Thomas, holding out his arms for me.
I could still have that. Thomas would forgive me, that I knew.
I had done my duty, spoken up, stood up for truth and justice.
I was free to go, to return to a life that seemed cut out for me.
Yes, the news of what I had done would follow me to Barbados
and make of me a pariah. But if Thomas could forgive me so
would, in time, everyone else. I had done my duty in speaking up,
confronting Papa. I was free to make that choice. I could not have
done so, had I not spoken to the prosecutor, for the guilt would
eventually have killed me.

But now, a different kind of guilt plagued me, sharp and relentless, a knife twisting within me: guilt towards Papa but of a deeper quality. No longer just the guilt of testifying against him, but the guilt of selfish motives.

*Had I betrayed my own father just so I could win George for myself?*

Was I such a manipulative person, so evil, so devious, that I was prepared to send my father to prison just to impress, and win, the man I loved? Was water thicker than blood? How could I live with myself, with George, knowing the terrible price I had been willing to pay? Could I ever forgive myself? Had I done the right thing? Where lay selfishness, unselfishness? Had I betrayed my own people, my own blood? But what choice did I have? Weren't truth and justice of more worth than ties of blood? Would I ever find peace again? What about Yoyo, the plantation? Miss Wright – would she stay, now that Papa was in prison? Had I betrayed her, too? All these questions swirled through me, tumbling over each other, tearing me apart. Where was the answer? Where? What was right, what was wrong?

I hid my face in my hands and wept. All the guilt, the emotion, the pressure of the last few weeks and the final climax here in this building of justice flooded through me, an ocean wave that found its only outlet in tears, in great heaving sobs that racked my body. George tried to hug me but I pushed him away; I had to walk this path alone. Yet I did accept the handkerchief he offered. Wave after wave washed through me and it seemed it would never end, that I would weep forever.

But finally the flood ceased, and then came the ebb, bringing peace, and final conviction. I looked up at George, whose last question still hung in the air, unanswered.

I looked up, and my voice broke, yet it was clear and firm. 'George: I'm sure. I'm not free! I can't – I just can't! I need to put things right first. I need to be there for Yoyo – she thinks she's grown up but she isn't. She's all alone now. I need to be there for her. She must hate me – I need to put that right! I have to go back to Promised Land – we girls will have to run the plantation for a while. I can't leave it in the hands of Mr McInnes, and Mr Smedley, and Yoyo just isn't old enough. I don't even know if I'm old enough. But I'll try.'

I reached out and grasped his hand, squeezed it.

'I'm more than ready for that fight, George. But I need to put my own house in order first. That's where my fight begins. Wait for me.'

# Epilogue

Telegram from Ruth Cox, Salzburg, to Winnie Cox, Tower Hotel Georgetown:

ARRIVING GEORGETOWN AUGUST FIFTH STOP SO SORRY LOVE YOU STOP MAMAX

# LETTER FROM SHARON

Thank you so much for reading *The Secret Life of Winnie Cox.* I do hope you enjoyed it as much as I enjoyed writing it.

When I write I am always thinking of you, the reader, and feel somehow connected to you. It's thrilling for me to know that out there you, a perfect stranger, are reading the words I wrote, following a story that came from my heart; somehow, this makes you not a stranger, but a friend. Isn't it wonderful how words, stories, can connect us all?

I'd love to know how you reacted to this story. Did it make you sad? Did it make you cry? Did it make you think? Did it take you back to the past? To a country that you perhaps did not know before? Which of the characters did you like the best, and which one did you love to hate? Did it make you see history from a new perspective? Did it change you in any way? **I'd be delighted to hear your reaction, and the very best way of getting back to me is through a review, even a short one.**

**Getting feedback from readers is always wonderful, and it also helps to persuade other readers to pick up this, or another one of my books, for the first time.**

I also hope you are eager to hear how Winnie's story continues – because it does! Yes – this is the first of a trilogy, and in the next two books you will find out how her life continues. Does she marry George? Does her mother return to British Guiana? Does Yoyo take over the plantation? All of these questions will be answered in my next book, coming out next year! And here's a big secret – you can take a sneak peek by jumping a few decades: you'll meet Winnie again as a wise Grandma in my previously published novel, *The Small Fortune of Dorothea Q*. She doesn't play the main role in that book, but she's there all right!

And if you'd like to keep up-to-date with all my latest releases, just sign up here:

http://www.bookouture.com/sharonmaas

I promise to only contact you when I have new book out, and of course I'll never pass your email on to anyone else.

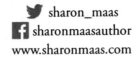

sharon_maas
sharonmaasauthor
www.sharonmaas.com

# ACKNOWLEDGEMENTS

The first person I'd like to thank is my Aunt, Zena Bone, who one starry night in the Pomeroon District of Guyana told me the fascinating story of my paternal grandmother, her former mother-in-law, Winnie Westmaas. I immediately knew that here was the seed not only for a new novel, but for several. The seed sprouted and grew: the result is *The Secret Life of Winnie Cox* and its follow-ups. Of course, in the writing, the story grew legs of its own – my Granny never lived on a sugar plantation, as far as I know, and all the details are completely of my imagination – but she did inspire the story as a whole, and so I thank her, too, posthumously.

It's not easy writing a novel set so far in the past, for research is necessary and the facts are sometimes hard to come by. But two people in particular answered my questions: Clem Seecharan, the author of *Sweetening Bitter Sugar Jock Campbell - The Booker Reformer of British Guiana 1934 –1966;* a book that became my Bible as I was writing. That book is dedicated to Ian McDonald, Clem's friend and a former Booker employee, and I was fortunate enough to meet Ian in Guyana. The Booker story seemed worth telling, and fiction is as good a way as any. How many readers know, for instance, that one of the biggest prizes in literature, the Booker, owes its existence, and its name, to British Guiana's oppressive Sugar Kings of centuries past (don't worry, that story does turn good!)? Between them, Clem and Ian helped me build up the setting for my book, and I am hugely indebted to them.

My good friend and fellow author Jan Lowe Shinebourne actually grew up on a sugar plantation on the Courantyne coast of British Guiana, and so she and her novels helped me to put myself there, to recreate the atmosphere – the smells, the sounds, the sights of a sugar plantation are one of a kind, unforgettable, and I hope that some of that ambience seeps through the words of this book.

I made it a point to stay for a weekend at Albion Estate (mentioned in the book) in one of my visits to Guyana, and I'd like to thank the many members of staff who showed me around and explained the industry to me. I have fond memories of staying at Albion as a child, as my Uncle Leonard worked there and lived in the staff quarters with his family, and it was fascinating to delve further into sugar's story.

However, none of us were alive in 1910 and so, in order to tell the story I also had to rely on imagination, and I admit to taking poetic licence here and there. Any mistakes I made in the setting and history are mine, not theirs.

Last but not least, I'd like to thank the wonderful team at Bookouture: Oliver Rhodes, who agreed to publish a book many agents had rejected, my gifted editor Claire Bord, (who is always right!), and Kim Nash, Bookouture's Publicity Manager, who I just know is going to put her heart and soul into making this book a success, just as she does with each and every one of our books. Thank you all for your faith, for your support, for your work!

Coleman Northwest
Regional Library

CPSIA information can be obtained at www.ICGtesting.com
Printed in the USA
LVOW07s1535021215

465056LV00021B/1320/P

9 781910 751510